THE RATIONING

THE
RATIONING

A NOVEL

CHARLES
WHEELAN

W. W. NORTON & COMPANY

Independent Publishers Since 1923

NEW YORK   LONDON

Copyright © 2019 by Charles Wheelan

For information about permission to reproduce selections from this book, write to Permissions, W. W. Norton & Company, Inc., 500 Fifth Avenue, New York, NY 10110

For information about special discounts for bulk purchases, please contact W. W. Norton Special Sales at specialsales@wwnorton.com or 800-233-4830

Manufacturing by LSC Communications Harrisonburg
Book design by Barbara Bachman
Production manager: Julia Druskin

Library of Congress Cataloging-in-Publication Data

Names: Wheelan, Charles J., author.
Title: The rationing : a novel / Charles Wheelan.
Description: First edition. | New York : W. W. Norton & Company, [2019]
Identifiers: LCCN 2018054654 | ISBN 9781324001485 (hardcover)
Subjects: LCSH: Political fiction.
Classification: LCC PS3623.H429 R38 2019 | DDC 813/.6—dc23
LC record available at https://lccn.loc.gov/2018054654

W. W. Norton & Company, Inc., 500 Fifth Avenue, New York, N.Y. 10110
www.wwnorton.com

W. W. Norton & Company Ltd., 15 Carlisle Street, London W1D 3BS

1 2 3 4 5 6 7 8 9 0

For the Americans who
died during the Outbreak.

CONTENTS

———

A NOTE ON SOURCES   *ix*

PART 1   Running the Yellow   *1*

PART 2   Do the Right Thing   *51*

PART 3   What If?   *139*

PART 4   It Hits the Fan   *183*

PART 5   The China Option   *211*

PART 6   Nature Fights Back   *253*

PART 7   Okay, Now What?   *279*

PART 8   The Hypothesis and the Ego   *331*

          Epilogue   *407*

ACKNOWLEDGMENTS   *411*

A NOTE ON SOURCES

———

THIS BOOK IS COMPILED PRIMARILY FROM MY RECOLLEC-
tions. I took notes in most of the important meetings. I kept a journal
on those rare evenings when I had enough energy after leaving the
White House to pen a few lines before collapsing into bed. To be
honest, though, most of the salient events are so firmly implanted in
my memory that they were not terribly hard to recall in vivid detail.
As a scientist, I recognize that the mind can play tricks. Whenever
possible I have verified my recollection of events with the principals who were in the room. My notes were helpful in reminding
me of the exact sequencing of events. During our long, contentious,
often meandering meetings, I made a habit of writing down who said
what, sometimes quoting them directly.

I took detailed notes because it was obvious that we were all
spectators to history. Taking notes also passed the time and helped
ease my frustration. (I noticed that the Secretary of Defense was a
chronic doodler; somewhere in the archives there must be hundreds
of drawings of buff soldiers operating impressive armaments.) The
point is that I was able to reconstruct the dialogue for this book, not
always word-for-word, but close enough to evoke the spirit of the
conversations.

For some of the public reaction outside of the Beltway, I have
drawn heavily on Gregg Brockway's series of articles in *Vanity Fair*
that have rightfully become the definitive contemporaneous account
of the nation's reaction to what will forever be known as "the Out-

break." Experts and historians will be parsing documents for decades, but no one will ever match Brockway's reportorial eye. While the nation arguably lost its collective mind, Brockway captured the extraordinary details that will forever illustrate popular reaction to the crisis, from Hollywood to Wall Street to some of the most obscure hamlets in Appalachia. We all knew that we were living something scary and extraordinary; Brockway was the guy writing it down.

For the meetings I did not attend, I have either interviewed the principals or drawn on their published memoirs. In cases where recollections differ, or where there are gaps in the public record, I have used my firsthand knowledge of the people and their personalities to infer what most likely happened. I have made use of some contemporaneous news coverage. These sources are generally cited in the text. However, I feel compelled to point out that a shockingly high proportion of the news coverage at the time was inaccurate—not incomplete, or misleading, or oversimplified, but just plain wrong. As my story will tell, we in the White House were partially responsible for creating the information vacuum that allowed this kind of misinformation to take root. Still, that should not give anyone, particularly the *New York Times* and the *Washington Post–USA Today*, the right to fill that vacuum with "news" that was not even tenuously connected to the truth. Many of the alternative news sources, with a few notable exceptions, were worse than that.

The publication of this book was delayed by nearly eighteen months of legal wrangling, as my lawyers did battle with various parties, including the U.S. government. (I often worked through disagreements with my own lawyers over what it would be prudent for me to reveal.) In that time, two fortuitous things happened. First, the Outbreak Inquiry Commission—the body created by Congress to investigate the crisis from start to finish—released its report, including material from closed-door hearings that had never before been made public. Second, WikiLeaks produced a huge trove of State Department documents covering this period, giving me remarkable access to the diplomatic wrangling behind the scenes. I do not condone such leaks; I can say that in this instance they have enabled me to tell a more complete story.

This is not the first book on the Outbreak. It is the most accurate. I am not a brilliant writer, but I am a scientist who happened to be in the right place at the right time (or the wrong place at the wrong time, depending on your perspective). I was in nearly every important science-related meeting at the White House during the crisis and in many of the political ones, too. In fact, I had greater access to the full scope of events than the President, since he was often consumed by other affairs of state and generally did not participate in the scientific meetings.

I am not writing to settle scores. I am not writing to burnish my leadership credentials or to make myself viable for the Iowa caucuses. (Yes, that is why some of the other books were written, and it explains why they were so ridiculously inaccurate and self-serving.) I was there. I understood the science. I watched our political process deal with an unprecedented crisis. This is what happened. It is not my story; it is our story.

PART I

RUNNING THE YELLOW

1.

WAREHOUSE 61 IS AT THE END OF A LOADING DOCK in the Port of Long Beach. Sometime between midnight and two a.m. on March 21, it caught fire. For reasons that may never be clear (given that it was a very warm night), a homeless man had set a small blaze in an oil drum near the truck entrance to Warehouse 61. The fire somehow spread to a pool of motor oil, setting ablaze the warehouse and several small maintenance buildings. No one was injured except for the homeless man, who was treated for burns at a Los Angeles hospital. The Long Beach Fire Department responded and put out the fire after several hours.

Warehouse 61 is owned and operated by the U.S. government. It is used to store materials coming and going across the Pacific, everything from sophisticated research equipment to school supplies for students in Guam. On March 21, the warehouse also held fourteen chimpanzees, which were being shipped from a government research facility in Hawaii to a private laboratory at Stanford. Thirteen of the fourteen chimps were killed in the fire; the fourteenth, a female named Bobo, was rescued by firefighters. Bobo became the story. Protesters descended on Los Angeles and Long Beach to protest animal experiments by the U.S. government. The President of the United States, the head of the National Institutes of Health, the President of Stanford, and assorted other officials were called upon to explain the necessity of doing research on primates, and, more immediately, why these particular chimps had been left unattended overnight in a warehouse.

Meanwhile, Bobo clung to life. She was attended to by a team of veterinarians, as well as several prominent burn specialists for humans. Money poured in for Bobo's treatment. By the time she regained consciousness several days later, still with serious burns and at high risk of infection, over $25 million had been collected to pay Bobo's bills. This prompted a wave of counterprotests by those Americans, myself included, who found it perplexing, if not absurd, that our fellow citizens lavished money on a burned chimp only six months after repealing (once again) the health care coverage for fifty million Americans. The health care debate became even more pitched when it was disclosed that the homeless man burned in the fire, who had third-degree burns over 20 percent of his body, had been quietly turned out of a Los Angeles hospital because he could not pay his bills. This left him at serious risk of infection, and the police without the only witness to the start of the fire. The homeless man would never show up again. Doctors and talking heads tweeted aggressively about who had been more seriously injured, Bobo or the homeless man. For three days, Home Depot Media made Bobo the feature story on all of its receipts and coupons.

The homeless guy was soon forgotten. Bobo got better. She was placed in the Los Angeles Zoo and became a hit attraction. Just last year she "mated successfully" (a term I now use with my married friends), and the world eagerly embraced the son of Bobo, Hanson, who was named for the Long Beach firefighter who rescued Bobo from the warehouse blaze.

2.

BOBO WAS A SIDESHOW, A DEVASTATING DISTRACTION. WAREhouse 61 also contained a shipment of research materials and pharmaceutical products that were en route from the naval laboratory in Honolulu to the mainland. That shipment included the core ingredients for twenty-five million doses of the drug transcriptin, which we now know by its commercial name, Dormigen. For anybody working anywhere in science or medicine—for people like me—the development of Dormigen was like the World Series and the Super Bowl rolled into one. Other kids dreamed of coming to bat in the ninth inning of the seventh game of the World Series with the score tied and the bases loaded. Guys like me cried when our mothers drove us to Little League practice. As I stood in right field, where the ball invariably came more than it was supposed to, I imagined inventing something like Dormigen—the most important breakthrough in medicine since penicillin.

Dormigen is an effective treatment for viral infections *and* bacterial infections *and* most parasites. If Dormigen were a person, he would play professional basketball, publish popular novels, and teach math at Harvard, all while dating a supermodel. I have given some thought to that metaphor. Just as we do not expect people who teach math at Harvard to play professional basketball, scientists had always assumed it was improbable, if not impossible, to find a drug that could be effective against all the different pathogens that pose harm to humans. Then we created Dormigen.

It was none too soon. By the 2020s, many traditional antibiotics were becoming less and less effective. The "golden half-century" of medicine—during which a cheap course of antibiotics would wipe out anything from venereal disease to tuberculosis—was over. We had collectively neglected what Charles Darwin taught us: pathogens adapt or die. Those that were not dying in the face of penicillin and its relatives were getting stronger and more dangerous. Pediatricians blithely passed out prescriptions for antibiotics to parents with screaming children, regardless of whether those drugs were necessary or even effective against little Ellie's ear infection. The grocery shelves were full of every imaginable antibacterial product. Never mind that soap and water worked better than most of them. The peak of this dangerous silliness was when Hanes and Jockey both released antibacterial underwear, almost immediately capturing 40 percent of the market. ("Germ-free fresh!")

The germs just kept getting stronger and more resilient. Evolution moves swiftly for organisms that can produce millions of offspring a day, any one of which could be the mutant strain equipped to live comfortably in antibacterial underwear. By 2024, public health officials were warning of a crisis. The number of fatal hospital infections from so-called "superbugs"—which are really just bacteria that have developed a resistance to our best antibiotics—had been rising steadily for a decade. Every public health meeting and conference included a breakout session on antibiotic resistance. The major medical journals wrote editorial after editorial pointing out the growing threat. I remember reading a dire warning in the *Journal of the American Medical Association* that concluded, "Without a major change in behavior, we will soon face a medical return to the pre-penicillin era, and that should scare us."

That did not scare us, apparently, at least not beyond the medical and public health community. By then, almost half of us were wearing antibacterial underwear. We were also using antibacterial sunscreen, buying phones with bacteria-resistant keyboards, and decorating our homes with antibacterial paint. All the while, the germs marched and drilled and produced more robust offspring; the number of Americans dying from drug-resistant hospital infections quietly eclipsed the number of Americans dying from HIV/AIDS and motor vehicle accidents combined.

And then Buster Bowman died. I liked him well enough; his music was popular in a "retro" kind of way when I was in college. The cable news networks played the announcement of his death over and over again. He had been admitted to a prestigious New York hospital for a routine procedure. The media and Bowman's die-hard fans had camped out on the sidewalk outside the hospital, hoping to snap some photos of him or to get an autograph on his way out. What they got instead was Bowman's physician, a white-haired fiftyish-looking man, who stepped out of the main doors of the hospital entrance in his blue scrubs to give them shocking news: "Buster Bowman died shortly after seven this morning," he said.

The doctor was so quiet that many of the fans sprawled on the sidewalk did not hear him. Most of the tabloid photographers were around the corner vaping. Those who heard the doctor's mumbled pronouncement rushed forward; the news spread through the crowd like an electric current. The reporters began yelling for the doctor to repeat his statement. They demanded more details. How does someone who comes in for a ruptured Achilles tendon end up dead?

Bowman's physician had the look of a man who had been awake all through the night. He composed himself and stepped toward the bundle of microphones now being thrust in his direction. "Is this okay?" he asked of no one in particular, giving the statement a sense of performance art. Then he delivered the stunning details: "Buster Bowman was pronounced dead at 7:05 a.m. He died of a massive infection that we were unable to control with antibiotics. That is all the information I can provide at this time, pending an autopsy and a hospital investigation."

My parents and their friends were devastated; Bowman was the rock icon of their generation. Public opinion toward antibacterial products changed overnight. Being spotted at the gym in antibacterial underwear was now only slightly more socially acceptable than wearing baby sealskin. But the pathogens were literally out of the bottle. Dormigen would have saved Buster Bowman, but it had not been invented yet.

3.

AL GOYAL, THE CEO OF CENTERA BIOMEDICAL GROUP, STARED at the spreadsheets arrayed on his desk. "This won't work," he said to his CFO, who was sitting opposite the impressively large and orderly desk. "We can't have another quarter like this."

Aditya "Al" Goyal was born in Mumbai, still Bombay at the time. He became Al at Harvard Business School, where he recognized that his classmates preferred their diversity in manageable doses. (At trial, his mother still referred to him as Aditya, causing some confusion.) Goyal knew his way around a balance sheet. He graduated from one of the prestigious Indian Institutes of Technology, which admit students based on the results of a single standardized test given across India. More than a half million students sit for the exam every year and fewer than ten thousand are admitted to the Institutes—making Harvard and Yale seem like community colleges by comparison.

Goyal joined McKinsey & Company, the prestigious consulting firm, in their Mumbai office. He was promoted to the New York office and then McKinsey sent him to Harvard, the business equivalent of finishing school, where he was a Baker Scholar (top 5 percent of the class). No one ever denied that Al Goyal was a very smart man, even after the trial. He was not necessarily brilliant, as that implies some creativity or exceptional skill. Goyal was most adept at running slightly faster than everyone else, jumping through whatever hoops happened to be placed in his path. He was not one to spend a lot of time questioning the direction he was being told to run, or why he was jumping through the hoops along the way.

"We might as well drop our trousers, bend over, and let Wall Street have their way with us," Goyal told his CFO. Goyal was not a crude man, but as part of the assimilation process he had adopted common colloquial expressions and sports references, not unlike transforming himself into Al. He was determined to be as American as the Americans around him—the professional equivalent of a chameleon changing its color.

"We can put off some capital spending," the CFO answered. "I've toyed with the idea of selling one of the plants and then leasing it back. We could book the revenue now. It's not obvious we should own the real estate anyway." The CFO, Johannes Swensen, was a neat, thin, athletic man. He did triathlons and the occasional marathon. Swensen had spent most of his career in his native Sweden, and then elsewhere in Europe. He had come to New Jersey when Centera Biomedical Group bought out the small genetic engineering firm he had founded in Stockholm. Swensen looked particularly pale and skinny opposite Goyal, who had the dark complexion of South India and the physique of an executive who had spent more time in airports than the gym. There was more than a little irony in the fact that the two men described on the cover of *The Economist* as embodying "The Low Point of American Capitalism" were both born somewhere other than America. When photographed together, the two of them—big and dark, thin and pale—looked like corporate villains designed by Disney animators.

"That's small change," Goyal muttered. "The analysts will see right through it."

"Small change adds up," Swensen said. "When the number hits the wire, that's what the market will react to. The rest of the story will dribble out later. Besides, there is logic to getting out of the real estate business. We make pharmaceutical products. We don't need to own the land under the plants. The analysts love that kind of thing. We can tell them there is more to come, this is just the beginning, lots of future cost savings, and so on."

"They're going to crucify us," Goyal said, tapping the spreadsheet distractedly. "The board will not tolerate another quarter like this."

"Well, this is the quarter we're going to have," the CFO answered, losing patience with the spreadsheet equivalent of hand-wringing.

"Then you and I need to take up golf—because we're going to have a lot of spare time on our hands when the board sees this," Goyal said.

"I don't like golf. It takes too long," the CFO replied. His attempt at levity fell flat. Goyal shook his head from side to side in disagreement, almost like a tremble. It was a distinctly Indian gesture that the Internet cameras liked to capture during the trial.

"We had a bad quarter. It happens. The board is smart enough to realize that," the CFO said. "We can brief them before the meeting. They don't like surprises, but they do tolerate bad news."

"What happened to the Dormigen revenues?" Goyal asked.

"We booked it all last quarter," Swensen said.

"Then why do we have this huge Dormigen expense now?"

The CFO explained the terms of Centera Biomedical Group's contract with the U.S. Department of Health and Human Services (HHS). Centera was chosen to provide the federal government with twenty million doses of Dormigen a year to be stockpiled in case of a virulent pandemic, a terrorist attack with a biological weapon, or some other widespread biomedical emergency. Epidemiologists have always considered this a possibility; the flu pandemic of 1918–19 killed some forty million people around the globe. If anything, we are more vulnerable to a pandemic now than we were a hundred years ago. An outbreak of some nasty disease in Ningde, China—or some other place you have never heard of—will not stay isolated, as it would have in 1915. One business executive visiting a T-shirt factory in Ningde can spread a killer virus to Manhattan or Tokyo in a matter of hours. And there are plenty of nasty viruses: polio, avian flu, Ebola, swine flu, HIV, MRSA.

Dormigen works against them all. Ironically, it was the HIV virus that inspired us to believe that something like Dormigen might be possible. HIV has a unique ability to change its form; when the human body produces antibodies to fight back, HIV modifies itself— actually changes its form—so that the antibodies become ineffective. As soon as the human body finds the right key to disable the virus, HIV changes the lock. Some bold researchers reckoned that antibodies could be engineered to do the same thing, only for the "good guys." Why couldn't we engineer antibodies that would change form until they were able to destroy whatever pathogen had invaded the body? These antibodies would show up with a whole ring of keys, like the janitor who lets me into my office when I lock myself out. He takes the huge ring of keys hanging off his belt and patiently tries one after another; eventually one of them opens my door. Ten billion dollars and fifteen years later, we invented the most powerful drug since penicillin: a giant antibody key ring.

"Dormigen is alive," Swensen told his boss at that fateful meeting at Centera Biomedical Group.

"It's a pill, right?" Goyal asked.

"Yes and no," Swensen offered. "It's a gel cap. But my point is that it's alive. It's a package of enzymes that we cultivate—"

"Never mind," Goyal said, literally waving away the science with a sweep of his fleshy arm. Obviously, if he cared more about the science, fewer people would have died. Dormigen is engineered by splicing several key human genes into a host embryo, usually a chicken egg. The process is not terribly complicated, but it does require twenty-one days for the genetically engineered cells to mature in their host embryos, after which they are harvested and grafted onto a common human antibody that can be injected back into the body and easily absorbed. As the Centera CFO correctly pointed out, Dormigen is alive. There is nothing unique or even terribly interesting about that; many vaccines are alive. It does explain, however, why Centera Biomedical Group was paid a lot of money to manufacture Dormigen, store it, destroy it—and then do it all over again.

"Dormigen has a shelf life of about a hundred and eighty days,"

Swensen explained to his overwrought boss. "We make twenty million doses, then six months later we destroy them. That's what we do, over and over again—unless there is a need for them, in which case the government would draw down the stockpile."

Goyal tapped a line item in the budget. "We'll spend a hundred and twenty million dollars this quarter to destroy something that cost us a hundred and twenty million to produce last quarter?"

"No," the CFO said. "We'll spend about fifteen million to destroy the old doses and a little over a hundred million making the new ones."

And that was when the plan was hatched. Both men denied any knowledge of it at first, when the FBI raided the headquarters of Centera at the beginning of the Outbreak. Later, at trial, each would blame the other for the scheme. The jury found neither convincing and convicted them both. In any event, their plan was simple and good for the bottom line: stop producing new Dormigen until revenues turned healthier, probably in just a few quarters. Goyal and/or Swensen decided to gamble. Rather than spending a lot of money to produce a new batch of Dormigen—vials that would sit in a warehouse only to be destroyed six months later—they would keep the old stuff around. "I never thought it would matter," Swensen explained during the sentencing phase of his trial. "We were just a safety valve."

That was the exact language in the contract: safety valve. Centera was only obligated to provide the Department of Health and Human Services with Dormigen after the government had exhausted 75 percent of its own stock. The U.S. government had tens of millions of doses, most of which went unused in a normal year. The Centera scheme was like loaning out the spare tire on your car for a few weeks. How often do you get a flat? There was virtually no chance that the government would need Dormigen *this quarter*, when Centera could really use the extra revenue. As soon as the business environment improved, the company could go back to making and destroying Dormigen without anyone being the wiser.

Goyal and Swensen were vilified as the embodiment of evil, two guys willing to sacrifice lives in order to goose quarterly profits. The truth is subtler. Goyal and Swensen cut a corner. They did something selfish and dishonest—but they did not believe anyone would get hurt. They did not run into a crowded stadium and start firing weapons. They did not drink pitchers of margaritas at happy hour and then drive home. Their crime was the corporate equivalent of running a yellow light. They lost perspective. They were three minutes late for an appointment that did not really matter in the grand scheme of things; when the stoplight went from green to yellow, they sped up—just a little, in their eyes. The rest of the world did not figure into that calculation. *Their three minutes were more important.* Who knew that a group of schoolchildren might enter the crosswalk? If you think about it, the people who run yellow lights are more dangerous than the people who run red lights, because there are so many more of us.

Goyal and Swensen were in complete agreement on how their fateful conversation ended. Goyal once again insisted that Swensen take up golf. "You can't run marathons forever. The knees are not made for it," the CEO said.

"There is no exercise in golf," Swensen protested.

"There is if you walk," Goyal insisted.

"Most people take carts."

"Not where I play, at the Wood Hollow Club. We have caddies. I can get you in like that," Goyal said, snapping his fingers. "Your kids can use the swimming pool."

"I don't see the point of trying to hit a small ball into a small hole from a long distance," Swensen joked with his CEO. The conversation drifted back to a familiar place. Levity crept into the room.

"That's exactly the point!" Goyal exclaimed. "When I focus on hitting the ball, my mind is purged of all this nonsense." He made a sweeping gesture across his desk.

"And then you get angry when you miss a shot."

"Now, that is true!" Goyal laughed heartily. "Still, it's yoga for the mind, I am telling you. This evening, I am going to the driving range. I am certain of that!"

Goyal walked his CFO to the door. According to his testimony at trial, Goyal did in fact hit two buckets of balls at the Wood Hollow driving range later that afternoon.

4.

MY PARENTS WANTED ME TO GO TO LAW SCHOOL. I TOOK THE LSAT my senior year in college just to placate my mother. I also took a summer job working for a Washington, D.C., firm that was litigating an enormous patent infringement case in the defense industry. As a college student, I was a peon—albeit a peon billed out to the client at $75 an hour. (I was paid $15 an hour, with no benefits.) I moved boxes around. I did some background research on missile defense systems. During one three-week stretch I put fifteen thousand trial documents in chronological order. The law school interns had only slightly less menial tasks, though they were billed out at $125 an hour. Even the young lawyers did not seem to be doing a whole lot of intellectually interesting work. Our collective paper pushing did not resemble the fancy courtroom dramas on television.

The case never went to trial. All of the work was just a prelude to a negotiated settlement, a very expensive and time-consuming bluff. The settlement was very advantageous to our client, and we were supposed to be excited. Instead, most of the team was exhausted and cynical. We knew it was not our brilliant legal analysis that had brought the case to closure; neither firm wanted to roll the dice with a jury trial. We had hired an expensive jury consultant who told us that twelve laypeople would have little ability to grasp the key technical details of the case. I could have offered the same advice more cheaply. At about the same time I was putting those fifteen thousand trial documents in chronological order—lab notebooks with pages of equations, long memos with detailed weapons specifications, and the like—I had to go to the Department of Motor Vehicles to get my driver's license renewed. As I looked around the DMV, I lost a fair bit of confidence in our prospective jury pool.

After the settlement, the firm had a massively expensive party in a ballroom at the Four Seasons, including a caviar bar and small Kobe beef sandwiches passed around on trays. There was a guy making martinis in the corner of the ballroom with boutique gins. (Unlike vodka, you really can taste the difference with gin.) I stumbled home with a perky second-year law student from Harvard whom I had been lusting after since the day I arrived at the firm. The next morning, while she was still naked in the bedroom of her small but charming Georgetown apartment, she rolled toward me and kissed me gently on the chest. I was expecting more great things. Instead, she said, "Promise me you won't go to law school."

That was not exactly a binding legal commitment. And it is not the story I told my parents about why I did not want to become a lawyer. Still, I did not apply to law school. I stumbled into virology almost by accident. My dad is an accountant; my mom was a marketing consultant until she quit to raise my sister and me. My people tend to be service providers, not scientists. I had never met anyone with a Ph.D. until I arrived at Dartmouth. Several years later I woke up as an economics major. The math was relatively easy for me; economics was considered to be the most direct route to Wall Street, or someplace equally lucrative and respectable. Anyone who graduated with a respectable GPA and decent social graces could tap into the impressive Dartmouth alumni network to become at least a mini-titan of finance. Guys who had spent a good portion of senior year drunk in fraternity basements were handling millions of dollars for hedge funds by homecoming of the following year (or so they said).

I am not one to shake up the social order, but it did strike me—even at the time—that most of the "career planning" going on senior year did not involve much planning, let alone introspection. Rather, it felt like a warm, comfortable current sweeping smart people gently toward investment banking, consulting, law school, and a few other low-risk, high-reward careers. When we entered as freshmen, our class dean pointed out in her matriculation speech that our class of roughly one thousand had three hundred and eleven high school valedictorians. We also supposedly had twenty-three soccer captains (which boggles the mind given the awful performance of the soccer team during my four years). I was surrounded by high achievers who, to that point in life, had excelled by doing a prescribed set of tasks faster or better than everyone else. High school is a brilliantly designed machine for beating the originality and creativity out of anyone. One does not thrive by creating original work, or inventing something, or questioning authority, or working well with others (cheating).

By senior fall at Dartmouth, all of this was bouncing around in my mind. The inner competitive streak among my high-achieving classmates had been unleashed full force. When McKinsey & Company* arrived on campus, it felt like the corporate equivalent of the Beatles' arrival in America. All conversation revolved around which members of our class had been selected for "closed" interviews—those that were offered by invitation only. In what struck me as a cruel gesture, McKinsey also offered "open" interviews to the first twenty-five students in line at Career Services on a particular Monday morning. Scores of students lined up the night before. The weather was so bad (it would fall below freezing that night) that students at the back of the line began to hope that those at the front would get sick and leave. They actually said that out loud.

I was having a small existential crisis when I arrived in Professor Huke's Biology of Parasites class at the beginning of the winter quarter. I wish I could say that I had scoured the course guide looking for a class that would take me to a new intellectual plane. In fact, my adviser had sent me an e-mail the previous week pointing out that I had not yet completed my laboratory science requirement. I had a keen interest in graduating, and I was running out of terms to finish my electives, so I decided to sign up for a lab science class. There were two choices. (Actually, there were six choices, but four of them either met before nine a.m. or were held in buildings that would have been a nose-hair-freezing walk from my dorm during January and February.) It had to be Bio 3 (Biology of Everyday Life) or Microbiology 32 (Biology of Viruses and Parasites). The Biology of Everyday Life was a known "layup," meaning that anyone who put in a modicum of effort could count on an A- or better. The bulk of the course consisted of collecting samples of living things and looking at them under a microscope. Other than the week on "bodily fluids," which was apparently pretty cool, the course was an embarrassment to the Ivy League. Still, three hundred people enrolled every time it was offered—most of the humanities and social sciences majors on campus—because it was an easy way to boost the GPA and fulfill the lab science requirement at the same time.

* Yes, this is the very same firm where Al Goyal worked early in his career.

On a Thursday night in the first week of the quarter, I had a conversation in the basement of a fraternity that changed my life trajectory, like a boulder dropped into a stream that sends the current coursing in a new direction. I ran into Sloan Hill near the beer tap in the Alpha Delta house. We talked for a while. One can draw a straight line, or series of lines, from my conversation with Sloan that evening to the Oval Office, where I would spend hours huddled with the President of the United States a decade later.

5.

SLOAN AND I APPROACHED THE BEER TAP FROM DIFFERENT directions and I offered to fill her cup. She was effortlessly cute: gray-blue eyes, short blond hair, no makeup to speak of, and a killer smile, especially when she was a little tipsy. Sloan squinted when she smiled, and that was cute, too. She was also "wicked smart," as we liked to say in New Hampshire, even in a sea of overachievers. She worked hard enough; the work came easy to her, as it did to a lot of those high school valedictorians wandering around campus. But what set Sloan apart were her impressively eclectic intellectual interests. While the rest of us complained about too much work, she found time to read for fun, even fiction. Her RealNews blastbox was filled every day with writers who ranged from counterculture to intellectually unhinged. ("We all need to know what they're saying," she explained to me once.) I explicitly remember her citing a column in the *Jerusalem Post* one day in the context of some meandering discussion on the Middle East. Who in New Hampshire reads the *Jerusalem Post* unless it is assigned for a class? (Even then, most of us tried to cut corners on the assigned reading.) I remember seeing Sloan at the bus stop one Friday afternoon, waiting for the Dartmouth Coach. She was headed to New York to wander through museums all weekend. "I just need to recharge," she said, looking comfortably alone with a small duffel at her feet.

Sloan was the student that we all should be, the student that our parents probably thought that we were. She took classes that interested her. She worked hard but was indifferent to grades. She visited her professors during office hours to talk about concepts in the class, rather than to haggle for more points. Sloan lived in my freshman dorm, just down the hall. We had become friends before she disappeared to date older guys and pursue different campus activities. Still, the bonds of freshman year are deep, and I really liked her. She was one of a handful of people whose opinions I valued. To my credit, I did not really spend a lot of time obsessing about what other people thought of me. I did care what Sloan thought.

As I filled Sloan's glass with beer from the tap, she asked, "So, what are you taking this quarter?"

"Monetary Policy," I said. "And a writing class that looks pretty good. I'm still shopping for a lab science."

"You're not taking Bio 3, are you?" she asked accusingly.

"No way," I said. It was the truth, as of that moment. Yes, I had sat in on Bio 3 twice that week, and it fit perfectly into my schedule, but once Sloan asked me that question, in that tone, I was not going to take Bio 3. "I'm thinking about that parasites course."

"Really?" she said, with more than the usual amount of enthusiasm for a desultory conversation in a fraternity basement. "Were you there this week? I didn't see you. I'm doing my Presidential Scholar thesis on the anthropology of contagious diseases, so I'm sitting in on the class."

The next morning I signed up for Microbiology 32. I could fulfill my lab science requirement; I also entertained visions of sitting next to Sloan every day in class, sharing notes, studying together. Sometimes I imagined that we would work together late into the night, and then when the readings no longer made sense, and we had grown punchy from too little sleep and too much coffee, I would lean over and kiss her. And she would kiss me back, because the bond developed over weeks of studying together was inexorable . . . There were a lot of variations on what happened next, though invariably we had sex in some public study space and then went on to ace the exam, after which we became a prominent campus couple.

Only the part about acing the exam had any approximation to reality. I worked hard in the class, for a bunch of reasons, one of which was to impress Sloan. I was never going to have sex with her in the rare books section of the library if we did not at least get to the studying part. And to get there, I would have to add some value to the study sessions. I went to class. I did the reading. I even went to see the optional documentary during the X-hour. I sat next to Sloan as often as possible, while still trying to make it feel like happenstance. Along the way, something else happened: I fell in love with pathogens, with their stunning evolution and adaptation, even the most awful among them.

I learned right before the midterm that Sloan was not taking the course for credit. We never did study together. Still, my career was launched. My path to the White House began with a drunken conversation in a fraternity basement and was nurtured by salacious thoughts of wild sex with my study buddy. Sad but true.

6.

"THE MARBURG VIRUS, WHICH IS CLOSELY RELATED TO THE Ebola virus, causes a hemorrhagic fever. After a brief incubation period, it attacks the body's major organs, the spleen, the liver, the pancreas, the testicles, the eyes, the spinal cord. In some cases, the victim will hemorrhage—bleed profusely—from all of the body's orifices. Somewhere between a quarter and ninety percent of human Marburg victims will die, and that's when the virus reveals how beautifully adapted it is."

That was how Professor Richard Huke began his first lecture in Microbiology 32. He did not call roll; he did not pass out the syllabus. He just started talking about the Marburg virus. I am paraphrasing him, but I remember the details vividly. I am certain he used the word "beautiful," because when someone describes humans bleeding out of every orifice and then goes on to speak admiringly of the organism responsible—well, that is something you remember. Huke had a point. The Marburg virus is spread through bodily fluids—blood, saliva, vomit, and so on. When humans die from Marburg, they become "disease bombs" (another Huke phrase). A single drop of blood from a Marburg-infected corpse can contain five million viruses. Remember, the victim dies bleeding from all those orifices. So his or her last act, post-death, is to infect the next of kin, like an uncapped oil well spewing viruses.

Marburg strikes primarily in Central Africa (though it's named for a German village where there was one outbreak, which is so sadly typical). In Central Africa, the most common funeral ritual is to wash the corpse and kiss it goodbye. The motivating belief is that the lack of a proper funeral will anger the spirit of the deceased and cause that spirit to seek vengeance. In the process of that ritual bathing, the five million Marburg viruses per drop of blood find their next victims. One has to appreciate the irony: the deceased exacts viral vengeance because his relatives do what they are supposed to do to avoid vengeance.

When Professor Huke said the virus was "beautiful" or "beautifully adapted" or whatever the phrase, he was right. Remember, we do not even agree on whether viruses are living things or not. We do know that they exist primarily to replicate themselves; the better a virus is at replicating itself, the better its chances of surviving for another hundred million years or so. Natural selection helps organisms that help themselves. When I was later thrust abruptly into the media spotlight, my first mistake was speaking like a microbiology professor. When I described *Capellaviridae* as "elegant"—I was at least politic enough not to call it "beautiful"—I meant only that it was well adapted from an evolutionary standpoint. My comment was meant to underscore the scientific challenge that we faced in breaking the chain of transmission. Obviously, with the risk of a pandemic hanging over the nation, I can understand how my comment was interpreted differently. I did not mean to be callous or indifferent. I have since apologized formally, but I will repeat the essence of that statement here: I was speaking as a scientist. I was speaking about a shockingly devilish and dangerous pathogen in the same way that a detective might describe a wily serial killer. I did not "admire" this raging virus, as Home Depot Media stupidly suggested. We had our work cut out for us—that was all. I assume, given my role in stopping the epidemic and saving untold lives, I can be forgiven my poor word choice.

7.

PROFESSOR HUKE FASCINATED ME. FIVE MINUTES INTO THE lecture, and I was already convinced that I should take the course, whether Sloan was in it or not. "Should you be worried about Marburg?" Huke asked the class. Most of the students nodded yes, but no one raised a hand to answer. "You're nodding 'yes,'" he said, making eye contact with a guy wearing a DARTMOUTH FOOTBALL cap in the second row. "Why?"

"Because I don't want to bleed out of every orifice," the guy in the football cap answered. There were titters from the class, as we each imagined bleeding to death out of our ears, nose, mouth, eyes, and asshole. Even Huke conceded with a little grin that the answer was clever, if not particularly deep.

"Fair enough. Do you think that's likely to happen?" Huke asked.

"Not if I stay out of Central Africa," Football Cap Guy said.

"What if it spreads? There are flights from Liberia to Brussels three times a week," Huke prodded. He let this prospect sink in, before turning in my direction. He made eye contact and took a half step forward. "Are you worried?" he asked. I was four or five rows back, usually far enough to be safe from this kind of thing. He just looked at me, not rudely, but it was clear he was going to wait for an answer. Some of the students in the rows in front of me turned and looked back.

"Well, I wasn't worried when I got out of bed this morning," I said. "Now I am, I guess." The class laughed again. Huke got the answer he was looking for.

"You can stop worrying. For all the horror of this virus, we're talking about a couple of hundred cases a year. Even in the places where it's endemic, the infection rate is extremely low," Huke explained. There was a brief clicking of keyboards as students made a note of this fact, which felt like it could turn up on the midterm.

"What if it were used as a biological weapon?" a girl asked at the end of my row. Huke wheeled excitedly in her direction.

"We've been close! The Soviets had that capacity during the Cold War. They never used biological weapons, thankfully, but they had

them. So, yes, you're correct. If the goal were to inflict mass casualties on a population in a particularly horrific way, Marburg would
be a good mechanism—as would a lot of the other organisms that
we're going to talk about in this class. So does that worry you?" The
question was directed back at the girl in my row. She was a soccer
player, tall and tan and fit, probably in KKG or one of the other popular sororities.

"Sure," she answered earnestly.

"Well, you can relax, at least about Marburg," Huke assured her.
"Transmission requires direct contact with a victim's bodily fluids.
We can contain that. The outbreaks are horrible, but then they fade
away as we sequester the victims. But smallpox, now, that's a nasty
little virus, far worse than Marburg because it spreads more easily."
There were clicking keyboards around the room. This stuff would
definitely be on the midterm. I was typing along with the rest . . . "an
airborne virus that can be inhaled, like the flu" . . . "the more serious
form of smallpox, *Variola major*, kills thirty or forty percent of those
who become infected" . . . "black pustules on the skin."

Huke paused; the clicking keyboards continued for a few seconds as we caught up. Then he delivered his carefully scripted finale,
the virus equivalent of that last burst of fireworks on the Fourth of
July: "In the twentieth century, smallpox killed at least three hundred
million people—more than the world wars, the Soviet purges, the
Great Leap Forward, and just about every other man-made catastro-
phe combined." He paused again. The typing stopped and most of
us looked up. Then, when he had our full attention, he continued,
"I was born in 1967. That year smallpox killed two million people
around the world."

"Holy shit," someone exclaimed up front.

"Yes," Huke answered. "That's about right. You know what's even
crazier? Edward Jenner had invented the smallpox vaccine a hundred
and fifty years earlier!" There was lots of clicking as Huke walked us
through the mechanics of immunization . . . "infecting an individual with cowpox, a milder relative of the smallpox virus, causes the
body to produce antibodies" . . . "wealthy countries developed mass
immunization programs . . ."

"What happened on October twenty-sixth, 1977?" Huke asked

with a dramatic flourish. I had no idea. I looked around the room; apparently no one else did, either. After the suspense mounted sufficiently, he told us: "The World Health Organization diagnosed the very last naturally occurring case of smallpox in Somalia. The very last case! After that, the WHO certified the global eradication of smallpox—the first and only time that we have completely triumphed over a major contagious disease." Huke must have given this lecture twenty-five or thirty times in his career. Still, he was not faking the excitement. He thought this stuff was so remarkably cool that we had no choice but to share his enthusiasm. *A disease that could kill two million people in a single year, wiped out by human ingenuity.*

Huke walked us through the details, which felt more like an adventure story than biology. The developed countries had already eradicated the virus through immunization. That left the disease lurking in some of the poorest, most war-ravaged places on the planet. The goal was to identify outbreaks in those places and then contain them. Teams of public health experts were dispatched with radios to these forlorn outposts so they could call in any outbreaks. At the first sign of smallpox, the vaccine was rushed to the scene and anyone who had come into contact with the victim was immunized. "In some cases, guards were posted at the doors of infected households so no person could spread the disease," Huke explained, relishing the detail. "The strategy was called surveillance and containment. And on October twenty-sixth, 1977, the very last case of smallpox on the planet was identified and isolated. That is how and why you live in a world free of that horrible disease."

This material would definitely be on the midterm, but almost no one was typing or writing. How can you forget something like that?

8.

THE PRESIDENT OF THE UNITED STATES WAS NOT A PARTICularly nice man. At times he could be kind of an asshole, to be honest. The curious thing is that I do not think that made him a bad president. If anything, it may be an essential characteristic for the job.

I met the President on the first of April. I know it was April 1 because it was my thirtieth birthday. That morning I was trying to fix the power source in one of our microscopes in the lab. The phone rang in my office, which was really just a small nook with a desk in a corner of the laboratory. I did not have a secretary; no one in the laboratory did. The microscope was disassembled all over my workspace, so I let the call go. Then my cell phone rang, and I ignored that, too. I figured it was someone calling to wish me a happy birthday and I could call them back. (The good news about a birthday on April Fool's Day is that people tend to remember.) But just a few minutes later a woman whom I recognized as the assistant to the Director walked into the lab. She looked around quickly, spotted me, and headed briskly in my direction: all business. "You need to answer your phone," she said.

"I was in the middle of something," I replied. I was more puzzled than defensive. I did not get a lot of important calls and none that were time-sensitive. I was paid to do research, not talk on the phone.

"The Director needs to see you right now," she said.

I felt a tinge of panic at that point, right in the pit of my stomach. Three days earlier, a college friend had sent an e-mail to my work address with a subject line that urged me to "TAKE THE TEST." I foolishly opened it, and the link led me to an Internet slide show with twenty pairs of bare breasts. In each pair, one set of breasts was real, and one was "enhanced." I did not even take the test—I was smart enough to know that—but as I rushed to close the screen, with two large sets of breasts plastered across the entire thirty-five-inch monitor, one of our lab assistants walked by my desk. "Nice," she said sarcastically. I closed the window immediately, but still . . . not good. And now, with the Director's assistant standing officiously in front of me, I thought, *Very bad. Very, very bad.*

The lab is funded almost entirely by the federal government. My computer was government property. Roughly 80 percent of the scientists are men; the Director, a woman, was appointed in part to send a signal about the importance of promoting women in science. I had been to three full-day seminars on gender sensitivity in the workplace. (Everyone at the National Institutes of Health had to do this; I was not singled out for any particular behavior.) Even without the sensitivity training, I was well aware that studying real and fake boobs on a government computer with a huge monitor at a federally funded laboratory was frowned upon.

Was it enough to get summoned to the Director's office? Maybe. I stood there for a minute, trying to remember if I had deleted the e-mail. The servers were all backed up, so it probably did not matter anyway.

"Hurry up. And bring your coat," the Director's assistant said. My coat?

"Where are we going?" I asked.

"I have no idea," she answered curtly. "They just told me to find you as quickly as possible and take you to the rear entrance. The Director is going to meet you there." At that point I knew this was not about trying to tell real boobs from fake boobs in a government laboratory. If anything, the pit in my stomach grew more intense. My chest felt tight, like someone was squeezing it from behind.

The Director was standing next to a black Town Car in the circular drive at the back of the building. As I appeared, she opened a rear door of the car and motioned me in. I slid across the seat and she got in beside me, slamming the door. The car pulled out immediately. The Director introduced herself and offered a handshake. Obviously I knew who she was, but I appreciated the gesture. Many of the people whom I would meet in the coming days did not extend the same courtesy, including the President. Then again, I suppose it is silly for the President of the United States to introduce himself, just false modesty.

"What can you tell me about lurking viruses?" the Director asked.

"What would you like to know?" I asked. She had asked a broad question, the virology equivalent of asking a historian to tell you about wars in Europe. "You should read my Ph.D. dissertation. You'd be the fourth person," I said, trying for humor.

The Director had a nondescript black trench coat folded across her lap. She pulled a copy of my dissertation from beneath the coat. I could tell from the binding that it was the copy from our library at the lab. "I flipped through it," she said. "You need to give me the basics."

"Where are we going?" I asked.

"To the White House."

"Has there been some kind of attack?" I asked. Anybody in my field knew the risks of biological warfare. The public tends to freak out about nukes, but if you put some of those nasty pathogens that Huke taught us about on a simple rocket—the kind that Hamas can build in a garage—you could kill, maim, and terrify a lot of people. Pathogens are easier to acquire than nuclear weapons and far easier to move across international borders. That was one reason our laboratory had been relatively well funded over the previous decade.

"It's more complicated than that," she said.

"Every lurking virus that I'm aware of responds to Dormigen," I offered.

"Yeah," she said in a strange, noncommittal kind of way.

Only later, when I was sitting on a couch opposite the President, with a White House steward offering me coffee or water, would I understand what she meant by that.

9.

THE FIRST KNOWN CASE WAS IN NATICK, MASSACHUSETTS. A thirty-seven-year-old man had been shoveling after a particularly heavy snowstorm in late March. He came into the house and complained of flu-like symptoms. By midnight he was in the emergency room with a 103-degree fever that would not respond to aspirin or ibuprofen. His white blood cell counts were elevated, but there was no obvious sign of infection or illness. At two-thirty a.m., after the fever climbed to 104, the attending physician prescribed Dormigen. The fever abated quickly and the patient was released from the hospital later that morning.

We know about that particular case only because the ER physician did what she was supposed to do, which was report the illness and its symptoms to a central database jointly maintained by the Centers for Disease Control (CDC) and the National Institutes of Health (NIH), my employer. True, the patient walked out of the hospital nearly recovered, and there were no recurring symptoms, but that had become a problem in the post-Dormigen world. Dormigen is effective against all known pathogens, meaning that doctors can cure a patient without having any idea what the underlying illness is.

This is a great thing—mostly. Public health officials also recognized it as a looming problem. If Dormigen were to go the way of penicillin and just about every other breakthrough antibiotic—as will almost certainly happen, unless we can somehow stop the process of natural selection—we might have no knowledge of the illnesses that had been afflicting us. Dormigen took us to a strange place in medicine. A physician can have no idea what is wrong with a patient, and yet a ready cure is never more than a prescription away: the doctor hits a key, a CVS drone drops the medicine at your door, and the disease is beaten back—whatever it may have been. Many health care experts pointed out, half seriously, that if you showed up in an emergency room with flu-like symptoms, the guy mopping the floor in the waiting area could treat you just as effectively as any of the professionals in white coats. "Here, take Dormigen," the janitor would offer before going back to his mopping. And it would work.

In a rare act of bipartisanship, Congress passed a law to deal with this potential problem. Physicians are now required to make a diagnosis before prescribing Dormigen. A doctor has to at least make some conjecture as to why your chest is covered with open sores. Then you get your gel caps. Yes, physicians still cut corners, offering vague, incomplete, and often inaccurate diagnoses (e.g., "tropical disease"), as I would if I were an overworked general practitioner with twelve and a half minutes to spend with each patient. Still, some information is better than none.

The same law requires that if a physician prescribes Dormigen without a firm diagnosis—if he or she really cannot identify the underlying illness—the symptoms have to be entered into a federal database. Doctors hate it; so do the anti-government folks. Big Brother now knows if you have a rash on your penis. Like many federal regulations, this one is imperfectly observed and poorly enforced. Nonetheless, on that snowy March evening in Natick, Dr. Helen Spellings typed a few vague lines into the Dormigen Prescription Without Diagnosis (DP-WoD) database at the end of her shift. The salient key words of the undiagnosed illness were "healthy male," "nonresponsive fever" and "flu-like symptoms."

In Tampa, Florida, at about the same time that Dr. Spellings was typing those vague symptoms into the DP-WoD database, Tom

Elliott, a management consultant from San Francisco, was spiking a fever as he prepared to give a presentation to the board of directors of a large auto parts manufacturer. Elliott did not seek medical attention, as far as we know. Our best guess is that his fever was around 102 as he rushed through his PowerPoint slides. He mentioned in passing at the beginning of his presentation that he was not feeling well. He later sent a text to his daughter saying he felt miserable—so bad that he was not sure he could tolerate the five-hour flight home. Elliott went back to his room at the Marriott Courtyard, presumably to rest. A hotel employee found him unconscious that afternoon when she went to clean the room. By the time Elliott was transported to a hospital, his major organs had shut down. He died less than an hour later. Tom Elliott was forty-three and healthy. As far as we know, he was the first fatality of the Outbreak.

Elliott's death, and what little could be pieced together of his symptoms, were entered in a different federal database, the Fatal Infectious Disease Surveillance Instrument (FIDSI). This database has been around longer; doctors take it much more seriously. Public health officials pay attention when otherwise healthy people die from unknown causes. On the same day that Tom Elliott died in a Florida hotel room, six other people died with similar symptoms: five middle-aged men and a female lacrosse player at the University of Vermont. But to spot that pattern, someone has to be looking for it.

10.

"WHAT DO YOU MAKE OF THIS?" TATIANA BOROVSKY ASKED her supervisor.

She had walked down the hall at the CDC on a Monday morning clutching a handful of papers and some rough statistical analysis she had done earlier that morning. The public would eventually know her simply as "Tatiana" after stories described her as the "discoverer" of the Outbreak. I suppose it was technically true, in the sense that Tatiana Borovsky was the first person to notice a statistical anomaly, the mathematical manifestation of an epidemic. If I were to be less generous, I would point out that the first person to discover it is raining is not necessarily a genius. The data, like raindrops, tend to fall on your head.

Tatiana was tall—nearly six feet—and exotic-looking. One has to wonder if she would have received as much attention if she had been a balding, middle-aged man, like her supervisor. She had an intriguing backstory, including family that hailed from the Balkans and Syria. (Her provenance tended to shift, depending on the news story.) Tatiana had long legs, long jet-black hair, and exotic if not necessarily beautiful features. As you may remember from some of the news stories, she also had a proclivity for skinny-dipping while on holiday at various destinations on the Black Sea. One lesson from the Outbreak is that if you are lanky, reasonably good-looking, and prone to post topless photos on the Internet, you are likely to garner undue attention. Tatiana walked down the hall on that Monday morning with data showing an increase in unexplained deaths that was two standard deviations above the norm. If one does a Google search of "Tatiana Borovsky and two standard deviations" the topless photos come up, along with a succinct explanation of what a standard deviation is, using breasts as a teaching tool. One standard deviation is significantly larger (or smaller) than normal. Two standard deviations is very unusual—as the photos illustrate. Very clever, I suppose. (To be clear, I never visited this site while using my government computer.)

"Probably just noise," Tatiana's supervisor said as he perused the data. "But those are big numbers." He had a small, windowless office with pleasant but artless photos of his second wife and their blended family. He most likely did not take photos of himself swimming naked, and if he did, no one would want to see them. "Check all the databases," he told her. "See if anything turns up in the OECD numbers."

This was basic epidemiological detective work. You look for patterns. The more data you have, the easier it is to spot them. Suppose six people driving the same kind of pickup truck die in traffic accidents in six different states. A police officer at each accident scene will investigate the crash and fill out the paperwork. Why would any one of those officers—just one person examining one crash site— suspect that the brakes on that particular pickup truck were faulty? Each report gets filed away. Maybe it ends up in a state database, one piece of a jigsaw puzzle. No one can do the puzzle without seeing the other pieces. But when a mid-level bureaucrat at the National Highway Traffic Safety Administration—Tatiana without the legs and exotic looks—gets a weekly report showing a cluster of fatal crashes involving a T-370 pickup, she is going to put down her coffee and walk that report down the hall. Someone is eventually going to take a look at the brakes on the T-370.

Tatiana did that. The rhetoric about her as "the hero" and "the Syrian savior" was not merely overblown; it was ridiculous. She had only one basic responsibility, which was to gather reports and look for anomalies. She was not a paper pusher, more of a paper catcher. The oddity she spotted was 107 unexplained deaths from flu-like symptoms in the previous week. All were otherwise healthy people. Most were under age fifty, including eight college students. Even in the era of Dormigen, there are periodic spikes in unexplained deaths. Most of them turn out to be statistical noise, but as Tatiana's supervisor rightly observed, 107 was a curiously high number for unexplained deaths among healthy people. Each of those deaths was its own tragedy; together they may have been the pieces of a more interesting puzzle. Or maybe not.

Tatiana plodded back to her cubicle and did three things as a matter of protocol.* First, she sent a blanket query to the public health entities in the other thirty-three OECD countries asking if they were observing a similar trend. (The Organization for Economic Cooperation and Development—OECD—is a consortium of the world's most developed countries that share data and cooperate on assorted things.) That is the fastest and easiest way to spot a global epidemic. True, any nasty pandemic is more likely to originate in Liberia than in France, but there are no meaningful data in the Liberias of the world, so the best we can do is spot a trend when it begins to appear in places where you can drink the water.

---

* Again, I feel compelled to point out that this was not heroism or genius on her part. It was her job. The NIH had binders spelling out in picayune detail exactly what low-level employees (e.g., Tatiana) were supposed to do in such situations. When Amazon put her photo on every digital receipt—dressed as a nurse, for no apparent reason—with "How many lives did she save?" splashed above her sultry pose, many of us in the scientific community answered, "Probably none."

Second, Tatiana requested follow-up data for each of the 107 deaths. There would be autopsy results for all of them because the cause of death was unknown. That is the law in most states, even if it is often skirted. She also requested the medical histories and treatment files for each case. This is trickier territory given the privacy issues, but doctors and hospitals typically comply if the identifying information can be stripped from the files. The sad irony is that the CDC—our first responder for anything that looks contagious—does not care at all about personal information. At the same time families and friends are reminiscing at funerals about intimate details— hobbies and weddings and crazy college stories—the CDC wants none of that information. The puzzle pieces do not need names, let alone golf handicaps or boyfriends.

Last, Tatiana accessed a different database to check for any unexplained increase in the prescription of Dormigen. If there were an epidemic afoot, particularly a flu epidemic, most patients would be treated successfully with Dormigen. They would stop by the doctor's office after a day or two of feeling miserable, or on the way home from work in the middle of the day. Neither doctor nor patient would ever know—or care—how bad things might have been in the absence of Dormigen. Still, there should be a record for each of those cases, even if the last thing a beleaguered physician wants to do at the end of the day is fill out extra paperwork. More puzzle pieces.

The bureaucratic gears turn slowly. Tatiana left for a short vacation in the Bahamas with her fiancé. Many of the European equivalents of the CDC were closed for assorted holidays (and, to be honest, they do not work at light speed even when they are open). The files were eventually shuffled and filed and analyzed, after which there was a clear pattern. Six of the OECD countries showed an anomalous rise in flu-like deaths among young, healthy adults. The spike in unexplained Dormigen prescriptions, both in the U.S. and in those six OECD countries, was also pronounced. The numbers were not huge, but they were significant. More reports were prepared. Meetings were held. Information was shared across countries—the usual administrative protocol. No one was particularly alarmed. The pattern was noteworthy but relatively modest in the grand scheme of things.

That changed in week three. Tatiana, back from the Bahamas,

sent an e-mail to the whole Contagious Disease Working Group: "Hey All, I just compiled the new data on global unexplained deaths, and there is something going on here. The numbers are still relatively small, but they are increasing at a rapid rate. Can we get together before the end of the day?"

In CDC-speak, that means "Holy shit!" Nobody in public health likes to see anything "increasing at a rapid rate." Epidemics do not meander along at fifty-five miles per hour. When a sick person has the potential to infect ten or twenty-five others, every sporting event or crowded subway car or day-care center becomes the disease equivalent of a cluster bomb. That was how forty million people died in the Spanish flu pandemic. There were three more deaths at the University of Vermont, all athletes. The media did not have access to the broader data, which was showing a rise in unexplained deaths across the country, but when three otherwise healthy college students die in the same place from an ambiguous cause, people notice. Google News blasted a segment on the "mysterious deaths" at the University of Vermont. CNN sent a camera crew to campus to interview alarmed students, thereby generating more alarm. The Internet was abuzz with theories.

The CDC Director asked Ron Justman, the head of Tropical Diseases, to lead a working group to coordinate our response to whatever was going on, this anomalous spike. There was no reason to believe it was a tropical disease, but Justman was senior and relatively competent. More important, he had some free time, having just rotated off of a task force working on an outbreak of dengue fever in Hawaii. The NIH sent over a handful of research scientists. Yes, there was a CNN camera crew at the University of Vermont, but in our world (though I was not yet involved) this felt like more of the same: another statistical aberration that would likely run its course.

The first meeting of the still-unnamed working group reflected this sense of business as usual. While the group waited for a conference room, the junior staffers discussed a new sushi restaurant in downtown Baltimore. "Do we really need another sushi restaurant?" one of them asked.

"It's totally different," a CDC staffer weighed in. "More creative stuff, a fusion thing. Pricey, though."

"A good date-night spot?"

"Perfect. It's in an old warehouse. Very cool space. If you sit upstairs you get a view of the harbor."

The conference room door opened and another team filed out, carrying papers and water bottles. They left behind a tray of semi-stale bagels and muffins. Justman's working group filed in, six or seven of them, with Justman taking a seat near the end of the small conference table. The bagels and muffins remained untouched until one of the NIH guys cut them into quarters, at which point they all disappeared rapidly, even the raisin bagels.

"Okay, what do we have?" Justman asked. He was forty or fifty (or maybe thirty-five or fifty-five), with a full head of unruly reddish hair and a matching mustache. The mustache was impressive; he could have passed for a state trooper if you gave him a decent haircut, the black boots, the uniform, and a cool hat. Instead, he was wearing a short-sleeve no-iron dress shirt with a breast pocket full of pens. One of the junior staffers turned on the projector, which illuminated a screen on the opposite wall, but he could not get the laptop computer to recognize his encrypted data pod. "Just walk me through it," Justman told him. "I don't need to see slides."

The junior staffer summarized the patterns that had emerged in the previous week: the increase in unexplained deaths; the corresponding spike in Dormigen prescriptions; similar anomalies in a few other developed countries; the cluster of deaths at the University of Vermont. "What are we seeing in the autopsies?" Justman asked.

"Not much, really," one of the CDC women answered. "It's not meningitis, not measles. Doesn't seem to be a strain of the flu. We can rule out most of the logical explanations."

"Just unexplained deaths," Justman said.

"Pretty much, yes."

"And we've got tissue samples here?" Justman asked.

"They're coming," another staffer offered. "We should have a decent number to look at by the end of the week."

Justman nodded in acknowledgment. All pretty normal stuff. A medical examiner in rural Colorado or suburban Chicago might never see a fatal case of malaria, let alone something more exotic. The NIH and CDC could do more extensive tests, with far more expertise as to what to look for. As grieving families around the country held memorial services and burials—all the more emotionally wrenching because these were healthy people struck down for no obvious reason—the tissue samples were making their way via FedEx and DHL to a nondescript federal laboratory just outside Atlanta. These samples were the disease equivalent of bullet casings and fingerprints: not always enough to find the perpetrator, but a logical place to start.

"Okay, so tell me about the University of Vermont," Justman said. This was a "cluster," a small group of deaths from which the working group might be able to draw some inferences. If there are three homicides in the same neighborhood on the same night, the first thing you want to figure out is what they have in common. Did the victims know each other? What did they do for a living? What were they all doing the day before they were killed? Diseases may not stalk their victim with a gun, but they each have a modus operandi, just like any other killer. If you figure out the MO, it will often lead you to the guy pulling the trigger.

"The UVM cases are kind of a head-scratcher," one of the CDC staffers began. She was Indian-American, slightly older than the others around the table. "They were all athletes but different sports. They didn't live together or take any of the same classes. I couldn't find any evidence that they'd ever met."

"It's a small campus," Justman said.

"True, but still nothing obvious. They weren't sharing water bottles. They weren't dating."

"Food, maybe," someone offered from around the table. "A dining hall, or the local sandwich shop."

"Maybe," the Indian-American woman answered, "but it doesn't look like a foodborne outbreak. These were healthy young people. It wouldn't explain why we are seeing a similar pattern in France and the UK. I don't know. I've got nothing."

"It probably is nothing," said the only guy in a tie, albeit with a collar he had forgotten to button. He was the statistics guru, with no background in epidemiology or public health. He was paid twice as much as the rest of us, which we knew because the NIH needed approval from Congress to waive the pay scale to hire him. In the era of "big data," every company was trying to digest terabytes of data to gain any possible advantage in the marketplace, whether it was pitching just the right vacation to divorced soccer moms in California or using online reading habits to sort the good credit risks from future deadbeats. Never mind that the NIH was using the same basic tools to save lives rather than sell shoes, the stats geeks were a hot commodity and we had to pay them a competitive salary. So we got Tie Guy (Marcus? Marc?). Word around the water cooler was that he could be smug and annoying, but it was hard to separate that from general envy of his highly publicized salary, like those college football coaches who make more than the university president. He did himself no favors by wearing a necktie in an office where the dress code consisted of matching socks, zipping one's pants, and trying to make sure each shirt button went into its assigned hole. (Some of our brightest scientists routinely failed one or more of these sartorial challenges.)

To be fair, Tie Guy was a trenchant thinker when confronting complex challenges. I had first met him at a brown bag lunch several months earlier when he presented his findings on the impact of a proposed Chinese railroad that would connect a series of mining sites in South Africa and Zambia with a major port. He started the presentation with a pretty darn good line (as I recall it): "Copper, gold, and diamonds are going to move more efficiently on the railway. People are going to move more quickly and easily on the railway. And that means the HIV virus is going to be riding, too. I don't know if the Chinese have named the rail line yet, but we should think about calling it the AIDS Express." He had color-coded slides showing how the increase in mobility would change the AIDS infection rate under different scenarios, including different prices for a third-class ticket.

"Most of these clusters turn out to be randomness," Tie Guy now told the members of Justman's newly formed working group. "Six kids get cancer near the fertilizer plant. Sometimes six kids just get cancer." Justman looked at him but said nothing.

"And sometimes the fertilizer company is dumping poison in the water," said a woman across from him.

"True, but where's our fertilizer plant here?" Tie Guy replied with confidence bordering on hubris. "If we can't find a pattern, then it's probably because there isn't a pattern."

"Let's see what the tissue samples show," Justman said. "Tatiana, can you speed that along and schedule something for all of us when we have data to look at?" Tatiana, who had been quiet for the whole meeting, nodded and made a note on her phone. "Thanks, everyone," Justman said, bringing the short meeting to a close.

That was it. Not a lot of drama or excitement, a fairly typical meeting for anyone in public health. I was not in the room. There was no reason I would be.* This group was still a long way from having any idea what was going on. Only then would they call me.

11.

I APPLIED TO PH.D. PROGRAMS IN MICROBIOLOGY AND WAS accepted at the University of Chicago. Sloan went to law school. My parents were convinced that microbiology was close to medicine, and therefore I could still become a doctor. I never gave them this idea, but I did not disabuse them of it, either. During my third year in the Ph.D. program, when I had already adopted and abandoned three or four different potential dissertation topics, I applied to get a joint degree in public health. What was another two years and $140,000 of debt? My parents gradually accepted the notion that I was not going to become a doctor, though they never fully accepted the idea that I was a scientist. I once overheard my mother tell a friend that I worked "in medicine." True, technically. Professor Huke's class stuck with me, and I winnowed my doctoral research down to virulent pathogens. I really liked the scary ones. In my third year, I was able to work with Ebola, meaning that I had to put on the full level-four biohazard suit. Some people climb mountains for the thrill of it, knowing that one misstep could send them tumbling down a

---

* The detail here comes from the Outbreak Inquiry Commission hearings, during which a group of Tea Party senators were obsessed with the idea that the NIH, the CDC, and the Federal Reserve had somehow—and for some reason that I never fully grasped—colluded to cover up early evidence of the Outbreak.

precipice. I felt that way when I put on two sets of gloves and entered the air-lock chamber. A little carelessness and I would be infected with a million viruses capable of making me bleed to death out of every orifice.

Dormigen changed that, obviously. By the time I was doing my fourth year of research, the most serious pathogens were no longer as excitingly scary, as if a giant net were installed around Everest to catch everyone who slips and falls. Still, the advent of Dormigen created a different kind of excitement. The research we were doing, particularly our growing understanding of the human genome, was producing giant strides in other areas of medicine. We reckoned that cancer was the next frontier (as it had been for several decades, admittedly). Dormigen did not work on tumors because they were not recognized as foreign DNA; cancer cells are mutant products of our own body, rather than invaders like the Ebola or Marburg viruses. But all of us working at that frontier were convinced that a Dormigen-type breakthrough was possible on the cancer front.

My doctoral research was intended to probe one possible link between viruses and cancer: the so-called "lurking virus." What makes this kind of virus fascinating—and dangerous—is that it lies dormant in a host for years or even decades. Then, for reasons that we did not fully understand when I began my doctoral work, the virus turns spectacularly virulent, killing a high proportion of the infected population. This is entirely anomalous behavior among the hundreds of thousands of viruses that have been identified and stud-ied. Viruses are usually benign or dangerous—not both. In the past, I have made the comparison—admittedly imperfect—to a workplace shooter. Some guy comes to work every day, settles into his cubicle, does his work, goes to the holiday party, complains about the Docu-Text scanner—normal to the point of fading into the background. That is even what witnesses sometimes say: "He was so normal" or "A very quiet guy." Then one day he shows up with a semiautomatic weapon and starts firing at his coworkers. We are left with one over-whelming question: Why? And even if we have some insight there, we ask, Why that day? What transforms a guy from someone whom colleagues struggle to remember into a killing machine? What was different that morning, or the night before, or whenever he decided to massacre his colleagues instead of making car loans or selling motor-cycle insurance? If we can understand that, we will have unlocked one of the deepest mysteries of the human psyche. And we may save a lot of lives.

So it is with lurking viruses. How and why does an organism that can live in perfect symbiosis with its host for years or decades suddenly turn deadly? *Even more bizarre, the same virus will often return to its benign state months or years later.* Imagine that the virus for the common cold suddenly became as virulent as smallpox, wiping out a large percentage of the infected population. Then a few years later the virus goes back to causing sniffles and a sore throat. *The exact same virus.* This is not a mutation, or a different strain. The guy goes to work one day and celebrates a receptionist's birthday in the conference room, sharing the cake and chuckling at the bad rendi-tion of "Happy Birthday." The next day he tries to shoot as many of his coworkers as possible. But then a year later, this deranged killer would ask his jailers, "Hey, when can I go back to work?"

As one of my graduate school professors once said, "It defies everything we think we know about evolution." A tiger is not sup-posed to change its stripes, at least not suddenly. And if there were a sudden change—some kind of major genetic mutation that bestows a reproductive advantage—why would the organism change back? A virus typically lives without doing serious harm to its host (the common cold), getting passed along successfully. Or it kills violently (Ebola), using the dead victim (bleeding from every orifice) as a virus bomb that propagates the deadly organism to more hosts. But not both. It was hard to reconcile what we observed in lurking viruses with the most fundamental tenets of biology.

The prevailing theory was that some kind of "trigger" causes a lurking virus to go rogue, and then later to return to normal, like some kind of genetic on/off switch. Obviously, if we could identify that switch, we could in theory turn dangerous viruses "off," or turn benign viruses "on." This was the potential cancer link. Tumors are benign cells that begin dividing out of control—workplace shooters. Might there be a similarity between the hypothetical on/off switch in lurking viruses and the trigger that turns normal human cells into devastating malignant tumors?

When I began my research, lurking viruses had never been found in humans. In fact, there had been no documented cases of a lurking virus infecting any warm-blooded vertebrate. The most common hosts are amphibians, particularly in the tropics. My research took me to the Amazon basin, where I spent ten months collecting data on two species of tree frog. My Dartmouth classmates, many of whom had gone on to business and law school, liked to joke that I had gone off to climb trees in the jungle. Their observation was not entirely inaccurate; both species of frog are easiest to find just below the canopy, where they are safest from predators. I did literally climb trees, usually with the benefit of a ladder. But the jungle comments also had a tinge of judgment, as if my doctoral research were some kind of escape from "real" work. I found it amusing when I was in a good mood—and irksome when I was not—that my peers who were finding better ways to sell snack foods, or engineering mergers between giant oil companies, had the chutzpah to tell me I was shirking my social responsibility.

Anyway, these two species (the Abiseo climbing frog and the black-eyed tree frog, for anyone who cares) were nearly wiped out by a parasitic virus beginning in the early 2000s. That was no big deal; species come and go, especially in the Amazon. But in 2016, a savvy Brazilian researcher made a startling discovery. These tree frogs had *always* been hosts for this parasitic virus—literally for millions of years—but for nearly all of that time the virus did not kill them. He had excavated a tar pit near an Amazon tributary where a whole ecosystem from two million years ago had been preserved intact—the biological equivalent of Pompeii. The site was (and still is) a treasure trove for biologists. The finding that interested me was just a footnote to the many other extraordinary discoveries. Two million years ago, these two tree frogs were infected by the same parasitic virus that would later nearly wipe out their species, but they were seemingly unaffected by it. The tree frogs trapped in the tar pit all carried the virus, but analysis of the preserved tissue suggested that they died *with* the virus, not *from* it. The relationship between the host and the parasite was innocuous, maybe even symbiotic, just like all the organisms inhabiting the human gut. Happy tenants.

So what changed? And why? Those were the central questions of my doctoral dissertation. The dissertation was mediocre by any conventional standard. That was one reason I could not find an academic job. I loved my work at the NIH, but I had "settled" when I first agreed to work there. Scientists have their own hierarchies. The researchers at the preeminent academic institutions are at the top: Harvard, Yale, and so on. The big state universities are next; what they lack in prestige they make up for in grants, facilities, and access to graduate students. Then there are the government research facilities, places like NIH and CDC, where the quality of research is good, but there are fewer freedoms than at a university. My research had its merits. I had thoroughly documented spells in which the Amazonian tree frogs had been harmlessly infected with lurking viruses and also periods during which the viruses had nearly wiped out the affected populations. Nobody had ever done this kind of fieldwork before. Still, when I gave my academic job talks (I did apply for openings in biochemistry at a handful of research universities), the faculty panels would always ask the same thing: "Why?" I had no answer, not even a compelling theory to test (which might have earned me a job at a second-tier university).

I was the guy who came in after a mass killing and explained exactly how the killer had behaved on the day of the shooting. I could outline exactly what happened and when—but not *why* some twenty-one-year-old decided to open fire on his professors and fellow students. And *why* is really what we care about, as that is what we need to know to prevent the next campus shooting.

I was cursed with a particularly unimaginative dissertation adviser, who discouraged a line of inquiry that might have led to more robust answers to these questions. This caused a profoundly uncomfortable moment at my dissertation defense. "I don't see how you have moved the research frontier," my adviser declared. I was standing at the front of a small seminar room filled with a smattering of fellow students, family members, curious faculty members, and the three professors who would determine whether I would become a Ph.D. or a failed graduate student, the dreaded ABD (All But Dissertation). My adviser was the chair of that committee and its most influential member.

"My work provides a deeper understanding of how lurking viruses function within their hosts," I answered.

"But it's not your work. You've summarized the work of others," my adviser pressed. He was sitting in the back of the room; the other observers turned to look at him, then turned back to hear my response, like an academic game of tennis. My mind was working furiously, trying to figure out if he was trying to screw me or just make me sweat a little.

"There were various strands of research on this topic, each isolated in its own way," I said with far more confidence than I was feeling. "When you bring them together—well, that's what I've done here— you get a more complete understanding of how the organisms interact." I was thinking, *What the fuck? This guy has been working with me for three years and now he brings this up?*

"Hmm," my adviser said with mild disdain. "You have successfully woven together work already published by others—"

"Much of this work was not published," I interrupted.

"Fine. That's an irrelevant distinction," he said haughtily. "You've taken Legos produced by other people and built something interesting." There was tittering around the room in response to the Legos metaphor. "I'll repeat my original question: Where is the original work? What Lego did you produce?"

In my mind: *Oh, my God, he is screwing me.*

I tried to compose my thoughts, but before I could respond the chair of the department interjected, "Enough of the Lego claptrap. The most valuable contribution one can make in science is to give voice to the work of others in a way that improves our overall understanding of a subject." I looked furtively at my parents, whose body language improved noticeably after this intervention. A few of the graduate students exchanged sly smiles; they recognized this was no longer about my dissertation. The chair of the department was a well-respected microbiologist, one of the first women tenured in the department. She was fiftyish and dowdy, neither attractive nor unattractive. She was a lousy teacher but a kind person and a good administrator, making her much appreciated by students and faculty alike. She was a relative superstar in her subfield of protozoology.

Also, she was my adviser's ex-wife. They had been recruited to the department together in the 1990s, both with tenure. Her publication record was more impressive than his, both before they arrived at the University of Chicago and after. He had an affair with one of his graduate students, leading to a separation and then a divorce. I have no idea why they both chose to stay in the department, but they did. The department was full of faculty who hated one another; these two at least had good reason.

Heads in the academic tennis match turned back to the rear of the classroom in anticipation of a response from my adviser. "And how have you improved our overall understanding of this subject?" he asked me. A softball. To those in the room without any understanding of the internal politics, like my parents, this whole discussion seemed to flow naturally. But to those of us who understood the Kabuki theater of academe, my adviser's ex-wife, who also happened to be a far more impressive microbiologist than he was, had just smacked him down. He was going to lose if he went back at her. I knew that. More important, he knew that. His softball question was a white flag.

I gave an innocuous answer, something more or less straight from my abstract. There were some other softball questions and then my adviser politely brought the discussion to a close. I walked out of the room along with the rest of the observers, leaving my committee behind to deliberate on my fate. It did not take long. Ten minutes later they filed out of the room and informed me that I was now a doctor of philosophy. "Congratulations," my adviser said woodenly.

His eyes betrayed what we both knew: I had been saved by the fact that he had been caught screwing one of his graduate students.

12.

JEFF YUN, THE HEAD PATHOLOGIST FOR THE CENTERS FOR Disease Control, was standing at the front of a conference room. Ron Justman's task force was assembled around the table. The lights were dim; a slide showing a single virus was projected on a screen on the far wall. "That's it," Yun said. "*Capellaviridae*." The organism was hexagonal, with short hairlike structures emerging from each of the sides. "Each of the victims had extremely high levels of the virus concentrated in their livers. As best as I can tell, that's the cause of death. The virus attacks the liver, and to a lesser extent the pancreas. Both organs shut down relatively quickly."

There were blank stares around the table. Justman shrugged, "A cappella?"

"*Capellaviridae*," Yun said.

"Never heard of it," Justman said. "Am I missing something?"

"No," Yun said. "No. That's the thing." He had a roundish, friendly face with closely cropped hair. Small beads of perspiration gathered on his upper lip. "It's a totally unexceptional virus, commonplace in temperate zones of the northern hemisphere. It didn't even have a name until twenty years ago." He looked around the table, inviting someone to make sense of this pedestrian virus turned killer.

"Are humans the only host?" Justman asked.

"We don't know. I'm telling you, nobody has ever studied this thing."

"And you're sure this virus is responsible for the deaths?" Tie Guy asked.

"I'm not sure of anything," Yun answered. "But the concentration of viruses that we observed in each of the victims is unlike anything I've ever seen. I spoke to my Canadian and European counterparts this morning. They've observed the same thing."

"Hold on," Tie Guy interjected. "Are we really sure of the causality here?" There followed a discussion of whether this virus, *Capellaviridae*, was killing people, or if people who were dying of something else were prone to becoming infected with *Capellaviridae*. Tie Guy lectured the room on what most of them already knew: many viruses are opportunistic, meaning they thrive when a host's immune system is compromised. A cancer victim may die of viral pneumonia, but to blame pneumonia for the death would be to miss the real problem.

Justman said, "In any event, we know that this virus is, at a minimum, a marker of the problem, yes? Maybe it's a dangerous pathogen, maybe it thrives when something else nasty is going on. Given how little we know, we should begin by focusing on *Capellaviridae*. Can we agree on that?" There were nods around the table.

"Is it harmful to animals?" the Indian-American woman asked. "We should at least know that."

"My people are testing that right now," Yun said quickly, not quite cutting her off. "I've got everybody working on this."

"Let's back up for a minute," Justman interjected. "The Dormigen database. We've seen a spike in prescriptions—"

"And those people, at least some of them, are testing positive for *Capellaviridae*?" Tie Guy interrupted.

"Yes," Yun said. "That appears to be why we're seeing the spike in Dormigen demand. Based on the limited data we have, it seems that most, if not all, of the increase in Dormigen prescriptions can be explained by some kind of epidemic related to *Capellaviridae*."

"And Dormigen is effective against *Capellaviridae*?" Justman asked.

"Yes, of course," Yun assured him.

"Hold on," Tie Guy said. "We still have not established that this virus is doing the harm. For all we know, it's an opportunistic pathogen that happens to manifest itself—"

"Yes, fair enough," Justman said, clearly impatient. "But whatever is going on responds to Dormigen. That's what I'm asking."

"Whatever is happening responds to Dormigen, yes," Yun said. As he answered, he reached into his jacket pocket and pulled out his phone. "Sorry, I should check this."

"Of course," Justman assured him.

Yun scrolled through a text of some sort and then ran his hand through his short hair, clearly perplexed. "Okay, this is interesting," he said as he looked at his phone. "I've got someone digging into *Capellaviridae*. Apparently it's just a run-of-the-mill virus, so common as to be unexceptional."

"What does that mean?" someone asked.

"That's just what he texted me: 'So common as to be unexceptional,'" Yun answered. He stared at his phone in silence for a few seconds and then looked up at Justman. "Let's take a break for a few minutes. Can we do that?" As Justman nodded agreement, Yun was already punching a number on his phone and walking out of the conference room. The participants around the table seized on the break to check devices, all eyes staring down as if it were some kind of choreographed dance. When Yun returned just a few minutes later, all eyes went immediately back to him.

"It's a common virus," Yun said, sliding his phone back into his jacket pocket. "That's why nobody has studied it. There's really nothing to study. It's an innocuous virus, found almost everywhere."

"Hardly innocuous," Tie Guy said. This was why people did not like him; it was not just his outsized salary. He always had to be the contrarian. One minute he was arguing that *Capellaviridae* might not be the real killer, the next he was refuting someone who said the same thing.

"Yes, innocuous, usually," Yun answered sharply. "This virus is everywhere. It's as common as bread mold."

"Obviously we're dealing with a different strain," Justman said.

"Not that we can tell," Yun said. He was starting to look a little flustered. More perspiration had gathered on his upper lip. "Here's the thing: My people in the lab tested themselves, and most of them are carrying the virus. On a whim, they tested a sample of soldiers at Fort Gail, and most of them are carrying it, too."

"They're all going to get sick?" the Indian-American woman asked.

"No, I don't think so," Yun replied. "My best guess is that this virus is innocuous for most people, most of the time. And now, for some reason, for some people, it's not."

"That's a big leap," Justman said. "It's more logical that we're dealing with a different strain."

"Hold on," Yun said. "I wasn't finished. The viruses are identical—from the victims and from my people in the lab. Indistinguishable DNA. But it gets weirder. We went back and looked at some old tissue samples that we have in the lab, ten or twenty years old. Most of them show traces of the virus, too. If I were to guess, humans have been carrying this virus around with no adverse effects for thousands of years."

"That doesn't make any sense," Justman said. A silence settled over the conference room. There was no panic, more of a puzzle. After all, Dormigen was there to handle the problem, whatever that problem might eventually shape up to be. This group was used to handling outbreaks: the flu epidemic of 2021, the Sam's Burrito *E. coli* contamination, and many more exotic things along the way. The formula was the same: treat the victims, find the source. It was always just a matter of time, and Dormigen could buy whatever time they needed.

Justman started thinking out loud: "We have a virus that is entirely innocuous, has been for decades, until it's not."

"A lurking virus?" a young woman offered. Her tone suggested uncertainty, but that was likely out of deference to those around the table rather than due to a true lack of knowledge. She was a staff epidemiologist, barely out of graduate school. In this case, youth was an asset. Most of the faces around the table were blank. She continued with more confidence. "I studied them in graduate school, just a bit. They are symbiotic with the host, then perhaps there is a trigger of some sort and they become virulent."

Yun gave a strange head nod, not a clear yes or a no, suggesting that he was familiar with lurking viruses while simultaneously discounting the theory.

"A lurking virus?" Justman asked.

"The pattern looks just like what we're seeing," the young epidemiologist continued. "An innocuous pathogen turns deadly, then, even more puzzling, they sometimes turn innocuous again."

Justman was clearly nonplussed that he had never heard of a lurking virus before. "In humans?" he asked skeptically.

"No, no," Yun said. "Not even in rodents. Only reptiles, as far as I know. Isn't that right?" he asked, looking at the young epidemiologist.

"I just read one paper in graduate school. It was salamanders or frogs. But the pattern looked just like what we're seeing," she said.

"What pattern?" Tie Guy interjected, prompting eye rolls around the table. "If we've established a pattern, I missed it. We do not have any sense of what's going on."

Justman looked at his watch. "Okay, we've run over time. We need to gather a lot more data. I think we can agree on that. In the meantime, we should notify the folks over at HHS that we are likely to see a higher than average demand for Dormigen in the coming months. We should probably also learn more about these lurking viruses."

The meeting broke up, and two things were set in motion. A formal notification was sent to the Department of Health and Human Services notifying the department of a projected spike in Dormigen demand—a so-called "Kaufman notice," named for the Congresswoman who wrote the bill requiring such notice. And the epidemiologists on the task force made some calls to inquire about the lurking virus. They called some people who called some people who called me.

13.

AL GOYAL, THE CHAIRMAN OF CENTERA BIOMEDICAL GROUP, was meeting with a group of Brazilian suppliers in the elegant sitting area of his office when his CFO appeared at the office door. "Al, do you have a minute?" the CFO asked.

"We're just wrapping up here," Goyal said.

"If you could just step out here for a second," the CFO insisted. The Swedish CFO of Centera Biomedical was not a pushy guy, and because of that, Goyal's impulse at that moment was panic. Perhaps there was a family emergency. He excused himself and walked briskly into the corridor with Swensen.

"We just got a call from Health and Human Services," the CFO reported. He stopped, as if that were all Goyal needed to know.

"Yes?" Goyal asked, perplexed.

"Health and Human Services," Swensen repeated. "They would like to exercise their option. The Dormigen. We owe them twenty million doses."

"Jesus Christ," Goyal muttered. "Why?" he asked.

"Why what?"

"Why do they want it?"

"I don't know," Swensen answered, growing more flustered. "They don't have to tell us that. It's a simple contract. If they exercise the option, we owe them up to twenty million doses."

"How much are they asking for?"

"All twenty million. Some of their stock was destroyed in a fire."

"Why do they need so much?" Goyal asked.

"I just told you, I don't know," Swensen said angrily. "It's not really important."

"We don't have twenty million doses," Goyal said, panic creeping into his voice.

"Well, we do. We do—but it's old," Swensen said.

There was some disagreement at trial over the balance of the conversation. Since Goyal and Swensen each blamed the other for hatching the original fraud, they also disagreed about the attempted cover-up. For the American public, it was a distinction without a difference. (The jury found likewise.) As I noted earlier, and most of the world now knows, Centera had burnished its balance sheet by keeping the old Dormigen, rather than destroying the stock and creating a new batch as the contract with the U.S. government required. Centera had more than twenty million doses of Dormigen in its warehouses,* but every one of them was past its date of expiration.

"Have you tested the effectiveness of what we have?" Goyal asked.

"I was waiting for your permission," the CFO answered. Centera policy had explicitly forbidden any testing of the Dormigen shelf life. If the drug proved effective for longer than six months, or could be reformulated to last longer, then Centera could no longer charge HHS for producing and destroying the drug every six months. More knowledge might mean lower profits.

"Do it now. Don't tell the lab why we need to know," Goyal instructed.

"Obviously."

"I'm sure it will be fine," Goyal said earnestly. He really believed it. After all, the government had imposed ridiculous padding everywhere else in life. Did we really need to know that our coffee was served hot? Would drinking milk one day after the expiration date do any harm? Goyal testified that he had purchased a lawn mower with a warning telling him not to use it to cut his bushes. The expired aspirin in his cabinet seemed to work fine, year after year. What difference would a few months make for Dormigen?

---

* Because Centera was trying to reduce costs by postponing the destruction of expired doses, the actual number was closer to forty million.

14.

A FEW MONTHS MAKES ALL THE DIFFERENCE, IT TURNS OUT. The FDA clinical trials had clearly established that seven months was the upper bound for the effectiveness of Dormigen and six months was the maximum recommended shelf life. Unlike aspirin, or even milk, Dormigen was alive. That is what made it such an extraordinarily effective drug. Dormigen was genetically engineered— human antibodies inserted into chicken embryos—and after about six months the medicine dies, literally.

Neither Goyal nor Swensen knew this, supposedly, which was the crux of their defense at trial. Neither was a genetic engineer; neither had any scientific training at all. In fact, not a single member of the Centera senior management had even a bachelor's degree in one of the hard sciences. Much was made of this fact in the months after the Outbreak—"the bean counters had elbowed aside the scientists," as the *Atlantic* described it. Much of this criticism misses the point, not because a science company does not need scientists in management, but because it lets the bean counters off too easy. There were thirty or forty scientists on the Centera payroll alone who could have told Goyal and Swensen that their plan would be deadly if the Dormigen doses were ever needed. Besides, one does not need a Ph.D. in virology to know that violating the terms of a contract with the federal government is a bad thing to do.

It is technically true that Goyal and Swensen did not willfully put the public at risk. They were not fully aware of what they had set in motion. The jury found this irrelevant. As the *Washington Post– USA Today* elegantly put it on the day of their conviction, "Neither Swensen nor Goyal knew that the gun was loaded when they pulled the trigger. But they also never cared to ask, which is just as awful in its own way."

Goyal and Swensen did understand one thing: Dormigen takes twenty-one days to produce. No one had ever found a way to shorten this process, in part because there had never been any need. The process was cheap and easy and foolproof, if you have three weeks. "We have to make more," a panicked Goyal told his CFO.

"I've already set that in motion," Swensen said. The two men were hoping the expired doses of Dormigen would still prove effective. If not, they would have twenty million new doses in three weeks. One has to give Goyal and Swensen some credit. When they found themselves in a hole, they did stop digging.

Swensen figured, and Goyal concurred, that they could always stall the delivery to HHS by three weeks. It was the federal government, after all. There were two weekends and a state holiday in those twenty-one days. "So, worst-case, we deliver it a little late," Goyal said, trying to reassure himself and Swensen. "Right?"

Under normal circumstances, he would have been correct. Of course, under normal circumstances, the federal government would not need twenty million extra doses of Dormigen.

PART 2

DO THE
RIGHT THING

15.

So there we were. The seven people in the world who appreciated the magnitude of what was happening: the President, his Chief of Staff, the President's Strategist, the Majority Leader, the Secretary of Defense, the Director of the National Institutes of Health, and me—the person who supposedly knew more about lurking viruses than anyone else in the world. The President was sitting at his desk reading papers as we filed in. He was wearing reading glasses; I had never seen him in glasses before. I later learned that he did not like to be photographed with his glasses on because he felt they made him look old.

There was no grand plan for this first meeting. No one spent hours figuring out exactly who should be in the room. The President convened a small group of people with relevant expertise, and, more important, whom he trusted. The Secretary of Health and Human Services should have been there, but she had become embroiled in a scandal involving her private investments in a pharmaceutical company. She would resign two days later. The Attorney General should have been involved from the beginning, but he was attending a conference in South Africa on post-conflict justice and could not be called home without attracting undue attention. The head of the Centers for Disease Control (CDC) would later claim, rightfully, that he was excluded for political reasons from the early White House deliberations. He was a holdover from the previous administration whom the President never fully trusted (mostly because he had a habit of leaking self-serving information to the press). And so on.

Meanwhile, there were some people in the room who literally did not know the difference between a virus and a bacterium. The Majority Leader was there because the President wanted some representation from the legislative branch. He and the President had developed a strong working relationship. The Senate Majority Leader, a former funeral director from central Illinois, looked much less impressive in person than on television. He was short and fat—not middle-aged heavy, but fat. When he put on his suit jacket, one did not notice as much, but when he took off his jacket and sat down, his prodigious paunch sometimes made it hard for him to pull his chair all the way to the conference table. Funeral directors are often pillars of the community. The Majority Leader had started his political career on the school board before making the leap to the state legislature and then to Washington. He never finished college; no one in the Senate had ever confused him for the resident intellectual. If anything, he was quick to criticize the "pointy heads." For all that, the Majority Leader was a brilliant politician, in the sense that he had a keen sense of the fears and hopes of people on the street. He was plainspoken, hardworking, and honest. In four decades of public life, he had made a lot of enemies, but no one had seriously accused him of breaking his word. Neither his friends nor his enemies ever doubted that he would use every tool in the legislative toolkit: flattery, bribery (the legal kind—a stadium here, favorable tax treatment there), persuasion, and threats (never idle).

The Majority Leader was a relatively new member of the Senate in 2024 when the final spasm of political realignment swept away what was left of the Republicans and Democrats. He was quick to jump on board with the New Republican Party, helping to shape it into the pragmatic, Main Street party that it is today. He could speak effectively, if not eloquently, about the needs and desires of small businesses and working people. "I don't have much use for books, other than political history," the Majority Leader told me once over a coffee break.

How does one respond to that? I was tempted to say, "If you read

more books, you might understand the difference between a bacterium and a virus." Or that when someone mentioned Willa Cather
in the course of discussion, you would not ask, "Who is he?" The
Majority Leader was also a big fan of simple solutions for complex
problems. He was skeptical of "fancy studies," as if there were some
logical alternative for advancing the frontier of human knowledge.

The Majority Leader was an unabashed patriot, so much so, he
said, that he never felt the need to leave our beloved country. When
he was younger, he made one trip with his high school Spanish class
to Mexico City. "That was enough," he told Rotary Clubs and New
Republican Party conventions. He said it in a way that made people cheer. Don't get me wrong: He was no buffoon. You do not get
elected to the U.S. Senate three times—not anywhere, not ever—
without some prodigious talents. He could talk in an informed but
vague way to Chicago business groups about "oppressive taxes and
regulations." He would rattle off some examples of wasteful federal
spending that were both telling and humorous, such as the earmark
in the farm bill to study the mating habits of potbellied pigs. That
always got a chuckle. As the laughter faded away, he would say, "I
can tell you how they mate for a lot less than two hundred and fifty
thousand dollars!" The audience would roar again.

He was not scary on social issues, so the suburbanites were
attracted to him. That was part of the Republican divorce. The New
Republicans got the low taxes, pro-business planks in the platform
and the Tea Party got the social issues: opposition to gay marriage,
abortion, and the like. (They had joint custody of guns.) The settlement was lopsided, at least with someone as politically adroit as the
Majority Leader atop the New Republican Party. "Let me see if I
can explain the difference between the New Republicans and the Tea
Party," he would tell his audiences. "Our number one *New Republican*
priority is making sure that hardworking people can earn a decent
living." He would pause, making eye contact around the room, big
or small. "Sometimes that means a little help from the government."
Another pause, more eye contact. "Sometimes it means keeping the
government out of your business." Pregnant pause. "I believe that
honest people deserve to make an honest living, and that we should
do whatever we need to do to make that possible."

There would be enthusiastic nods of approval—not whoops or cheers, but heartfelt agreement. And then he would go in for the kill. "Now, the *Tea Party*, they are going to work just as hard. I do not doubt their passion or commitment, not for one second. I agree with them on a lot of things. These are good people, many of them, at least." There would be some chuckles. "The difference is priorities. They are going to spend every waking moment trying to get Washington to tell you what you can and can't do—in your bedroom, in the hospital, in the bathroom, at school—sometimes even in the bathroom at school." Lots of laughter. "I'm pro-business, they are all up in your business!" This last line did typically provoke cheers of approval. It was a brilliant strategy, allowing him to transcend the social issues that had previously been a political fault line. He could tell the social conservatives that he shared their beliefs. They were tired of being mocked and disrespected by the liberal establishment. Yet he could also tell libertarians and liberal suburbanites that he was not going to politicize those same social issues.

The Majority Leader eviscerated the Tea Party in Illinois, and later marginalized them nationally when he became Majority Leader and de facto national leader of the New Republicans. After he delivered high-speed rail to the Midwest and found federal funding for a third airport in Chicago, he was untouchable. He and the President had a better relationship than one might expect. True, they did not share a political party, but they both were creatures of Washington. The President envied the Majority Leader's ability to connect with Main Street, even as he mocked his lack of sophistication. The President frequently referred to him behind his back as "Lyndon," as in Lyndon Johnson, because of his coarse manners and savvy political machinations. "Tell Lyndon we need to get this out of the Senate without any amendments," he would say at the end of a staff meeting. The irony, of course, is that the Majority Leader would have considered the LBJ comparison nothing but a compliment.

The relationship was made easier by the fact that the Majority Leader had no designs on the presidency. "I'm too fat and too short," he would tell people who asked. It was a brilliantly disarming answer, mostly because it hewed so closely to the truth. He had seen the polling data (as had the President and others): most Americans were willing to elect a president without a college degree, but they could not get past his body type. Focus groups would hem and haw when asked to explain why the Majority Leader "did not look presidential." If the discussion went on long enough, or if the participants were asked to write comments anonymously, they would just come out and say it: "He's fat," then adding some tortured reasoning as to why a man who had functioned brilliantly for seven years as the leader of the U.S. Senate would not be able to serve effectively as Commander in Chief because he weighed too much.

Unlike the real Lyndon Johnson, the Majority Leader did not lust for what he could not have. He had a love and appreciation for politics—not just winning elections, but also the legislative give-and-take. He had a long memory but also a thick skin. He never forgot a political defeat, but he was not apt to take the setbacks personally. Instead, every loss, big or little, was a lesson on how to do it better next time. "This isn't powder puff," he would tell his audiences, whether it was a Rotary lunch or a group of CEOs. His one intellectual passion was political history and he could recount in detail, more accurate than not, the political failures that had brought great civilizations to their knees.

Others have written in great depth about this unlikely "bromance" between the Majority Leader and the President; there is not much for me to add, other than underscoring that the two of them got along well because they had so little in common. There was no margin on which they viewed themselves in competition with one another. The President called frequently on the Majority Leader to chat informally about the political viability of various ideas. "How can I sell this in the Midwest?" the President would ask earnestly. For his part, the Majority Leader was flattered to be so important to the White House.

The Secretary of Defense was in the room because he had been at the White House for a different meeting and the President asked him to stay for a few minutes. Like I said, no grand strategy—not at the beginning. The Secretary of Defense had spent his career making tough decisions in the face of uncertainty. He and the President had a respectful if somewhat guarded relationship. The President had not served in the armed forces; he recognized that as a weakness and did what he could to remedy it. Still, there was more to the relationship between the two men than that. The Secretary of Defense was a straight shooter who often saw the world differently than the President and did not hesitate to speak candidly to his Commander in Chief. He was loyal, too. The President had come to appreciate the honesty and loyalty in a town where both virtues are oddly rare. "Can you stick around for a few minutes?" the President asked the Secretary of Defense as a meeting on the newly restarted North Korean nuclear program was breaking up. "We've got some problem at HHS with our stock of Dormigen." One has to appreciate the innocence of that moment, because that is really all the President knew: "some problem at HHS"—seemingly just like all the other little fifteen-minute annoyances that made up each of his days at the White House. A treaty here, an angry African leader there.

"I don't know anything about Dormigen," the Secretary of Defense replied.

"Neither do I. But if you don't mind, I'd like you to sit in, just fifteen minutes or so."

"Of course, Mr. President."

There were pleasantries as the participants filed into the Oval Office. The President and the Majority Leader, taking advantage of a moment together, conferred briefly over some matter. The Majority Leader took a pen and small blue notebook from his breast pocket and made a small notation, a note to himself, presumably. The technology was so old that I found it striking at the time. "Okay, where are we on the lurking virus thing?" the President asked, trying to call the meeting to order.

"One minute," his Chief of Staff said, looking at her phone. "Are we going to invite Prime Minister Abouali to the White House while he's in D.C.?" She was a petite, athletic-looking woman with short dark hair that was going gray in streaks. She wore dark-rimmed reading glasses that she put on when she consulted her notes or her phone and then took off as she spoke to the President, almost like a nervous habit. She could have passed for a school librarian, albeit in a very well-funded school district.

"Sure. Why not?" the President asked.

"The Jordanians have asked that we not grant him a formal meeting," the Chief of Staff explained. Her tone with the President was respectful but far from obsequious.

"How about a walk-through?" the President said.

"That will have to be end of day Thursday—"

"Fine," the President said, cutting her off.

"Remember, I won't be here," the Chief of Staff said, prompting the President to look at her quizzically. "It's Maddie's lacrosse banquet," she explained. "The whole family will divorce me if I miss this one."

"I'm sure the Prime Minister will understand," the President said sarcastically. I don't know if he was attempting humor; if so, it fell flat. The two of them seemed oblivious to the rest of us standing awkwardly in the Oval Office. I felt like I was watching my parents squabble over whose turn it was to walk the dog.

"I put it on the schedule eight weeks ago," the Chief of Staff said firmly.

"I understand," the President replied. His tone, however, suggested that he could not fathom why anyone would leave work—at the White House or anywhere else—to attend a high school lacrosse banquet.

"I'll let the Prime Minister's people know," the Chief of Staff said.

The President looked up at the rest of us, as if he were noticing us standing there for the first time. "Do we really have to spend time on this lurking virus thing?" he asked. He was not being insouciant. He had no sense of the crisis at that point. The Chief of Staff had put this briefing on his daily calendar, over which he had less control than one might think. At the end of every day, as he headed up to the family quarters, he would get a single typed card with his schedule for the next day, neatly divided into fifteen-minute increments. In the President's mind, there was no crisis, not yet. Yes, a high proportion of the government's Dormigen supply had been destroyed, and now the contingency stock was compromised—but in three weeks everything would be back to normal. Might the situation spin wildly out of control during that window of vulnerability? Of course—but that was true of nearly every fifteen-minute headache on the President's schedule, day after day. The impending Dormigen shortage did not feel like it was a crisis because it was *impending*. If you are wandering in the desert and I tell you that your water supply will be cut off next Tuesday, you will not feel thirsty, even if you should be panicked.

Most of the matters brought to the President's attention involve problems that are already manifesting themselves: a bridge collapses, a leader is assassinated, a police officer shoots an unarmed black man. The problem is lying there on the ground—literally, in some cases—for everyone to see. In the Oval Office that first day, however, no one was feeling thirsty. Not yet.

The situation—this sense of calm in the face of something that would inevitably go wrong—reminded me of a time I ran out of gas on an interstate in the middle of New Hampshire. I had flown into Boston after midnight and picked up my car in the remote parking lot. I opted not to get gas as I left Boston; I figured I might need a break from driving after an hour or two. I discovered—too late—that the gas stations along I-89 were closed after midnight. Not a single oasis. The gas light on my dashboard had been glowing orange since the New Hampshire border. The trip computer, one of those fancy gadgets I rarely paid attention to, was counting down the miles left until my tank was empty: forty, thirty, twenty. Then I saw a road sign; the next exit was forty-two miles away. I could not beat the math: I was going to run out of gas.

But the car was running fine. That was the thing. I was moving along a beautiful New Hampshire highway at sixty-five miles an hour on a clear night with a bright moon and almost no traffic. It was a lovely time for driving. A passenger in the backseat would have had no sense that a problem was imminent, that the math would inevitably catch up with us. Everything would be fine—for fifteen miles, or thirteen, or seventeen—at which point the engine would cut out and I would end up stranded on the side of the road. That was what I could see coming. So it was on that first morning in the White House. The people in that room were the first ones who would get a glimpse of our equivalent of the trip computer. The math.

Many of my NIH and CDC colleagues knew what was happening with the lurking virus—but they had no idea the country might run short of Dormigen. For them, *Capellaviridae* was a curious intellectual puzzle. Meanwhile, over at Health and Human Services, the Secretary and several of her deputies were aware that the nation's surplus Dormigen stockpile might run low for a few weeks—but they had no idea the nation might need those stocks. It was *surplus*, after all. When Centera Biomedical Group failed to produce its twenty million doses after the Long Beach warehouse fire, the department set in motion several contingency plans. Federal prosecutors were notified so that civil charges could be filed against the company and criminal charges against its top executives. The missing doses would be replenished in three weeks. The HHS models predicted that even with the warehouse fire and the Centera debacle, the doses on hand would be sufficient. Canadian health officials offered to transfer up to two million doses to cover any shortfall. Nobody at HHS had ever heard of *Capellaviridae*. They looked out the window and saw a warm, sunny day—perfect for a picnic. No one told them that a hurricane was bearing down, so they continued to plan for their picnic.

Five minutes into that first meeting, those of us in the Oval Office—and only those of us in the Oval Office—could see the totality of what was happening, the confluence of the Dormigen shortfall and whatever was happening with *Capellaviridae*. We could see the trip computer counting down: forty, thirty, twenty. "The numbers are not looking good," the Chief of Staff said.

"What is that supposed to mean?" the President asked. "And why don't we have someone here from HHS?" he asked.

"We are trying to keep the number of people involved small at this point," she replied. "This is starting to look like a potential public health crisis."

"If it's a public health crisis, then we need definitely someone from HHS," the President said sharply.

"I will brief the Acting Secretary," she said. The Chief of Staff quickly outlined the situation: the Dormigen stocks were running low; the *Capellaviridae* virus presented a potentially fatal threat to a significant percentage of the population in the absence of Dormigen. There had already been 171 deaths in cases where the virus had been left untreated, usually because the victim had not sought medical attention. She read from her notes: "Thirty-one in New England. Twenty-five in the New York metro area. A handful in Ohio, Indiana, Minnesota—"

"How does it spread?" the President demanded. We were sitting on sofas. He was at his desk, signing documents of some sort. I noticed for the first time that he was left-handed. No one answered. "How does it spread?" the President repeated impatiently, looking up from the papers he was signing, as if to say that we were wasting some of the precious fifteen minutes we had been allotted. The other participants on the couches looked at me.

"It doesn't spread, actually," I said. "That's what's so curious. The virus is very common. Most of us are probably carrying it now. It's just that for some people, under some circumstances, it turns lethal."

"Which people and under what circumstances?" the President asked.

"We don't understand that yet," I said.

"Jesus, what the hell else is there to understand?" the President said, tossing his pen onto the desk. "That's pretty much all that matters."

"We have a team of people working on this around the clock," the Director of the NIH interjected.

"How quickly is it spreading?" the President asked.

"We don't like to use the word 'spread,'" I answered. I did not feel comfortable correcting the President of the United States, but this was a crucial point. I continued, "It implies that there is some kind of contagion, that people catch it from one another. That's not really how this thing works. You have it or you don't. And it turns deadly or it doesn't. It's more like cancer than the measles."

"But it's a virus?" the President asked.

I answered, "Yes, it's a virus, but—"

"People are not going to understand that," the President's Strategist interrupted. "No fucking way. There is no way we can explain to the public that there is a virus killing people but that it's not contagious."

"I just explained it," I said.

The Strategist laughed dismissively. "Twenty percent of the country does not understand that the earth rotates around the sun. This is going to be fucking mayhem."

"It seems to me that we need to stockpile more Dormigen," the President directed. "And we need to figure out what the hell is going on with this a cappella virus."

"*Capellaviridae*," I said. The President did not dignify my correction.

The Director of the NIH said, "We've reached out to all the OECD countries to borrow enough Dormigen to cover our gap until our stocks are replenished. But, frankly, we're getting a little pushback because most of these countries are either seeing the same increase in *Capellaviridae*-related illness, or they're afraid they will soon. They're hesitant to make a firm commitment."

"So what's the number?" the Strategist asked of no one in particular.

"What number?" the Chief of Staff replied.

"How many people will die?" he asked.

"It's not that simple," I offered.

"Yes, it is," he said. "We have some estimate of the rate at which this virus turns fatal, right?"

"A guess," I said. "It's pretty rough."

"Well, it's going to get less rough as we get more data," the Strategist said, indignant that this had to be explained. "For now, we have an estimate?" he asked. I nodded yes. He continued, "Okay, based on that estimate, we can project what the demand for Dormigen is likely to be and when our stocks will run out, if they will." He looked around the room. "Am I not speaking English here?"

"These are all very inaccurate projections," the Director of the NIH said, visibly annoyed by the Strategist's reductionist logic.

"For fuck sake, people, an inaccurate projection is better than nothing. We need to know what might happen here, even if it's just our best guess."

"He's right," the President said. "We need to put some numbers against this. What kind of problem are we talking about?"

"There are a lot of variables," the Director of the NIH explained. "What is the rate at which the virus turns fatal, how much Dormigen will we need for other health issues around the country, how much Dormigen can we borrow—"

"Obviously," the Strategist interrupted. "So we build a model with our best estimate for each of those variables. Then we update the model as our information gets better." He looked around the room as if he were teaching fractions to fourth-graders. "Yes?"

"That's exactly what we do," the Secretary of Defense agreed. "We'll never have all the information we need, but there is no excuse for not making a plan with the best information we have at any given moment."

"Thank you," the Strategist said. He was not being sarcastic or deliberately mean. He simply felt relieved when others finally caught up. "That model is going to spit out one number that counts: How many people die from this sleeping virus, or whatever the fuck it is, because we run out of Dormigen? That's it, one number, that's what matters here—like I said five minutes ago."

"Right now that number is zero," the NIH Director said, trying to reassure the room. "We have likely commitments from enough OECD nations that we should be able to cover the Dormigen deficit."

"What exactly is a 'likely commitment'?" the President asked.

"Sounds to me like a military treaty with the French," the Secretary of Defense offered.

"We're still working that out," the Chief of Staff said. "The disruption at HHS has made things more difficult."

"That's why we need somebody from HHS in this group," the President repeated.

The Secretary of Defense offered, "In my experience, commitments become wobbly when the shooting starts. I think the relevant number here is how much Dormigen we have in our possession, not what's been promised."

"I agree," the President said.

The Chief of Staff nodded, making notes on a legal pad in an elegant leather case with the White House logo on it. Yes, I was sitting in the Oval Office, but the meeting felt like every other meandering group discussion I had been a part of—until this point. "Okay, then," the Chief of Staff said, "I will brief the Acting Secretary at HHS. We need to firm up the Dormigen commitments from OECD allies. The *Capellaviridae* task force needs to speed up their work and get us an estimate on the rate at which this thing is spreading—or whatever we want to call it. We'll use that to build the model we discussed." As she ticked off each item, she pointed her Montblanc pen at the person responsible, who would nod in acknowledgment. "Anything else?"

Silence. "Okay, then let's meet again tomorrow," she said.

"I don't need to be in the room for that," the President said.

"Let's see what we learn," the Chief of Staff replied. With that, she stood up and we followed her out. The President did not look up as we left. From that point on, we were talking about "the number."

16.

THE PRESIDENT WAS TALL AND THIN, HANDSOME IN A POLITical kind of way. He had good hair. He kept it long to emphasize that, I suspect. He had been a high school basketball star in Virginia, where he still holds the high school record for most points in a single season. His team did not win the championship that year, as many commentators have pointed out. "He's the kind of guy who yells at you if you don't make a shot," one of his teammates said years later. (In my limited experience, that is exactly what makes mediocre players clutch up and shoot worse.) In any event, the President was smart, refined, and politically savvy. He may not have had the natural political talent of the Majority Leader, but he made few mistakes. Every decision was put through a fine political filter, beginning in his early twenties. He was accepted to Yale Law School but attended the University of Virginia instead. I spent enough time pretending that I was going to law school to know that Yale is a better law school— arguably the best—but the University of Virginia is a better place from which to launch a political career in Virginia.

He married a law school classmate. She helped him run his first few campaigns for the state legislature. They divorced during his first term in the state legislature, without children. To her (Marnic's) credit, she kept a low profile during the presidential campaign, always politely refusing to make any comments about her ex-husband. "It was a long time ago, and we grew apart. I wish him the best, both personally and professionally. He's a good man and will make a good president," she would say. She never deviated from that line; eventually the press left her alone. The "mainstream media" recognized that she was not really a legitimate news story. The less reputable news organizations eventually got bored. There are only so many times you can follow a plain-looking fifty-year-old woman to the supermarket while the stories that generate clicks are happening elsewhere. It would be a real journalistic fumble to follow the President's uninteresting ex-wife as she weighs kiwis when, just across town, a drunken celebrity has crashed his car through the front wall of a yoga studio with a prostitute in the passenger seat.

The President's political career marched steadily on. Now single, he was elected governor of Virginia and then to the Senate. Not surprisingly, he showed up periodically on the glamour blogs as one of America's most attractive single men, that kind of thing. If you believe the rumors, Washington was his sexual playground, particularly young lobbyists and staffers, but since he was not married there was no scandal. He eventually married the CEO of Kraft Foods, a forty-year-old corporate star, who had also been divorced a decade earlier and had no children. She was a fashion icon and a strikingly beautiful woman, albeit with a reputation for ripping people's eyes out if it would improve cash flow. The most famous bloodbath for the bottom line was the "Mac 'n' Cheese Massacre," a mass firing of twenty-one hundred people three days before Christmas. A ham-handed PR executive tried to minimize the damage by releasing a statement saying that laying off employees before Christmas was the humane thing to do because it would help them budget more realistically for the holidays. This became a punch line for late-night comedians, at which point the PR executive was fired, too. The President and his CEO wife became one of America's most glamorous power couples. Their wedding gained some notoriety when two tabloid helicopters nearly collided while filming the reception at a borrowed ranch in Santa Barbara. Had the helicopters gone down in a flaming wreck on the tent below, it would have taken out some of America's smartest, richest, and most beautiful people.

The first time I met with the President one on one, I was ushered into the family quarters of the White House. He was in his small study, dressed casually, eating a piece of toast. I was struck that I was watching the President eat. "So you're a hotshot scientist," he said. I felt pretty damn important. "I understand you went to Dartmouth," he continued.

"I did," I said. I told him the year I graduated.

"Harold Scott wasn't still there, was he?"

"He was." Harold Scott was a legendary basketball coach who had been at Dartmouth for three decades. He turned the program around and went to the NCAA tourney a handful of times. The Ivy League champion always gets a bid, but Harold Scott's teams actually won a few NCAA tournament games. My senior year they bumped off Kansas State in the first round. "Do you play?" the president asked.

"Basketball? Just for fun and exercise," I said.

"We should throw it around sometime," he offered.

The President of the United States wanted to play basketball with me. One-on-one? Or maybe it would be a pickup game with some other White House insiders. What does one wear to play basketball with the President? I could not rush out and buy all-new stuff, or I would look like a newbie. On the other hand, I could not show up in running shoes. There I was sitting in front of the President of the United States, trying to remember if I had kept my Converse basketball shoes from graduate school. Might they be in that box of stuff I left in my parents' basement? *Because the President wanted to play basketball with me.*

"I don't know if you have a girlfriend, or anything like that, but this might be a tough stretch. I appreciate your willingness to help out," he said.

"I am seeing someone," I offered.

"At some point, when this is over, I'd like to meet that person to say thank you."

I realized that the President was referring to "that person" because I hadn't specified that I was dating a woman. "Ellen," I said.

As if he cared. I eventually learned that I would not be playing basketball with the President. Nor would Ellen and I be dining with him and his CEO wife. Rather, the President had a unique ability to speak with a relative stranger for a few minutes and leave him or her feeling like an important friend. It is an impressive skill, though it stings when you eventually see through it. Several days later I overheard him referring to me in a conversation with his Chief of Staff as "the guy in the brown shoes." I was wearing a black belt for that first meeting, and I had been self-conscious that my belt did not match my shoes. It was an odd thing to worry about when thousands of people might die from an uncontrolled epidemic. I do not know if the

President had noticed that my shoes and belt did not match; maybe the brown shoes were just my most distinguishing characteristic. In any event, he had no idea what my name was. And I know he did not spend a lot of time thinking about whether I was dating a man or a woman.

17.

THE CHIEF OF STAFF HAD COME FROM HARVARD, WHERE SHE was dean of the Kennedy School of Government for over a decade. When I looked around during our meetings, she often struck me as the only "real" person in the room, in the sense that she had a life beyond Washington. She had kids who got sick, or had to be picked up after band practice. Obviously she had people to help her deal with that kind of thing, but she acted like someone you might run into at a school potluck. Her husband was a pediatrician, one of the nicest guys I met in Washington. They were both from Minnesota and conformed to every stereotype of the Midwest I had ever encountered, particularly the wide-eyed cheeriness and optimism. The Chief of Staff had been a star researcher at the University of Minnesota in the field of child and family poverty. Much of her work followed the effects of the 1996 Welfare Reform, and then the 2021 law that further curtailed benefits. Harvard hired her away to become dean of their policy school and she proved to be the rare academic who was also a good administrator.

When the President spent a stretch at the Kennedy School after losing a tight election for Governor of Virginia, they struck up a friendship—some said more, but I never saw any sign of that. During his second gubernatorial race (he won), she advised him on social welfare issues. Later, when he was in the Senate, she coordinated all his policy work, and when he was elected President, she became Chief of Staff. It was probably a mistake. She did not have the thick skin or the political experience necessary to operate effectively in that job. She should have been his domestic policy adviser, but the President was often accused of being a lightweight on policy, and a Chief of Staff from the Kennedy School at Harvard was supposed to address that weakness. I always found myself happy that she was in the room. Once she baked cookies. They were not great, if I am being honest, but she brought in this wobbly paper plate heaping with oatmeal chocolate chip cookies. The White House staff always gave us whatever we needed, including lots of cookies, but this homemade gesture, no doubt baked after the kids had done their homework and gone to bed, was one of the most human gestures that emanated from the cabinet group during this stretch, even if the cookies were not very good.

By the time the two of them reached the White House, the Chief of Staff had already made her permanent mark on the President's career, and also on the trajectory of American politics. She had helped him run successfully for the Senate from Virginia as a conservative Democrat. He won by huge margins in suburban areas, particularly with women and college-educated voters. The handsome senator was fiscally responsible but not scarily so. He believed in climate change (and the scientific method more generally) without ever asking voters to do anything uncomfortable about it. When he began thinking about the presidency, however, he had a problem. The Democratic Party was in complete disarray nationally, with a deepening split between the progressives, who were trying to pull the party sharply to the left, and the moderates, who believed the future of the party lay in winning the American political center.

The Democrats had developed a "Tea Party problem." Just as the Republicans were finalizing their divorce, leaving the New Republicans free to run without pandering to the Tea Party, the Democrats were still trapped in a bad marriage. Progressive Mommy and centrist Daddy were fighting incessantly, and it was killing their White House prospects. Every national Democratic candidate would kowtow to the progressives, especially to raise money in New York and California. They would promise a $20 minimum wage, a carbon tax, and a whole bunch of other things that would then sink them in the flyover states. When Elizabeth Warren received the nomination in 2024, she went on to lose forty-nine states in the general election, even New York because she had so antagonized Wall Street. It is a special achievement for a Democrat to lose New York.

What was a smart, handsome, ambitious Democratic senator

from Virginia to do? He polled well nationally, but the progressives distrusted him (rightfully). And without the progressives he could not win a Democratic primary. More irony: he could probably win a general election for president, but there was no obvious way for him to get on the general election ballot. There was talk of him switching to the New Republican Party, but voters hate that kind of opportunism; when pollsters asked about it as a hypothetical, his numbers plunged.

The Chief of Staff found a way through this political labyrinth. Her motivations were entirely altruistic; she had decent instincts for politics but no love for the political game. "I want to bounce an idea off of you," she said one night on a private plane, returning from a dinner speech somewhere in western Virginia.

"What?" he said, somewhat rudely. He had been dozing lightly. The plane cabin was dark. The two were alone on the flight except for the pilot and copilot. The President was more introverted than most political types. Political events often left him enervated, particularly at the end of a long day.

"One term for one nation," the Chief of Staff said.

"What the hell is that supposed to mean?" he asked. He often spoke like that. He had been rude to subordinates for so long that he no longer recognized how rude he was.

"That's the campaign slogan."

"For the presidency?" he asked. "I pledge to serve just one term?"

She nodded. "That's part of it. And you run without a party."

"As an independent? You've got to be kidding me. That's a terrible idea. No one can win the presidency as an independent." He closed his eyes and settled back into his seat.

"George Washington did."

"I don't have time for this," he said without opening his eyes.

She had thought about it more than she let on. The two ideas in that simple slogan resonated with voters who were tired of partisan politics and organized interests. In one stroke, this campaign could transcend both: a candidate with broad centrist appeal would leave his party and pledge to serve a single term. No more fundraising once he was in office. No more obligations to a political party. *One term for one nation.* The George Washington comparison was not entirely spurious. One could make a reasonable argument, in 1789 or 2028, that a president should transcend political parties, representing all of America.

It was the right message at the right time. The Chief of Staff put some polls in the field to test hypothetical candidates. A candidate with the profile of the senator from Virginia did reasonably well. More important, the "one term for one nation" message tested off the charts, especially after voters were reminded that George Washington had been elected without a party. (They were not reminded that he had served two terms.)

"Have we all forgotten about the Electoral College?" the President grumbled when he was presented with the data. "I've seen strategies for student council elections that were more sophisticated than this."

"I can make it work," his Strategist said. "You will win." Others in the meeting rolled their eyes. The Strategist did not say, "You might win" or "You can win." He said, "You will win." The Strategist was everything that you have probably read about, almost to the point of being a caricature of himself: rude, brilliant, abrupt, funny, socially inept, and brutally honest. But he was not mean, at least not intentionally. If anything, he could be sweet in a childish kind of way when he was not saying remarkably harsh things. I remember the first time I encountered him in a meeting in a small conference room in the Eisenhower Executive Office Building. "Nice tie," he said. I looked down at my tie self-consciously, assuming he was being sarcastic. That was the kind of thing my college friends would say if the tie had some garish paisley pattern, or if it had a giant ketchup stain. But the Strategist was entirely serious. "The green pattern makes it more interesting," he said as he walked past and took a seat at the far end of the conference table.

I tried to remind myself of that exchange at later meetings, when he would say things like, "That's a horrible idea," or "You have no idea what you are talking about," or my personal favorite, "If you were smarter, this would make sense to you." I will leave it to others to speculate about whether the Strategist was "on the spectrum." In any event, the President had enormous respect for his analytical abilities, both the political acumen and the policy smarts. The Strategist formulated a strategy—abetted by a healthy dollop of good luck—that delivered the President 274 electoral votes, and perhaps more impressive, a narrow majority of the popular vote. Others have written more extensive accounts of that unlikely victory. The important thing to recognize is that the Chief of Staff conceived of the audacious idea that an independent could win the White House. The Strategist developed a plan to make it happen. The President played his role without messing up the lines.

18.

I WAS DATING ELLEN AT THIS POINT, AS I HAD TOLD THE President when I was still under the impression that he might care about these kinds of things. My personal life may seem irrelevant to the larger story that was playing out, but since it would later be dragged into the open, I should put those developments in context. I first met Ellen in a bar, though that is somewhat misleading. We were both there for a Dartmouth wine-tasting event. Ellen had come with her roommate, who was a Dartmouth alumna two classes behind me. (Ellen went to Duke.) Ellen and I had a nice time that evening. We met for breakfast the following Sunday with some mutual friends. I was single. Ellen was single. Our friends knew each other. There was a certain centripetal force to the relationship; it kept moving in one direction because no force intervened to send it in a different direction.

By the time we moved in together, Ellen was doing public relations for a big firm. It was totally vapid work, if I am being honest. Why does a bean dip need a PR campaign? (She really did have a client that made bean dip, or frozen nachos—one or the other.) Ellen accused me of belittling her work, which was scary given that I had only verbalized a small fraction of my cynical thoughts. She had little or no interest in my work at the lab and not enough background in science for me to explain why my work mattered. By the time I realized that Ellen did not know the difference between RNA and DNA—and had no interest in learning—it was obvious that we were not meant to be together for the long run. I suspect she was thinking the same, but neither of us had done anything about it. We had a comfortable routine.

The *Capellaviridae* crisis created new tensions. I was almost never home. The White House obviously forbade us from talking to outsiders about the crisis, so when I was home, I was not able to explain what was happening. I was not even able to say that I had been to the White House for a meeting. "I'm working on something really important," I told her one night when I came home after midnight.

"I know," she said sympathetically. "It's hard when we're both this busy."

The bean dip? I thought. *You are comparing the public relations strategy for a bean dip to a deadly epidemic?* "No, like really important," I said. That was a mistake, obviously. I will not relate the balance of the conversation. We were done at that point; it was just a question of making it official. I did not have time to move out, but that was where things were clearly headed.

So when the thing happened with Jenna, it was not as bad as a handful of blowhard members of Congress made it out to be.

19.

TIE GUY HAD THREE HUGE COMPUTER MONITORS ON HIS desk. They were arranged like a dashboard, making his small dark office feel like the bridge of a spaceship with him as the captain. The light from the screens reflected off his face. "I'm not seeing anything," he said. I was standing behind him. There was not room for a second chair in his office.

"We need to pick up the pace on this," I said. We both knew that was a ridiculously unhelpful thing to say, like telling someone to "think harder."

"To begin with, the data are complete shit," Tie Guy said. We both knew that to be true. The public health community—doctors and nurses and hospitals and even coroners—had no reason to believe that *Capellaviridae* was anything more than a nuisance. By that point we had roughly three hundred deaths that could be linked to *Capellaviridae*. One big plane crash. Plane crashes happen, I told myself. Besides, those people would have been fine if they had just gone to the doctor. Nearly a thousand people had died in car accidents over the same stretch. Yet I knew there was a problem with these rationalizations. *It was not just one plane crash.* It was one plane crash with evidence to suggest that hundreds of other planes with the same design flaw might soon start falling out of the sky. It could even be thousands of planes.

And our problem was trickier than planes. With a plane crash, an FAA investigator shows up at the site of the crash, does a preliminary investigation, and says, "You need to ground every plane that might have a defective Y-hinge holding the rear engine in place." Nobody panics because swapping out the Y-hinges will prevent more planes from falling out of the sky. With *Capellaviridae*, there was no "Y-hinge." We had no idea what was happening. Nor was there any obvious behavioral response that would minimize the public risk (like flying less). What does that press conference look like? "Hey, everyone, we just want you to know that you are all at serious risk from a pathogen with the potential to cause a pandemic at a time when our Dormigen stocks are running low. We do not understand why or how this is happening, and there is nothing you can do to avoid it, but we felt you ought to be aware of the situation. We won't be taking any questions at this time, because we don't have any answers." How would that go over?

We had a dilemma: If we did not tell the medical community how serious *Capellaviridae* might be, they would continue to send us the same lousy, incomplete information. They would not test for *Capellaviridae*. Or if they did and prescribed Dormigen, they would neglect to enter it into the database. And so on. Our public health detectives would get fewer clues and less cooperation because the public would have no idea that a serial killer was on the loose.

Or, we could do the medical equivalent of announcing that the building was on fire and cause people to run screaming for the exits—only there were not any exits.

"Look at this," Tie Guy said, pointing at the middle screen on his desk. It was a map of the United States with yellow and green dots scattered across it with no discernible pattern.

"What am I looking at?" I said.

"The yellow dots are deaths, the green dots are cases we know of that have been treated with Dormigen. Do you see anything interesting?" he asked.

"Not really," I said.

"Neither do I. The data are totally worthless. We know almost nothing about these people."

"What *do* we know?" I asked.

"The people who are dying tend to be young and healthy. A surprising number of college students. What do you make of that?" Tie Guy asked, the frustration lingering in his voice.

"They were probably just too stubborn to go to the doctor—thought they were invincible," I answered.

"Could be," he said. "In that case, we don't even know who is most at risk, we just know who is too stupid to go to the doctor."

"We need an estimate," I said. "How often does this thing turn fatal?"

"I saw the e-mail," he said angrily. "You know as well as I do that we can't begin to answer that question with any degree of certainty."

"This could be an epidemic," I said.

"Fine," he snorted. "Run a public service announcement telling people to go to the doctor. Give them Dormigen. Collect real information. Then ask me what is going on."

"What if we were to run out of Dormigen?" I asked, skating just to the boundary of what I should be saying.

"Then we're fucked," he said. "And if North Korea fires a nuke at California, then we're also fucked. This is not what I get paid to think about."

"What if we were to sample an MSA?* Do it right. Collect all the meaningful info for you to do some real analysis."

He laughed. "Good luck finding a budget for that."

"If I can find the money, how long would it take?"

---

* Metropolitan Statistical Area, such as the Chicago metropolitan area.

He turned from the monitors to look at me. "What's going on?" he asked.

"Nothing," I said. "I've got people leaning on me for answers. How long would it take?"

"Well, there's nothing difficult about the analysis if you get me decent data. A couple of days, maybe."

I could see it in his eyes: He knew something was up. Maybe he saw it in my eyes. "Set everything else aside," I said. "This has to be top priority."

"Yeah, I'm getting that impression."

"I'll be in touch," I said, turning to go.

"Hey," he said. I paused in the doorway and looked back over my shoulder. "If you can really get the money to do this right, we should sample a couple of different places. And we should do it several days apart, maybe even a week or more. There's no reason to assume the rate at which this virus becomes fatal is constant. Right? It could easily be changing, for some reason."

"That makes sense," I said. He held my gaze for an uncomfortably long time, until he was persuaded that I was not going to say anything more.

"Do you know why I do this?" he asked.

"Well, I asked you . . ."

"No, *this*," he said, motioning around him to indicate the broader job.

"You like statistics, data," I offered. I knew my answer was just filling space. He was going to answer his question for me.

"I like what the data can tell us, you know? Do police officers disproportionately target black motorists? Let's ask the numbers. They won't lie."

"There is the whole lying-with-statistics thing," I said foolishly.

"*People* lie with statistics," he said. "The data scream out for us to pay attention."

"Right," I acknowledged. I realized in that moment that we could not keep a lid on this thing forever. There is only so long you can ask smart people to drop everything before they sense a crisis.

And information starts to leak, on purpose or even by accident. So if I had not messed up, someone else would have.

20.

I WAS DUE AT THE WHITE HOUSE AT SEVEN-THIRTY A.M. THE security process takes a while at that hour, as employees and visitors queue up at the gate. I did not want to be late, and as a result I was ridiculously early. To kill some time, I bought a cup of coffee and a *Washington Post–USA Today* at a kiosk on Dupont Circle. I perused the front page in one glance (a benefit of a real newspaper, as opposed to the online version that I usually read): flooding in Alabama; more evidence the Russians were violating their treaty obligations in the Arctic; a bad harvest in West Africa, probably caused by climate change; the new Afghan president vowing to expel the last American troops within two years; D.C. transit workers threatening to strike. *Those are all the President's other fifteen-minute meetings*, I thought. I may have said it out loud, because a woman drinking coffee nearby looked over at me. This was what the President was going to be dealing with today, even the stupid transit strike, since funding for the system was federal and a strike would effectively shut down the capital. I wanted to tell that woman, who was still looking at me, "This is just the stuff that is public. It's even worse than you know!"

Those first White House meetings had settled into a pattern. The President, usually preoccupied with something else, would say, "What do we know?" The rest of us would report out on our designated tasks, usually prompting the Strategist to declare that we had fallen short in some way, or that we failed to understand something, or that we were not asking the right questions—all usually valid points, but exasperating nonetheless because he seldom had any assigned responsibility himself. It was like the Strategist showed up to these meetings with a pin, relentlessly popping the balloons that the rest of us had spent the previous twenty-four hours working to inflate. Pop, pop, pop. Then the President would say, "He's right," and we would be left with even more difficult tasks before the next morning meeting.

The Acting Secretary of Health and Human Services had joined us. He had the least formal power of anyone in the room but often projected the largest presence. His boss, the Secretary of Health and

Human Services, owned stock in some company that supposedly got preferential treatment in the drug approval process, or something like that. It had none of the allure of a good sex scandal. The HHS Secretary owned only a hundred shares of the stock in question, meaning that if the sordid accusations were true, she made *at most* $642 in illicit profits, before taxes. No matter. Once the blowhards in the House began using the phrase "principle of the matter," she might as well have started packing up her office. The President hung her out to dry, like some kind of human sacrifice to placate his most rabid political opponents on the right. When the scandal reached its apex (among the three hundred people inside the Beltway who were following it), the President released a statement: "I am grateful for the service that the Secretary of Health and Human Services has provided to my administration and to the people of the United States." There was no mention of "confidence" or "continued service" and she resigned almost immediately—tossed out of the boat. As any Washington insider might have warned, the effect was not to placate the President's critics, but rather to encourage them with blood in the water.

The President appointed one of her deputies to take over as Acting Secretary. He had been briefed on the *Capellaviridae* situation. The Acting Secretary was a black man, probably sixty-five or so, with an infectious laugh. He weighed about 250 pounds, with the build of the former football player that he was. The Acting Secretary was strikingly impervious to politics—not oblivious, just mentally resistant, as if the sordidness of Washington rained down around him but he somehow stayed dry. He just did not care, or he managed to project that impression. The Senate was not going to confirm him as Secretary—for reasons that had nothing to do with his qualifications and everything to do with a small group of Tea Party senators who were in an ongoing pissing match with the President. The Acting Secretary's wife—not him, but his wife—had run a state chapter of Planned Parenthood, twenty or thirty years ago, and apparently that was enough to make the whole family toxic to the political right forever. A group of five senators had vowed to use every procedural tool in the Senate rule book to prevent a confirmation hearing.

"I can't help you on this one," the Majority Leader told the President. Of course, he *could* help him. He could go to bat for the nomination. He could use the tools at his disposal to wreck those five intransigent senators politically. The President did not call him "Lyndon" for nothing. But it would not be a wise move in the long run, and the Majority Leader always played the long game. The President, too, played political chess, and he knew well enough not to press for this favor, so the Acting Secretary was bound to remain "Acting" for the foreseeable future. What did he tell the *Washington Post–USA Today*? He said, "It won't affect my pension." That's it. That was the only thing he said for attribution. The cub journalist writing the story thought it was a great quote, but almost certainly for the wrong reason. Anyone outside the Beltway reading that story would think the Acting Secretary was some kind of bureaucratic functionary, watching the clock every day and counting down the years—including a bonus for accrued vacation—until he could retire at a small ceremony (on government time) and move to a sad little condo in Florida. In fact, the pension quip to the *Washington Post–USA Today* was a rifle shot at the political establishment. This was a guy who spent forty years working in many ways to make people's lives better; whether you called him "Secretary" or "Acting Secretary" did not make a whit of difference to him.

The beautiful thing about the Acting Secretary was that the political types could not bully him. Even the President did not intimidate him. The Acting Secretary was respectful of the President, even deferential, but never cowed. He was fond of saying, "I have six grandchildren, a pension [always the pension], and a decent set of golf clubs. What do I need this nonsense for?" Every time he said that I got a little thrill because it was really a polite way of saying, "Fuck you." Do you remember in middle school when some jackass would make fun of you for something, and your parents would say, "Don't let him get to you"? The logic is that no one can make fun of you—for anything, really—if you have no respect for his or her opinion. They cannot injure you by not inviting you to the party if you genuinely have no interest in going to it.

Middle school works that way, and so does Washington. There is a certain gravitas that comes from being able to stand apart from the day-to-day politics. The Acting Secretary of HHS had that figured out. If the President fired him tomorrow morning, he would be on the golf course with his grandchildren by afternoon—a point he repeated often, and to good effect. In fact, he would periodically elaborate on how much better his golf game would be if he had more time to practice chipping and putting. "It's all short-game," he said to me after one of these soliloquies. I recognized this comment as the finale to his public drama, so I nodded in agreement.

The Acting Secretary attended his first working group meeting on a Sunday morning. I remember it was a Sunday because the D.C. streets were sleepy as I walked out of the Metro (no transit strike yet) and toward the White House. The morning was sunny and already warm. Several cafés had set up outside tables that were crowded with young professionals having brunch outdoors before the day turned oppressively humid. In these days before the Outbreak became public, I was always struck with some variation of the same thought: *They have no idea. Most of these people laughing over their eggs Benedict are carrying* Capellaviridae. *I am walking to the White House because we know the Dormigen stocks are going to run out. If we do not come up with a fix, some of you are going to die. Enjoy your eggs and wish me luck.*

In the Oval Office, the principals were dressed casually, including the President, and I remember thinking that was strange, too. So arbitrary. The same people doing the same work in the same place, but one day a week none of us had to wear suits. It was the first time I had seen the Secretary of Defense out of uniform. The Strategist was wearing an interpretation of casual that one would have to see to believe: the pants from a pin-striped suit with black leather dress shoes and some kind of short-sleeve floral Hawaiian shirt. He had shaved, but not well; there was a small strip of whiskers running down one cheek.

The President was more engaged than usual, probably because he had nothing else on his schedule. He sat on one of the couches rather than at his desk. "Okay, where are we?" he said.

"The Canadians shipped us five hundred thousand doses," the Chief of Staff said.

"Good," the President said.

"Didn't they pledge two million?" the Strategist asked.

"They're monitoring their own situation and will release more if conditions allow," the Chief of Staff said, consulting her notes.

"That sucks," the Strategist said.

"India? Australia?" the President asked.

"They're both saying they need parliamentary approval to ship Dormigen out of the country," the Chief of Staff explained. "It takes time, and obviously it would be public. We've cobbled together some smaller contributions from a number of countries: Israel, Mexico, Colombia, Latvia—"

"Jesus Christ, did you just say Latvia?" the Strategist interjected. He was eating a Danish, and he chewed several times, though not quite enough, before continuing. "Latvia? If any part of our response depends on Latvia, we are completely fucked."

The President shot him a look, as if to say, "Dial it down."

"But seriously, Latvia?" the Strategist said, calmer for the moment. He took another bite of Danish.

"It all adds up," the Chief of Staff said. "It's a numbers game."

"Latvia," the Strategist mumbled, loud enough for those of us close enough to him to hear.

"Speaking of which, where are we?" the President asked. He meant "the number." We had bandied this concept around for several days, but the data were still trickling in, so for all the urgent talk we did not actually have a figure yet, much to the ongoing annoyance of the Strategist. Perhaps subconsciously we did not want to put such a fine point on the situation. It is hard for me to convey the surreal nature of the crisis. This was the opposite of Pearl Harbor or 9/11, when tragedy struck and the public demanded a response. We were watching the planes in flight, reckoning what would happen when they reached their targets. But nothing was burning yet. The public was having brunch on a sunny spring day. So rather than being forced to action, we had to press ourselves ahead when the natural impulse was to do as little as possible and hope the planes turned around.

"We are pulling a model together," the Chief of Staff said.

"It's not that hard," the Strategist said. "There are only a handful of variables. I can do it on an Excel spreadsheet."

"We are doing some in-depth sampling to learn more about *Capellaviridae*," the Director of the NIH offered.

"Great, but you must have some assumptions now," the Strategist said, more calmly than usual. "My understanding was that we were going to build this model right away—take our best guess at the situation and then update it as we get better data."

"That's what we agreed to," the Secretary of Defense said.

"So why aren't we doing that?" the Strategist asked. He was genuinely perplexed.

"Let's have that done for tomorrow," the President suggested.

The Secretary of Defense said, "With all due respect, sir, we are going to run out of 'tomorrows.' If we have the information, let's put it together. I appreciate that we are dealing with a lot of unknowns here, but that's always the case. I've never met a military planner who felt he'd started planning for anything too early."

"All we need is an Excel spreadsheet," the Strategist repeated. He was sitting on the couch opposite me. As he spoke, he grabbed a laptop from a coffee table in front of the Chief of Staff, who was sitting next to him, and flipped it open. I could see her shocked expression. "What's the password to unlock the screen?" he asked, oblivious to the strange looks around him.

"White House one two three," she said. "No capitals, all strung together."

"Wow, the Chinese will never figure that one out," he said, typing. "Okay. When can we expect the next batch of Dormigen to be done?"

The Chief of Staff looked at her phone. "April sixteenth," she said.

"I don't care what the date will be. Just tell me how many days from now," the Strategist said, shaking his head in exasperation.

"Twelve."

He walked the room through the other variables: the doses remaining; the doses on hand solicited from other countries; the expected demand for Dormigen to deal with other illnesses. "Okay," he said. "We're reasonably confident of all that, yes?"

"I think we can expect far more help from the international community," the Chief of Staff said.

"Fine. This will be a conservative estimate. Now I need some estimate of the number of *Capellaviridae* cases we are going to need to treat in the next twelve days, right?" There were nods of approval all around. "So what's that number?"

"We don't know yet," the Director of the NIH said. "We're doing intensive sampling. We'll have those numbers in two days."

"What's our best guess now?" the Strategist said in a tone that bordered on mockery.

"It would just be a shot in the dark," I said.

"Then give me a fucking shot in the dark!" he spluttered. "Come on, people, am I the only one who sees icebergs floating out there?"

I said, "We can have our stats guy do an estimate tomorrow, maybe a couple of scenarios: best-case, worst-case, and so on."

"Tomorrow? Am I talking to myself here?" the Strategist asked the room. "Call him now."

"It's Sunday morning," I replied. "I have no idea how to reach him."

The Strategist ripped a sheet of paper from his legal pad. He thrust it at me. "Write his name down and whatever else you know about him." I did as I was told. The Strategist took the paper from me without saying anything and walked out of the room. Even now I am not sure where he went.

The rest of us looked at each other until the President broke the awkward silence. "He's right. We can't wish this thing away."

The Director of the NIH shifted somewhat uncomfortably in her seat. She and I made eye contact, acknowledging to each other that it would be more sensible to wait for better data. I raised an eyebrow, as if to say, "What should we do?"

The Director of the NIH, to her credit, pushed back against the President. "We'll have to treat this number with skepticism," she warned.

"We know that," the Secretary of Defense said. "This number is not going outside this room. It's a start. We'll build a more sophisticated model when we get better data. For now it's something, and something is better than nothing."

The Strategist walked back into the room. He handed the piece of paper back to me with a phone number scrawled on the bottom. "It's a cell phone," he said.

I looked at the number, trying to make out the last four digits.

The writing was tiny and childlike. "You can use my small office," the President offered as I was trying to decipher the handwriting.

"Is that a one or a seven?" I asked the Strategist, pointing at the penultimate digit.

"Sorry," he said, genuinely apologetic. "It's a seven. Four-zero-seven-nine. Sorry." At that moment, I had what I can only describe as a burst of awareness. There were many other times when the gravity and bizarreness of the situation struck me: the first time I walked into the Oval Office; the first time the working group looked to me for an authoritative opinion. But this was different—less intellectual and more emotional, like looking up at the stars on a clear New Hampshire night and *feeling* the incomprehensible size of the universe. Of course, any middle school graduate understands that the universe is enormous and expanding, but there is something about those special moments when a bright night sky makes one appreciate emotionally what it really means. And then the feeling passes, as quickly as it arrived.

So it was as I tried to read the Strategist's handwriting. His chicken-scratch penmanship was so banal, yet the reason he had written down the number was so significant. The combination of the comic and the scary gave me this momentary emotional sense of what was happening. "You can use my small office," the President repeated.

I called what was apparently Tie Guy's cell phone. It rang four or five times and then went to voice mail. I left a short, cryptic message telling him to call me back immediately. The White House operator had given me an outside line. I did not know whether the number would show up on caller ID as "White House" or "blocked" or maybe something else. On a hunch, I waited a few moments and dialed again. Tie Guy picked up this time. "Hello?" he said. I had not woken him up, but his tone suggested surprise, or maybe wariness. I tried to walk the line between urgency and panic, explaining that I needed him to give me some estimates for the likely trajectory of the *Capellaviridae* epidemic. "That's why I'm doing the sampling," he said. "I told you, I'll have numbers on Tuesday."

"I need something now," I said.

"It's Sunday morning," he answered, more perplexed than annoyed.

"I know. I'm in a meeting and I need our best estimate for the number of *Capellaviridae* fatalities if the virus were not treated with Dormigen."

"Why?" he asked.

"That's not important," I said with faux-authority.

"Well, it's obviously important to someone."

"The Director. She's in the meeting. She wants numbers. *Now*."

"Is this some kind of terrorist thing? Is that what's going on?" he asked.

"No," I said firmly. "It's a lurking virus that has turned virulent. That's what they do."

"Yeah, but a terrorist group could have figured out how to trigger the virus."

The thought had occurred to me, but there was no country, let alone a terrorist group, with that kind of scientific expertise. "No," I said, with real authority this time. "Look, I'm in a meeting. The Director is literally in the other room waiting for me to get off the phone. I need you to give me your worst-case scenario, your best-case scenario, and what you think is the most likely fatality rate. Give me those three numbers."

"You want me to make something up?"

"No. I want you to give me an informed inference based on what you have seen so far."

"Okay, can I think for a second?" he asked. His tone had turned modestly more cooperative.

"Of course."

There was a brief silence. "But we have Dormigen, right?" Tie Guy asked.

"Yes," I lied. "We're just trying to get our mind around the virus— to isolate what's happening there. So give me your best estimate of what would happen without Dormigen."

Tie Guy gave me his numbers. I wrote them down on the same sheet of paper, right below where the Strategist had scrawled the phone number. I did not really process the numbers as I wrote them down. The conversation had meandered, and I was feeling pressure to get back to the meeting. Also, I was not privy to the Dormigen supply calculations (mostly because I had not asked), so the figures

Tie Guy gave me had no context. I walked back into the Oval Office and handed the sheet to the Strategist. He looked at them, betraying no emotion, and then typed them into the spreadsheet.

The Strategist read out the results with a similar lack of emotion, which is eerie in hindsight. "Worst-case: three-point-two-five million. Best-case: seven hundred thousand. Most likely: two million." The room was silent, until the Acting Secretary of HHS asked, "I'm sorry, I'm the new guy here. Two million what?"

"Two million deaths," the Strategist said.

"No, that's not right," the NIH Director said quickly. "Those figures have no basis in reality."

The Strategist looked at her. He started to say something and then stopped himself. The room went silent again. I had a feeling that the President was the only person who could speak next, which turned out to be correct. "We have commitments for enough Dormigen to deal with any of those scenarios," the President said.

"Commitments," the Strategist said.

"Mr. President, you need to start working the phones," the Chief of Staff said.

"Clear my schedule tomorrow. I'll make the calls."

The Acting Secretary of HHS looked around the room. He had an uncharacteristically dazed expression. After a moment, he said, "Again, I know I'm the new guy here, but if I'm hearing what I think I'm hearing . . ." He paused to gather his thoughts. "Well, we've got a serious situation." The rest of us had become desensitized to what was happening, the policy equivalent of the frog being slowly boiled alive. One meeting had led to the next, and while each one was serious, the progression left us oddly inured to the magnitude of what was going on. The Acting Secretary had just given the room a collective slap in the face. In that moment, I felt both terrified and relieved—terrified by the number of planes that might fall out of the sky, and relieved that I was no longer the only one seeing it.

"These numbers are nonsense," the NIH Director said.

"Do you have something better?" the Strategist asked.

"We will on Tuesday."

"What if Tuesday's numbers are worse?" the Strategist replied.

"You are creating needless panic," the NIH Director said.

"I would argue the opposite," the Strategist replied calmly. "Now we know how bad this could get."

The Strategist and the NIH Director were slowly developing an antagonistic relationship. The Director was the heart of the group, always offering up an optimistic spin, even when the facts did not necessarily support her case. The Strategist was all brain. If anything, he tended toward pessimism. "Everything in this town turns out worse than you think it will," he once told me during a break. We were standing at adjacent urinals. He turned to me and said that, apropos of nothing, and then went back to his business. I could not think of an appropriate response. I don't think he was looking for one.

The Acting Secretary was visibly shaken. "With respect, I'm the new guy here," he repeated. "But I hope we can agree on a couple of things."

"Go ahead," the President said.

"First, I think we need more people in the room. Is this it?" he asked, looking to his right and left. "Are we the only ones who know what's going on here?"

The Chief of Staff answered, "We have several groups working on different pieces of the situation. There is a large team from the CDC and NIH working on *Capellaviridae*. We are learning more by the hour. And we have a team at the State Department who are gathering Dormigen commitments from across the OECD, India, other countries. But yes, the people in this room are the only ones who have a complete understanding of the situation."

"Given the magnitude of what I just heard, this just doesn't feel right," the Acting Secretary said.

"I take your point," the President said. "On the other hand, we can't afford mass panic."

"What about the Speaker?" the Acting Secretary asked. The President leaned back in his chair and stared at the ceiling for a moment, visibly frustrated, and then quickly regained his composure. I knew from reading the newspaper that the President's relationship with the Speaker of the House was notoriously bad, sometimes openly hostile. His reaction suggested it might even be worse than that.

"We'll take that under consideration," the Chief of Staff said.

"What was your second point?" the President asked.

"Maybe you've already discussed this, but it seems like somebody—maybe all of us—needs to think about what happens if we don't have enough—enough Dormigen."

"Isn't that what we're doing right now?" the President asked.

"No, I mean if we come up short—"

"That's not going to happen," the NIH Director said sharply. The Strategist exhaled loudly, causing everyone else in the room to look in his direction, at which point he rolled his eyes.

The Acting Secretary continued, "Yes, I understand we're going to do everything we can, but in the event we were to come up short . . . well, who gets what we have?"

The question just kind of hung there.

21.

THE SPEAKER OF THE HOUSE. WHERE TO BEGIN? HOW ABOUT: She was the meanest, most calculating person I have ever met. I know some nasty people, but most of them are a little thick and not particularly strategic. They are impulsively mean, often because they do not know any better. The Speaker of the House was mean in a strategic, long-term, highly intelligent kind of way, like one of those predators on the Discovery Channel that tracks its prey for hours before seizing exactly the right moment to leap from behind a bush and sink its teeth into the jugular. She rose in California politics as "a Latina small business owner." There is nothing about that phrase—not the Latina part, not the small business owner—that was true in spirit. Both descriptions were technically accurate, I suppose, but I am shocked the media did not push back more aggressively on her political narrative. She grew up in suburban Connecticut, born to upper-middle-class parents. Her maternal grandfather, a Harvard Law School graduate and prominent appellate court judge, was Colombian. The Speaker of the House took from him a gift that kept on giving: a Hispanic surname. As a twenty-two-year-old graduate of UC Berkeley, an age when most of the rest of us are hoping to find some reasonably steady form of income, a rental apartment without roaches, and a roommate who is not psycho, she changed her last name from Ryan to Rodriguez. How many people are planning a political career at age twenty-two with that degree of seriousness?

The small business part was arguably bogus, too. She and a business partner bought a large chain of California health food stores. The businesses were already up and running; she spent her days at the corporate headquarters, not behind the counter selling fish oil. Yes, each store was a small business, but to describe the Speaker as a small business owner was like saying that Henry Ford tinkered with cars. Everything she did was political, and I mean *everything*. The President could not stand her, and it was mutual. The Speaker had entered the 2028 presidential primary as the solid favorite of the progressive wing of the Democratic Party. She had California locked up. She built a solid organization and was a terrific fund-raiser. The polls were saying that she could steamroll any centrist opponent in the Democratic primaries. Meanwhile, the Republicans had just split into the New Republicans and the Tea Party, leaving them without a candidate who could unite the two. The Speaker was convinced, not unreasonably, that she had a clear path to become the first female president, and, if you buy the narrative, the first Hispanic president, too.

Then the President declared he was running as an independent—the whole "one term for one nation" campaign. The Speaker's well-laid plans imploded. The centrist wing of the Democratic Party abandoned her for the independent Virginia senator, since he was far more likely to win the general election. Meanwhile, the New Republicans figured he was almost as good as anyone they could field, so they tossed him their support, too. And so on. Yes, the Speaker won the early Democratic primaries handily, but the polls showed her getting trounced in the general election. Rather than face humiliation, she dropped out before Super Tuesday.

After the election, the Speaker and the President tried to patch things up, but it was a superficial effort. To her mind, he was sitting in the seat that should have been hers. The animus was compounded by genuine ideological disagreements. She was coming from the California left; he was coming from the Virginia center. There was plenty of potential common ground, of course, but the first one hundred days—what the President believed should have been his honeymoon—turned into a pissing match with the House of Representatives, for lack of a more accurate description. The Speaker introduced two explosive bills, one proposing a $22-an-hour minimum wage and the other setting aside $100 billion for slavery reparations, a fund that would be dispersed (somehow) among the descendants of American slaves. Neither bill had even a remote chance of passing the Senate, but the President was forced to oppose both of them, which infuriated progressives on the hard left. The Speaker clearly designed the whole effort to strangle the President's support among her progressive base, and she succeeded brilliantly. To what end? That is what infuriated the President. It was not like low-wage workers or African-Americans emerged from this legislative charade any better off. It was just a lot of political churn to get nowhere.

"She's not decent," the Chief of Staff said at one point, almost rhetorically. The Chief of Staff was always more grounded than the others in the room, going home every night to a husband and two teenagers who had homework, acne, boyfriends. More important, she had a heartfelt desire to make the world better. Politics was a way of doing that, but not an end in itself. The Chief of Staff used the word "decent" in a way I had never heard it used before. To her, it was a binary measure of whether one was using government for good or for ill, regardless of ideology or intelligence or political circumstances. The Chief of Staff might meet with a right-wing legislator whose views were completely out of sync with her own, particularly on social issues, but she would return to the White House and say, "He's decent." She did not mean it in a begrudging or half-hearted way; it was a serious compliment. What she meant was that this person was intellectually honest and committed to making the world better, even if his or her definition of "better" was not one she shared.

Conversely, she might walk out of a meeting with a lawmaker or lobbyist—even those ostensibly "on her side"—and declare, "He's not decent," which meant this guy could not be trusted, or his motives were impure, or for some other reason this person had not come to Washington with the intention of making Americans better off.

The Speaker of the House was not "decent" in the eyes of the

Chief of Staff, but come Monday she would be sitting in the Oval
Office with us.

22.

MONDAY FELT LIKE SOMEONE TURNED UP ALL THE DIALS.
Everything was going faster, bordering on panic for the first time.
Because of time zone issues, the President had been up much of the
night speaking on the phone with Asian and European leaders. At
a "meeting before the meeting," set up primarily so we could speak
among ourselves before the Speaker arrived, the Chief of Staff briefed
us on the calls. "It's not good," she said. "Most of the countries with
meaningful stocks of Dormigen have some *Capellaviridae* issues of
their own, or they're convinced they might. They're not going to ship
Dormigen out of the country until they have a better sense of what's
going on. Honestly, I don't blame them. The only countries with
enough stock to close our gap are India and China."

"It's a shit show," the President said. He looked paler than normal, with dark circles under his eyes. His body language suggested
he really needed a nap. India and China, with over a billion people
each, had enormous stocks of Dormigen. Meanwhile, neither country was seeing the same *Capellaviridae* trends that we were. Either
one of them might be able to cover our shortfall.

But, as the Strategist cleverly put it, "India and China are the
opposite of Latvia." What he meant was that Latvia had offered up
a paltry quantity of Dormigen as a gesture of solidarity and goodwill. The country was too small to do anything more. On the other
hand, India and China were big enough to make all the difference,
but the Dormigen donation would not be about solidarity or goodwill. Each was looking to exact a pound of flesh, or, more accurately,
a metric ton. Our initial concern about India was that their Parliament would have to ratify the deal, making everything public. We
had now reached a point where we could deal with the publicity
if it would solve our shortage; our concern about bad publicity felt
quaint. The problem was that India's populist Prime Minister had

thrown down a new roadblock. "He wants $100.4 billion," the President explained wearily.

"My goodness," the Secretary of Defense said, with a little whistle afterward.

"That's an oddly precise number," the Strategist said.

"The licensing deal," the President said. His comment meant nothing to me, but the Chief of Staff and the Strategist both nodded in recognition. The Chief of Staff explained to the rest of us. Dormigen was still governed by a patent held by an American firm. The drug itself is strikingly cheap to produce. A lifesaving dose of Dormigen can be manufactured for less than the cost of a large cup of coffee. But that is not what the pills cost to buy—not even close. A full dosage was typically priced between five thousand and seven thousand dollars. The economists had no problem with such an extraordinary markup. The pills may cost just a few dollars to produce, but the intellectual property—the research and development that made this medical miracle possible—cost billions. Somehow the pharmaceutical company had to earn back that overhead. If we deprive them of huge profits now, we will not have blockbuster drugs in the future, the economists explained.

But a 250,000 percent markup? The ethicists were not so sure. Politicians in developing countries like India were apoplectic. Here was a drug that could transform their public health systems, potentially wiping out diseases ranging from tuberculosis to malaria for just a few dollars a pill. The U.S. patent holder had denied these poor countries the right to produce the drug without paying a hefty licensing fee. When the Indian Prime Minister had declared several years earlier that India would violate the patent and produce the drug without paying the licensing fee, the U.S. government had threatened to levy huge economic sanctions. The Indian Prime Minister accused the U.S. government of "going to bat for big pharma" (true). The President, who was in the Senate then, justified the huge licensing fee as "necessary to protect intellectual property and future innovation" (also true). In the end, the Indian government was granted a steeply discounted licensing fee to produce Dormigen, but the dispute obviously still rankled. The Congressional Budget Office had estimated that the economic sanctions threatened against India (but never implemented) would have cost the country $50.2 billion—exactly half what the Indian Prime Minister now was asking for the Dormigen doses.

"What a prick," the President said.

"He's got a point," the Strategist said. "If you look at it from his perspective—"

"Yeah, I get it," the President snapped. The Indian Prime Minister had been swept into power atop his party as a populist, railing against elites within the country and the perfidy of the "club of rich countries" beyond the borders. He had been a pain in the President's side ever since. He backed out of several treaties, expelled a handful of U.S. diplomats, and even canceled the license that had allowed the U.S. Embassy to import liquor duty-free. The last one had delighted the Indian press because the U.S. Embassy was subsequently required to document all of its liquor imports in customs—right down to the vermouth—for public scrutiny. "Americans Drink Martinis as Indian Economy Stumbles," one headline screamed.

"What about China?" the Secretary of Defense asked. His tone suggested he knew the answer would not be any better.

"Do you want the good news or the bad news?" the Chief of Staff asked.

"It's all bad," the President interjected.

"They'll give us two million doses free," the Chief of Staff explained.

"Nothing with the Chinese is ever free," the Defense Secretary said.

"Of course not," the Chief of Staff replied. "They will ship the doses tomorrow if the President cancels his trip to Australia."

"That can't happen, sir," the Defense Secretary said quickly.

"I know that," the President snapped. He was as ornery as I had seen him. Several of us looked to the Chief of Staff, who explained the geopolitics of what was going on. The administration had been working for months to reinvigorate an alliance of Pacific nations—Australia, Vietnam, the Philippines, South Korea, and a host of small countries—to push back against Chinese encroachment in the region. The President was scheduled to fly to Australia later in the week to sign the agreement. But it would not be just any flight.

The U.S. Navy would be sailing the Sixth Fleet through international waters into the South China Sea—an area illegally claimed by China, according to the U.S. and its allies—where the President was going to land on an aircraft carrier. The leaders of the other nations would join him on the carrier, at which point they would all sign the agreement. It would be the clearest, boldest, and broadest effort to push back against China's persistent encroachment in the region. "Am I even going to be able to make that trip?" the President asked.

"You have to, sir," the Secretary of Defense said. "If you don't show up, the whole thing will collapse."

The President had already canceled a short trip to Mexico. There were no diplomatic repercussions, but it had raised the antennae of the White House press corps. Word had also leaked out that the President was meeting daily with the Senate Majority Leader and the Secretary of Defense. These three were known to have a close relationship, so their regular meetings were not necessarily newsworthy, but now that the Speaker was joining them, the press corps would quickly figure out that something big was happening. "Where are we on *Capellaviridae*?" the President asked. As news turned sour among the Dormigen donors, our focus naturally turned in a different direction. Maybe the scientists would rescue us.

"I'm headed to meet with the working group after this meeting," I answered.

"Tell them to pick it up over there," the President said. "It's time to figure out what the hell is going on." He was tired and cranky and under enormous pressure. Still, I was reminded of the description of him as the kind of guy who would yell at you when you missed a shot—something that rarely helps the next time down the court. Telling scientists to "hurry up and discover something" is not generally a recipe for success, either.

23.

I HAD ACCESS TO THE WHITE HOUSE MOTOR POOL, ONE OF the many strange rituals to which I was becoming slowly accustomed. I signed my name in the log and a Secret Service agent called up a car for me. When the Town Car pulled into the driveway, I told the driver to take me across town to an office building where the NIH had a suite of offices. I slid into the backseat and tried to digest everything I had just heard. My Town Car privileges are relevant only because of an unfortunate coincidence. As my car pulled up in front of the NIH offices, Tie Guy was also arriving. He waited for me in front of the building and we went in together. "How's it going?" I asked.

"Okay," he said. "I'll know a lot more tomorrow." He did not ask why a mid-level scientist had arrived in the backseat of a black sedan, but he was a guy paid to draw inferences from patterns and was starting to see one. We took the elevator up to the third floor, where the task force had set up camp. I was, in theory, returning to my comfort zone—back with the scientists. I had left behind all the talk of "projecting strength in the South China Sea" and other concepts entirely foreign to my experiences. Except that at the NIH office I still felt alien, as if I were staring at the scene from outside a window on a dark night. Yes, I recognized most of the task force members sitting in cubicles and conference rooms arrayed across the floor, but their body language and the pace of their work made me feel estranged from them. Two of the younger staff members were laughing at something on a screen; when I walked closer I could see it was a YouTube video of baby giraffes. This was just another workday for them. Yes, it was an urgent task force, but these kinds of "urgent assignments" come and go. These people would all head to the health club after work, or maybe go out for drinks. They had no idea what was happening. I did, and that set me apart from them, almost like a physical separation.

Justman wandered up to me and shook my hand. "Guess what?" he asked cheerily.

"What?"

"Dust mites."

"What about dust mites?" I asked.

"That seems to be the transmission mechanism for *Capellaviridae*."

"Why didn't you text me?"

"Sorry, I didn't want to bother you over the weekend," he said apologetically. "Yeah, it's dust mites. They don't usually bite, but there is a subspecies of the American dust mite that apparently does. And it's a host for *Capellaviridae*—"

"That's the transmission mechanism?"

"Yes. Man, you wouldn't believe how many animals we've been testing: deer, squirrels, five species of mosquito—"

"But we still don't know what triggers the virus to turn fatal," I said.

"No," Justman replied, visibly disappointed that I was not more excited by his news. "But now we know the vector. That's huge. At least we know where this thing is coming from. It explains the patterns we're seeing—why everyone has it in some places, no one has it in the tropics, that kind of thing."

He was right. Understanding the "vector"—the mechanism by which a virus is carried and spread—is a huge deal. Because viruses cannot live independently, they must have a host. For smallpox, that was humans, and only humans. No other animal carries the smallpox virus, which is why we were able to wipe out the disease. On the other hand, a disease like Ebola is much harder to contain because bats and monkeys are also hosts. Even when we stop an Ebola outbreak in humans, as we did in Liberia and Sierra Leone in the 2010s, and again in the Congo in 2018, the virus still resides deep in the jungle, ready to leap back to the human population the next time some poor soul eats flesh from an infected monkey ("bushmeat") or gets bitten by an infected bat. So yes, in Justman's world, the dust mite discovery was a huge, exciting, relatively speedy development. In my world, we had a spreadsheet telling us that a lot of people were going to die if things did not move much, much faster.

One of the executive assistants clapped loudly to get the attention of the room. Justman and I paused our conversation to see what was going on. "Okay, everyone," the young woman said, projecting her voice across the open work area. "Today is Saurav's birthday." There were some claps and cheers from the room. "We have cupcakes in the kitchen, if you are hungry."

"Do you want a cupcake?" Justman asked. "They're really good. They come from a little bakery around the corner."

"No, I'm fine," I said. "Look, we need to know why *Capellaviridae* turns fatal for some people and not others."

"I know, I know," Justman assured me. "We'll get there, but this is huge progress. I've got people working around the clock here."

"Thank you, I appreciate that."

"Tomorrow we'll have all the sampling data analyzed. You'll be at that briefing, yes?"

"Of course."

"That will be another piece of the puzzle," Justman said confidently. "We'll figure this thing out. We just need a little time." He gave me a little encouraging pat on the shoulder.

"I understand," I said.

"Are you sure you don't want a cupcake?" he asked.

"No, I'm fine, thanks."

24.

WE MET IN THE OVAL OFFICE AGAIN THAT AFTERNOON. There was no new information, but it was the first official meeting with the Speaker of the House present. We started nearly forty-five minutes late because the President had to do a short news conference. An ex–police officer had shot thirteen people in a Cleveland shopping mall and then killed himself. The motive was not yet clear. Because the shooter was African-American and a former cop, it did not fit the pattern of previous shootings. The President made his statement, extending his condolences to the victims and their families, offering up all available federal resources, and so on. When he arrived back at the Oval Office, we already had a problem. The Speaker had been briefed that morning on the *Capellaviridae* situation and was told to keep all the information in the strictest confidence. Yet she turned up at the White House with her top aide. "He knows everything," the Speaker declared. "He might as well sit in." And so it began.

The President, already emotionally spent from dealing with the Cleveland shooting, was apoplectic. "We ought to just arrest her," he spluttered when the Chief of Staff told him what was going on.

"None of this information is technically classified," the Chief of Staff replied. "The intelligence agencies are not involved." She had a calming effect on him; that was part of her job.

"Okay, fine," the President said. "She can bring her mother if she wants to. Let's go."

The tenor of the meeting was entirely different from previous days. There was an odd mix of formality and passive aggression, with periodic bursts of comic interruption by the Strategist, who liked the Speaker even less than the President did. "We'll know a lot more tomorrow when we get the results of the NIH sampling," the Chief of Staff said, directing the remark to the Speaker.

"Yes, I got the briefing," the Speaker said. "Aren't we neglecting the real elephant in the room here?" she asked. The rest of us looked at her blankly until she continued. "The Health Research and Infrastructure Bill?"

"Just tell us what you're talking about," the Strategist said impatiently.

The Speaker continued, "That was the bill that outsourced our production of lifesaving drugs to private companies like Centera Biomedical Group."

"Okay, that was a mistake, obviously," the Strategist said. "But the horses aren't just out of the barn on this one, they're shitting up and down Main Street."

The Speaker fixed her stare on the President. "You supported it."

"Probably," the President answered, throwing up his hands. "That was, what, eight years ago?"

"Seven."

"Okay, what's your point?" the President asked.

"We knew that bill was a bad idea at the time," the Speaker said.

"Who's 'we'?" the President asked. We were five minutes into the meeting and he already sounded beleaguered.

"The progressive caucus," she answered stonily.

The Strategist started to clap, slowly and loudly. "Cut it out," the President snapped. He turned back to the Speaker. "Do you realize what we're dealing with here?"

"Of course I do. I'm just saying that some part of our response must involve facing up to how we got here."

"A government warehouse caught on fire in Long Beach," the Chief of Staff said.

"And?" the Speaker prompted.

"We've already arrested the Centera executives," the President said. "Obviously we can't publicize that."

"What about those of you who entrusted America's health to a greedy pharmaceutical company?" she asked.

"Oh, for fuck sake," the Strategist blurted out. This time the President did not cut him off. "Is there anything with you that is not political? *Anything?*"

The President was calmer. Perhaps he had been bracing himself for this. He turned to the Chief of Staff and asked, "What's the number?"

"We're still waiting for the NIH data, so it hasn't changed—"

"I know. What is it?"

The Chief of Staff opened up her laptop and looked at the screen. "Actually, several big Dormigen shipments have come in from Europe. One from Brazil."

"What's the number." It was not really a question, the way he said it.

"Just over 1.3 million."

The President turned back to the Speaker. "Do have any comprehension of what that means?" He spoke slowly. His voice was tinged with anger and disrespect.

"My understanding is that the Chinese have offered enough Dormigen to cover the gap," she said.

"Yes, if we want to abdicate our foreign policy to them for the next fifty years," the President replied with just a hint of sarcasm. "I don't think that's a very good idea."

"You're not going to let 1.3 million Americans die, I assume," the Speaker replied confidently.

"That's why we're here!" the Chief of Staff yelled. "That's what we're doing right now. That's why we've been meeting every day for hours on end. We're looking for a way forward." She grew calmer as she spoke, but I could see that her hands, still holding the laptop, were shaking slightly.

"Of course, I understand," the Speaker said, offering up her best impression of sincerity. "Thank you for all your hard work on this."

The President, provoked by the patronizing tone, shifted uncomfortably in his seat. "Can we just cut to the chase here? What is it you want?" he asked.

"This is not about me," the Speaker said calmly. "Can't you see what is happening here? The country is in the midst of what may become the worst crisis of the twenty-first century, and you have locked yourselves in this room, as if the rest of the government has no say in what's happening." She looked slowly around the room before continuing. "You cannot possibly think this is okay."

The Chief of Staff said, "We have a tough balancing act. We are trying to deal with the situation without causing a panic."

"Maybe you've convinced yourselves of that," the Speaker said. "Here is what I see: A small group of people trying to cover up a crisis that the President and all the other corporate lapdogs in Congress set in motion. You put the health of the nation in the hands of a greedy pharmaceutical company, and now here we are."

"Very nice," the Strategist said. "Have you run that language by a focus group? I bet it tests very well."

The President said, "Let me ask again, because time is really important here: *What do you want?*" He enunciated each word in the question slowly and clearly.

"It's not what I want, it's what needs to happen. This is not about me," the Speaker said, prompting smirks around the room. The Strategist laughed out loud. The Speaker turned to him and said sharply, "I'm not seeing the humor here."

The President stared at the Speaker stonily, waiting for her to continue, which she eventually did. "Two things need to happen," she said. "First, Congress needs to be involved. This is a matter of national importance. The people in this room should not be making these kinds of decisions alone. Also—"

The Secretary of Defense interrupted, "With all due respect, Madam Speaker, nothing that we're discussing here falls within the purview of Congress. Health and Human Services manages the Dormigen stock. That's an executive agency. The President has complete authority to negotiate with other governments. Congress has no authority over any of this."

"You are completely missing the point," the Speaker answered sharply. "Congress is the elected representative body of the American people." She turned suddenly to look at the Strategist, who had begun humming "God Bless America."

"Seriously?" the Speaker asked incredulously.

"Congress can't paint a hallway in less than a month," the Strategist said. "And five hundred and thirty-five people cannot possibly keep anything confidential. We are running out of Dormigen and a million people could die if we don't figure out what the hell to do. *One million people.* We invited you here because we want and need your input. But there is no way that Congress can make these decisions. It's just not realistic."

"Congress needs to be meaningfully involved," she said.

"I appreciate that," the President offered noncommittally. "What was your second point?" I had long since forgotten that she had a second demand.

The Speaker continued: "When this situation is resolved, there has to be a public accounting of how we got here."

"What does that mean exactly?" the Chief of Staff asked.

"It means that if we dodge a bullet here, as I fully expect we will, the American people need to know how close we came to complete disaster. And who was responsible, obviously."

"I'm glad you think we're going to dodge the bullet," the President said.

"One phone call to Beijing and it's all over," the Speaker said.

"It's that simple, is it?" the President asked facetiously.

"Okay, thank you, everyone," the Chief of Staff said. "We'll know more tomorrow when we get the NIH data. Thank you, Madam Speaker. We will take all this under advisement."

As the participants filed out of the room, the Strategist pulled the President and the Chief of Staff aside. "We need to get our legal counsel on this," he said.

"I know," the President acknowledged. "And the National Security people, if there is any chance we may be doing some kind of deal with China."

"I'll set up the meetings," the Chief of Staff said.

The Strategist nodded toward the door of the Oval Office, where the Speaker was talking to the Secretary of Defense. "You know what she's going to do with this," he said. "This is one big political gift for her. It's what she's been waiting for her entire life. She's going to ride in on a government-issued horse—"

"Yeah, I picked up on that," the President said tartly.

"I'd say we have about twelve hours before this starts leaking," the Chief of Staff said.

"That will be a complete clusterfuck," the Strategist said.

"We need a communications strategy," the Chief of Staff answered, a new level of weariness creeping into her voice.

"There are already too many people involved," the President said.

"I know," the Chief of Staff agreed. "But if this thing leaks and we're not prepared, the public reaction will be a complete disaster."

The Strategist chuckled sardonically. "I've got our message: 'Don't worry, America, only one million of you are at risk of dying.' Or maybe we should put a more positive spin on it: 'Three hundred and thirty-nine million Americans probably won't die.'"

The President smiled, grasping at the humor. "Or we can just loan the Chinese the Sixth Fleet for a while. How bad could that be?"

"I'll work up something with the Director of Communications," the Chief of Staff said.

The President nodded in acknowledgment. After a moment he asked the Strategist, "Did I really vote to privatize the Dormigen production?"

The Strategist shrugged. "I can't remember. It was a huge bill. I have no idea what all was packed in there, but I suspect the Speaker did her research on this one."

"Yeah."

25.

AS THE PARTICIPANTS FILED OUT OF THE MEETING, THE President walked to the window of the Oval Office that looked out on the Rose Garden. He did that sometimes, separating himself from the group but not yet ready to sit down at his desk and get back to work. The Majority Leader paused in the doorway and then walked back and joined the President by the window. "Welcome to my world, Mr. President," he offered. The President looked at him somewhat quizzically, neither welcoming his presence nor sending him away. "The Speaker," the Majority Leader continued. "I have to deal with her more often than you do. Just about every goddamn day, and sometimes she still amazes me." The President nodded and smiled slightly, implicitly welcoming the Majority Leader's presence. "Can I offer you one piece of advice?" the Majority Leader asked.

"About the Speaker?" the President replied.

"Mm-hmm," the Majority Leader confirmed.

"Wrap her in a carpet and drop her off a boat twenty-five miles out to sea," the President suggested.

The Majority Leader gave a deep, genuine laugh. "Oh, I've felt that urge," he said, still chuckling. "But I'll give you a different nautical metaphor. You've got to let her run away from the boat."

"I have no fucking idea what that means," the President said, albeit with an odd warmth for him.

"You're not a fisherman?" the Majority Leader asked.

"My idea of fishing consists of going to Whole Foods and buying whatever is on sale," the President replied. "Now I can't even go to Whole Foods," he added.

"If you're fishing for game fish, like tuna or swordfish," the Majority Leader explained, "they can take hours to land after you've hooked them. If you try to wrestle them into the boat too quickly, you'll wear yourself out, or break the line."

"One more reason to buy tuna at Whole Foods."

"True enough. But if you like the fight, what you learn is that you have to let the fish wear itself out. Sometimes it dives deep, or swims away from the boat. That's what I mean by letting it run. It doesn't feel right, to let the fish get farther away from you, but eventually that fish is going to exhaust itself. That's when you reel it in."

"I like the idea of putting a hook in the Speaker's mouth, if that's what you're suggesting. Other than that, I still have no idea what the hell you're talking about," the President said. His tone was not hostile; rather, it invited the Majority Leader to continue.

"One thing I've learned about people like the Speaker is that sometimes it's better to let them talk than to try and shut them up," the Majority Leader explained. "We had this nasty fellow back in Pekin. He was an out-and-out racist, but he was generally smart enough to dress up his repugnant thoughts in respectable clothing. He was making all kinds of trouble at the high school—stuff about how our kids needed to be taught by teachers who were 'culturally similar,' which was really just veiled talk about race. He didn't want any black teachers. The problem was, people were starting to listen."

"And?" the President asked with genuine interest.

"I was president of the school board and I kept trying to figure out how I could shut him up. One day over Sunday supper, my dad says, 'If you let him talk long enough, people will see him for what he is.' So I invited the guy to address the Rotary Club, to make a recommendation about what kind of teachers would be most appropriate for Pekin High."

"That was bold."

"The first fifteen minutes, I thought I'd made a horrible mistake. He had fancy slides and test score data. Everyone in the room was nodding along. But then he kept going. He started talking about how some races are genetically inferior and should be relegated to certain low-skill professions."

"He was running away from the boat," the President offered.

"You're telling me," the Majority Leader said, pleased that the President had embraced his metaphor. "I could feel the room turning. The longer he talked, the more mortified they became. I could see it in their eyes. I didn't even have to offer a rejoinder. At the end of his talk, I just said, 'Thank you for coming today. I'm pleased you all could get a deeper understanding of Mr. Mason's views on this subject.' The guy never caused any serious trouble again."

"Okay, but the Speaker is wily and we don't have much time," the President said. "She could really do a lot of damage here."

"I agree. But you have to resist the impulse to try to muscle her into the boat," the Majority Leader warned.

"You've caught a lot of tuna in your day, have you?" the President suggested.

"I do pretty well."

26.

I ARRIVED AT THE NIH OFFICES BEFORE DAWN. SOMEHOW I had lost my key card, and I had to search the lobby for a security guard to buzz me in. "Something's going on up there," he said as he tapped his pass on a pad beside the elevator. "They've been working all night." Tie Guy met me at the elevator. He had not shaved in several days and his face had an oily sheen. He was not wearing shoes. "Do you want me to get you a cup of coffee or something?" I asked.

"That's the last thing I need," he said. "If I have any more caffeine I might have a heart attack." I looked around the floor. A few people were working at computers, but most of the people I could see were loitering happily, as if they were working on a group project in graduate school—which, as far as they knew, was broadly similar to what they were doing. A young woman walked toward us, typing intently on her phone. When she noticed Tie Guy she said, "Hey, we're going out for breakfast. You want to come?"

"No, thanks. I need to review the slides," he said. We had agreed that Tie Guy would brief me as soon as he was finished analyzing the new data. At eight, the NIH Director would arrive and we would do a more formal briefing for her. The Director and I would then do a briefing at the White House later that morning.

"How does it look?" I asked.

"The data are pretty good," he said. "The numbers are more or less what I expected. No huge surprises, but there are some quirky patterns. We might be able to exploit the patterns to get some traction."

My phone beeped, not my normal phone, but the secure TransferPhone that the White House had given me a few days earlier. It was text from the Chief of Staff: "Please keep briefing to four or five slides, eight tops." I looked at my watch. It was five-fifteen in the morning. How long had she been up?

Tie Guy nodded at my clunky black device. "So you're carrying one of those now, are you?" he said.

"So it would appear," I replied, hoping to defuse the situation with humor. "Looks like we'll need a short version of the presentation, maybe five slides."

"Are you fucking kidding me?" he asked incredulously, almost yelling. "I've been up all night. My deck has one hundred and seventeen slides."

"We need a summary," I said.

"Who is 'we'?" he asked.

"It's a working group the Director pulled together," I said.

"Five slides?"

"Yeah. Maybe seven or eight, if you really need them."

Tie Guy looked at me, shaking his head as he processed the request. "Either these people are really, really important, or they're complete fucking idiots."

"They're not complete fucking idiots."

"Then I've got work to do," he said, walking away angrily.

"Show me what you have," I said, following him. "I can help you winnow the slides."

Tie Guy walked into a small conference room littered with the detritus of meals past. He moved a half-empty coffee cup out of the way and opened his laptop. Without looking up from the screen, he motioned to an open pizza box with one slice left in it, the cheese hardened and congealed. "There's pizza if you want it," he said.

"I'm good, thanks."

Tie Guy projected his presentation on the white wall, clicking quickly through some introductory slides: the team members, a mission statement, and so on. "Cut all that," I said. He nodded, still refusing to make eye contact with me. He clicked through a few more slides, stopping at a map of the United States with a purple blotch running across the northern part of the country from west to east, starting at the Rockies and stretching all the way through New England. "Do you know what that is?" he asked.

"No clue," I answered.

"That's where you find *Dermatophagoides mensfarinae*. Dust mites. A subspecies of the American dust mite, to be exact." He advanced to the next slide, which was a highly magnified image of a dust mite. It looked like some nasty invader from outer space in a bad horror film. "That's it," he continued. "Endemic to North America."

"The dust mite is the vector."

"Okay, but now watch this." He clicked to the next slide, which had the same map of the United States with the purple band, only now there were large green patches that roughly overlapped with the purple. "Those are your counties where more than twenty-five percent of the population tests positive for *Capellaviridae*."

"That makes sense," I said. "Where you find the dust mite."

"Okay, now watch this." He advanced to the next slide, which had the map of the United States, the same purple band, and myriad red dots spread randomly across the map with no obvious pattern. "Do you see a pattern?" he asked.

"With what, the red dots?"

"Yes."

"What are they?"

"Just tell me, do you see a pattern?"

"Well, the red dots—whatever they are—seem to be pretty random," I said.

"Exactly," Tie Guy agreed. "I ran the numbers, and there is actually a negative correlation."

"You still haven't told me what I'm looking at."

"Sorry," he said, growing more excited. "The red dots are the deaths and serious cases: the people who died of *Capellaviridae* or became sick and were treated successfully with Dormigen."

"That doesn't make any sense at all," I protested. "There is no obvious connection with the dust mite."

"I know, crazy, isn't it? The people most likely to get sick don't live anywhere near the dust mite that transmits the virus—except for five or six places where there seem to be concentrated outbreaks."

"That can't be right," I said. "It makes no sense. Are you sure you have the right vector? Maybe it's a coding error. You guys have been working all night—"

"Watch this," Tie Guy said, now nearly squirming in his seat with excitement. He tapped a key on his computer, though as far as I could tell, the next slide looked exactly the same: the map of the United States, the purple band, and the red dots. "Just watch," Tie Guy said, sensing my puzzlement.

Slowly the red dots began moving on the map, one at a time, from their random locations into the purple band. The pace picked up; the red dots moved more quickly into the purple band. After a few seconds, the motion stopped, with nearly all the red dots in or near the purple band. "Not so random anymore, right?" he said. "That's where those people lived for an extended period of time before moving away."

"So they were infected before they left?"

"Presumably, yeah. Remember the cluster at the College of Charleston?"

"No."

"There were two deaths and three or four people who got really sick. Charleston is five hundred miles from anywhere you'll find that kind of dust mite, but each of those students came from somewhere else—Michigan, New Hampshire, upstate New York."

"Okay," I said, trying to digest what he was telling me. "So they acquired the virus at home, and got sick in Charleston. That's indicative of the pattern we're seeing."

"Yes."

"Go back two slides," I told him. Tie Guy tapped aggressively on the computer and once again we were looking at the red dots strewn randomly across the map. "But if I'm seeing this right," I said, "people *are not* getting sick in the places where the virus is most common, other than a few clusters."

"Right."

"How can we possibly explain that?" I asked.

"No idea," Tie Guy said, shaking his head. "One of the strangest things I've ever seen."

"And what about those clusters—the few places where the virus is common and people are getting sick?"

"Nothing," Tie Guy conceded.

In all the excitement over the utterly bizarre pattern of disease, I had forgotten to ask him for the other crucial piece of information: the incidence rate. "So how bad is it?" I asked. "What's the incidence rate?"

"That's modestly good news," he said. "It's a little lower than I predicted." He clicked quickly through several slides. "There. About two million new cases per month. If anything, I would expect it to fall slightly over time. It's a big number, but totally manageable. Dormigen works everywhere. The deaths are all people who didn't seek treatment, or for some reason didn't get Dormigen." He waited for my reaction, adding, "It's not a crisis, if that's what you want to know."

"About five hundred thousand new cases a week," I said.

"Yeah, two million a month—five hundred thousand every week. It's leveled off."

I did the math quickly in my head. We would still be about three hundred thousand doses short based on the last numbers I had seen.

"Right?" he asked.

"Right what?"

"It's not a crisis," he said. "We can manage the disease for now and then either deal with this dust mite or work up a vaccine. As long as people are smart enough to go to the doctor, we're fine."

"Sure," I said. "This is good news." After a moment, I asked, "Who is most likely to get sick?"

Tie Guy leaned back in his chair and stretched. "No pattern at all, as far as I can tell," he said. "I looked for every possible correlation: young, old, black, white, preexisting illness. I have no clue who gets sick from the virus, or why. The people who die are the ones who are too stubborn to get treated, but we figured that already." Tie Guy was in a better mood now, pleased with his work. He said, "I'll trim it down to five or six slides. Can I at least put in the photo of the magnified dust mite?"

"If you want," I said.

"It's a sick photo." He looked up at the food and other garbage spread across the table. "I'll clean this up before the Director gets here."

"I don't think she'll care," I said. It felt like the first completely honest thing I had said that morning.

27.

THE DIRECTOR ARRIVED ABOUT TWO HOURS LATER, AS planned. The office was nearly abandoned; most of the team members who had been working all night had gone home. Tie Guy went through the same slides, still excited by the work he had done. "Do you have a slide with the incidence of *Capellaviridae* outside the United States?" the Director asked.

"I've got a couple of things like that," Tie Guy answered. After a few seconds of flipping quickly through the slide deck, he stopped at a slide titled "*Dermatophagoides mensfarinae* Endemic Areas" with a map of the world. There was the familiar purple pattern in the U.S. and a few purple patches in other countries with similar latitudes: Canada, Northern Europe, a few places in Russia and China. "Those are places where you find the vector, the dust mite. It's just not that common outside the U.S." I knew why the Director was asking: How much Dormigen was the rest of the world going to need? The less they needed, the more they could give us.

"What about incidence of *Capellaviridae*?" I asked.

"It's about what you'd expect," Tie Guy answered. He projected another slide with a map of the world and red dots randomly distributed across it. The only obvious clusters were in major population centers. "The international data are not great, but it seems to be the same pattern as in the U.S. The people who get sick are the ones who have spent time in an area where the dust mite is endemic and then moved to a place where it's not."

The Director asked Tie Guy to assemble his team in the bigger conference room. People were beginning to trickle back into the office, looking showered and somewhat refreshed. The Director (or more likely her assistant) had ordered a catered breakfast, which was being set up hurriedly by two young guys wearing brown shirts that read GILLIAN'S CAFÉ. It was not the usual stale muffins and not-from-New York bagels; there was a tray of nice-looking breakfast sandwiches and a huge bowl of fresh raspberries, strawberries, and blueberries—not even watered down with tasteless chunks of unripe honeydew and cantaloupe. The Director saw me eyeing the food. "Grab a plate," she said. I had not had breakfast. I could not remember if I had eaten dinner the night before. I had fallen into the habit of eating whatever food the White House put out during our meetings, whenever that happened to be.

As the last few task force members filled plates at the makeshift buffet, the Director called the room to order. "I don't want to ruin your breakfast with a long speech," she said, prompting modest laughter. "Thank you. Thank you. That's really all I have to say. I know how hard all of you have been working. I really appreciate that effort. The American people thank you—or they would if they knew how important this work is. Fifty years ago, a disease like this could have been devastating. Thanks to the work of people like you— steady progress at every turn—science is making our lives safer and better. Too often this kind of work is overlooked, especially the little discoveries and insights, but those little insights add up to huge discoveries over time. I'm here this morning to tell you that the work you are doing is really important. So thank you. Now eat!" There was some awkward applause and then a collective attack on the breakfast sandwiches.

I was impressed, not just by the Director's foresight in ordering the breakfast, but by the poise she brought to her talk. It was not the Gettysburg Address, but I could tell looking around the room that her words mattered. She was what my mother would describe as "put together," though it sounds less patronizing and sexist when she says it than when I write it. The Director was fiftyish and fit, if not necessarily thin. She wore a nicely tailored navy-blue skirt and jacket and a gold necklace of some sort. She looked professional, which I mean not in the bland, meaningless sense of the word, but rather that the people in the room looked to her and believed that she was someone who should be in charge. I had never thought much about leadership, but in that moment I had a sense that I had just seen it, and it felt different than what I had previously envisioned.

The free food mattered, too, not because the people in the room could not afford a good breakfast sandwich, but because they spent their days doing work that most of their friends and family could not understand, getting paid far less than their dafter college classmates who went to Wall Street or Silicon Valley. Finally someone had shown up and explained to them convincingly that what they were doing really mattered. It never would have dawned on me to do that. I was even more impressed when we climbed into the back of the Director's car. She slumped against the seat and exhaled audibly. For the first time, I could see how much effort she had mustered to give her little breakfast talk. After a moment I said, "It's reasonably good news, don't you think?"

"I suppose," she said quietly. The tone of her response ended the conversation for thirty seconds or so. Eventually she continued, "There's no way to prepare a vaccine in the time we have?"

"Anything is possible," I said. "But, yes, it's hard to imagine how that would happen. We have no handle on who is most likely to get sick, so we would have to vaccinate everyone. That would be logistically difficult in ten days, even if we had a vaccine."

"That's what the CDC people said."

"It's still worth working on," I offered.

"There is a team doing what they can."

We pulled into the portico at the White House and made our way to a small West Wing office to get ready for our briefing. The Director sat down and immediately began responding to e-mails on her phone. After fifteen minutes or so the Strategist appeared in the doorway, unshaven and looking somewhat harried. I distinctly remember wondering how anyone could look so disheveled before nine-thirty in the morning. "We have a situation," he said. "The briefing is going to have to wait."

"A situation?" the Director asked in amazement. "Are you kidding me? This is the situation." The Strategist did not reply. He just turned and left.

28.

THIS SOON BECAME ONE OF THE MOST FRENETIC DAYS OF the crisis. We sat in our conference room for more than an hour, like two patients in a dentist's office wondering if our appointments had been forgotten. The door was open and we could see a flurry of officious staffers passing briskly by. At one point, the Chief of Staff appeared in the corridor and the Director leaped out of her chair to ask what was happening. "I'm so sorry," the Chief of Staff said. "The President is in the Situation Room. Everything is backed up. Maybe an hour or so?" As always, I was impressed by her courtesy and grace amid the craziness.

It would be closer to three hours before we filed into the Cabinet Room. Only later was I able to infer what had been going on. There had been a coup attempt against the Saudi royal family early that morning by a surprisingly well-organized Islamic extremist group. The President and his team found themselves walking a fine line between protecting the Saudi government, a dependable if oppressive ally in the region, and being seen as a prop for yet another illegitimate regime. The Israelis, who often found common cause with the Saudis because they shared a common enemy (the Iranians), were pushing aggressively to put American troops on the ground in Saudi Arabia to protect the monarchy. The President had refused to commit troops; he had also warned the Israelis against any involvement other than intelligence sharing. According to one account, the President ended up in a shouting match with the Israeli Prime Minister. But I read about all this much later, at the same time everyone else did. For us, on that day, it just made for a lot of waiting.

The Chief of Staff eventually showed up at the door to our small office and invited us into the Cabinet Room. Our slides had already been loaded and were projected on small screens in front of each participant. The NIH Director walked quickly through the presentation, six slides including Tie Guy's highly magnified photo of *Dermatophagoides mensfarinae*. (I was eager to tell him that his "sick" photo made the final cut.) The group had grown larger. I recognized the White House Director of Communications and the National Security Adviser from photos. As we waited for the President to appear, my cell phone beeped with a text. I would have ignored it, but we were just waiting anyway, so I checked. It was from Justman, head of the *Capellaviridae* task force, and said simply: "Call me." I got the attention of the Chief of Staff to ask if there was a place where I could make a call. Before she could answer, the President walked in. The participants around the table stood up quickly.

"Sit down," the President said sharply. It was not a "Thank you for standing up but now please be seated." It felt more like he was annoyed that we had stood up in the first place.

"It's the task force," I mouthed to the Chief of Staff. She pointed to a door behind where I was sitting and motioned that I should make the call from there. I got up, drawing a look from the President, and walked out of the room into a small corridor. Justman answered right away. "You told me to call with news," he said apologetically.

"Of course. What is it?" I asked.

"I think we finally have a little good news," he said. "The fatality rate seems to be lower than we thought. We got another wave of data last night: public health clinics, a sampling of government workers—"

"Sorry, I'm in a meeting here. Can you just summarize for me?"

"A lot of people are fighting this thing off on their own," he explained.

"So what's your best guess on the fatality rate?" I asked.

"Best guess—probably three to five percent," he said.

"Is there a pattern as to when it's most likely to be fatal?"

"That's about what you'd expect," Justman said. "It's most likely to be fatal for people who are weak or immunocompromised to begin with."

"But there is no pattern as to when, where, or why *Capellaviridae* turns fatal in the first place?"

"Not yet," Justman answered. "That could be more or less random. For now, it probably makes sense to think of it like the flu. You don't really know who is going to get it, but among those who do get sick, it's those who are weak to begin with—the very old, the very young, that kind of thing—who are most likely to succumb."

"What about the college students?" I asked. "The UVM athletes?"

"If they don't seek any treatment at all, this is still a pretty nasty illness," Justman reminded me.

"Right," I said. I was becoming aware of how long I had been away from the Cabinet Room. "I've got to go. I appreciate this. Please text me again if you learn more."

"No problem."

I turned the knob on the door to the Cabinet Room as quietly as I could, hoping to slip back into my chair without drawing undue attention. That was not to be. The Speaker of the House was asking something about Ohio when I walked in; the President turned to me and said acerbically, "Thank you for joining us."

I instinctively looked to the Chief of Staff, who gave me a look that said, "Just ignore it," like my dad turning around from the front seat of the car and admonishing me to ignore my sister's repeated jabs in the rib cage. The NIH Director was briefing the room on our meeting with Tie Guy that morning, working her way through the six slides. I never did figure out what the Speaker had been saying about Ohio.

"We're still looking at a huge number here," the President said.

"It could be much worse," the NIH Director said.

"I have some good news on that front," I interjected. I explained what Justman had just told me.

"We're still looking at a huge Dormigen shortfall," the President said. "Where are we on that?"

"We're stalled, Mr. President," the National Security Adviser said. She was a black woman, surprisingly young-looking, who had risen through the ranks of the military. She was teaching at West Point when the President asked her to join the administration. Perhaps it was my imagination, but everything about her seemed slightly more impressive than the rest of us: she was fitter, she spoke more forcefully, she even sat straighter in her chair. "With regard to India, sir, we have moved backwards."

"India?" the Strategist asked, genuinely perplexed. "They wanted a hundred billion dollars. How can we move backwards from there?"

"Now they are not even willing to do that," the National Security Adviser said.

"They've taken that offer off the table?" the President asked.

"Yes, sir. They claim they have many untreated illnesses. The Prime Minister feels it would be inappropriate—"

"Politically stupid," the Strategist interrupted.

The National Security Adviser looked at him sternly, clearly annoyed at being interrupted. She continued, "The Prime Minister believes it would be inappropriate to ship Dormigen out of the country at a time when there is still unmet need within the country."

"Come on," the Strategist said. "There is unmet need because the Indian health system is corrupt and inefficient, not because they don't have enough Dormigen. They just can't get it to where they need it."

The National Security Adviser looked at the President as she answered, "Be that as it may, we cannot count on receiving any Dormigen shipments from the Indian government."

"Not even for a hundred billion," the President said.

"No, sir."

"Isn't this just a negotiation?" the Secretary of Defense asked. "Like hiring a taxi in Delhi?"

"Perhaps, sir," the National Security Adviser said. Her speech was as crisp as her white, starched shirt. She spoke in perfect sentences. "However, my sense is that the Prime Minister is not willing to take the risk of putting the interests of the United States ahead of those of his own people. In fact, if we do enter into some kind of negotiation, there is a risk, knowing the man, that he might walk away without consummating a deal and use the whole situation to his own political advantage."

"He'll walk away and make the whole thing public?" the President asked.

"Yes, sir. It would be a huge publicity coup for him. He would be seen as standing up to the United States on behalf of the people of India."

"That's his shtick," the Strategist said.

The National Security Adviser continued, always addressing her comments to the President, "As you know, there is an ongoing corruption investigation in India into military contracting. Several ministers have resigned. The opposition has seized on the situation to go after the Prime Minister. He's on the political ropes. This would be a great distraction for him."

"Okay, where else? What are our other Dormigen options?" the President asked.

"We need to discuss China, sir," the National Security Adviser said.

"Not yet," the President said. "I want to know what our other options are."

"We've hit a wall," the Chief of Staff said. "There are a few more loose commitments, but in terms of Dormigen shipments, there aren't any more big ones to report. We're about where we were yesterday."

"How about Latvia?" the Strategist asked, deadpan.

"Latvia shipped us seven hundred fifty doses," the Chief of Staff answered, trying to suppress her annoyance.

"I don't understand," the Speaker of the House said. "We're looking at a massive epidemic and we can't get our allies to loan us a week's worth of Dormigen? Have we pointed out to them that we invented the drug in the first place? If it weren't for us—"

The President interrupted, "Look, I've made fifty phone calls in the last few days. It's hard to get any responsible leader to ship a meaningful quantity of a lifesaving drug out of the country, especially with the *Capellaviridae* epidemic out there."

"Most of these countries are not seriously affected by *Capellaviridae*," the NIH Director said.

"That could change tomorrow," the President answered. "Then they go down in history as the leader who shipped their Dormigen to the U.S. just as a major epidemic hit. No politician wants to take that risk."

"So they're afraid of the politics?" the Speaker of the House asked. It was like she was wearing different glasses from the rest of us, with special lenses that saw only politics, wherever she looked.

"I don't think you heard what the President was saying," the Chief of Staff said. "I've listened in on a lot of the calls. They're afraid of making a huge, deadly mistake."

The National Security Adviser spoke up forcefully: "There's one other thing, ma'am, if I may be frank here."

"Of course," the Chief of Staff said.

"There's a lot of anger out there, a lot of pent-up frustration with the United States."

"We invented Dormigen!" the Speaker interjected. "The United States is the only reason they have any Dormigen at all. Billions of dollars of American taxpayers' money for all the research and development. What exactly are they frustrated about?"

"Well, Madam Speaker, they are frustrated by a lot of things," the National Security Adviser responded. She turned slightly to face the Speaker and spoke in complete sentences, even when she was angry. "They are frustrated that we withdrew half of our funding for the United Nations. They are frustrated that we shut our borders to immigrants from Yemen and Syria and Turkey. They are frustrated that we are the richest country in the history of civilization, but we refuse to allow the world's poorest countries to sell us their products." The National Security Adviser paused for effect, and then finished her delicately crafted paragraph. "Those would be a few examples."

She might as well have reached across the table and slapped the Speaker across the face. Even I—with a political knowledge gleaned mostly from the Internet while searching online for more interesting things—was aware that the Speaker had spearheaded all of the policies the National Security Adviser had ticked off, along with several others that could have made for a second paragraph. After Donald Trump's political success with his "America First" agenda, opportunistic politicians across the political spectrum had rushed to create their own knockoffs, the policy equivalent of those fake handbags spread across the sidewalk in New York City. Who cares who designed the original product if people like it? The Speaker had asserted her leadership of the progressive wing of the Democratic Party in large part by dressing up the Trump agenda in left-wing clothing. She had argued, for example, that we could not help the poorest Americans if we were shipping "a huge chunk of our tax revenues" to corrupt countries overseas. She said it was unreasonable for Americans to make sacrifices to deal with climate change while "the most polluting countries in the world are doing nothing." And so on. Her relations with the Tea Party were frigid but when it came to votes in the House, they often voted together, a new voting bloc of the populist left and right. The President had run for the White House in part to fight against this new isolationism. Like so much else he had done, the Speaker considered it a personal affront and a political assault.

"What about privatizing Dormigen production?" the Speaker asked defensively.

"Yes, that came up in a few of the conversations, but no one seems to care why we have a shortage," the Chief of Staff answered, somewhat ruefully. She looked at the President. "Do you remember what Cedrek told us?"

"The French President," the National Security Adviser interjected for the benefit of the rest of us.

"No, I don't remember," the President said.

The Chief of Staff continued, "He said—I even wrote it down . . ." She flipped through a legal pad and then continued, reading from her notes: "'The Americans have been stealing our lunch money for fifty years and now you come asking to borrow some change.'"

"Stealing their lunch money?" the Speaker said incredulously. "That has no basis in reality. Half these countries have been free-riding off of our military for the last century. South Korea? Please tell me that South Korea has shipped us Dormigen."

"South Korea has been very generous," the Chief of Staff said.

"They should be, given all we've done for them," the Speaker declared.

"I'll mention that to them," the President replied.

The National Security Adviser said calmly, "With all due respect, Madam Speaker, many of these countries perceive that the United States has been insensitive to their needs, especially in recent years. Whatever the objective reality, their perception is what matters here. You are welcome to tell them they should feel more grateful, but I suspect that will just make the problem worse."

"What about killing them with kindness?" the Senate Majority Leader said. He had been largely silent since our early meetings. In the Cabinet Room, he sat with his jacket buttoned, his huge paunch creating what looked like an Olympic ski jump onto the table. But now his inner LBJ had been activated. "Everybody is willing to make some kind of deal, if we sweeten it enough."

"I'm not sure that's true in this case," the Chief of Staff said. "This is more about national pride."

"It could actually make things worse," the National Security Adviser added. "If a leader is seen as taking a big payoff from the U.S., and then they come up short on Dormigen in their own country, even just a few deaths, it would be a political nightmare. Why take the risk?"

"Maybe we make them a deal they can't refuse," the Senate Majority Leader said. "These countries don't really want to be on the wrong side of the United States." The room was silent as the participants around the table absorbed the Majority Leader's thought. He continued. "They've got a surplus of Dormigen—"

"Maybe they have a surplus," the Acting HHS Secretary interrupted. "They can't be sure exactly what they will need."

"Okay, fine," the Majority Leader continued. "They are *likely* to have a surplus and we need what they have. With the resources of this government, I find it hard to believe we can't make some kind of deal happen." He shook his head in mock amazement, as he had done so many times to such great effect at Rotary Club speeches and sports banquets and Fourth of July parades.

"Remember, we've already collected over a million doses," the Chief of Staff answered. "Our allies have contributed what they think they can afford to do without. Now it gets harder."

"Then isn't this really just about China?" the House Speaker asked, though it did not really sound like a question. "Isn't that what we should be talking about? That offer is on the table. That one solves our problem in one stroke." We had been briefed that morning on the President's upcoming visit to the South China Sea. If he was going to make that trip—land on the carrier, as our Pacific allies were expecting—he needed to leave in about forty-eight hours. One meeting in Hawaii had already been stripped from the schedule; there were briefings in Guam and the Philippines that could be canceled as well, buying more time. But two days was the max before Air Force One had to be wheels-up to make the South China Sea Conference, the culmination of America's effort to build a bulwark against Chinese meddling in the region. The South China Sea Agreement had been in negotiation, on and off, since the Obama administration: nine signatory nations; 711 pages, including addendums on fishing, mineral rights, endangered species, even fighting piracy; *and one high-profile landing by the U.S. President on an aircraft carrier to put a fine point on it all.* No wonder the Chinese were willing to give us a million doses of Dormigen to ditch the whole thing.

The President slapped the conference table, somewhere between a tap and a bang, and said, "Why are we not making more progress on the virus? I don't understand that. That's where we need to beat this thing. We should not be begging the rest of the world to fix this problem. I need better options."

The NIH Director answered quickly, perhaps a tad too defensive: "Mr. President, we've got three teams working around the clock on this thing, and they've made remarkable progress in a short amount of time. Usually it takes decades to confront a disease like this. We have weeks."

"Then this is when you need to dig deeper, think differently," the President demanded. "Can you not see the stakes here? What we need is the Manhattan Project and what we're getting is a government task force." The President looked around the room as he made his motivational speech, or whatever it was. He never made eye contact with me, but I could feel my neck and face flushing. I was, after all, the only one in the room specifically because of my purported expertise on viruses.

The Strategist said, "To be fair, the Manhattan Project took at least a couple of years." He typed quickly on his phone. The President ignored him. After a moment of silence, the Strategist read from his phone, "Yeah, four years, one hundred and thirty thousand people. You got to love Wikipedia, right?"

"Maybe we should take a short break," the Chief of Staff said.

"Fine," the President agreed. "But I'm telling you, these options are not good enough."

"One thing," the Acting HHS Secretary said, raising his hand slightly. "I've said this before, but I think we need to discuss what happens if we come up short on Dormigen. I'm not saying that's going to happen, but I think we need a plan."

"I agree," the Secretary of Defense said.

"That's for Congress to decide," the House Speaker said.

"No, actually, it's not," the President said.

The Speaker replied, "Since when does Congress not have a say—"

The Chief of Staff cut her off: "I'll put it on the agenda for this afternoon."

"One more thing," the Communications Director interjected, speaking for the first time I could remember. Mostly he just sat at the end of the table checking his phone, reading and typing messages. He was a former cable news political correspondent, trimmer and younger than the others in the room, with a full head of hair and a nicer suit. He and the President were the only two who consistently looked good on television. "The blogosphere is starting to heat up," he said, looking at his phone. "I'm getting some inquiries."

"What exactly?" the Chief of Staff asked.

"The President canceled the Hawaii meetings, the Speaker has been at the White House for three days in a row, that kind of thing. They're starting to smell a story."

"Are there any leaks?" the President asked.

"Not yet."

"Well, what are we supposed to do?" the President asked in the same impatient, ornery tone that he had been using for most of the morning.

"I've got some ideas," the Communications Director assured him.

"Like what?" the President asked.

"We don't need the whole group for that," the Chief of Staff said, closing her leather legal pad holder. "Okay, everyone, let's come back in twenty minutes."

The participants stood and whipped out their phones and other devices. I got up and wandered over to a table with cookies and coffee, more out of a need to do something than because I needed cookies or coffee. The President's comments had struck a chord. Were we really working as aggressively as we might on *Capellaviridae*? For all the effort, we still had no new insights on lurking viruses. We had no clue what triggered *Capellaviridae* to turn fatal, not even any decent theories. I was the one who was supposed to be making progress on that front.

I made one call during that break and sent one text. The call was pure genius. The text turned out to be a complete disaster.

29.

DURING THE BREAK, THE COMMUNICATIONS DIRECTOR USED his phone to show the Chief of Staff a short video clip of the Speaker of the House arriving at the White House. "CNN is running this over and over," he told her.

"Do you think she tipped them off?" the Chief of Staff asked.

"Maybe. It makes her look presidential. Why else would a camera crew happen to be there when she arrived?" the Communications Director suggested.

"We can't prove it," the Chief of Staff said.

"Of course not. I just thought you should know." The Communications Director was still looking down at his phone. "Oh, fuck," he said.

"What?"

"Fox is reporting that there is some crisis related to the Saudi coup attempt." He continued to read, and then said, "Where do they get this crap?" He began to read from his phone: "Sources close to the White House are reporting that Saudi Arabia's nuclear strike force has been put on high alert in the wake of a coup attempt, prompting other nuclear powers in the region to respond in kind." Saudi Arabia had only been a nuclear power for a handful of years. After Iran acquired the bomb, the other major powers in the region scrambled to even the playing field. The Saudis had the resources to spend freely, so they were the first to get the bomb (allegedly with the assistance of the Israelis, who believed that a nuclear Saudi Arabia would be the best counterweight to a nuclear Iran). Egypt followed soon thereafter. Given the instability of the region, there was a chronic fear of some kind of nuclear incident. A press person for the Joint Chiefs of Staff had refused to comment on the Fox nuclear alert story, which merely incited more interest.

I stood in a corner of the conference room, sipping coffee idly. The President's admonition was replaying itself in my mind. We really did need the virus equivalent of the Manhattan Project. There was no excuse for not doing everything—anything—that might be remotely productive. With that in mind, I called Dartmouth's Department of Biological Sciences, where I spoke to a friendly administrative assistant. Professor Huke had retired several years earlier, but he was still living in the area. She gave me his phone number. I gathered my thoughts for a moment and then dialed. Professor Huke's wife answered. He was outside working in the garden, she said, and would call me back as soon as he came in.

I wandered over to the Chief of Staff and told her what I was thinking. Huke was not an expert on lurking viruses, but he did have an excellent grasp of the broader field. Maybe we were too deep in the rabbit hole and needed to pull our heads out and look around. Huke would be a guy who could help us do that. "Of course we should talk to him," the Chief of Staff said. "We can bring him to Washington or we can fly you up there."

"How do I do that?" I asked. I was still learning all the protocols.

"Go this afternoon, after this meeting," she instructed. "We'll get you an Air Force plane. Just let me know the closest airport."

Huke called back just as the participants were making their way back to the Cabinet Room. He did not remember me; I had not expected that he would. I briefly explained the work I was doing at NIH and that we were facing a new threat from a lurking virus that could infect humans.

"That's curious," Huke said.

"Exactly," I agreed. "It's potentially dangerous. I'm hoping I could speak to you in person about it, as soon as possible."

"I'm not an expert on lurking viruses," he protested.

"I know, but we need to take a step back on this one. Our thoughts have gone stale."

"Sure. I'm retired now, so you pick the time and place."

Huke did not react when I asked if we could meet early the following morning. He knew enough about viruses to recognize that public health situations are often time-sensitive. I offered to meet him in a Hanover coffee shop, but Huke suggested that I come to his house instead.

While this conversation was going on, I got a surprising inbound text. It was from Sloan, my Dartmouth infatuation, whom I had last seen at a friend's wedding six or eight months earlier. It said, "In DC. Can you get coffee?? So eager to see u." The meeting had resumed in the Cabinet Room, so I stepped out of the room to send a quick reply. Sloan had that effect on me.

30.

I DID NOT LEAK ANYTHING. THIS WAS THE CONCLUSION OF both congressional inquiries. My answers to the commissions were entirely truthful, if somewhat misleading. (In the eyes of the law, that is not a crime.) Still, the reality is that my meeting with Sloan inadvertently set in motion a series of events that I deeply regret.

Sloan lived in New York City. We had drifted apart after graduation, but we still saw each other at weddings, reunions, and the like. We never dated in college, but we did "hook up" briefly during senior week—the week prior to our graduation from Dartmouth when classes were over, our diplomas had been earned, and we were left to do in seven days everything we wished we had done over the previous four years. Sloan and I had a long conversation after a class picnic on one of those June evenings when the sun seems to linger forever, the light getting softer and more beautiful before darkness finally falls and the temperature plunges. We were both drunk, not sloppily so, but enough to precipitate a long, meandering, lovely conversation about life's big questions: our regrets at Dartmouth; our plans after graduation; the state of our families; the role that Turkey could play in promoting peace in the Middle East. (I said it was meandering.) Sloan leaned close to me, in part because it was getting cool, but also because our body language reflected the intensity of our conversation and the depth of the bond that we had built over four years—the kind of bond, really, that it's hard to build at other points in life. And, as I mentioned, we were drunk. At one point two asshole lacrosse players began tossing beer at one another. I pulled Sloan out of the path of an arcing plastic cup of cheap beer and ended up with my arms wrapped around her from behind. My nose just dusted her hair and I could smell the flowery fragrance of her shampoo. I inhaled deeply.

I am a scientist, not a romance novelist. As a scientist, I can say that a hundred million years of natural selection was telling my body that I should reproduce, which tends to produce a physical reaction. A romance novelist might simply point out that my dick was harder than the pine picnic table. Sloan was wearing jeans; nothing made her look better or more alluring. When she sensed the physiological response of my reptilian brain, she pushed gently back against me, and that sensation—her clearly sexual response after my years of platonic longing—remains one of the more pleasant sensations I have experienced in life.

"Will you walk me home?" she asked.

My answer should be obvious. Our walk home has social significance because of two things that happened, which is why I have gone to great lengths to explain how the night unfolded. We headed from the picnic area toward Sloan's off-campus apartment, but then took a detour onto a well-worn path that led through a small pine forest and up a hill to an open field that housed the college observatory. It was a lovely spot; the night was crisp and clear. The observatory was obviously there for a reason. We were hours from a major city, so the night sky was brilliantly illuminated. There is no better brew for inspiring contemplation about the meaning of life for a pair of twenty-two-year-olds than college graduation, alcohol, and the endless bright expanse of a starry night. "So tell me what you're going to do with your life?" Sloan asked.

By then we were sitting on a bed of pine needles at the edge of the clearing. I was leaning against an old stone wall and Sloan was resting in my arms, which was both a natural continuation of what had happened at the picnic and an instinctive response to the crisp New Hampshire night. "I'm going to be a scientist," I said. "And I want to teach at a place like this." We loved Dartmouth. For all our griping over the years, we had talked often about some of our more inspiring professors and our unique opportunities to interact with them, rather than being treated like the academic equivalent of cattle, herded into a huge lecture hall to listen to a teaching assistant with a tenuous grasp of English.

"It's an amazing lifestyle," Sloan said. Only she would be prescient enough to think about lifestyle at that point. Our peers were rushing off to take jobs with hedge funds and investment banks, eagerly boasting about the ninety-hour weeks that they would work. It would take until our tenth reunion for many of them to admit that their lives were a wreck.

"What kind of lawyer are you going to be in twenty years?" I asked.

"I won't be a lawyer," she said emphatically.

"Does Harvard Law know that?" I asked. Sloan had been accepted to Harvard Law (and every other law school to which she applied). She had deferred for a year to travel and write columns for a small Vermont newspaper.

"I'm going to be a writer—journalism of some sort, probably

political journalism," she said. She had been the editor of the Dartmouth newspaper, so that was hardly a stretch.

"So why law school, then?" I asked.

"Because it will set me apart." She paused, staring at the stars. "Because I'll have some substantive knowledge, rather than just being able to write. There are lots of good writers in the world, and there are plenty of Harvard Law grads, but there aren't many who are both."

We sat at the edge of that clearing watching the stars for a long time. If I could relive several hours of my life, kind of like the play *Our Town*, these would be the hours I would choose. The night sky was indescribably beautiful. I was holding in my arms the girl I had both loved and lusted after for nearly four years, who nuzzled closer as I buried my face in her hair and ran my hand gently across her breasts. The college chapter of our lives was drawing to a successful close; we had everything to look forward to—both in the next hour or two, at least for me, and then beyond.

I held her hand as we wound our way through a narrow wooded path that led to her building. When we reached the front door she turned and wrapped her arms around my neck. We kissed—not the platonic pecks that we had exchanged a hundred times over the years—but a deep lingering kiss. Her mouth tasted of beer and spearmint gum, which I remember her popping in as we left the picnic. The moment was wonderful, and we had done something that we had never done before, but I recognize now that it was not particularly passionate, at least not on Sloan's part. After the long kiss, during which my hands roamed up and down like some kind of time-sensitive geological survey, Sloan pulled back and gave me a peck on the forehead, a much more familiar gesture. "Good night," she said. "This was wonderful. Perfect." She did not invite me in.

Sloan's career plan was uncanny, because it unfolded pretty much as she described that night. She spent two years writing and traveling (deferring Harvard for a second time) while building up a portfolio of work. She ground her way through Harvard Law while working summers in the newsroom at the *New York Times*. Between her second and third years, she was the personal assistant to Barack Obama, helping to draft his columns. Sloan's postgraduation job search worked out exactly as she had planned: she was a Harvard Law grad applying for prestigious journalism jobs, setting her apart from other aspiring writers. Meanwhile, her super-smart law school classmates were slashing each other's eyes out competing for clerkships and positions at prestigious law firms.

Sloan was clever. She was also ambitious, in the old Shakespearean pejorative sense of the word, which I did not fully appreciate until I became a victim of that ambition.

31.

WE RECONVENED AFTER LUNCH IN THE CABINET ROOM, BUT the meeting broke up almost immediately, before the President had even taken his seat. The Communications Director, tethered as always to his phone, said, "Hold on, can we have five minutes here?" He huddled in the corner with the President, the Chief of Staff, and the Strategist. Something had obviously broken in the news. I did a quick search on my phone. The top story was that teen pop star Onyx was reportedly pregnant. Obviously that was not delaying our meeting—but I clicked anyway. "Hollywood sources" were saying that Ryan Seacrest, who had to be nearly sixty, might be the father. I restrained myself from clicking on that, too.

I scrolled down. There was a study purporting to show that one donut a day could lower your blood pressure. That was not why the President was huddled in the corner, either. I scrolled further. The script for an Oscar-nominated film was allegedly plagiarized. Two convicts had escaped from a New York state prison, one of them for the second time. (According to a poll on the subject—who conducts polls about prison breaks?—a solid majority of Americans were pulling for the escapees.) And then, near the bottom of the page: "News Outlet Reports Nuclear Standoff." Some Middle East news agency that I had never heard of, perhaps because it was really just some Arab guy sitting in his underwear in his parents' basement, was reporting that Saudi Arabia had threatened "nuclear retaliation against the state sponsors of the recent coup attempt." The story hinted that

Iran was behind the coup and that the Saudis had Tehran in their nuclear crosshairs. Even I knew that made no sense. The Iranians are Shia Muslims; the coup plotters were radical Sunnis. Besides, the President had been with us since our morning delay, so my sense was that that situation was under control. I clicked around. Other news outlets had picked up the story from the Middle East Affairs News Outlet. All of the coverage mentioned that the President had been sequestered in the White House for days with the Secretary of Defense, the Speaker of the House, and the Senate Majority Leader. They did get that right. A cub reporter on a high school newspaper could tell that something was afoot, even if it did not happen to be a nuclear standoff in the Middle East.

I was amazed by the speed with which the cameras were set up on the White House lawn. Each major news outlet gave the crisis a name, because every disaster of any sort must now have a name. Fox News tossed subtlety aside and went with "Countdown to Armageddon." NBC went with "Nuclear Nightmare?," which deserves honorable mention for inviting panic while simultaneously adding the question mark to signal they really had no clue what was happening. The nuclear story was taking on a life of its own, crowding out nearly everything else on the political page (though Onyx's alleged pregnancy was still a far more popular story overall). Another story at the bottom of the Netflix politics blog caught my eye. The Speaker of the House had told a group of political reporters that the U.S. approach to China "may be overly confrontational." I was still a political neophyte, but even I could see her long game on this one. China had the Dormigen; the Speaker was going to be the one to get it.

The President, the Chief of Staff, and the others had wandered back to the table in the Cabinet Room, still discussing the nuclear situation. "It buys us time," the Communications Director was arguing.

"Great," the President said sarcastically. "It might also set off a real nuclear conflict. The last thing we need is a bunch of unstable regimes believing that the Saudis and the Israelis are conspiring to launch an attack."

"No government is going to take this seriously," the Communications Director said.

"The hell they won't," the President snapped. "Have you spent any time in the region? Have you? The place runs on conspiracy theories, not to mention that there are twenty different groups that will use this to advance their agenda, whether they think it's true or not. *This story needs to die now.*"

"Then how do we explain it?" the Communications Director said, motioning to the rest of us standing and sitting around the conference table.

"That's your job," the President said unhelpfully. The Chief of Staff called the meeting back to order, but no more than three minutes later the Communications Director interrupted, "Sorry, can I have five minutes alone with the President?"

"You just had twenty," the President said. "Unless you can get me a million doses of Dormigen, we need to be right here."

"I agree with the President," the Speaker of the House said. "We still don't have a grasp on what's happening here."

"Give me five minutes," the Communications Director insisted. "I can kill this nuclear story right now. Can we talk with the First Lady?"

"What does she have to do with this?" the President asked, genuinely puzzled.

"Five minutes, everybody. Sorry," the Communications Director said.

I was not privy to the subsequent meeting. I admire the First Lady for her willingness to play a role in a very clever misdirection scheme. Then again, no one ever doubted the First Lady's toughness. The Communication Director's plan can best be described as media tai chi. "You cannot fight a story, no matter how ridiculous it is," he told me later. "You can only redirect the frenzy." Buried in the news that day was another story—made up wholesale by some Internet troll—that the President was having an affair with a South American diplomat. The story had no legs whatsoever. The page had ninety-one views when the Communications Director stumbled across it. It was wedged between a headline proclaiming that a cream made from avocado pits could cure skin cancer and another alleging that the former Federal Reserve Chair had stolen two tons of gold during his tenure—purloining bars one at a time from the vault under the New York Federal Reserve Bank, hiding them under his desk (which was in Washington??), and eventually sneaking it all out in the family minivan.

Later that afternoon, the Communications Director released a statement proclaiming, "The President and First Lady have a rock-solid marriage," and that any reports of extramarital affairs were "damaging and unsubstantiated." Every press person immediately recognized the "nondenial denial," which in media-speak means that the Communications Director had not denied the affair. He had merely described it as "damaging and unsubstantiated," which means, "Yeah, it's true, but my boss made me say something." Over the next hour, the original South American affair story had fifty-two thousand hits, at which point the server went down.* At about the same time, the *Washington Post–USA Today* reported that a "senior White House official" had "acknowledged the possibility" that the President was embroiled in a salacious sex scandal with "a member of the foreign diplomatic corps." The genius of this misdirection was twofold. First, the nuclear story went away. (The cameras on the White House lawn were disassembled almost immediately and dispatched to camp out at various embassies across Washington.) Second, the mainstream media could pass off this sex scandal as real news, rather than just salacious gossip, because it involved a foreign diplomat, no doubt a spy. *Obviously, the public has a right to know if the President is giving up national security secrets in exchange for sexual favors.*

The news "analysts" quickly pieced the story together: the nuclear situation was just a cover for the President's sexual misdeeds, which were so serious that he had assembled the top officials in the government, including the Speaker of the House and the Majority Leader, to discuss the possibility of his resignation. When this rumor frenzy

---

*   Unfortunately, the former Chair of the Federal Reserve was also forced to deny that he had stolen two tons of gold, a rumor that dogs him to this day. As anyone who has served in Washington knows, these kinds of rumors can never be fully scrubbed away, no matter how outlandish they may be. I remember a college-educated friend telling me at a bar mitzvah years later, "Of course he denied stealing the gold. What else was he going to say? They never searched his house. Why not? Because all these guys are crooks. They're in cahoots." I considered telling him that it's hard to get a search warrant based on an Internet rumor, but instead I just excused myself and went to the bar.

was at its peak, the Communications Director leaked a photograph of a voluptuous, ethnically ambiguous, thirty-something woman to a Spanish-language television network. Much like that first iconic picture of Monica Lewinsky in the beret, this lovely Mediterranean or Arab or Hispanic woman became the face of the crisis. The press camped out at the twenty-plus embassies most likely to have a sexy spy with a vaguely olive complexion. In reality, the photo was computer-generated: a composite of several attractive celebrities, including a Lebanese jazz singer and a Brazilian soccer star, all melded together by a young computer whiz at the NSA. It was just an unfortunate coincidence that the computer-generated photo bore a stunning resemblance to Maria de la Campos Rivera, the head of the political section at the Colombian Embassy. Telemundo made the discovery, after which the press corps followed her doggedly. This turned out to be doubly tragic, since she was, in fact, having an affair with the married Cuban ambassador.

Roughly 60 percent of the American population still believes that the President was passing secrets through this Colombian mistress to the Cubans. That is ten times the number of Americans who can correctly locate Saudi Arabia on a world map.

32.

BACK IN THE CABINET ROOM, WE STILL HAD NOT ADDRESSED the two most contentious issues: China and a possible "rationing plan" for Dormigen if we were to come up short. Before we plunged into that, the Chief of Staff updated us on assorted other small developments. The U.S. military had identified a stash of Dormigen in Germany, some forty thousand doses, that would be shipped back stateside immediately. The Canadians were monitoring their Dormigen usage on a daily basis; demand was falling short of their projections, so they shipped us a hundred thousand doses and projected they might be able to donate more in the coming days. The better news came from a working group at the Centers for Disease Control. Doctors there had lowered the likely fatality rate for those sickened by *Capellaviridae* to a range between 0.5 to 1.1 percent—which they described as "on par with a virulent strain of the flu." The earlier estimates were based on data from victims who had not sought treatment. Those who showed up at a hospital were likely to do better, even without Dormigen. The CDC experts wrote in a short memo, "If victims are treated with fluids and antibiotics to deal with possible secondary infections, the likely fatality rate would be appreciably lower than our earlier estimate." The report also noted that the pattern of fatalities would be similar to a bad flu: the very old, the very young, and the immunocompromised. Our intuition was confirmed: the early fatalities—clusters of college students and young, otherwise healthy men—were not the most vulnerable populations; they were the ones who were too stubborn to seek treatment.

Despite the protestations of the Strategist, we had abandoned "the number" and were now working with a "likely range" of deaths. Experts typically use confidence intervals when projecting outcomes. "The number" had been a bizarre and artificially precise construct. Still, I would emphasize how important it was in those early days to quantify the risk we were facing. We should be grateful to the Strategist, his personal foibles aside,* for his unwillingness to bury his head in the sand. The dominant sentiment in those early meetings was denial, which was the worst possible response.

Our range had settled at seventy-five thousand to a hundred and fifty thousand likely deaths. "Most of these people are going to die anyway," the Strategist said.

"So are we," the Acting HHS Secretary said.

"You know what I mean," the Strategist said. "Most of these people are very sick to begin with. You read the CDC memo."

"Not the very young," the Acting HHS Secretary replied.

"Right," the Strategist conceded. "But we can give them the Dormigen we have."

---

* The Strategist was arrested in D.C. for solicitation eight months ago, and then again for the same offense three weeks later in Buffalo, New York. This made him a target for late-night comics, not merely for the prostitution arrest, but because it happened in Buffalo. He later made a compelling argument that prostitution should be legalized. (You can watch the YouTube video.) Like so many other things he argued, it was eminently sensible once you stripped the emotion away from the issue.

The Chief of Staff interrupted the exchange. "Hold those thoughts," she said. "We need to talk about China first."

"That Dormigen offer is still on the table?" the Senate Majority Leader asked.

"Of course it is," the President answered. "This is the best thing to happen to them since the British left Hong Kong."

The Chief of Staff turned to the National Security Adviser. "Can you update us on where we are on the South China Sea Summit?"

"Yes, ma'am," she replied crisply. "We can buy ourselves another two days. I've spoken to most of my counterparts in the other signatory nations. Rather than landing on the carrier at the beginning of the summit, they feel it would have the same effect if the President were to leave from a carrier after the agreement is signed."

"We just do it at the end instead of the beginning," the President said.

"Exactly. Two things need to happen," the National Security Adviser answered confidently. "The President needs to be there to sign the agreement. And we need to have some show of military presence in the disputed area to signal our collective resolve. Our allies feel—and I agree—that there is no substitute for an American carrier group clearly staking out international waters."

"So we sail an aircraft carrier along the China coast?" the Speaker of the House asked indignantly.

"No, ma'am," the National Security Adviser answered, not betraying any change in emotion. "We sail the carrier group through international waters that the Chinese government has heretofore illegally claimed to be their exclusive—"

"Okay, okay," the Speaker said. "But we're still talking about a big military pissing match over a bunch of islands in the South China Sea."

"No, that is entirely wrong," the President interjected. "This is an agreement we have been negotiating for twenty years. It covers everything from fishing rights to human trafficking. It is the cornerstone of our entire defense strategy in the region."

The Secretary of Defense added, "I want to underscore what the President said on this. Our allies are counting on us to be the anchor of this agreement. China has not proved to be the responsible actor on the international stage that we had hoped. We need a multilateral effort to contain a variety of illegal and aggressive actions on their part."

"I don't even know what that means," the Speaker said. "We're talking about a bunch of uninhabited islands ten thousand miles from here."

"We are talking about much more than that, ma'am," the National Security Adviser said.

"Enough to let Americans die?" the Speaker asked. "We are unwilling to ask for the medicine that will save all those lives? That just feels like testosterone run amok."

The President said, "If we back down on this, it will be Yalta all over again. We will pay a huge price in that part of the world—all over the world, actually—if we capitulate to Chinese aggression."

The Speaker replied, "Yalta? You know what it feels like to me? Vietnam. Your team has some deluded notion that terrible things are going to happen if we don't project strength thousands of miles from our borders. Are we willing to let tens of thousands of Americans die for that?"

The Senate Majority Leader, who normally sat impassively for these conversations, added, "Mr. President, I have to agree with the Speaker on this one. It would be awfully difficult to explain to my constituents back in Illinois that their loved ones are dying from a preventable disease because we're trying to protect Vietnamese fishing rights. I can't sell that to a Rotary Club."

"You know this is about much more than Vietnamese fishing rights," the President said sharply.

"I do," the Majority Leader answered. "But that doesn't mean I could sell it to a Rotary Club back home."

"Here's what you say," the Strategist offered. "You tell them that you don't think we should subvert America's interests to an authoritarian regime for the next hundred years in order to save people who are likely to die soon anyway. You sprinkle in some historical references to the times when the democracies were too timid to stand up to authoritarian bullies. Then you finish with an overview of how the United States led a coalition of democracies that successfully contained the Soviet Union."

"Maybe I'll just have you give the talk," the Majority Leader said, chuckling.

"This is a decision Congress should make," the House Speaker said tartly.

The President waved the comment away with a dismissive sweep of his hand. "Congress will do whatever helps most in the midterm elections," he said. "There is no long-term vision there. That's why we don't make military decisions in the legislature."

"With respect, Mr. President, Congress will do what the American people want them to do," the Speaker shot back.

The Strategist offered, "Roosevelt had to drag the country into World War II. We would have watched the Holocaust from afar if it weren't for Pearl Harbor."

"Let's not pretend we're dealing with the Holocaust here," the Speaker said.

"I think the point is that popular opinion is not always a great gauge in these kinds of situations," the Secretary of Defense interjected. "The South China Sea Agreement is very compelling. We've done it right. It has the backing of all our key allies. We have bipartisan support in the Senate—"

"Not if they know the price we have to pay," the Majority Leader said.

"Obviously," the Defense Secretary continued. "I'm just saying that if we are going to sit here tossing historical examples back and forth, this is not some unilateral muscle-flexing."

"Like Iraq," the President said.

"Correct. This is not Iraq. To the contrary, the world is looking to us on this one. They want us to lead in the region," the Defense Secretary said.

"Can we just go back to India for a minute?" the President asked. "Because then we wouldn't have the South China Sea problem."

"We've hit a dead end there, sir," the National Security Adviser said.

"I don't understand that. The world's biggest democracy—how are we not getting more help from them?" the President asked, almost pleading.

"The Prime Minister is in political trouble," the National Security Adviser explained (though we had been over this ground before). "His coalition is breaking up. He thinks this would be political suicide for him. He cannot be seen as shipping medicine out of the country."

"Saving hundreds of thousands of lives is bad politics?" the President replied in frustration.

"When we canceled the trade deal with India, it provoked enormous hostility there," the Secretary of Defense answered. "We were their biggest export market. The perception is that the U.S. is indifferent to the country's welfare."

"What about the military angle?" the President asked. "We can revisit the Boeing deal."

"Sir, we rejected that deal for sound reasons," the Secretary of Defense answered, looking somewhat alarmed by the subject. "The Prime Minister has been very bellicose toward the Pakistanis. The Islamabad government is hanging by a string. Sending advanced fighters to India right now would destabilize the region. Pakistan is a nuclear power. The last thing we need—"

"Yeah, okay, I got it," the President said. "You're telling me we can't do some kind of secret deal with Delhi? Send him money to a Swiss bank account if we have to."

"That government is worse at keeping secrets than we are," the Secretary of Defense said.

"Are we really talking about a Swiss bank account?" the Speaker asked. "Really?"

"It's just an example, for fuck sake," the President snarled. "But yes, now that I think about it, I would ship briefcases full of cash anywhere in the goddamn world if I could get the Dormigen without selling out our country to the Chinese."

There was a brief lull in the conversation. The participants around the table instinctively looked to the President. "Give me something better," he said.

PART 3

WHAT IF?

33.

URING OUR SHORT BREAK, THE HOUSE SPEAKER approached the President and told him she was prepared to force his hand on the China situation, either by congressional action or in the courts. Their conversation was calm enough that none of the rest of us even knew it was happening. The President calmly rebuffed her. Congress has no authority to conduct diplomacy, he said. The White House Legal Counsel joined their sidebar conversation. "You have no grounds for action in the courts, either," he pointed out. "You can sue the President to stop him from doing something—if he were giving away American Dormigen, for example. But you can't sue to make him *do* something, at least not in this case."

The Speaker's top legal adviser, who had been following her around silently like a lapdog ever since she attended her first meeting, nodded in agreement. The Speaker stared malevolently at the President. "You are making a huge mistake," she said. "Thousands of people are going to die, and it will all be on you."

"I haven't decided anything yet," the President said. "But as always, I appreciate your input." The Speaker turned abruptly and walked away. We do not know exactly where she went, or who she called. We do know that shortly thereafter, Claire Yegian, the most notoriously dogged member of the White House press corps, texted the Communications Director for a comment on "the Hawaii tragedy" with a link to a local news story: three children, all under seven, had died from "flu-like symptoms." Their father, a widower who had moved the family from Cleveland to Honolulu for a new start after his wife was killed in a car accident, was demanding an investigation. The tragedy of three dead children, combined with the father's allegations that some dangerous disease was afoot, was getting traction.

The Communications Director texted back, "President sends deepest condolences, but this is clearly not WH [White House] business."

Yegian's chilling response came right back: "I have it on highest authority that it is."

The Communications Director called her. "Who's your source?" he asked, without exchanging pleasantries.

"Give me a break," Yegian said, miffed that he would even ask.

"Then let me ask you this: Might it be someone who wants to run for president herself?"

"Something's going on," Yegian insisted. "That I know. Now I've got three dead kids under strange circumstances and a high-level source saying the White House knows something—"

"You can't corroborate that," the Communications Director said tersely.

"Not yet."

"The President sends his deepest condolences for this family tragedy," the Communications Director said, and then hung up. He walked quickly to the corner of the room where the President was speaking with the First Lady. I had not noticed her come in; this was the first time I had seen her in person. She was taller than I thought, maybe because of the heels, and elegantly made up, with dark black hair pulled back in a tight bun. She was wearing large diamond stud earrings. Later, when she appeared in public, they would be gone. I was watching the couple from across the room, unaware of what they were talking about, when the President wheeled in my direction and pointed at me. There was fierceness in his eyes, more than just anger, that I had not seen before. "I thought you said this was like the flu," he said loud enough to stop other conversations. I found myself walking, almost involuntarily, to where the Communications Director was huddled with the President and the First Lady. "Three kids—three little children—all dead. That's not the flu," the President repeated as I joined them.

"Focus," the First Lady snapped at him. And then, more calm and measured: "These things happen. Tragedies happen." In that moment I appreciated what it means to be the partner of someone who carries the weight of the White House.

"The Speaker is leaking like a sieve," the President said angrily. "Now goddamn Claire Yegian—"

"You just need time, honey," the First Lady said. "I can buy you time."

"Three children?" the President repeated. "The guy loses his wife and then all of his children? That's not the flu . . . His whole family."

"Did they seek treatment?" I asked. The President ignored my response. The Communications Director shook his head no, leaving me confused as to whether he was answering my question or trying to tell me to stop talking.

"Do you have any idea how bad this could get?" the President asked. We all recognized it as a rhetorical question.

"You need to keep doing what you're doing," the First Lady said, almost sternly. I realized that the architect of the "Mac 'n Cheese Massacre" was no stranger to hard decisions, if in less deadly situations. "Okay?" she added.

"I think this is a bad idea," the Communications Director said.

"Nobody asked you," the First Lady answered. Under different circumstances this might have been funny, as the Communications Director's entire job consisted of offering advice on these matters.

"Are you sure?" the President asked.

"Twenty minutes," she replied.

Having walked into the conversation, I had no idea what was afoot. But roughly twenty minutes later I understood. The First Lady held an impromptu news conference on the White House lawn. "I have just two short statements," she began. "First, the President and I would like to extend our heartfelt condolences to Cliff Barnhill for his tragic loss in Honolulu. The President and I read this story and were so deeply saddened. Please, please let this be a reminder to all Americans to seek treatment immediately if you feel ill—always better to err on the safe side. The flu season is not over, and we are working with Hawaii public health officials to learn why the illness was so virulent in the Barnhill case.

"Second, the President and I will be spending some time apart." There was an audible gasp from the assembled press corps. The photographers and camera operators pressed closer. "I will be leaving immediately to spend time with my parents in New Hampshire. I would ask that you respect our privacy with regard to this situation." She paused and grasped the podium, as if for emotional support. One of the photographers, paid to notice the small things, realized that she was not wearing her wedding ring. He moved toward the podium and shot a close-up of the ringless finger. It was unseemly, so close that a pale band was visible where the ring had shielded her finger from the sun, but this was the money shot. Home Depot Media began blasting out the image three minutes later.

The First Lady's motorcade left the White House with a parade of media vehicles in tow. Claire Yegian's editor texted, "Go to NH."

34.

THE STRESS AND FATIGUE WERE EVIDENT AROUND THE CON-ference table. On breaks, the White House staff would swoop in to clear away plates and cups, but the room still had the stale feel of a common area in a college dormitory during finals. The Majority Leader had finally taken off his jacket. The Strategist had loosened his tie and unbuttoned the top button of his shirt. The room was cool, but many of us looked like we had been sitting in the same place for too many hours (and probably smelled that way, too). I wanted real food, some exercise of any kind, and a shower. It was not going to happen anytime soon. As soon as I left the room, I would have to get on a plane and fly to New Hampshire.

The Chief of Staff called us back to order. "I want to thank the Acting Secretary for bringing up the issue of how we might distribute our stock of Dormigen if we were to come up short," she said. "I know we hope it will not come to that, but I agree that we ought to plan for every contingency."

"Don't we have some system for allocating scarce medicine?" the Strategist asked.

"No," the Acting HHS Secretary said. "We have situations where individuals cannot afford the medicines that are available, but we do not have any policy governing scarcity. It's just not something that typically happens."

"What about donor organs?" the Strategist asked.

"That's a whole separate system that has a lot to do with matching the tissue type of donors and recipients. It really doesn't offer us much guidance."

"So how do we distribute Dormigen right now?" the Strategist asked. It was interesting to watch his mind work, like a precocious child who cannot help but ask more questions. Others in the room were clearly eager for the Acting Secretary to start his presentation, but the Strategist was oblivious to the looks that were being exchanged across the table.

"Dormigen is no different than Band-Aids or aspirin," the Acting Secretary answered. "It's expensive, yes, but it's plentiful. When the supply is running low, you order more. And when you order more, it comes. No one has ever considered anything different."

The Chief of Staff steered us back on track. "Why don't you tell us what you have in mind?" she said to the Acting Secretary.

The Acting Secretary stood and buttoned his suit jacket over his sizable stomach. It was a gesture of formality that I found oddly affecting, as it seemed to signal some kind respect for the moment. "Mr. President, members of the Cabinet Working Group, thank you for this opportunity to present my ideas. I'm particularly appreciative since, as you all know, I'm merely a placeholder in this position." These opening remarks were not as stilted as they may now seem. Like the small gesture of buttoning his suit jacket, the formality of the Acting Secretary's remarks gave a certain gravitas to the moment, which was all the more noteworthy because of his normal levity. The Acting HHS Secretary had been the person least in awe of the President throughout this process, yet here he was showing the most deference to our situation when it came his turn to make a recommendation. "I don't have a fancy presentation," he continued.

"Good," said the President. "Just tell us what you want to tell us."

The Acting Secretary nodded respectfully. He looked around the table slowly, almost as if to generate suspense. "My idea is very simple, though don't for a second think I haven't given it a great deal of thought. I propose that the available doses of Dormigen be allocated to those who need it based on a lottery. Everyone with a Social Security number is eligible. We will draw numbers—electronically, I assume—and the persons with the Social Security numbers selected will receive the available doses."

"People are going to live or die based on a lottery?" the Speaker asked scornfully.

"My dad went to Vietnam because of a lottery," the Acting Secretary said, not missing a beat. He had obviously anticipated that question.

There was silence around the table, and not even much movement, as if the cabinet had been frozen in place, or was posing for one of those old-fashioned photos that required stillness for twenty seconds. The Majority Leader spoke first. "A lottery? That doesn't feel right."

"Which one: for Vietnam or for Dormigen?" the Acting Secretary asked pointedly.

"Hold on a second," the Strategist interjected. "Why don't we just sell the stuff? Supply and demand. That's what we do when we have a shortage of anything else."

"You can't be serious," the House Speaker said.

"Why can't I be serious?" the Strategist said. I could not tell if he was being literal, or if he was just trying to provoke her.

"You propose that we give a lifesaving drug only to those who can afford it?" she said, genuinely incredulous.

"Hello! Welcome to America!" the Strategist said loudly, almost yelling but not quite. "That's what we've been doing with health care for the last eighty years."

"It's not the same thing," the Speaker said.

"Really? I passed at least four homeless guys on my way here this morning. Do you think those guys are sleeping on the street because they have a special affinity for the outdoors?" The Strategist was more visibly emotional than I had seen him. I could not tell if he was angry because of the social injustice of the situation, or because the Speaker refused to accept his logic.

"They're mentally ill," she said. "They have substance abuse problems."

"Then why don't they get treatment? Because it would conflict with their regular golf game?"

The Speaker paused, taking a breath to calm herself before she responded. "I have supported higher funding for those programs at every turn. I sponsored many of those bills."

"Did they pass?" the Strategist asked.

"Ask the President about that," the Speaker replied tartly.

"Did they pass?" the Strategist repeated.

"Usually not," the Speaker answered. "I don't understand where you're going with this."

Because the room was so quiet and still, we all noticed as the President shifted in his seat and took off his reading glasses. He stared at the Strategist with an expression I had not seen; his whole bearing seemed to soften, as if the White House porters had whisked away the anger and frustration of the past week along with the coffee cups and dirty plates. "John, I appreciate what you're saying," the President said. He rarely called staffers by their first names, so I noticed when he did. "You're right. You are absolutely right."

"Don't patronize me," the Strategist warned.

"I'm not patronizing you," the President said. "God knows I've learned that lesson." There was some chuckling around the table. Even the Strategist smiled slightly. The President continued, "There is no doubt that we have a system in which . . ." He paused to gather his thoughts. "Life is not fair."

"Life is not fair anywhere, Mr. President, but it is uniquely American to deprive poor people of basic necessities that we as a society could easily afford to provide for them." The Strategist was calmer now, having had a chance to express his thoughts. The President nodded in acknowledgment but said nothing. I could not for the life of me figure out what was happening. The Strategist was no flaming leftie; if anything, he had been the most caustic critic of some of the Speaker's proposals. He described the $22 minimum wage proposal as "a policy designed by a kindergarten student who had been hit on the head during block-building hour." That was his exact comment. For obvious reasons, journalists loved interviewing the Strategist, and for equally obvious reasons, the White House tried to make sure it happened as infrequently as possible.

I looked at the Chief of Staff, but her expression betrayed nothing.

Finally, the President spoke again, "John, how is auctioning off Dormigen going to make any of that any better?"

"It would hold a mirror up to society," he answered. "It would say, 'This is what we have become. We are the richest society in the history of civilization, but if you can't afford the basic necessities of life, you're fucked.'" The Strategist was emotionally taut. He was speaking like a first-year college student in a late-night bull session, but his thoughts were coming from a much deeper, more emotional place. I thought he might cry, which seemed almost inconceivable based on all that I had seen and read about his detached, ironic view of the world.

Some of us began unconsciously looking down the table to the Acting Secretary of HHS, perhaps because he still technically had the floor, but more likely because he had the highest emotional intelligence of the group. Maybe he was the guy who could say the right thing as we confronted this awkward situation. The Acting Secretary fixed his warm gaze on the Strategist. "John, I wish you could have met my dad," he said. "Let's just say that when he came back from Vietnam, he was one angry man. Actually, if I'm being honest, he was pretty angry on the way over, too, but when he came back—*one very angry black man*. Because, shit, if it's bad to be poor and white in this country, it really sucks to be poor and black."

"Yes," the Strategist said, inviting him to continue.

"He'd watch the news and read his newspaper, sitting in this big armchair with a footstool, right in front of the television. And he would tell anyone in earshot everything that was wrong with the country. I'd be running around the house looking for a chemistry book or my football cleats, and he'd insist on reading some article out loud. He'd yell, 'Did you see what that clown Bush did?' And then he'd read me the article, stopping after every paragraph to offer commentary, like some kind of talk radio show in our living room.

"So one day my mom comes home and tells us she's running for the school board. Truth be told, there were three open seats and only three candidates, so really she volunteered for the school board. But her name was on the ballot, and we all went together and voted for her, and then she was on the school board. Bless my mother, she was a kind soul, never one for direct confrontation, but don't get me wrong, that woman could get her point across. So when my dad started grumbling about some injustice or another, she would say, 'Can you read that to me when I get back, honey, because I've got a meeting to get to.' My sisters and I would look at each other and smile, because we knew what she was really saying was, 'If you're so upset about the situation, why don't you get your big fat black ass out of that chair and do something?'"

The Strategist smiled, as did others around the table. The Acting Secretary continued, "Something changed after my mom joined the school board. She served for fourteen years and she made a lot of difference. We could see it. She'd say one night over dinner, 'We need a better library,' and then two or three years later, we'd be sitting at some ribbon-cutting for a new library. Don't get me wrong, my dad still spent a lot of time in that chair. He died there. *I mean he literally died in that chair.* But he lived to see me get elected mayor, and he lived to see Barack Obama become president. I spent the better part of a day trying to get him a ticket to the inauguration, and we went together. When it was over, and we were still sitting in our seats, he turned to me and he said, 'You need to keep doing what you're doing.'

"Now, to be clear, he was right back in his chair the next week, yelling at the television. But that's the phrase that stuck with me: 'You need to keep doing what you're doing.'" The Acting Secretary paused and looked around the table. "I'm sorry. I've gone on for too long." He turned to the Strategist. "John, I am sorry about your brother. I really am. For what it's worth, that's exactly the kind of thing that would get my dad all riled up. It's just plain wrong. But you know, and I know, that this is not the time to make that point."

"I know," the Strategist said. "Thank you."

"And as bad as our situation is here, we got to keep doing what we're doing," the Acting Secretary added.

No one said anything. It was as if only the Acting Secretary and the Strategist had permission to speak. What could any of the rest of us add? The tenor of the room had changed for the better, though it would not necessarily last. In that moment, I felt part of something bigger. We would do our best to muddle through. We would join the ranks of other Americans who had muddled through. *Maybe sensible people trying to muddle through is the best we can hope for*, I thought. Muddling through won World War II. It got us through the Great Depression and the Trump presidency.

At the time, all this was just a feeling. I could not have articulated those thoughts in the Cabinet Room. Even now I struggle to put words against that fleeting sense of goodwill and purpose. The scientist in me says that the Acting Secretary's inspiring speech caused a little burst of dopamine in my brain. But maybe that, too, is part of muddling through. Eventually the Chief of Staff said, "I think we all need a short break."

I was growing more politically aware, noticing subtle cues and comments that had escaped me just a few days earlier. Our short break, which on the surface looked like any other group of adults lingering near coffee and pastries, was in fact more like a group of political animals gathering near a watering hole. The Majority Leader, with a Danish in each hand, was huddled in a corner with the Secretary of Defense. As I walked by, they were discussing some kind of defense appropriations bill. The Defense Secretary was making a passionate case for something, and the Majority Leader seemed to be agreeing with him.

The National Security Adviser stood alone on one side of the room, a solitary creature in this political tableau. Her work typically rose above this kind of political give-and-take, and she was too disciplined to eat pastries just because they happened to be there.

The Chief of Staff had made herself a cup of tea and was now using the break to answer as many calls and e-mails as possible. The mundane details of governing did not stop just because we were in crisis. She sat in a chair by the wall speaking on her phone with someone I assumed to be her assistant. "No, no, no," I heard her declare emphatically. "Tell the Prime Minister if they announce more settlements, the President will veto the whole foreign aid bill. Period." She listened for a brief time and then issued more instructions. "Fine. Add Chile to the itinerary and cancel the fundraiser. What else?" She listened again and then exclaimed, "You've got to be kidding me! That's the only open appointment they had this month.

Tell her if she can't make it to the orthodontist, I'm taking her phone away all weekend." I was struck by how similar the Chief of Staff's tone was in dealing with the Israeli settlement-building and her teenage daughter skipping an orthodontist appointment. In both cases, I found her threats to be entirely credible.

If the pastry table was a political watering hole, the Speaker was the predator loitering on the periphery, looking for an opportunity to strike. A coffee break was not to be wasted on tea or phone calls; it was ten minutes to be used for political advantage. I watched her watching the room, like I was on some kind of political safari. Her gaze settled on the Acting HHS Secretary, who was talking to the Strategist. The Acting Secretary had his arm draped over the Strategist's shoulder in a supportive way. I could hear snippets of what they were saying, something about the Vietnam War. From across the room, the Speaker watched intently, waiting for the right moment. It wouldn't surprise me if her breathing slowed and her pupils dilated. After about a minute, the Acting HHS Secretary said, "Get something to eat, John." The Strategist nodded and turned toward the pastry table. Almost immediately the Speaker walked briskly toward the Acting Secretary, who was now standing alone near the wall. The Acting Secretary took a step toward the coffee and pastries; the Speaker quickly inserted herself between him and the food table, making it appear that they came face-to-face by serendipity. In my mind, I could hear the narrator on the Discovery Channel explaining (with a cool South African accent), "The Speaker, an adept hunter, has injected herself between the Acting Secretary and the pastries, cutting him off from his fellow cabinet members and leaving him effectively pinned against the far wall of the room."

The Speaker got right to the point. "We're wasting our time here," she said.

"How's that, Madam Speaker?" the Acting HHS Secretary replied respectfully.

"This is a matter for Congress to decide," she said in a tone that bordered on accusatory.

"You've made that point," the Acting Secretary replied without emotion. "Would you like some coffee?" He took a step to move around her toward the table, but the Speaker moved quickly to block his path. He was a large man and she was a relatively small woman, so the effect was almost comical. Still, he was not going to get his coffee unless he physically moved her out of the way. "What do you want?" he asked, losing patience.

"Look, you're new at this," the Speaker said with transparent insincerity. "Maybe you're a little over your head." The Acting Secretary laughed loudly, drawing looks from elsewhere in the room. (There was not a lot of other laughter.) The Speaker leaned closer. "What's so funny?" she challenged.

"I spent seventeen years working with a city council," the Acting Secretary said. "The people in this room, they're just like the city council. Some are smarter. Some are meaner. They're all better dressed. But at the end of the day, politics is politics."

"I can make things very hard for you," the Speaker said.

"Really?" the Acting Secretary replied. His tone suggested he was unsurprised by the threat but curious what form it would take.

"You may be an executive branch appointment, but don't think for a second that I couldn't make your job go away."

"Like today?"

"Like that," the Speaker said, snapping her fingers to emphasize the point.

The Acting Secretary exhaled audibly, acknowledging the threat, and then took his cell phone out of the breast pocket of his jacket. He pushed a single button, presumably speed dial, and waited for an answer. The Speaker looked on, wary and confused. The volume on the Acting Secretary's phone was loud, perhaps on purpose, and I could here the answer: "Pro shop, Dustin speaking."

"Hey, Dustin, it's Charles Mingo here. How do things look this afternoon after three?"

"I've got three-ten, three-twenty, or three-fifty?" Dustin replied.

"Fantastic," the Acting Secretary said. "Will you hold three-ten for me and put my clubs on a cart? Looks like I'm going to get fired, in which case I really want to take advantage of this beautiful spring day."

"Sure thing, Mr. Mingo."

The Acting Secretary hung up and put the phone back in his pocket. "Now all my bases are covered," he said jauntily to the Speaker.

"You don't know who you're dealing with," she challenged.

"Oh, I do. I most certainly do."

35.

MAYBE I WAS THE ONLY ONE IN THE ROOM WHO DID NOT know what had happened to the Strategist's brother. During the break, after the Acting Secretary arranged for his tee time, I did a quick Internet search; the details were easy to find. The Strategist's older brother had spent his career in Army intelligence, doing two tours in Iraq and one in Afghanistan. During the Afghanistan tour, he had been riding in an armored vehicle that drove over an improvised explosive device. Everyone in the vehicle survived. The injuries were not life-threatening, but the Strategist's brother had taken a serious blow to the head. After he returned to the States, he began to suffer crippling headaches, mood swings, depression. There was a lot of finger-pointing after the fact, but the gist of the story is that he never got the treatment he needed—a sadly typical story, as the Strategist would say. I could not tell from my quick reading whether his brother fell through the bureaucratic cracks, or if there simply were not enough resources to provide the support he needed. (I suppose the Strategist would argue that it is a false distinction: if you put enough resources against a problem, there will be fewer cracks.) In any event, it ended badly. His brother was shuffled through various facilities, eventually to a group home in New Jersey where no one was responsible for monitoring his daily meds. On a particularly cold night in February, he walked out the front door and disappeared. Three days later, the police found him frozen to death on a park bench.

The Acting Secretary resumed his presentation, the essence being that any temporary shortage of Dormigen should be managed by lottery. "We are talking about a couple of days here, at most," he reminded us. At that moment, the door to the Cabinet Room opened and the President's scheduler stepped demurely into the room. She signaled to get the Chief of Staff's attention, but it was the President who responded. "What?" he said impatiently.

"Prime Minister Abouali's people want to know if this is still a good time for his impromptu visit," the scheduler explained.

"Oh, Christ," the President said. At the same time, the Chief of Staff looked quickly at her watch; an expression of panic swept across her face. The President continued, "It's hard to imagine a worse time, frankly."

The National Security Adviser said, "Sir, given the Saudi situation, we need to give Abouali some face time. It's important to his credibility in the region. He just needs to be able to tell his people that he met with the President of the United States—"

"Five minutes in the Oval Office," the President agreed. "That's it."

"That will work just fine," the National Security Adviser assured him.

"Okay, five minutes, everybody, while I try to make the Palestinians feel better about themselves," the President announced.

As the President and the National Security Adviser walked out of the room, the Chief of Staff motioned subtly to the President's scheduler. The two of them walked to a corner of the Cabinet Room. "Can you call Dan and tell him that I won't be able to make the lacrosse banquet?" the Chief of Staff asked the scheduler.

"Of course."

"Please order a bouquet of balloons for Maddie—you know, the big helium ones," the Chief of Staff instructed. The scheduler made a note to herself on her phone and the Chief of Staff continued. "And get one balloon for each of the five seniors. There is a list with their names on my desk."

"Where is the banquet?" the scheduler asked.

"Dan can give you all that information."

"Got it," the scheduler said officiously. "Anything else?"

"Can you find me a new family?"

"Pardon?"

"I'm kidding," the Chief of Staff said with more sadness than humor. "Thank you for this. Make sure it doesn't get charged to the White House. Dan can give you a credit card number."

"Of course."

36.

WHEN THE PRESIDENT RETURNED TO THE CABINET ROOM, he made an offhand comment about the political incompetence of the Palestinians, and then, for the third time, the Acting Secretary of HHS gave a brief summary of his plan to allocate Dormigen by lottery should a shortage arise. "Hundreds of thousands of people will be affected," the Senate Majority Leader said.

"Yes. Some will get Dormigen, some won't," the Acting Secretary explained. "But if you do it by lottery, or some other random mechanism, at least it will be fair and transparent."

"It's so callous," the House Speaker said.

The President interjected impatiently, "There's not really a kind-hearted solution here. If we don't have enough Dormigen, we don't have enough Dormigen. That problem is not going away."

"But some people are sicker than others," the Chief of Staff said, though she made it sound like a question.

"Yes," the Acting Secretary answered. "I think it would be up to the medical establishment to screen out anyone who doesn't really need Dormigen."

"Or those who are too sick to benefit from it," the Strategist added.

"That's right," the Acting Secretary agreed.

"Every citizen is eligible?" the House Speaker asked.

The Acting Secretary answered, "That's for the people in this room to decide. I would propose that all citizens be included, maybe everyone with a Social Security number."

"Just a little background here," the Secretary of Defense interjected. "We have two million prisoners in this country. With the exception of a small number of illegal immigrants serving sentences for violent crimes before they are deported, every one of those prisoners has a Social Security number."

"Of course," the Acting Secretary said. "Every American citizen has a Social Security number, as do all permanent residents, temporary workers, and so on."

"So you're proposing that all of these folks are eligible for your Megaball drawing?" the Defense Secretary asked.

"I said nothing about a Megaball drawing," the Acting Secretary said, firmly but respectfully.

"Megaball, Powerball, Dormigen-ball. We can call it whatever we want," the Secretary of Defense said dismissively. "If it's a big deal when the Powerball jackpot gets to four hundred million, I can assure you that when we draw numbers to save lives, it's going to attract a lot of attention. We can get that cute girl to prance across the stage and pull balls out of the giant drum—"

"What's your point?" the President asked.

"My point is that where I come from—and probably where all of you come from—we've got guys in prison who raped little girls, cut them up into pieces, put them in a car trunk, and then set the car on fire."

"We get that," the President said.

"That is not hypothetical. I did not make that up. That was an actual case that went to trial while I was an officer at Fort Benning." The Secretary of Defense looked around the table before his gaze came to rest on the Acting HHS Secretary, who returned the gaze but did not reply. The Secretary of Defense looked around the table again, clearly agitated by the silence. "You understand my point, don't you?" he asked to no one in particular.

"Go on," the Acting HHS Secretary said.

"What do you mean, 'Go on'? Is this not obvious? These guys have Social Security numbers. *Child molesters have Social Security numbers.*"

"Yes, that's correct."

"And there are ninety-five-year-old men with Alzheimer's in nursing homes who don't know what century this is who have Social Security numbers."

"Yes, assuming they are citizens or legal residents," the Acting Secretary answered dispassionately.

"Oh, for Christ sake!" the Defense Secretary said, looking down the table at the President. "What happens when those numbers get pulled? What happens when the media gets wind of the fact that we've got a finite amount of Dormigen, and we're giving it out to some of society's least attractive characters—people on death row?

Just think about that irony for a minute! Just the notion that we would even consider putting those lives ahead of productive citizens . . . Where do I begin? How do I explain to some law-abiding, hardworking American taxpayer that his children have less chance of being protected against this terrible disease because we decided to protect murderers and rapists?" Again, the Defense Secretary looked slowly around the table, locking eyes with each participant as his gaze went around the table. He finished with the President. "Am I wrong here?"

The Acting Secretary broke the silence. "Obviously I've thought about all that."

"And you still proposed this idea?" the Defense Secretary asked, followed by some kind of grotesque chuckle.

"It could be a starting point," the Chief of Staff interjected. "The lottery has a certain fairness about it. There is no reason that we can't put some limitations on who would be eligible."

"Like murderers and child molesters?" the Defense Secretary asked sarcastically.

"It's harder than it sounds," the Acting Secretary answered.

At that moment, the door to the Cabinet Room opened and the President's scheduler reappeared. The conversation paused and all eyes turned in her direction. "Who's dropped by this time?" the President said angrily.

The scheduler, clearly uncomfortable, looked at the Chief of Staff. "I'm sorry to interrupt, ma'am. The florist says their helium tank is broken. They can't do balloons."

The President exclaimed, "The helium tank is broken? It's just one fucking crisis around here after another." This was not an attempt at humor, though there was some uncomfortable laughter around the table.

"Just do flowers for all of them," the Chief of Staff said, ignoring the President.

"Okay. I'm sure that will be very nice," the scheduler said, withdrawing from the Cabinet Room as quickly as possible and pulling the door closed behind her.

"Now that we've managed the helium shortage successfully, where were we on Dormigen?" the President asked. That's one thing about the President: he could be articulate in a brutally cutting kind of way. Most in the room turned their attention back to him, but I could not help but continue to look at the Chief of Staff, whose expression betrayed some combination of sadness, anger, and resolve. If I were to guess, she had come to an agreement with herself years ago: she would forgive the President's rude outbursts because they were a response to the stress of a job that most other people could not or would not take on. The sad part was that the flowers were not going to mollify her daughter anyway (nor would helium balloons, for that matter).

The Acting HHS Secretary continued, "I was saying that it's difficult to make a blanket determination as to who deserves to get Dormigen and who does not."

"I don't think it's that hard at all," the Secretary of Defense said angrily. There were subtle nods of approval around the table.

"It's harder than it sounds," the Acting Secretary repeated. His voice betrayed not a hint of frustration. If the Speaker of the House was a carnivore who lay in wait for weak members of the herd and then leaped for their jugular, the Acting Secretary was an entirely different kind of predator, but a predator nonetheless. In a Discovery Channel context, he would be one of those large insects that disguises itself as a branch or a leaf and then stays absolutely still until its prey does the nature equivalent of flopping onto a dinner plate. That afternoon in the Cabinet Room, some of the smartest people in the world were walking into an ambush, without a hint of what awaited them.

"I'm perfectly willing to go there," the Defense Secretary said confidently. "And based on the reaction around the table, so is everybody else."

"Do you agree that there is some merit to the lottery idea?" the President asked.

"Absolutely. I commend the Secretary for getting us to that point," the Secretary of Defense said.

"Acting Secretary," the Acting Secretary corrected him, causing laughter around the table.

"Well, I would vote to confirm you," the Defense Secretary said earnestly. The tension from their previous exchange had evaporated.

He continued, "I believe that we ought to place limits on eligibility." Again, there were nods of approval around the table.

The Acting Secretary was still standing. "Fair enough," he said. "Since I still have the floor and there seems to be a consensus that a simple lottery is not a good idea, I would propose that we discuss who would be eligible and who would not."

"I think that's a good idea," the Chief of Staff said.

The Acting Secretary walked to a corner of the room and dragged a whiteboard closer to the conference table. "I'm on record as proposing that everyone with a Social Security number be eligible for the Dormigen drawing."

"Wow, it even has alliteration: Dormigen drawing," the Senate Majority Leader interjected.

The Acting Secretary smiled and then continued. "Why don't we use this time to identify the broad groups who should be excluded from eligibility." He turned to the whiteboard and wrote *Child Molesters* in red marker.

"It's broader than that," the Secretary of Defense said, mildly peeved again. "There is no reason we should be giving out scarce medicine to anyone who has committed a serious crime, a felony."

"So, felons?"

"Fine."

"What about ex-offenders?" the Acting Secretary asked.

"What do you mean by that?" the Defense Secretary asked.

The House Speaker answered, "Someone who committed a crime, did the time, and has now returned successfully to society."

"Once a felon, always a felon," the Senate Majority Leader answered.

"Not in the eyes of the law," the House Speaker said. "They have done their time and returned successfully to society."

"That's not the point," the Secretary of Defense responded. His tone had turned analytic, more like for a military briefing, or at least how I would imagine a military briefing to be. "Suppose you have a deadly conflict going on around you. You have a bunker, but there is not enough room to keep everyone safe. Who goes in the bunker? It's not about fairness, necessarily. Lots of people deserve a spot in that bunker. It's about who you want in there with you, and more important, who you want with you when the conflict is over. *Who comes out of the bunker to rebuild society?*"

The President said, "We're talking about a few days without Dormigen. We are not going to have to rebuild society here."

"Yes, but I take the point," the Acting Secretary said. "You're saying we should try to choose the strongest and most capable. This should be about merit, of some sort," the Acting Secretary said.

"Yes, that's it. Thank you," the Defense Secretary answered, relieved that his point of view was finally getting some traction. It was not, of course. The Acting Secretary was merely disguising himself as that twig, luring everyone in the room closer and closer, until they realized at the last moment that he was in fact an insect disguised as a twig, and then it would be too late.

"Once a felon, always a felon," the Acting Secretary repeated. "Are we in agreement?" There were nods of assent around the table and he wrote *Felons* on the whiteboard.

"Well, no," the House Speaker said. All heads turned in her direction.

"If we can't agree to exclude felons, we're not going to get anywhere," the President said.

The Senate Majority Leader added, "There is no way I can defend any plan that puts felons ahead of law-abiding citizens."

"Felons or ex-felons?" the Chief of Staff asked.

"Both," he said.

The House Speaker said, "It makes me uncomfortable, given the racial makeup of our prison population. But let's go on. We can come back to this."

The Acting Secretary continued, "Based on our earlier discussion, I suppose we need some kind of age limit. Is that right?"

"I don't think it makes a lot of sense to be giving scarce medicine to eighty-year-olds," the Senate Majority Leader offered.

"Those are the people who need Dormigen the most," I reminded the group. "They are the ones for whom *Capellaviridae* is most likely to be fatal."

"But still," the Secretary of Defense insisted, "there's just not a lot of runway there, if you know what I mean."

"So what's the cutoff? Sixty-five? Seventy?" the Acting Secretary asked the group.

"I'm not sure we have to choose that now," the Chief of Staff said.

"When are we going to do it?" the President asked, essentially correcting her.

"Let's say sixty-five," the Speaker of the House suggested.

"That feels kind of young to me," the Senate Majority Leader said, generating chuckles around the room, since we all knew he was well north of sixty-five. "Seriously, there is a lot of human capital invested in folks over sixty-five."

"So seventy?" the Acting Secretary asked.

"Let me take the other side of that," the Defense Secretary answered. "Every time you give a dose to a sixty-nine-year-old, there is one less dose for a thirty-nine-year-old, who has a lot more life ahead of him."

"Sixty-five?" the Acting Secretary asked.

"Let's just say sixty-five and move on," the Senate Majority Leader offered.

"Agreed," the President said.

"There is a case to be made that it should be lower," the Defense Secretary said.

"Make it sixty-five for now. Move on," the President said, more emphatically this time.

The Acting Secretary wrote >65 in red on the board.

"Just to clarify, does someone who is sixty-five get the Dormigen or not?" the Chief of Staff asked.

The Acting Secretary answered, "As I've written it, only folks over sixty-five are excluded. So if you're sixty-five, you get the Dormigen, but we could say that you have to be under sixty-five."

"I was just asking," the Chief of Staff said.

"Boy, that would make your sixty-sixth birthday really suck, wouldn't it?" the Strategist interjected. "Happy birthday, Grandpa, I bet you wish you were one day younger." He was back to his old self.

"Okay, next," the Acting Secretary said, looking around the table. "Or are we done?"

"Who else do you want in the bunker?" the Defense Secretary asked.

"College graduates?" the Chief of Staff asked.

"That would exclude about sixty-five percent of the country," the Speaker of the House pointed out, after which a silence settled over the table.

"Do you want college graduates in the bunker with you or not?" the President asked.

"I've met plenty of college graduates who couldn't find the entrance to the bunker if it had a sign over it," the Senate Majority Leader said.

"You can say that again," the Defense Secretary added.

"Well, what about high school dropouts?" the Chief of Staff asked, hoping to move the discussion along.

"Have we made a decision about college graduates?" the Acting Secretary asked, his red dry erase marker poised over the big whiteboard propped up on the easel.

"It might be easier to think about this going the other direction," the Chief of Staff said. "Maybe high school dropouts are excluded?" Her tone suggested some reservations with the idea.

"You can't get into the military without a high school degree," the Defense Secretary pointed out.

"There is a significant difference between getting into the military and getting the medicine that might save your life," the Speaker of the House said sharply.

"I was just providing information," the Defense Secretary said.

"Do you know what the impact would be on our minority populations if we were to exclude high school dropouts?" the Speaker asked.

"I'm not sure this should be about race," the Defense Secretary said.

"Pardon me?" the Speaker of the House said, her faux-Hispanic hackles clearly up.

"We're trying to decide what to do here based on what's best for the country. I don't see what race or ethnicity has to do with it," the Secretary of Defense said calmly.

"Of course you don't," she replied accusingly.

"Easy," the President warned.

The Strategist said, "If I may state the obvious, passing out Dormigen using any kind of educational credentialing as a criterion is going to have a huge adverse impact on every minority population in this country. The same is true if we exclude felons. Your 'bunker' is going to be full of old white guys."

"They can't be over sixty-five," the Acting Secretary interjected with flawless timing. There were uncomfortable smiles around the table.

"We are not excluding anyone from receiving Dormigen based on race, sex, or ethnicity," the Defense Secretary said firmly. "I'm proposing a criterion based strictly on educational attainment. That's entirely defensible. The racial implications are what they are."

"You don't think it would be a problem if our stocks of Dormigen went disproportionately to white middle-class Americans? Or is that the point?" the Speaker asked.

"That's out of line," the Defense Secretary said.

"I agree," said the President.

The Strategist interjected, "There are a fair number of people, especially minorities, who don't attend college, or don't graduate, because they can't afford it. Obviously we would be compounding that disadvantage."

"I agree," the President said.

"On the other hand," the Strategist continued, "the Swedes and the Canadians, and I think some of the other Nordic countries, have built their entire immigration strategy around this idea of giving preference to the most desirable. You get points for having an advanced degree, points for having a job, points for speaking the language. You literally add up the points to see if you qualify for a visa." This was one thing the Strategist was famous for: holding elaborate arguments with himself.

"That's different," the Chief of Staff said, almost reflexively.

"Is it?" the Strategist asked. "I'll be honest, I'm still agnostic on all this. But those are some pretty enlightened societies. They have a finite allotment of visas, and they have no problem giving preferential treatment to those most likely to succeed."

"If you define success strictly in economic terms," the Chief of Staff said.

The Strategist replied, "It's not like high school dropouts are knocking it out of the park in other respects."

"And you die if you don't have enough points?" the House Speaker asked.

The Strategist shrugged. "I'm just saying: It's not crazy to give advantage to the most productive citizens. We're trying to put people in lifeboats here and we don't have enough seats."

"Perhaps we should set the education question aside for a minute," the Acting Secretary said. The eyes around the table turned back to his whiteboard, which still had only two criteria on it, age and felony status.

"Dropping out of high school is different," the Senate Majority Leader said. "That's a personal decision, and it tends to have a high cost for all of us."

The Chief of Staff stared thoughtfully at the whiteboard. "I just need to say that I'm uncomfortable with this 'bunker' idea that we've implicitly adopted. I'm not sure it's our job to pass out a lifesaving medicine based on merit."

"You can choose whatever metaphor you like," the Defense Secretary said. "We've just got to pass out a finite amount of Dormigen."

The Chief of Staff said, "We don't administer any other kind of health care that way. That's not how an emergency room works. If there has been a shoot-out, and a police officer and a gangbanger get brought into the ER at the same time, nobody asks who is who."

The Strategist said, "It's usually pretty easy to tell."

"Come on, you get my point," the Chief of Staff insisted. "With triage, we always ask who needs care most urgently, not who deserves it most. The drunk driver gets care, right next to the family he crashed into."

"That doesn't make it right," the Senate Majority Leader said. "Most of my constituents would say that we ought to leave the drunk driver lying on the table until everybody with even the smallest scratch has been treated."

"Hold on," the House Speaker said. "When did high school dropouts become drunk drivers?"

The Senate Majority Leader replied, "I'm just saying that I don't necessarily have a problem using merit as a criterion here."

The President leaned forward in his seat and tapped his pen several times on the table. He did it unconsciously—the pen-tapping—

but the rest of us had learned, perhaps unconsciously as well, that he did it right before he was about to speak. "This situation is different than an emergency room," the President said. "The thing about an ER is that you don't have time, and some people are always in worse shape than others. So it makes sense to use scarce resources wherever they are likely to do the most good. We have some time—not enough, but we can make a plan here that prioritizes who gets care, if we so choose."

The Acting Secretary pointed at the whiteboard with the marker. "What about disabilities?" he asked.

"What do you mean?" the House Speaker asked.

"Should that disqualify someone from getting the Dormigen, or make them lower priority?" the Acting Secretary asked, his voice perfectly steady, so as not to offer any opinion one way or the other.

"What kind of disabilities are we talking about?" the Senate Majority Leader asked.

"We're not talking about anything yet," the Acting Secretary said, "but I guess I would start with profound physical or mental illness."

The House Speaker exclaimed, "That's repugnant. It's like Nazi Germany." Someone entering the room might mistake the Acting Secretary for a staffer, the designated scribe for the group. Yet he had deftly steered the discussion in the direction he had hoped it would go. The group was marching steadily along the branch to where the stick bug had disguised itself, waiting silently.

The Strategist said, "Well, letting a healthy sixty-seven-year-old die is no picnic. The bottom line here is that we don't have enough Dormigen—"

"We *might not* have enough Dormigen," the President interjected. "This is all hypothetical."

"It's making me sick," the House Speaker said. "We should agree to the China deal right now. This is horrible, horrible—and unnecessary."

The Chief of Staff said calmly, "We need to have this discussion in order to frame our options."

"Let me just add one thing." At first I could not tell where the voice was coming from—not from the table. The White House Legal Counsel had been sitting against the wall, behind the President. This was the first time he had spoken, other than private conversations with the President and the Chief of Staff. He was slim, with a neatly trimmed gray beard, almost overly neat, like an affectation. He had been an appellate lawyer with a long and distinguished record of arguing cases in front of the Supreme Court before the President asked him to join his staff. I had a vague recollection that they knew each other from law school, or perhaps college. Those of us around the table turned toward the voice; the President had to turn his chair around. The White House Counsel continued, "I do not believe any plan that excludes felons would pass constitutional muster."

"Oh, Christ," the Senate Majority Leader exclaimed.

The President nodded, acknowledging the possibility. "Okay, walk us through that," he said.

All eyes went back to the White House Counsel, who paused for a moment as he gathered his thoughts. "Denying felons Dormigen, or ex-felons, would be perceived—correctly, to my mind—as part of their sentence," he explained. "You have been sentenced to two years for assault, for example, and now, in addition to that prison time, we are making you ineligible to receive a lifesaving drug. In the eyes of any federal judge, liberal or conservative, that amounts to changing the sentence for a crime after the fact. That would be constitutionally prohibited, for violating due process and probably for creating a law ex post facto."

"This would be considered part of the sentence, and you can't change the sentence after the fact, especially after someone has already served their time," the Strategist said, translating the legal-speak for the rest of us.

"Yes, more or less," the Legal Counsel said.

"Now you're telling us that?" the Senate Majority Leader said, exhaling audibly.

"What about using an age limit of some sort?" the President asked.

"I think you would be on firmer legal ground there," the White House Counsel answered. "But it's not bulletproof."

I looked to the other end of the room, where the Acting Secretary was still standing near his whiteboard and easel. For all our meandering discussion, there were still only two items on his list:

>65 and *Felons*. Now, without saying anything, he drew a red line through *Felons*.

The sun had dropped low on the horizon, creating a softer light in the Cabinet Room and reminding us of how long we had been in that room. "Should we stop to order dinner?" the Chief of Staff asked.

"I think we can finish up," the President said. "I'd like some closure here."

"Maybe a short break?" the Chief of Staff asked.

"Let me float an idea first to see if we can get some consensus," the President replied, more genial than usual. "Remember, we are only adopting a contingency plan. We are not recommending a course of action. We can decide what we want to do vis-à-vis China in the morning—or, I guess, by the end of day tomorrow, is that right?" The Chief of Staff nodded yes, and the President continued. "So this would be our recommendation if we have to ration the available Dormigen. We will do everything in our power—everything responsible in our power, I guess I should say—to avoid such a situation. But this would be our plan, should the need arise, yes?"

The House Speaker said, "I still believe this is a decision for Congress. I want that to be clear."

"You've made that abundantly clear," the President said. "Believe it or not, I agree with you." The House Speaker looked surprised, and then vaguely suspicious. The President continued, "A decision of this magnitude ought to come from Congress, even if that's not where the authority over the Dormigen technically resides. On the other hand, I think any discussion in Congress would be longer, more contentious, and less productive than what we've been sitting through this afternoon." The President looked at the House Speaker and then the Senate Majority Leader. "Would you agree?" he asked.

"I think that's right," the Senate Majority Leader said.

"What are you saying?" the House Speaker answered, wary of walking into a trap.

"I would propose that this group make a recommendation for Congress to approve. Maybe it's an up-or-down vote. Maybe there could be some modest amendments. I would leave that to the two of you."

"What exactly are we recommending?" the House Speaker asked.

"We're not there yet," the President said. "This is just about process. I want to agree on a process first."

"I would be comfortable with that," the Senate Majority Leader said. "I think it's a sensible approach."

"What about China?" the House Speaker asked. "That's how we make this whole problem go away. There is no need to be rationing anything."

"China is my decision," the President said firmly. "Congress has no authority over foreign policy decisions, and, frankly, I don't have confidence that Congress would be in a position to weigh the long-term implications of our complete capitulation in that part of the world."

"But you can?" the House Speaker said.

"I don't have to get reelected," the President asked.

"Maybe that's a problem," the House Speaker said.

The President ignored her and continued, "As I was saying, if we get into a position where we have to ration Dormigen, I would like this group to make a recommendation with regard to how we allocate the available Dormigen, and I would like Congress to ratify that decision, perhaps with modifications—I'll leave that to the two of you." He looked first at the Speaker and then at the Senate Majority Leader. The latter nodded in agreement; the Speaker waited warily to hear more. "There is no way Congress can take up this issue from scratch, in a short amount of time," the President said. "I think the Acting Secretary has made a powerful point here this afternoon, namely that any attempt to ration Dormigen using anything more than the most basic criteria is fraught with problems. If necessary, I propose that we ration Dormigen based on age alone, drawing a cut-off as necessary depending on the size of our shortage." The President paused and looked around the table to take stock of the room.

After a moment, the Secretary of Defense said, "In my heart, I believe there has to be a better way, but for the life of me I can't seem to pin it down. I'm persuaded that we ought to keep it simple. I support what you're proposing." The others nodded in agreement.

The President continued, "If the plan to ration by age is rejected, either in the courts or by Congress, then I think the only alternative is to use some kind of lottery. We should make that explicit up front." The President looked to the Speaker and the Senate Majority Leader. "Would you be comfortable taking that to the Congress?" he asked.

"It would be an unnecessary tragedy to get to that point," the Speaker said.

"One step at a time," the President said. "I need to be wheels-up for Canberra at about this time tomorrow."

"I would be comfortable presenting that plan to the Senate," the Majority Leader said.

"Yes," the House Speaker agreed.

There was a moment of palpable goodwill in the room, a sense that we had taken a long journey and arrived at our destination. Although the view at the top may not have been as glorious as we had hoped, we were nonetheless standing there together. I began to admire the President's style. He did not row, he steered. The rest of us thrashed about, hour after hour, as he sat at the end of the table saying relatively little. Then, when the destination was in sight, he pointed toward a spot on shore and urged us to make the last few strokes necessary to get there. The Chief of Staff said, "Thank you, everyone. I know it's been a long day. We're going to talk through the China option in the morning—"

The President cut her off, his geniality gone. "We're not done yet. How bad is it? What's our death toll?" There was no answer from the table. "From *Capellaviridae*," he added. "I assume we have data on this."

"Our Dormigen stocks are still robust everywhere," the Chief of Staff assured him.

"But they're not going to the hospital," the President said emphatically, almost yelling. "This family in Hawaii . . ." He looked to the Director of the NIH. "How many?"

"The data are very rough," the NIH Director replied. "Any estimate at this point is just an approximation."

"How many?"

The NIH Director looked at her phone and took a shallow breath. "Somewhere in the range of twelve hundred."

"Jesus Christ," the President exclaimed. The collective body language around the table suggested similar shock.

"It's worse than we thought?" the President asked.

"I wouldn't say that—not the virus," the NIH Director responded. "Our behavioral models . . . we may have overestimated how likely it is that people who fall sick would seek treatment."

"*Because you've covered it up!*" the Speaker yelled. "People don't know it's a problem because you're hiding it from them."

The President said calmly, "The First Lady made a statement about seeking treatment—"

"Hah!" the Speaker retorted. "I'm sure that's what the public will remember from that dishonest circus show. You've killed twelve hundred people—"

"That's enough," the Chief of Staff said.

The Speaker was not to be deterred: "You've killed twelve hundred people, and that's before the Dormigen stocks run out. When that happens, twelve hundred is going to feel like a rounding error. We're talking tens of thousands of deaths—an American Hiroshima. Tell the American people what is happening, accept the offer from China, and make this problem go away. Anything else is totally irresponsible."

All eyes around the table turned to the President, who remained silent. Maybe I saw doubt in his eyes; some of the anger appeared to have dissipated. And then, from the other end of the table, "Ninety thousand." It was the Strategist, reading from his phone. "Hiroshima deaths. Between ninety and one hundred and forty thousand. A lot of it was radiation sickness—"

"We're not going to have an American Hiroshima," the President said firmly. There was another long silence, during which many of us did the math. For all the Speaker's hyperbole, her Hiroshima comparison was not wildly off base.

"Telling people could make it worse," the Strategist said, as if he were thinking out loud. "Yes, it probably would."

"Says you?" the Speaker challenged.

"Anyone with the sniffles would rush to get a prescription," the Strategist explained.

"We'd blow through our Dormigen stocks even faster," the Chief of Staff said, "and a lot of it would be wasted."

"I'm sure the nation will be grateful to you for keeping them uninformed," the Speaker said bitterly.

"Where are we on the virus?" the President snapped. Before the NIH Director could answer, he continued, "The brightest minds in the country can't do better than this? We're going to sit here tomorrow morning and try to decide whether Americans are going to die, or if we're going to go hat in hand to Beijing and cede half the world to an authoritarian regime. That's a shitty decision that I really don't want to have to make. Give me something better."

The goodwill in the room had dissipated quickly. The President stared at the NIH Director, though it was not clear if he was expecting a response. She offered one in any event. "We have a complete genetic sequence of *Capellaviridae*," she said. "We have a medical team working around the clock to test treatments other than Dormigen. As soon as we finish here, Max is headed to New Hampshire to speak to one of the world's foremost virologists." The heads around the table turned toward me. I had said virtually nothing in these meetings, other than answering the occasional technical question, or passing along requests to the research teams.

"Why weren't you talking to this guy last week?" the President asked.

It was clear I had to say something, but my tongue felt awkward and I had the sensation of looking down on myself in the Cabinet Room, struggling to formulate an answer. I am no great athlete, but I played enough Little League to know what it feels like to choke, the physical sensation of the body tightening up in the moment when it needs to perform some task that should be simple, but for the pressure: throwing from shortstop to first base with two outs or tapping in a two-foot putt to win a match. I understood the physiology; I had read articles on it in graduate school. Now I had that choking feeling, struggling to form a basic sentence. By thinking about the act of speaking, as opposed to just answering, the act became all the more difficult. It was as if someone had pushed me onto a stage in front of ten thousand spectators and said, "Tell them a joke. *And make it funny.*"

The silence probably felt longer than it was. The NIH Director cocked her head slightly, as if to indicate, "Say something."

"Viruses are like criminals," I began. "We piece together clues that explain how they operate, why they do what they do. As the clues accumulate, we close in." I realized, even in the moment, that I was speaking just like Professor Huke. That was exactly what he would say; maybe it was something he had said.

"Yes, well, this is a serial killer on the loose, so I would appreciate it if you could convey the urgency of the situation," the President said.

"I'm confident Professor Huke will be able to help us," I replied. Of course, I had no such confidence.

37.

IT WAS DARK WHEN I WALKED OUT OF THE WHITE HOUSE. Some of the humidity had gone out of the day. Most of the staff had returned home and there was an unusual calm. I was aware of the click of my shoes on the asphalt as I walked toward the waiting car. I had packed a bag early that morning, but I had been rushed. Now I tried to remember if it had the things I would need, which was not much, really. As I approached the car, the driver opened the rear door and took the small duffel from my hand. "I've got to catch a plane—" I began.

"Yes, sir. I have the directions," he replied.

I was bone-tired. The car was already cool; the driver must have had the air-conditioning running, which was not environmentally friendly but felt really good. I slumped back against the seat and fell asleep before we left the driveway. I was awakened when we reached the security perimeter at Joint Base Andrews. The driver spoke briefly to the soldier manning the gate, who peered through the window at me in the backseat and then waved us through. I do not think I had ever been on a military base, and I know I had never been on a private plane. We drove around a perimeter road to another gate, where the driver used a passkey to let us onto the tarmac.

"Right there, sir," the driver said, pointing to a soldier standing stiffly near a small Air Force jet. As I got out of the car, the driver moved quickly to take my small bag from the trunk and hand it to the waiting soldier.

The soldier, now holding my duffel, said, "This way," and motioned toward the jet. The door was open and the stairs were down. "You can go ahead and climb aboard," he directed. The plane had six or eight seats. I sat down on one of them near the front. Almost immediately the Captain emerged from the cockpit and introduced himself. "We're headed to Lebanon, New Hampshire, tonight. Is that right?" he asked. I nodded yes. I remember seeing some humor in the question. What if I got on the wrong plane? Would I wake up after a long, comfortable flight and see Beirut out the window? The Captain continued, "We have a beautiful night for flying. It should be about two hours. Make yourself comfortable. My copilot is doing some paperwork, but he'll be back to introduce himself shortly." The soldier who had met me on the tarmac climbed aboard. With a remarkable economy of effort, he pulled the stairs up and shut the plane door. It could not have been more than a minute before we were rolling along, headed for a tiny airport in New Hampshire.

"Welcome aboard," the soldier said as he buckled himself into a seat on the other side of the cabin.

I was self-conscious of being the only passenger with three crew members. "Sorry to make work for the three of you," I said.

He waved his hand dismissively. "We have to do the training hours anyway. Might as well take someone where they need to go."

The plane accelerated along the runway and we were airborne almost instantly. I looked out the window and marveled at the beauty of D.C. by night. I tried to locate the White House, thinking that the President was probably still there meeting with different advisers, maybe the China group, or maybe the Saudi experts, or maybe staffers discussing some challenge I knew nothing about. Then I fell asleep.

I woke up when we touched down for landing. As we taxied, I recognized the Lebanon airport—one tiny single-story building, smaller than most houses. A woman in a fluorescent yellow and orange vest motioned for our plane to park near the terminal building, which was dark but for one light over the door. The soldier handed me my duffel as I walked down the stairs onto the dark, empty tarmac. The

Captain cut the engines, and then it became quiet, too. The woman in the fluorescent vest walked over to me. "The terminal is locked up," she said. "You'll have to walk around. Do you have a ride?"

I did not. I was not accustomed to flying into an airport that had been locked up for the night. "I'll call someone for you," she offered. Twenty minutes later I was in my room at the Hanover Inn, opposite the Dartmouth College green and a short walk from Professor Huke's house. I had not packed anything to sleep in, or my toiletries, but there were some clean clothes for the next day. The front desk sent me up a toothbrush and a razor. I lay down and tried to figure out what I was going to ask Huke in the morning. The truth was that Huke knew less about lurking viruses than I did—my fake optimism in the Cabinet Room notwithstanding. He was the scientific equivalent of a general practitioner; I was the specialist. But maybe his broad view could help. Maybe I was so deep in the tunnel that I needed someone on the surface with a view of the whole landscape who could tell me that I was burrowing in the wrong place. I was groping at straws, I knew. Yet those sanguine thoughts would prove eerily prescient.

38.

SPRING WAS IN THE AIR ON THE DARTMOUTH CAMPUS, IF not necessarily visible. The trees were bare, and the grass was still brown, but the weather was unseasonably warm. This was "mud season" in New England, when the snowmelt and new rain made a mess of things before the trees and flowers finally caught up with the rest of the country. The day was sunny and the few students walking across the green opposite the hotel were dressed more for July than for April; I suppose that is part of the optimism of spring, having just emerged from a New England winter. Much to my surprise, there was a *New York Times* box just outside the hotel in the same place it had been when I was a student, perhaps for the old alums who liked the sensation of reading a real newspaper. I paused to peruse the headlines, noting with amusement that some members of Congress were calling for hearings to examine whether the President had passed classified information to his Colombian mistress.

I had been to Huke's house once before, when he invited our senior seminar to his home for dinner. It was not far from campus, about five or six blocks up a hill leading out of town. The day was perfect for walking. I let my mind wander as I went, trying to formulate questions to steer the conversation. I turned down a narrow street with small, well-kept houses relatively close together. There was no sidewalk but also no traffic, so I walked in the middle of the road. As I approached Huke's house, he emerged from the side yard pushing a small wheelbarrow. He waved hello and hustled over to greet me. "Isn't it too early to plant?" I asked as he approached.

"Oh, yes," he said jauntily. "Nothing goes in the ground until Mother's Day, but it's never too early to start cleaning up. We don't get many days like this in April."

Huke's house was a small ranch with a sunroom in the back. I had spent so much time in "McMansions"—soaring foyers and enormous great rooms—that Huke's house seemed quaint by comparison. Yet it was so comfortable and tidy that I found myself wondering why anyone would want anything bigger, especially if one could just stroll to work in the morning. I was reminded of Sloan's comment long ago about the "academic lifestyle." I paused near a set of bookshelves, perusing the eclectic titles. "You can have anything you want," Huke offered. "I have boxes more in the basement. I had to clean out my office when I retired."

We sat at a small table in front of a window looking out at the woods behind the house. Professor Huke's wife brought us tea and croissants. "They're from King Arthur Flour," she offered. It was a little café across the river in Vermont, where I used to go to work when I was a student.

"So, you have a virus puzzle, have you?" Huke asked. He nodded as I explained what we had learned about this lurking virus: the numbers, the regions affected, the dust mite vector, the bizarre pattern of cases that turned virulent. "Very exciting!" he said, slapping his knee. I had not told him about the Dormigen shortage, or the twelve hundred people who had died so far, or the marathon meetings at the White House, or the looming decision about the South China Sea Agreement—so of course he would think *Capellaviridae* was exciting. I found his scientific exuberance refreshing despite the circumstances.

"And you're certain that you're not dealing with a mutation?" he asked.

"We've sequenced the virus when it's benign, and we've sequenced the virus when it turns virulent—identical DNA."

"The vector, the dust mite, that's a subspecies?" he asked. I nodded yes and Huke continued, "You do have a puzzle on your hands." There was a pause as Huke sipped his tea, and then stared out at the woods behind the house. Eventually he said, "If this were a midterm, what would I ask?"

I felt a pang of annoyance at the pedantic nature of the question. I was tempted to point out how far this was from an academic exercise. "It's been a long time since I've taken an exam," I demurred.

"My classes were always about viruses, not people," he said. "Sure, humans were often the hosts, but viruses were the stars. So, what I would ask you on a midterm is: 'What's in it for the virus?' Right? Viruses exist to propagate themselves, as do other species—like this dust mite, so I might look there, too. What's in it for them? How is this a successful evolutionary strategy?"

"That seems to be the mystery with all lurking viruses," I answered. "Why would you kill your host when you've got a perfectly good thing going? The lurking viruses seem to turn evolution on its head." Huke made eye contact, acknowledging my point. I continued, having found what felt was a perfect metaphor: "It's like you're living free in someone's house. They do your laundry. They cook your meals. And then one day you get up and kill the owner of the house. It makes no sense."

"I agree. That's not how nature works," Huke said firmly. "We're missing something." He was growing excited and he slapped his leg again. "I envy you!"

I laughed. "It's been a lot of work, to be honest."

"*Capellaviridae* kills its host some of the time, but not usually," Huke mused. "That's a clue."

"Yes."

"One of the species involved has to benefit from this strange arrangement," Huke prodded. "Maybe it's *Capellaviridae*, maybe it's this dust mite. Something here has to help one of them reproduce more successfully in the long run. Start with first principles, right?"

"What if that's not what's happening?" I asked.

"Then you have no hope," he said with a laugh. "It's like solving a murder with no motive. You have no idea where to begin looking. But that's not usually the case, is it? Always start with the jealous boyfriend!"

We chatted amiably for a while longer before I excused myself. "I'm off to physical therapy," Huke said. "My shoulder. Last year it was my knee. That's what happens when you get old." He walked with me to the front door and then out into the front yard. The sun was higher and the day had continued to warm up. "Not bad for April," Huke said. I offered thanks and promised to pass along whatever I learned. His excitement was still palpable.

I turned and walked self-consciously across the damp front lawn toward the road, my dress shoes sinking into the grass. Just as I reached the asphalt road, Huke said loudly, "Wait a minute. One more question." I turned and took a few steps back toward him. "The dust mite, it bites, yes?"

"That's right," I said.

"Most dust mites don't bite."

"Correct."

"So what happens if you get bit by this particular dust mite, other than the virus?" he asked.

"We've been focusing on the virus," I said.

"Does it itch?" Huke asked.

"The dust-mite bite?"

"Yes."

"I don't know," I admitted.

"For goodness' sakes, find out!" Huke advised. "Because if this dust mite is a real pest, humans will try to get rid of it. And when that happens, nature always fights back!"

I thought about Huke's parting comment as I walked back to the Hanover Inn. A taxi was waiting for me; the bellman had already put my duffel in the trunk. As soon as I got in the backseat, I called

Tie Guy on his cell phone. "I have a different angle," I said without exchanging pleasantries. "This dust mite: How do you get rid of it?"

"It's too late for that," he said. "People are already infected—"

"No, no, no," I said. "I just want to know what people have been doing to try to get rid of the dust mite."

"Okay, I'll take a look," he replied, obviously puzzled.

"Because nature always fights back," I added.

"I have no idea what you're talking about," he said.

39.

I MET SLOAN AT A STARBUCKS IN BETHESDA. SINCE GRADUA-tion, we had seen each other infrequently and usually as part of a large group: weddings, reunions, and so on. We had swapped the occasional e-mail, but for all intents and purposes we had fallen out of touch. We never spoke about the night during senior week when we crossed the platonic boundary. Sloan had suggested the Starbucks because it was near her hotel. In hindsight, everything about the meeting was wrong. After I landed at Joint Base Andrews, I had to take a taxi across Washington at rush hour; she walked a block. And why a coffee shop, when we had years to catch up on? I should have at least suggested dinner. I was starving, not having eaten anything since the croissants with Huke. In any case, I had overeagerly accepted Sloan's invitation, and now here I was accepting all of her terms.

During law school, Sloan had dated a guy a class ahead of her who was the editor of the *Harvard Law Review*. If the media reports were correct—and I have no reason to believe they were not—she also had a "serious romantic entanglement" with her constitutional law professor in her third year. None of these relationships left Cambridge with her. In New York, she had taken up with a prominent staff writer for *The New Yorker*, which is highly relevant for all that came next. I took a $65 WeGoNow and arrived at the appointed Starbucks about fifteen minutes early. I lingered near a professional couple sitting opposite one another; both were working their devices frenetically between large sips of coffee. They seemed more likely to get up and leave than the elderly couple a few seats over, whose cups were empty but seemed in no rush to go anywhere. The professional couple soon stood up to leave, and I took their table. (I was right about the elderly couple. They were still sitting there when Sloan and I left.)

Sloan was more or less on time. She spotted me and offered a beaming smile. After waiting in line for a black coffee, she made her way to the table and gave me a big hug. "This is great!" she said. "So how are you?" We did the usual catching up. It was a delightful conversation, diminished only slightly by the fact that Sloan glanced at her watch periodically. I would have stayed there all night, even as I grew ever hungrier. I explained the rudiments of my Ph.D. dissertation and talked about my work in the lab. "But you're not teaching?" Sloan said. The tone suggested it was a question, but it was more of an observation, and it had layers and layers of significance. This was the first reference either of us had ever made to that starry night during senior week when we had pronounced our life plans.

There was so much implicit in what Sloan had just asked, or said. On that lovely evening, she had predicted that she would go to law school and then enter journalism. And here she was, a Harvard Law grad, checking her watch because she was due back at the *New York Times*. I had said I wanted to teach at a place like Dartmouth, yet the closest I had been to a classroom on campus since graduation was my meeting with Professor Huke. I knew, even if Sloan did not, that my job talks at various colleges and universities had not gone well. My only offer had been at the University of Nebraska—not even at the main campus in Lincoln, but one of the satellite campuses. My work at the lab was, in the eyes of most academic scientists, significantly less prestigious than a post at a top research university.

"I really like what I'm doing," I offered, trying hard not to sound defensive.

"That's great," she said. The reply felt slightly patronizing, or maybe I just perceived it that way.

"I like applied science," I explained. "I get to work on real problems, stuff that affects people's lives."

Sloan nodded, smiled, and sipped her coffee. "Do people ever move from what you're doing into teaching posts? Could you still end up at Dartmouth?" she asked.

"I don't think I'd want to do that," I answered.

She raised an eyebrow skeptically. "Really?"

"It's too academic," I said. I paused, because somewhere in the recesses of my brain there was a safety alert telling me to stop talking. I felt a physical warning from my body, as if I were getting too close to a steep ledge. I kept talking anyway. I felt an overwhelming need for Sloan to appreciate my work, to acknowledge that I had not failed the grand plan that I laid out on that inimitable, sex-charged evening during senior week. "I was with the President yesterday," I said.

At that point, the dam holding back my urge to say too much had broken.

"Of the United States?" Sloan asked with a quizzical look.

"What other president would it be?" I asked facetiously.

"That's cool, like a photo op?" she asked.

"The whole day."

Sloan put down her coffee. She never looked at her watch again. "What were you doing?" she asked.

"I can't say," I replied. "I don't mean to be a jerk about it. All I can tell you is that something is happening and I'm right in the middle of it. I never dreamed that my work would have this kind of significance." That was *all* I told her about what was going on. The reality, of course, is that Sloan is smart and ambitious. She could put two and two together, especially with all the resources of *The New York Times* at her disposal. More important, she was dating a staff writer at *The New Yorker*, which was where the first piece on "the Outbreak" would run. I was not quoted in that piece, directly or indirectly. When I was asked at the first congressional inquiry whether I had had any contact at any time with any person representing *The New Yorker*, I answered no—truthfully. To this day, I do not know if the meeting with Sloan was a coincidence or not. The whole journalism community knew that something was afoot at the White House. The cleverer ones realized it was probably something more than a presidential mistress. If Sloan had seen a leaked copy of the White House logs, she would have recognized that I was spending time there. And if I was at the White House, it was probably *not* to help the President of the United States disentangle himself from a relationship with a Colombian diplomat.

Our strategy throughout the crisis had been to keep each part of our response compartmentalized. Tie Guy knew about *Capellaviridae* but had no idea about the looming Dormigen shortage (despite his ongoing suspicions that something was up). The senior management at Health and Human Services knew about the Dormigen shortage but had never heard of *Capellaviridae*. With two sentences I had delivered to Sloan a journalistic gold mine. I was "the guy" on lurking viruses; she knew that. *It was the crucial puzzle piece.* All the others were in plain view. The warehouse fire in Long Beach was a matter of public record. Presumably some quick research turned up the fact that the fire that had seriously injured Bobo the chimpanzee had also destroyed a large proportion of the government's Dormigen stock. The Centera arrests were not publicized but they were still public record. Sloan walked out of the Starbucks with a Rosetta stone for the whole story: the connection between Long Beach and Centera and the lurking virus. Since each involved party was unaware of the larger crisis, they all spoke freely when contacted by reporters. When Sloan called Professor Huke the following morning, he talked to her for half an hour about "this thrilling new virus." And so on.

Sloan and I said a pleasant goodbye outside Starbucks with another platonic hug. We vowed to stay in touch. Once the story broke, the White House dictated whom we spoke to in the media and what we told them. Later, when the various inquiries and commissions began their work, my lawyers would not let me speak with Sloan. When those verdicts arrived (paving the way for this book), I finally was in a situation where I could just pick up the phone and call her. By then, she had been promoted and was coordinating all of the *New York Times* investigative pieces. I left a message—a semi-rambling request to catch up "after all this." She did not call back. I sent a text a week or so later and did not get a reply to that, either. Once I called her office at the *Times*, where an intern dutifully took a message. I never heard back. I have since learned that Sloan married the guy from *The New Yorker*. I was not invited to the wedding.

PART 4

IT HITS
THE FAN

40.

THE PRESIDENT HAD FLOWN TO LOS ANGELES THAT AFTER-
noon, where he spent several hours before Air Force One took off for
Australia, with a refueling stop scheduled in Hawaii. The national
security team had made no decision with regard to the Chinese Dormigen offer, but they had decided that he should make the trip to
Asia to preserve his "optionality." If nothing else, flying to the South
China Sea Conference would give the President a little leverage. We
all recognized that if the Chinese understood the scale of the *Capellaviridae* crisis, the price for the "free" Dormigen would rise pre-
cipitously. The President was en route to Australia in part to keep
up appearances, like an unhappy couple who put on a good face for
Thanksgiving. Maybe the President would sign the South China Sea
Agreement; maybe he would take the Chinese Dormigen instead.
Flying to the region kept all the options open. Obviously we were in
constant secure contact with him.

At about four a.m. on the day after I met with Sloan—one a.m.
on the West Coast—*The New Yorker* posted a short "breaking story"
on its website. In just a few paragraphs, the piece outlined the Dormigen shortage and the fatal outbreak of *Capellaviridae*. Because *The
New Yorker* deemed the story "enormous and urgent," the magazine
had immediately enlisted a consortium of print and media news outlets to assist in the follow-up reporting. Just about every news outlet

in the nation, and subsequently the world, was following up on *The New Yorker* story within an hour of the original post.

Some crucial details in those early stories were incorrect—fabulously so. First, most posts described *Capellaviridae* as "spreading," giving the impression that it was a contagious disease. Second, some of the early reporting by Home Depot Media quoted unnamed "national security" officials who described the situation as "most likely a highly sophisticated terrorist attack." The unnamed officials speculated that a hostile government or a terrorist organization ("or several such entities working in collaboration") had introduced the *Capellaviridae* virus into the U.S. and was also responsible for the Long Beach warehouse fire that had caused the Dormigen shortage. Because the September 11 attacks had been unexpected and unusual, the public was primed to believe the next big attack could be equally imaginative and unprecedented. One anonymous official at the Department of Homeland Security laid out a grim scenario: "The worst case is that a hostile government or terrorist organization has introduced a pathogen that will kill us on a scale previously unimaginable. The best case is that the group responsible has an antidote and will hold us hostage until they get what they want." This was what America woke up to.

In Asia, where it was late evening, government leaders were suddenly made aware of the magnitude of what was happening in the United States. China's President Xing was addressing a convention of farm equipment manufacturers in Shanghai when an aide walked onto the stage and delivered him a note. President Xing excused himself, walked off the stage, and never returned.

41.

I WAS SLEEPING ON MY COUCH WHEN EVERY DEVICE I OWNED began to ping or beep. I had fallen asleep the night before after two beers, having watched mindless television as I mulled over my conversation with Huke, searching for clues. My thoughts kept skipping to the encounter with Sloan instead. The first text I saw was from the Chief of Staff: "Call me immediately. Urgent." My mind raced, in part because I was trying to figure out where she was texting from. The President would have taken off from California some hours earlier, so the only possibility was that she was on Air Force One somewhere over the Pacific. That assumption turned out to be correct. Air Force One had taken off from Los Angeles around nine p.m. California time, midnight on the East Coast, so the President and senior staff, including the National Security Adviser and the Secretary of Defense, were nearly to Hawaii when the first *Capellaviridae* stories began to break. The Communications Director was on board, but it was one of his aides—with no knowledge whatsoever of the crisis—who first spotted the stories as she perused the first headlines of the day. The early stories seemed so bizarre that she ignored them, but within minutes credible news organizations were reporting more details. She woke the Communications Director, who immediately woke the Chief of Staff, who woke the President. This cascade of "who woke whom" would have been amusing under different circumstances.

Immediately after waking the President, the Chief of Staff sent orders to turn the plane around, hoping to get back to the mainland before the story spiraled into national chaos. She, like all of us, had known in the back of her mind that this moment would come, though it was difficult to imagine a worse place for the President to be when the story broke than over the Pacific Ocean. The Captain notified the Chief of Staff that there was plenty of fuel to return to Los Angeles; with favorable winds and a higher airspeed, the plane could be on the ground in less than three hours. The Captain never asked why the President had to return urgently to the mainland. One has to appreciate the integrity of that chain of command. An order was given on behalf of the President and the Captain turned the plane around.

The President and his senior advisers—those on board with a knowledge of the crisis—gathered hastily in the Air Force One conference room. Others on the plane, all the junior staffers and the traveling press, were awakened as the hulking 797 banked sharply and began its 180-degree turn. Even the most junior reporter recognized that a U-turn on Air Force One was likely to be newsworthy. As the media folks picked up their devices to report what might be a mechanical failure, or perhaps a medical issue on board, they received frantic incoming messages from stateside editors and producers. The fact that Air Force One was now turning sharply back toward California was evidence, if somewhat circumstantial, that something potentially massive was afoot.

I called the Chief of Staff, still not aware of the breaking news. The call went straight to voice mail. I left a short message and then sent her a text acknowledging her text to me. As I waited for a reply, I scrolled through the headlines on my phone, immediately recognizing what had happened. A few seconds later, I received a return text from the Chief of Staff: "Give me a few minutes." Those few minutes grew to ten, then twenty. I fidgeted on the couch, recognizing that the longer the story bounced around without some adult supervision from the White House, the less recognizable it would become. Eventually the Chief of Staff called on my secure phone. I answered immediately. "I've seen the news," I said, trying to appear calm.

"We need to get a better scientific understanding of the virus out there," the Chief of Staff said breathlessly. "We are working on a statement right now, but we are going to need you to do a press conference. We need a scientist to calm people down."

"Of course," I said.

"I'm going to have to call you back," she said suddenly, and hung up. I sat on the couch waiting for another call. I turned on the television, flipping to CNN, where a somber anchor (no one recognizable in the studio at that hour) was sitting solo above a huge red image on the screen: "BIOTERROR STRIKE, POTENTIALLY NATIONWIDE." I found it hard to watch; the story was completely inaccurate, and I, who could set the record straight, was sitting on the couch in my boxer shorts. I walked to the bathroom, balancing my secure phone on the sink so I could answer it if it rang while I was in the shower. The call finally came while I was shaving. (I distinctly remember putting the phone to my left ear to avoid the lather on the right side of my face.) "Get yourself to the White House," the Chief of Staff instructed. "Someone will meet you there. We need to get you on camera for the morning programs."

"Is there a car coming?" I asked.

"Take a taxi." She hung up. I finished dressing as quickly as I could, slipping a tie in my jacket pocket to put on later. I walked briskly out of the house into a light rain, prompting me to wonder if I should go back to get an umbrella so I would not be soaked when I went on camera. I decided against it, but then realized I had also left my White House badge behind. I rushed back inside—thinking about the fact that I had not seen any cabs—and grabbed both the badge and an umbrella.

The streets were empty and dark, save for the streetlights reflecting off the damp pavement. I recalled a film professor in college who pointed out to us that cinematographers always hose down the pavement before filming their night scenes to give the shots a glistening effect. That thought lasted just a split second. I jogged half a block to Nineteenth Street, looking both ways. There were no headlights, let alone taxis. I stood there briefly, my mind now spinning with what I knew from basic statistics: if there were no cabs now, the chances of one coming along anytime soon were slim. I patted my breast pocket and realized that I had left my regular cell phone back on my coffee table. I had checked the WeGoNow app back in my apartment, but the closest car was twelve minutes away, which seemed like an eternity. I must have set the phone down after that. I considered waking up one of my neighbors, but I did not know many of them, and the ones I did know did not have a car. Or I could go back to my apartment to get my phone, but there was no reason to think a WeGoNow driver would be any closer. I had deleted my other ride-sharing app after it was reported that their algorithm used crime data, which effectively steered drivers away from low-income neighborhoods.

I saw headlights behind me—no taxi light, but maybe I should flag it down anyway. I stepped into the street, waving my hands. The car swerved away and accelerated. No one was going to pick up a stranger at four in the morning, not even a white guy in a suit (with a tie stuffed in my pocket).

I called the Chief of Staff, figuring that getting a White House car might be the only hope here. "What?" she answered sharply.

"I can't get a car," I said. "I've been on the street for—" She hung up, or we were cut off. I assumed it was the latter and that she was too busy for me to try calling back. My best bet at that point was a hotel. There was a Marriott about ten blocks away, not close, but what else was I going to do?

42.

ON BOARD AIR FORCE ONE, THE PRESIDENT WAS HUDDLED with his senior advisers. A television set mounted on the wall of the conference room was broadcasting the semi-apocalyptic headlines, all still with a terrorism theme. Some of the more familiar anchors had begun to appear on camera, no doubt roused from bed as I had been. By all accounts, the President was poised and calm. Perhaps that was the athlete in him, exercising an ability to screen out distractions in the midst of a situation that one participant described as "trying to play chess at night in a sandstorm."* The President and Chief of Staff, in consultation with others around the table, had agreed on four key priorities: (1) refute the terrorist story; (2) correct public misunderstanding of the virus (my job); (3) get the President on air to reassure the nation; (4) reach out to our Asian allies to reassure them (perhaps falsely) that we remained "steadfastly committed" to the South China Sea Agreement. It was a laudable strategy given the unfolding chaos, but, as the Communications Director told the Chief of Staff, "When your top two priorities involve the words 'refuting' and 'correcting,' you're pretty much fucked."

A new face appeared on one of the cable channels, the first "outside authority" to go on camera after the story broke. The Communications Director unmuted the sound so the room could hear "Retired Virus Expert" Dr. Vikram Banerjee: "The terrorists have most likely introduced a virulent virus, such as MERS—"

"That would be Middle Eastern Respiratory Syndrome," the host offered.

"That's correct," Banerjee said confidently. "It's a potent virus

---

* Martin "Bo" McCormick, *The Source of My Courage* (New York: Little, Brown, Simon & Schuster, 2032).

because it is airborne and can spread quickly via almost any kind of human contact."

"What would you advise for Americans right now?" the host asked, his hand perched under his chin in a way that suggested grave concern.

"The key is to stay away from other people or any other place where the virus might spread," Banerjee advised.

The Communications Director let out something between a growl and a shriek, muting the sound once again. "Where did they find this douchebag?" he asked to no one in particular.

"We need to get on air," the Chief of Staff said. "We have to get the real story out."

"I've got the President booked on all the morning shows," the Communications Director said. "We can do it using the video uplink on the plane."

The President interjected, "No, it should be an address. I don't want to be answering questions. I want to make a clear, uninterrupted statement about what is happening—and what is not happening."

"You're going to have to answer questions," the Communications Director said.

At that point, a junior staffer walked into the conference room and handed two sheets of paper to the Communications Director. "Oh, Christ," the Communications Director said as he read.

"What?" the President asked.

"The Speaker just issued a statement," the Communications Director answered. He began reading aloud as his eyes raced down the page. "'The House of Representatives and I stand ready to provide leadership . . . blah, blah.' Oh, my God: 'Now is a time for us to reach out to our allies—'"

The National Security Adviser said, "She's making the China play."

"Of course she is," the Chief of Staff said. "She's going to deliver the China Dormigen."

"Did she at least say it's not a terrorist attack?" the President asked.

"Second-to-last paragraph," the Communications Director said as he continued reading. "'I want to emphasize that at this point we have no evidence of a terrorist attack.'"

The Chief of Staff exclaimed, "That's it? *No evidence of a terror attack?* How about, we know for certain—"

The Communications Director cut her off, "It gets worse. Last graph: 'After we have confronted this crisis, I will personally lead an investigation into how America allowed its Dormigen stocks to become so disastrously low. I am especially troubled by the privatization of our Dormigen production.'"

The President said loudly, "Why does she have a statement out before we do?" The room was silent. "Put out a fucking statement! We are already twenty feet underwater on this."

"We are going to have a comprehensive statement out in the next ten minutes," the Chief of Staff assured him.

"We don't need a dissertation," the President snapped. "We just need to get some facts out there so we don't leave a vacuum for all this crap."

In the brief silence that followed, the Communications Director's phone chirped lightly. He looked at the screen, read for a moment, and then hurled the phone across the room at the opposite wall. It splintered into several pieces, one of which bounced back onto the conference table, settling in front of the Secretary of Defense. As the others in the room stared at the shattered cell phone, the Communications Director said, "The satellite uplink isn't working. We can't send video from the plane."

"Can we fix it?" the Chief of Staff asked.

"I don't know," the Communications Director answered.

The President said, "I need to be on television. I need to address the country."

"We can do radio," the Chief of Staff offered.

"I'm not fucking FDR," the President snapped.

"The safest option is to get you on the ground in Hawaii," the Communications Director offered. "That would be about an hour shorter."

"Or we could fix the uplink," the Chief of Staff said.

"Who?" the President challenged. "Who on this plane knows how to fix a satellite uplink?"

"Then we need to go to Hawaii," the Chief of Staff said. "Right? That gets us on the ground an hour earlier." The President nodded assent. For the second time in half an hour, Air Force One made an aggressive 180-degree turn. And for the second time, the Captain did not ask why. In the back of the plane, the press corps *did* wonder why the plane was once again making a U-turn. Unfortunately—and arguably unfairly—the metaphor for the White House response was born: Air Force One flying in circles over the Pacific.

43.

TWO BLOCKS BEFORE THE MARRIOTT, WHEN I COULD SEE THE bright lights illuminating the circular driveway in front of the hotel, I looked back over my shoulder and spotted headlights coming toward me. I could see the bright taxi light as the car drew closer. I stepped aggressively into the street to hail the cab. By this point I was damp from the mist, not soaked, but also sweating despite the cool early morning. I reached for the back door of the taxi and pulled the handle; it was locked. I instinctively looked to the driver's window, which buzzed down about halfway. The driver was an enormous black man with short salt-and-pepper hair. He stared out the window, locking eyes with me but not saying anything. I had never hailed a cab in D.C. at four-thirty in the morning. I suppose it makes sense that a sensible driver does not let just anyone jump in the back. "I need to go to the White House," I said. The driver cocked his head slightly, still saying nothing. "It's really important," I added.

"Have you been drinking?" he asked without irony. I presume he could tell from looking at me that I was not going to stick a gun in the back of his head, but it was entirely plausible that I had been drinking all night and might vomit in the back of his cab. I fished into my pocket and pulled out my White House badge. I held it up in front of the window.

"It's important," I repeated.

"Okay, get in." I heard the locks pop.

The cab dropped me at the northwest gate, where I usually entered, but I did not recognize the guard. Nor did I recognize the woman sitting in the lighted booth behind him. I flashed my visitor badge. "Who are you here to see?" the guard asked.

"I'm not sure," I said.

"Your name is not in the visitors log," he said.

"It's an emergency."

"Someone still has to sign you in."

"Okay, hold on." I dialed the Chief of Staff, but there was no answer. I texted her: "Someone has to sign me in to the White House." The rain began to fall a little harder, and I moved under the eaves of the guardhouse. I dialed the Communications Director, unaware that his phone was strewn in pieces around the conference room of Air Force One. No answer. I turned back to the guard. "Who's inside already?" I asked. "Who can sign me in?"

"I can't tell you that." His tone suggested I should know as much, and he grew more suspicious just for the asking. My secure phone buzzed; caller ID showed it was the Chief of Staff. "I'm at the White House but I can't get in," I said.

"There has been a change of plans," she explained. "We don't want you to look political. You're supposed to be the voice of science. We want to put you on camera somewhere else—not the White House."

"My cab just left. I'm standing outside in the rain."

"You'll need a car."

"Where am I going?"

"We don't know yet. Does the NIH have TV facilities?" the Chief of Staff asked.

"Maybe, but there won't be anyone there to run the equipment," I said.

"Just stay there," she said, hanging up. No one said hello or good-bye that day. After about five minutes a young woman in blue jeans and a sweatshirt came walking briskly down the path from the West Wing, two pieces of paper flapping in her hand. She opened the gate from the inside and thrust the papers toward me. "We just issued this release," she said. I looked at her quizzically. She continued, "I'm the Assistant to the Deputy Communications Director. We listed you as the scientific contact on the release. Reporters are going to start calling, so you need to think about what you are going to say."

I held up my secure phone. "On this number?"

"No, on your cell phone."

"I left my cell phone at home," I said.

"Fuck." She exhaled audibly. I began to read the release. The first paragraph explained that the *Capellaviridae* virus was a common virus that had recently proven dangerous to humans. The statement declared in bold letters: "**There has been no terrorist attack. *Capellaviridae* is a common virus found in nearly all American households.**"

The second paragraph explained that the White House was going to "extraordinary measures" to procure sufficient doses of Dormigen to deal with the virus threat. Near the bottom of the page, the release explained that *Capellaviridae* was "spread by the bite of a common dust mite found in most—" I stopped reading. "We can't say 'spread.' You've got to redo this."

"It's gone out," she said, mildly annoyed, as if I did not appreciate the magnitude of what was going on. "I was told to get something out immediately."

"We can't say 'spread,'" I repeated. "We cannot have people thinking that they're going to catch this thing. It's not contagious . . . You're either going to get it, or you're not. We can't—"

"I can do an update. What am I supposed to say?" she asked.

"I don't have my phone, so you need to change the contact number anyway."

"Fine. Tell me what to write."

"Just say . . ." I was thinking as I spoke, but not fast enough. "Say it's not contagious," I instructed. "Leave the dust mite out. Just tell people . . . say it's not contagious. Say that nearly all Americans are infected by—no, don't say 'infected.' Say that many Americans are hosts to *Capellaviridae*, and in the vast majority of cases, the virus is benign." She was just staring at me. "Write this down," I said sharply. Neither she nor I had a pen. As I patted my jacket pockets, the guard, who had been standing near us the whole time, offered a ballpoint. I continued, "Say that we are—that scientists, the nation's top scientists, are working around the clock to determine why *Capellaviridae* turns virulent—"

"No one knows what virulent means."

"Fine, say 'dangerous.'"

She offered her phone to me. "Take this," she said. "We'll use my number as the contact number on the updated release." Just as she handed me her phone, my secure phone beeped with a text from the Chief of Staff: Get to the CNN studio. The Communications Assistant read the text at the same time I did. As I stood there paralyzed, she grabbed her phone back from me. "I'll get you a car," she said.

44.

ON BOARD AIR FORCE ONE, THE PRESIDENT AND SENIOR staff monitored the news after the release of the White House statement. News directors all over the world had been waiting for any information from the White House, so they rushed out the first thing to come over the wire. The revised statement, issued after my exchange with the Communications Assistant, was ignored. Almost no one noticed the absence of the word "spread" in the second release, and once we had mentioned the dust mite, there was no way of unringing that bell. Sure enough, CNN broadcast a huge graphic of the North American dust mite, just like the one Tie Guy had been so enamored of days earlier. Prime-time anchor Linda Schuham was alone on camera, presumably having been roused from bed and rushed through makeup. (When I appeared on camera forty-five minutes later, I would not look so put-together.) The electronic banner below the anchor desk read, "Bioterror Attack?"

"At least now we have a question mark," the Strategist commented sardonically. The Communications Director was calling news outlets, one after another, demanding that they remove any reference to terrorism. His smashed phone—which had been cleaned up, but for the occasional piece that turned up on the carpeted floor—was turning out to be a huge problem. That phone had all his contact numbers; worse, it was the number recognized by the people who needed to be answering his calls. Now he was fighting his way through layers of gatekeepers with each call, screaming things like, "I'm standing next to the President, you fucking peon! Put me on with your producer now or you will never work in the news business again!"*

* Sam Williams Wainwright, *In Service to My Nation* (New York: W. W. Norton, 2031).

Fox was now running a banner at the bottom of the screen: "White House denies terror attack." In focusing on the terror angle, however, we had made no progress in disabusing the nation of the belief that *Capellaviridae* was spreading. By six a.m. on the East Coast, over two thousand school districts had canceled classes. Universities were telling students to stay in their dorm rooms and avoid common areas—even as students rushed to common areas to watch the news warning them to stay out of common areas.* Americans in the Midwest woke up to reports that most schools and workplaces in the East were closed, further embedding the notion that some kind of plague was sweeping across the nation. Fox News cut to a "Contagious Disease Expert" via satellite, a well-coiffed woman sitting at a desk in an academic office. She explained to viewers, "The dust mite bites an infected person and then bites someone else, thereby passing along the deadly virus." The Strategist, holding the remote control, was shaking his head no as he listened.

"What advice would you offer?" the anchor asked earnestly.

"Obviously you stay away from other people, since we don't know who is already infected."

"And what about the dust mites?"

"Vacuum anyplace they might be found. Wash all sheets and towels in hot water and bleach."

"Would it be better to burn them?" the anchor asked.

"That's a good option, if you can do it safely," the expert advised.

The President roared,[†] "Where's our guy? Why are we not on-screen?"

The Communications Director looked at his watch and answered, "He'll be up on CNN in about four minutes."

The Chief of Staff said, "Mr. President, we are going to be in

---

* Sociologists would later note a sharp reversal in a decades-long trend: Americans were more likely to gather news related to the Outbreak in those early days on television rather than from the Internet. They speculated that the nature of the crisis was such that humans felt an unconscious need to share the news with other people as the situation unfolded.

† The President himself described "roaring" at aides throughout the Outbreak: Robert Evan Steans, *Leadership in a Time of Crisis* (New York: Crown, 2034).

Hawaii in an hour. We have broadcast facilities set up at the air base. We need to start drafting your remarks."

"I want to see this," the President said, looking at the television.

The Strategist changed the channel to CNN, where the anchor was talking to a terrorism expert, and then changed it again, this time to MSNBC, which was showing aerial footage of a massive backup on the George Washington Bridge as drivers rushed to leave New York City. "Where do they think they're going?" the Strategist asked no one in particular. Of course, we now know the answer. Many of these drivers would show up at campgrounds in Vermont and Maine—not willing to risk a motel—where they set up tents or slept in their cars, often completely unprepared for the cold. A young couple from New Jersey wandered into the woods north of Bangor, where there was still snow on the ground, and died of exposure hours later. Hikers found their bodies in June. This urge to drive somewhere was one of the stranger aspects of the Outbreak. An urge to move. *To do something.* And then there were the gun deaths. A high proportion of Americans believed that repelling *Capellaviridae* was somehow like fighting zombies. More than three hundred people died from gun accidents in the three days after the *Capellaviridae* news broke. How exactly was one supposed to fight a lurking virus with a shotgun? People tried, apparently. There were also tragic homicides as paranoid individuals shot neighbors who had come to check in or offer help. Another fifty or so people died in house fires after they tried to burn "contaminated" sheets and towels indoors, sometimes in the bathtub.

Last year Princeton University convened an interdisciplinary conference on the Outbreak: public health officials, virologists, national security experts, and so on. I spoke on some panels, but I also sat in on sessions with scholars who had examined the crisis through a different lens. A psychology professor from the University of Illinois[*] spoke about the unique nature of the Outbreak, namely that all Americans perceived themselves at risk, but none, save our political

---

[*]   Simran Shankardass, "Don't Just Do Something, Stand There: The Emotional Need for Volition During the Outbreak, *Journal of Social Psychology* 169, 1 (2033): 123–146.

leaders, were in a position *to act*. One passage from her paper (which she summarized at the conference) has stuck with me, as it helps to make sense of the country's utter craziness in those first hours:

> On September 11, after all the planes had been grounded, Americans could reasonably (if not always rationally) infer that some places (e.g., Omaha) were at lower risk for future attacks than others (Los Angeles). Even when these assumptions were wrong or irrational, the residents perceived that they were in a position to minimize their own exposure.
>
> Americans were also presented with an array of options to "strike back" at Islamic terrorism. Many of these efforts were fruitless, or even counterproductive. Some promoted intolerance; some were illegal. My focus here is not on whether the responses were appropriate. My point is that that *there was an opportunity to act* [emphasis added]. From a psychological standpoint, this action provided an enormous relief. The Outbreak, on the other hand, put every single American more or less equally at risk and gave them no course of action with which to channel that anxiety. The result was often psychologically devastating.

Of course, many people did act, just not in ways that made the situation any better. One reality we overlooked before the crisis went public is that the bulk of the nation's Dormigen supply was unsecured. It was a drug with no recreational value, like aspirin or antibiotic lotion. In most hospitals, the Dormigen was in places easily accessible by all: in the examining rooms, at the nurses' station, in hallway cabinets, and so on. In the immediate hours after the Outbreak became public, doctors and nurses and pharmaceutical reps and warehouse attendants and anyone else with access to the drug realized that they were potentially in possession of a lifesaving resource that would soon disappear. *We had done nothing to secure the supply.* A truck driver in Virginia was rolling along I-95 when he heard the first reports of the Outbreak on the radio. He had left a hospital supply warehouse in Georgia two days earlier. On a hunch, he pulled off the highway and parked his eighteen-wheeler in the far corner of a truck stop. He slid open the back door, revealing ninety-seven cases of Dormigen—a cargo that was now more valuable than heroin. The truck later turned up empty in Pennsylvania. The Dormigen, like so much of the supply, was gone—sold on one of the black markets that popped up everywhere. The Outbreak Inquiry Commission subsequently calculated that roughly 17 percent of the nation's Dormigen supply was purloined in the twelve hours after the crisis became public.

45.

I ARRIVED AT THE CNN STUDIO JUST AFTER SUNRISE. THE morning sun was reflecting sharply off the shiny exterior of the building as the black sedan dropped me at the entrance. News of the Outbreak was palpable. The street was mostly deserted. Many of the stores and shops had handwritten signs on the door saying they would not be opening DUE TO CIRCUMSTANCES or UNTIL FURTHER NOTICE. Later, when we had made some headway convincing the public that *Capellaviridae* does not "spread," stores and shops began to open as an act of solidarity and strength. Starbucks was the first company to issue a statement saying that all of its stores would be open, as "this is a time for Americans to come together, not to rush away from one another in fear." It was an important step in our efforts to stem the panic. Still, some 40 percent of Starbucks employees called in sick in those first few days.

The CNN building was abuzz with activity, in striking contrast to the eerie, semi-deserted street outside. A producer was waiting for me in the lobby. She, like most of the other people scurrying across the lobby, was wearing a white face mask. "I know you'll understand if I don't shake your hand," she said.

I laughed involuntarily, causing her to take a half step back. "It's not even the right wrong response," I said.

"What do you mean?" she asked, perhaps offended but also deferring to me as "the expert."

I explained, "Most of us are already carrying *Capellaviridae*, so there is no point in trying to protect ourselves from the virus. But even if for some strange reason you were not infected, the virus is transmitted by a biting insect, so there is no point in wearing a face mask. See? It's the wrong wrong response."

"Say that on camera," she said. "That's perfect. We need to get you into makeup." She used a badge to swipe me through security and pushed me gently toward a bank of elevators. An elevator door opened and we stepped inside. Two other people joined us, both wearing face masks. They spread out to the corners of the elevator, keeping us all as far apart as possible. "Eleven. This is us," the producer said. "Have you ever been on television?" she asked.

"No," I said.

"Just have a conversation. You'll do great."

Makeup was a small, harshly lit room with several barber-type chairs. "He's yours," the producer said, handing me off to a very large man in a tight white T-shirt sipping coffee. "I need him back in five."

"Five?" the makeup attendant exclaimed with mock indignation. "I've got a lot of work to do." As if to put a finer point on it, he turned to me and said, "Get in the chair, you're a mess." My suit was wet, as was my hair. My face was damp with perspiration. "Where to begin?" he asked. I pulled the tie out of my pocket; it was creased at two-inch intervals from having been wadded up for hours.

"Should I put this on?" I asked.

"No! No, that is not going to work," he said, taking the wrinkled tie from my hand and literally tossing it aside. "You'll be fine without it. But we need to get that jacket dry or it's going to reflect on camera." He used a blow dryer on both my jacket and my hair. Then, with striking efficiency, he applied makeup to the shiny places on my face and combed my hair, spraying it with something to hold it in place. The producer appeared in the doorway holding a clipboard and looking slightly anxious.

"Okay, I need him," she said. The producer steered me around a corner into a large studio with banks of desks arrayed across the open floor. At the far end of the room, I could see the familiar CNN news desk illuminated by bright lights. The room was a hive of activity, with reporters and producers scurrying back and forth off camera. The familiar Linda Schuham was sitting at the anchor desk, interviewing someone whom I did not recognize. There was a large map of the United States illuminated behind the anchor desk; both Schuham and her guest pointed at the map on occasion. An older man with a long gray ponytail stepped beside me and said in a raspy voice, "I'm going to mike you up." I could smell tobacco on his breath as he clipped a microphone on my lapel, wrapped the extra cord around a small transmitter, and then slid it inside my jacket pocket. "You don't need to do anything," he said. "I'll turn it on from here. Just remember to give it back to me when you're done." The White House had been emphatic about the three points I needed to make: (1) no terrorist attack; (2) the virus does not spread; (3) we have the capacity to keep the country healthy. The last point was clearly debatable, but panic was not going to do anyone any good. I would do my best to make the situation feel under control as Americans woke up to the *Capellaviridae* news.

The Communications Director had given me a pep talk as I rode to the studio in the sedan. "Stick to the talking points," he said. "Do you know what that means?"

"I want to make sure I get those points across," I answered.

"No. That means you are not going to say anything else. Those three points, over and over. That's it. If Linda Schuham asks you what your favorite color is, you say, 'What's important to understand right now is that there has not been a terrorist attack.' Got it?"

It seemed easy enough until I found myself gazing across the room at the news desk, with cameras surrounding it from all angles. The producer said, "We're going to break in thirty seconds and then I'll take you up there." I did one more mental checklist of the points I needed to make. The producer must have seen the concentration on my face, because she said, "Don't overthink it. It's just a conversation. You're going to have about three minutes."

"Three minutes?" I asked, incredulous. It had never dawned on me that I would have so little time.

"That's actually long for a news segment at this hour," she said. "Remember, follow Linda's lead and have a conversation."

Of course, that was the opposite of what the Communications

Director had advised me, I thought, recalling his final admonition: "I don't care what the fuck she asks you. Don't even listen to the question. When her lips stop moving, you give the answer you want to give." The program went to break. The guest stood up to leave, a different producer escorting him off the set as I was steered into the bright lights. A young woman rushed up to Linda Schuham, handing her a bottle of water while conferring about something. The producer guided me to my seat on the set. I felt awkward and stiff compared to what seemed like the fluidity and ease of everyone around me. The lights were bizarrely bright, giving everything on the set a fake plastic feel. Linda Schuham shared a laugh with the woman who had brought her the water and then turned to me and said in a surprisingly chipper voice, "Thanks so much for coming on. Just explain to me what's happening like you were talking to your mother."

"We'll just have a conversation," I offered.

"Exactly," she said.

From somewhere behind the bright lights beating down on me, I heard, "We're on in five-four-three-two, and live."

46.

THE PRESIDENT AND HIS SENIOR ADVISERS WATCHED ON THE television in the conference room on Air Force One. Linda Schuham looked somberly into the camera and delivered her introduction: "Many of you are waking up to the news that America is suffering a potentially devastating public health crisis: a previously benign virus, widespread in America, has turned deadly. This is happening at a time when America's supply of Dormigen, the one drug that can be used to treat this virus successfully, is in short supply. Our guest is one of America's top scientists and an adviser to the White House." She turned to me and said, "Welcome to the program. Why are we just learning about this now?"

"That's a good question, Linda," I said, trying to buy myself time. *It really was a good question.* As the chaos had unfolded that morning, I found myself wondering if our secrecy had done more harm than good.

On Air Force One, the Communications Director yelled at the television, "No. No, that is not a good question. *Do not answer that question.*"

It felt awkward, almost rude, but I went with the talking points. "The most important thing to realize is that there has been no terrorist attack—"

She cut me off: "The White House put out a statement to that effect. If that's true—"

"It is true," I said firmly.

On Air Force One, the Communications Director continued his commentary: "Okay, good, good."

Unfortunately for me, Linda Schuham had faced more than a few guests who showed up with talking points in their pockets. "Back to my original question," she pressed. "How long has the White House known about this virus, and also about the looming Dormigen shortage?"

The Communications Director pleaded with the television, "Do not go down that rabbit hole."

I answered, "The most important thing right now is to manage the public health situation. What people need to realize is that the *Capellaviridae* virus is extremely common. Many of us are already carrying it. Only in some small fraction of cases will it become dangerous."

The President, watching with the others, said, "That's good."

"Nice pivot," the Communications Director added.

Linda Schuham took the conversation in my direction. "So I might have the virus right now? Or you might have it?" she asked.

"Yes, we're probably both carrying *Capellaviridae*," I said.

"Might the virus be spreading through our studio as we speak?" she asked in mock alarm.

"No. Absolutely not," I answered. "That's the wrong way to think about *Capellaviridae*. The virus is already out there. You and I have probably been carrying it around for twenty or thirty years, maybe since we were born. The danger here is more like cancer than the flu."

On Air Force One, the Strategist asked loudly, "Did he just say 'cancer'?"

"Fuck me," the Communications Director said.

Linda Schuham asked, "Cancer? Is that supposed to make people feel better?"

I tried to climb out of the hole. "What I mean is . . ." No one heard the rest of the answer, during which I tried to explain how lurking viruses work, without actually understanding how lurking viruses work.

Linda Schuham threw me a lifeline. She asked, "When *Capella-viridae* turns dangerous, Dormigen is effective, yes?"

"That's right," I said.

"And yet the nation is running out of Dormigen. How did that happen? How many people might die as a result?"

She put talking point number three on a tee for me. I explained, "The White House and all federal agencies are working around the clock to bolster the nation's Dormigen supply. Our allies have shipped us millions of doses. We are working on alternative ways to treat the virulent form of *Capellaviridae*. We are managing this public health challenge."

On Air Force One, the Chief of Staff said, "That's a strong finish."

The Strategist replied, "But you can't mention the *c*-word. That's going to be the headline: an epidemic of cancer, spreading."

"Cancer doesn't spread from person to person," the Chief of Staff said. "That's why he made the comparison."

"No one's going to understand that," the Communications Director complained, shaking his head in frustration.

"At least we're beating back the terrorist story," the President offered.

In fact, the terrorist story was alive and well. We had not yet even seen the worst of it. In a nondescript suburb of Houston, Tony Perez was just finishing his work for the day. He had been up early, about four-thirty Central Time, digesting the news of the day and then, as he would tell the Outbreak Inquiry Commission, "Putting a different spin on it." In fact, Perez was the reigning king of fake news: creative, compelling, prolific, and shockingly well read. In a burst of imagination that morning, Perez had reported that a Latino separatist group had introduced *Capellaviridae* to the United States and would provide an antidote only if Congress agreed to their demands.

47.

I WALKED OUT OF THE CNN STUDIO INTO THE BRIGHT MORN-
ing sunlight, not sure what to do next. The rain had cleared and the
day was pleasant in an early spring kind of way. There was no car
waiting for me. I heard nothing from the Communications Director
after my segment. Maybe that was because he was displeased with
me; more likely it was because there was so much else going on. I
knew I should not have used the cancer analogy. I felt that even as I
was saying the words. My impression had been reinforced by Linda
Schuham's reaction as I made the comparison. I saw a glimmer of
surprise in her eyes—recognition that she had knocked me off my
talking points and unearthed something newsworthy in our conversation. That is what CNN paid her a lot of money to do.

I sat on a bench across from the CNN building, taking in the surreal scene around me: harried, concerned people walking purposefully on a beautiful spring day. Now what? I looked at the cell phone
the Communications Assistant had given me. There were 151 voice
messages—so many that it seemed pointless to return any of them.
Tie Guy had left me a text on my secure phone: "Call me ASAP." I
had not spoken to him since the news broke. I figured he wanted to
hear firsthand what was happening, or maybe he wanted to critique
my CNN performance. (No one appreciates how difficult it is to stay
on message in a very short conversation with a host who is working
hard to steer the discussion somewhere else.) Or he might be angry,
given that I had been less than forthright with him. In any event, I
was not eager to have any of these conversations, so I did not call him
back. Instead, I sat on that bench in the sunshine, watching people
in face masks scurry by while I waited for someone to tell me what
to do next.

Tie Guy sent me a second text on the secure phone: "Call me
ASAP. It's important re: Capellaviridae." This time I decided to call
him back, but as I was searching for his number in my contacts, the
Communications Director called. I answered immediately: "Hey, I'm
sorry about the cancer comparison—"

separatist group, the so-called Latino Liberation League (LLL),* had also engineered an effective antidote for the virus. According to Perez's initial story, the LLL was offering the antidote to the President and Congress in exchange for the creation of an independent, Spanish-speaking nation to be carved out of parts of New Mexico, Arizona, and West Texas. Perez's story had two graphics: a map showing the proposed borders of the new independent nation, Estado Latino Nuevo, as well as a larger map of the United States with eleven red dots indicating where the virus had been deliberately introduced.

For all the fiction embedded in the story, there was one pillar of truth sufficiently strong to keep the story alive: There had been talk in previous years, mostly among fringe groups on the far right and far left, about a Latino independence movement. One Arizona community, some little town with 350 residents, had voted to make Spanish its official language. Never mind that no one had ever articulated what an "official language" really means at the town level; this quirky development was enough to inflame the imaginations of both right-wingers (who feared the country was being hijacked by Mexicans) and left-wingers (who were advocating for more explicit political rights for the nation's Hispanic population). When Perez tossed *Capellaviridae* into this political maelstrom—a fake news grenade— he hit the readership jackpot. For the President, who was preparing to address the nation from a military base in Honolulu, it meant that a shockingly high proportion of Americans believed the country was under bio-attack from a domestic terrorist group.

The President was scheduled to address the nation at noon Eastern Time, six a.m. in Hawaii. He and his principal advisers were not the only political leaders for whom the crisis was top of mind. In China, Premier Xing had been huddled with his senior staff since the *Capellaviridae* story broke. It is not hard to infer what they were discussing: What ought to be the price for the Dormigen that America was now desperate for? And when exactly should that offer be made?

---

* Perez told Congress that he came up with this name, the LLL, while waiting for his burrito to heat up in the microwave.

PART 5

———

THE
CHINA OPTION

49.

HAD THE SECRETARY OF STATE BEEN DELIBERATELY excluded from our Dormigen discussions, as she would later allege? I saw absolutely no evidence of that. True, the only credible alternative explanation—that no one thought to include her—suggests an almost unfathomable incompetence. In her congressional testimony, the Chief of Staff took responsibility for this oversight, explaining that the Secretary of State would have been briefed before any meetings began in Australia. The National Security Adviser was more direct: "I just assumed she knew," she testified.

I can attest that there was never a grand strategic plan with regard to who was in the room. One thing just led to the next. The *Capellaviridae* challenge was compounded by the fact that the principals making decisions always felt that a solution would present itself—that the planes headed for their targets would turn around, figuratively speaking. They believed—*we* believed, if I am being honest—that something would save us: an antidote, more Dormigen from our allies, or something else at the eleventh hour. Or with one call to Beijing we could make the *Capellaviridae* problem go away. With the China option on the table, the Secretary of State should have been involved from the beginning. In fact, she boarded Air Force One for the flight to Australia with no knowledge of the crisis the White House was trying to manage. She learned about the Outbreak only when the story went public and Air Force One started doing 180-degree turns over the Pacific.

Imagine the Secretary of State's surprise and dismay when she was awakened abruptly, ushered into the conference room, and told for the first time that the South China Sea Agreement might be scrapped because China was the only country with enough Dormigen to save the Americans afflicted by a deadly virus. She would later write in her autobiography, "At first I thought I was dreaming. This had to be some kind of nightmare. I had spent the previous week in Tanzania and Kenya. I was still taking anti-malaria medicine. One of the benign side effects of that drug (Malarone) was particularly vivid dreams. What other explanation could there be? Would the President of the United States really withhold this information from his Secretary of State, even as we were flying to sign the most significant international agreement of his presidency?"

Yes. Though I am not convinced that "withhold" is really the right word, nor that gender had anything to do with it, as the Secretary of State has often alleged. In any event, this bad situation was made worse by ongoing turf battles between the Departments of State and Defense and a personal animus between the two Secretaries. The Secretary of Defense had been involved in the *Capellaviridae* meetings from the beginning, in part because of his close personal relationship with the President, but mostly because he happened to be at the White House on the morning of that first meeting. The Secretary of State, paranoid on the best of days, rejected that benign explanation. The suspicion between these two cabinet members was inflamed by political differences. The Secretary of Defense was a New Republican; the Secretary of State was a Democrat. (The President's cabinet was a mix of independents, New Republicans, and moderate Democrats.)

To put a cherry on top of it all, the Secretary of State was highly sensitive to being treated differently as a woman. By all accounts, including everything I experienced, the President was gender-blind, in a good way. His appointments going all the way back to his early days in Virginia were always reasonably inclusive. There was nothing to suggest he would exclude a senior cabinet member from some discussion because she was a woman. (He had, after all, picked her for one of the most important jobs in the cabinet.) Having said that, I should say also that the Secretary of Defense was more, well, old school. He had been dogged with charges of sexism for much of his career, including his infamous remark (disavowed aggressively at his confirmation hearing) that women are less fit for senior military positions because "maternal instincts could cloud their judgment in the heat of battle."* That is really what he said; I have watched the video.

Also, one could not help but notice that the President and Secretary of Defense—both tall, fit, middle-aged white guys—gave off a certain fraternity brother vibe. If you were to see them chuckling comfortably as they walked into a room together, you might assume they had just come from a weekly squash game. All of this is relevant if one is to understand the dynamic on Air Force One in those first hours after the Outbreak became public. The Secretary of State had gone to sleep after a light dinner, assuming she would wake up when the plane landed in Australia. As America's top diplomat, she would accompany the President as he signed the South China Sea Agreement, arguably the most significant international agreement of the twenty-first century.

The Secretary of State had spent much of her earlier career working to reform the United Nations. She had negotiated on behalf of the U.S. for the enlargement of the Security Council and the adoption of an updated charter that breathed new life and relevance into the UN. There was serious talk that she might be awarded the Nobel Peace Prize, most likely to be shared with some of the world's other senior diplomats, for having revitalized multilateral diplomacy and repaired much of the damage done during the Trump presidency.

The reality on board Air Force One turned out to be radically different than the Secretary of State's serene expectations. She walked

---

* My inner scientist compels me to point out that recent research has found clear gender-based differences in decision making, particularly in life-and-death situations (or the simulation thereof). There is no evidence to substantiate the Secretary of Defense's assertion that women are less capable military leaders. However, his implicit suggestion that there might be systematic differences between how men and women make battlefield decisions is defensible. Of course, it is entirely possible—and perhaps likely, according to my amateur reading of history—that less testosterone makes for much better military leadership.

into the conference room and encountered a handful of adrenaline-addled advisers trying to manage a situation that was spinning out of control. The Chief of Staff briefed her quickly on the Outbreak and the impending Dormigen crisis. We do not know exactly what was said, other than that the Secretary of State used "inappropriate language," as she would later describe it. We know for certain that the Secretary of State quickly joined the other foreign policy advisers in making the case that the President must continue on to Australia to sign the South China Sea Agreement. Any other tack, she argued, would alter the course of international affairs in ways that would limit American influence, sell out our key allies in the region, and give a green light to some of China's most nefarious activities.

These arguments had been made before, but the Secretary of State brought three things to the room. First, she knew the South China Sea Agreement better than anybody on the American team. She had been negotiating the most niggling details for years; she could literally recite the rise in carbon emissions that would result if the harmonized carbon tax among the signatory nations were not implemented.* Second, the Secretary of State was walking into the room with fresh eyes. Those of us who had been involved from the beginning were partially blinded by a "fog of war." We had made decisions, told each other those decisions were sensible, and then made more decisions based on what we had done earlier. The Secretary of State described this as going "deeper and deeper into a maze." That seems overly harsh given the unprecedented nature of what we were dealing with. Still, the Secretary of State brought new and much-needed perspective to the situation. We were slowly persuading ourselves that it would be unacceptable to let Americans die if the Chinese were will-

---

* Unless you are a policy wonk, you may not have any interest in this: One feature of the South China Sea Agreement was a uniform carbon tax to be implemented in all of the signatory nations ($42 per ton of CO_2 emission, to rise at 2 percent annually). Commonly called a "pollution tax," this was a measure that economists had recommended for years as a tool for discouraging the most carbon-intensive activities. The signatory nations also agreed to impose a "carbon tariff" on countries that did not adopt a similar carbon tax—namely China. The net effect was likely to be a huge reduction in carbon dioxide emissions, albeit at a high cost to Chinese manufacturing.

ing to throw us a lifeline. This was a moral calculation, not a political one. The Secretary of State dismissed our reasoning almost as soon as she walked into the conference room. "By that logic, Churchill should have cut a deal with Hitler," she said. "That would have saved English lives, right? Does anyone here believe that would have been the right thing to do? Look out the window, people. There is a reason we fought at Kiribati and Guadalcanal."* By all accounts, she paused and stared intently at the President before continuing. "With all due respect, sir, your responsibility is to do what is best for the *long-term interests* of the country, and that may well involve extraordinary sacrifices in the short run. Abraham Lincoln was not—"

"Okay, I get it," the President said, cutting her off. The Secretary of State's historical references may seem facile in the retelling. The reality is that the third thing she brought into that stifling little room was a powerful intellect and unparalleled global experience. Her parents had both been American diplomats, moving from posting to posting every couple of years. The Secretary of State spoke Swahili, Arabic, and enough Hindi to delight any Indian audience. Perhaps more important, she had attended local schools in many of those postings, picking up a visceral understanding of the needs and wants of local families. She could tell humorous stories about bouts of dengue fever (Indonesia), or winning a goat in an elementary school spelling bee (Tanzania). The Secretary of State was not, however, a natural politician. Twice she had run for office, once for Congress in a suburban Maryland district and once for the U.S. Senate, also in Maryland. Both times she was trounced in the Democratic primary, having delivered long monologues on "America's unique leadership role in the post-industrial world" that caused voters' eyes to glaze over. She declared bitterly at the end of her Senate campaign, "Americans have stopped caring about the rest of the world." There was a grain of truth in that, but it was also true that the Secretary of State had difficulty speaking about issues in ways that made normal people care. A *Washington Post–USA Today* political columnist described her

---

* As a matter of basic geography, Air Force One was still east of Hawaii, so no one was going to see Kiribati or Guadalcanal out the window. But, to paraphrase the iconic twentieth-century film *Animal House*, she was "on a roll."

stump speech: "Imagine your worst college professor. Then take away the excitement." A YouTube video of the Secretary of State speaking about a Brazilian antipoverty program went viral, apparently because college students had turned it into a drinking game.

For anyone willing to listen, the Secretary of State offered a deep understanding of the sweeping forces of history. She did not see international affairs as a stark, ongoing battle between good and evil, as the Secretary of Defense was wont to do, but she did believe that history offered up repeated cases in which "the forces of liberalism and enlightenment must face down our darker human impulses or face the awful consequences." She had lived in Rwanda and Cambodia, both places where the effects of genocide were still palpable. To put a fine point on all this, the Secretary of State viewed the South China Sea Agreement as a historic inflection point. She did not consider China to be an evil regime on par with the Khmer Rouge or the Nazis. Rather, she compared the Beijing government to the Soviet Union during the Cold War: an enormously powerful and influential nation that was steadily pulling the world order in a bad direction—flouting international agreements, trampling civil liberties, selling weapons to despots, despoiling the environment at a historically unprecedented pace, and demonstrating to bad governments around the globe that they could get away with it all. "The South China Sea Agreement will redirect the course of the world order, as NATO and the United Nations did after World War II," she had told the Chicago Council on Global Affairs—one of her many appearances as she stumped for the agreement across the country.

The Secretary of State was flabbergasted that the President was seriously considering selling out the future world order to get through a short-term public health crisis. "The Dormigen shortage is, what, five days?" she asked. "Capitulating to the Chinese would be *the next century.*" The President respected her judgment, though he found her to be pedantic and insufficiently respectful of his domestic political constraints. Sometimes, after a sour encounter, the President would tell anyone in earshot, "She couldn't get elected to a school board." For her part, the Secretary of State was often impatient with the President's lack of interest in detail and his poor grasp of history, particularly Asian and African history.

I should point out that none of the senior advisers on Air Force One had eaten in many hours. The Chief of Staff, recognizing the combined dangers of sleep deprivation and low blood sugar, asked the Chief Steward to bring breakfast. The crew on board, having expected a jubilant, unrushed breakfast upon the approach to Australia rather than a tense meal in the middle of the night, had planned an omelet station for senior staff. There was no other food readily available, so the Chief Steward directed the chef to set up a buffet, including the omelet station, in an alcove outside the conference room. This explains one of the more scurrilous charges to emerge in the aftermath of the Outbreak—that the President and senior advisers had been blithely dining on pastries and omelets while the country was overcome by plague, like Nero if he had had his own 797. Yes, there was literal truth embedded in the story. There were croissants and fresh fruit; there was an omelet station. But the reality is that the Chief of Staff was trying to feed a staff who had been working around the clock with the food that happened to be available.

As Air Force One made its final descent into Honolulu, the President told the Secretary of State, "We have not made any decision about the South China Sea Agreement."

"What are you going to tell the country?" she asked.

"First, we just need to explain what's happening," he said.

"Is the Chinese Dormigen offer for real?" she asked.

"As far as we can tell, yes," the Chief of Staff answered.

The Secretary of State said, "They are going to do everything they can to exploit this situation."

She was correct.

50.

THE PRESIDENT'S ADDRESS TO THE NATION WAS SCHEDULED for twelve p.m. Eastern Time. For once, the administration did not have to wrangle with the networks to get them to cover the speech. Upon landing, the President was hustled to a studio at Fort DeRussy in Honolulu. Almost immediately the schedule began to slip. The President was traveling with a single speechwriter, who had been brought along to draft valedictory remarks after the South China Sea Agreement was signed. Instead, she was awakened in the middle of the night and told to write a fifteen-minute national address on a subject she knew nothing about. The President angrily rejected the first draft, which was heavy on Pearl Harbor imagery. He snarled, "Pearl Harbor was the beginning of World War II. What I'm trying to convey here is that everything is going to be okay." The Communications Director wrote a short draft himself, but the President was unhappy with that as well, taking a Montblanc pen in his left hand and crossing out the whole first paragraph, then, as he read on, the whole second paragraph, before tossing the whole thing aside. "I need something short, straightforward, and reassuring," he said. "Do I have to write this myself?"

Shortly after five a.m. Hawaii time, the President was ushered into a small, secure conference room at Fort DeRussy along with the Strategist and the Chief of Staff. There were still no draft remarks. The Communications Director was working frantically with the studio crew to find an appropriate backdrop for the talk, something that would approximate the Oval Office. The television studio at Fort DeRussy had a digital background; the producer could manipulate the scene behind the President with the click of a mouse, like changing screensavers. The Communications Director leaned over the producer's shoulder as they tried out backdrops, most of which had been designed for military briefings. The first digital background showed the Pearl Harbor Memorial, with an expanse of ocean and blue sky. "That's the U.S.S. *Missouri* Memorial," the producer explained.

"Are you fucking kidding me?" the Communications Director exclaimed. "That looks like the President of the United States is on a Hawaiian vacation." The producer clicked on his console, bringing up a new digital background: dark wood bookshelves, lined with serious-looking books, like a cozy academic office.

"Maybe that?" the producer offered.

"What are the books?" the Communications Director asked.

"Pardon?"

"The books. What are the titles of the books?"

"They're not real. They're just digital images."

The Communications Director spluttered, "I understand that. I am not an idiot. But they still have titles, fake or not. Make it bigger, so I can read them." The producer enlarged the image, so that the fake titles on fake bookshelves became readable. After a few seconds, the Communications Director muttered, "No . . . no . . . no. Clausewitz? Counterinsurgency. They're all military books."

"That is what we do here," the producer said, finally pushing back. "It's a military base."

"This looks like the President is getting ready to invade some small country."

"I can blur the titles so they're not readable. It might look a little strange—"

"It will take five minutes before some douchebag living in his mother's basement unblurs them, and that will become the story. What else do you have?" The two of them finally agreed on a simple background with the presidential seal and an American flag, after which the Communications Director asked who would load the remarks into the teleprompter.

"We don't have a teleprompter," the producer said.

"Jesus. Does the President know that?"

"I don't speak to the President."

Of course, there were no remarks to be loaded into a teleprompter at that point anyway. The President, true to his word, had begun drafting a short speech, longhand on a legal pad. When the Communications Director called the President from the studio control room to tell him there would be no teleprompter, the President read him his draft remarks over the phone. It was a short, simple speech that again emphasized the three key points we were trying to make: no terrorism attack; the virus does not spread; the Dormigen shortage is manageable.

"It's good, but don't say 'terrorism,'" the Communications Director said.

"How the hell am I supposed to deny that there has been a terrorist attack without using the word?"

"You can't say terrorism. It gives credibility to the rumor," the Communications Director explained. The two men knew each other well enough that the President waited for the Communications Director to propose alternative language, which he did. "Just say that this is a common virus that has always been endemic to the United States. No hostile parties, foreign or domestic, have played a role in this public health challenge."

"Isn't that denying that it's terrorism?" the President asked.

"Yeah, but you can't use the word. You can't say 'terrorism.'"

At about that moment, the Chief of Staff, who had been talking on her own phone, handed the President a note. "Holy shit," he said to the Chief of Staff, but loud enough that the Communications Director could hear.

"What?" the Communications Director asked.

"I'll call you back," the President said, hanging up.

The Chief of Staff's note was short but powerful: "Our model now shows lower bound on deaths at 10,000." The NIH Director had called with the first really good news of the crisis: Nations around the world, recognizing the severity of what was happening in the U.S., were willing to dig deeper into their own Dormigen supplies. She had spoken personally to senior government leaders in Australia and other signatory nations of the South China Sea Agreement to inform them of the China dilemma. If these governments wanted to protect the agreement, she told them, they needed to help render the China Dormigen offer unnecessary. Hence the note that the Chief of Staff slid to the President: With the new Dormigen pledges, the NIH model was showing a range of "excess Dormigen-preventable deaths" from ten thousand to sixty-five thousand, depending on six or seven key variables in the model (e.g., the severity of any other disease outbreaks in the coming days).

The President and his advisers were obviously focused on the lower end of that range. It was tantalizingly close to zero, as the President grasped immediately. If somehow that lower bound were to go to zero—with more Dormigen pledges or more optimistic forecasts for other variables in the model (e.g., less flu)—the President could credibly tell the nation that the situation was under control. "We have to get that to zero," the President said.

"We're working the phones," the Chief of Staff said.

"I mean *now*. Before I give my address."

"We're doing everything we can," the Chief of Staff assured him.

"It's got to go to zero," the President repeated. "Get the NIH on the phone and tell them the lower bound needs to get to zero."

The Chief of Staff said, "They can't just change the model."

"Look, I spent five years as a consultant building these kinds of models. If you change a few assumptions, you can get the earth to spin backwards."

The Strategist added, "It's true. They don't have to do anything dishonest. Just tell them to 'reexamine the assumptions' to see if anything may have changed. Just a fresh look."

"We only have twenty minutes before you go on air," the Chief of Staff replied.

"Push it back, if we have to," the President said firmly. "I want to be able to tell the American people that we can manage this situation without any incremental deaths."

"It's still just the lower bound," the Strategist pointed out.

"I understand that," the President said. "Just make zero a possibility."

"I will ask them to do what they can," the Chief of Staff said, stepping out of the conference room to make the call.

They all recognized, of course, that the President would be addressing not just the American people, but also the international community, and the Chinese leadership in particular. The less desperate he appeared to Beijing, the better. While the Chief of Staff spoke with the NIH about "taking a fresh look" at their model, the President asked to be connected with both the Senate Majority Leader and the Speaker of the House. Congress was in recess, but both chambers had called emergency sessions; representatives and senators were rushing back to the Capitol to deal with the Outbreak, or at least give that impression. In a matter of minutes the President was on speakerphone with the two legislative leaders.

"You had to know this moment was coming," the Speaker said after some terse pleasantries. "You couldn't keep something like this from the public forever."

"Now we need to manage the situation," the President replied.

He described his proposed remarks. "I need you both to assure me that Congress is going to be a constructive partner as we work through this."

The Senate Majority Leader said, "The Senate is going to be like a teakettle—lots of steam getting blown off. I will do everything in my power to steer that emotion in a constructive direction. You have my complete support." As an amateur historian and a powerful senator who knew he would never reach the White House, the Senate Majority Leader was anticipating his shining moment. If he could help steer the Senate, and therefore the nation, through this crisis, history would be kind to him. He was a man vain enough to aspire to have parks, streets, and schools named after him, but honorable enough to feel he ought to deserve it. He continued, "Send me your draft remarks and I will issue a supportive statement. The Senate is going to be mayhem for a few hours. We're going to have to let that run its course, but we'll eventually get down to business."

"I think that's unrealistic," the House Speaker said. "The anger . . . My members are talking about impeachment. The nation feels like we were kept in the dark. Why weren't they told earlier?"

"You know darn well why they weren't told earlier," the President said angrily. "It would have provoked the panic we're seeing now—to no good end."

"There is a huge trust deficit, Mr. President," she warned.

The Strategist had been pacing around the small conference room, rolling his eyes at the Speaker's melodramatic lamentations. Finally, he could contain himself no longer. "Can we just save all that for your campaign?" he said.

The President signaled for the Strategist to keep quiet. "Madame Speaker, when the House comes back into session, can you please try to forestall any actions that would be counterproductive to what we are trying to do here?" the President asked earnestly.

"What are you trying to do?" she asked dramatically. "I have no idea what you are trying to do. The response seems rudderless."

The President answered, "We are gathering additional Dormigen commitments. We are continuing our work to understand the virus. We are urging anyone who is ill to seek treatment. And we are evaluating all other reasonable options."

"Those are just talking points," the Speaker said.

The Senate Majority Leader interjected, "I appreciate your leadership on this, Mr. President."

"The NIH model is now showing that we might not have any incremental deaths," the President said. "The lower bound on their estimate is zero."

"Near zero," the Strategist said, instinctively protecting his boss.

"What does 'near zero' mean?" the Speaker asked. "Thousands of people have died already."

"From idiocy," the Strategist said in the background.

"Preventable deaths," the President clarified. "It means that with a little more work on our part, or a lucky break, we may get through this thing without any deaths for lack of Dormigen."

"What about the China option?" she asked.

"We are still looking at that. There is a consensus among my foreign policy advisers that it would be far too steep of a price to pay in the long run. You heard some of those discussions."

The Senate Majority Leader asked, "Is the China offer public information at this point?"

"No," the President said emphatically. "And I'd prefer to keep it that way. Among other things, we don't actually have a firm offer in hand."

The House Speaker said, "I cannot in good conscience withhold that information from the House, or from the public. If China is offering lifesaving medicine, the public needs to know that."

The Chief of Staff walked back into the room and thrust a piece of paper in front of the President. It had a big "0" written on it—nothing else. The President understood immediately. He said sharply into the speakerphone, "We're now at zero deaths. I have a speech to give. All of the discussions with the Chinese are confidential. If you so much as hint at that in your public comments, I will personally have you arrested." He poked at the console on the speakerphone, trying to end the call, but he hit the wrong button, causing a loud beeping noise. The Strategist quickly stepped beside him and hit the correct button, hanging up on the Speaker and the Majority Leader.

The Chief of Staff began explaining: "The NIH revisited their projections for the number of people who would seek—"

"I don't want to know," the President said, walking out of the room. "Let's do this."

51.

I FOUND MY WAY TO THE RADIO STATION IN PLENTY OF TIME, even before the President pushed back the time of his address. The studio was smaller and less elaborate than the CNN facility. I waited in a sitting area with three large flat-screen televisions, each tuned to a different news station. A handful of station employees stood idly watching with me, waiting for the President to appear on camera. The address was postponed another five minutes as the President's staff (unbeknownst to the public) wrestled with the teleprompter issue, or more accurately the lack of a teleprompter. The President's handwritten remarks had been quickly typed up, but the font was too small for him to read without his glasses. There was a debate among the staff over whether it would be better for the President to wear his glasses, something the public had never seen before and might distract from the message, or to have the speech printed in large enough font for him to read without glasses. The latter seemed an easy fix, but the font turned out to be so large that there were only a few sentences on each page, creating a strange effect whereby he had to flip rapidly through many pages while saying relatively little. "It looks like he's reading a speech written in crayon by a kindergartner," the Communications Director said. In the end, the President wore his glasses. The reading glasses produced no meaningful public reaction. However, the public had been so conditioned to leaders using a teleprompter that there was some comment on the fact that the President read from an actual speech, looking down at the pages and then up at the camera.

In the studio, a producer sidled up to me as I waited for the President's speech to begin. "Have you ever done a satellite tour before?" he asked.

"I don't even know what it is," I said.

The producer pointed to a chair opposite a microphone in the middle of a small room surrounded on three sides by soundproof glass. "You're going in there. I'm going to be in the booth. We're going to do fourteen segments in about ninety minutes, mostly AM news programs, a few public radio segments. All live. If you mess up, just keep going. After you finish each interview, keep quiet and I'll patch you into the next one."

The President began his address and we all turned toward the televisions. Someone scrambled to find a remote to turn on the volume. The producer said to me, "When he's done, we're going to go right into the studio. You'll be fine."

I looked down at my phone as the President's voice boomed into the room. Tie Guy had sent me another text: "Nature strikes back. Call me!" I quickly texted back that I would call him after I finished my radio interviews. Nature strikes back? Why was he quoting Huke to me?

The President's speech was clear and authoritative, if somewhat short on artistry. There were no ringing phrases like "a day that will live in infamy" or the "axis of evil." Instead, the President did what he had to do, explaining *Capellaviridae*, the nature of the Dormigen shortage, the need for anyone who felt ill to seek treatment, and most important, the ongoing government response. The penultimate draft included the line: "I will do everything in my power to ensure that no American lives are lost." The Secretary of State had pleaded with him to remove or change the line. "It will make it that much harder to stand firm with the Chinese," she argued. Both the National Security Adviser and the Secretary of Defense concurred.

"People have died already," the Chief of Staff reminded him.

"Obviously," the President snapped. "This is about the Dormigen shortage."

"Maybe we need to say that," she suggested.

The television networks were getting impatient, as they had already interrupted their scheduled programming for nearly half an hour. "How about this?" the Strategist offered. "I am confident that we can weather this crisis without any preventable loss of life."

"Yes," the President agreed.

"That's a bit of a stretch, isn't it?" the Chief of Staff asked. "How about 'preventable loss of life from the shortage—'"

"Too clunky," the President said. "I'm comfortable with this. It's what people need to hear right now. Today is about quelling the panic."

"Sir, I think that leaves you in a better position with regard to the Chinese," the National Security Adviser said.

The Chief of Staff, still uncertain, said, "Only the lower bound of the model shows no loss of life. Everything has to go our way."

The President said, "The speech says, '*I am confident* we can weather this crisis without any loss of life.' It's about how I feel right now. *I am confident* that we are going to get through this without any preventable loss of life. That's what I'm asserting."

"Yes, that's right," said the Strategist.

The President, no doubt feeling a rising surge of adrenaline, said impatiently, "I'm ready. This is the speech I'm giving." I do not believe it is a coincidence that the President was an extraordinary basketball player. He had the ability to harness his anxiety in a way that elevated his performance, rather than smothering it. He may have looked somewhat awkward reading his speech off the printed page, but his demeanor and the message were pitch-perfect. I watched with a small, nonrepresentative group of people in the radio studio, but the feeling in the room after the President had spoken was different than it had been just seven minutes earlier. The brevity of the speech gave it additional power. The President did not have the eloquence of FDR or JFK, but he explained clearly what was happening and made a short but compelling case that the situation was under control. The immediate headlines suggested a public reaction similar to mine. Even before the President was done speaking, Bloomberg posted a one-paragraph summary of the speech under the headline: "President Urges Calm, Predicts No Loss of Life in *Capellaviridae* Crisis." The stock market, which had plunged more than 5 percent on the initial reports of the Outbreak, regained most of the losses.

Let me address the elephant in the room: Did the President lie to the American people? The Outbreak Inquiry Commission was equivocal on this point. The two pages in the report devoted to the President's Honolulu address are a mishmash of ambiguous phrases and tortured use of the passive voice. My view is much clearer: The President believed he was doing the right thing by presenting the most optimistic view of the situation in that moment. As I have noted, the NIH model was showing a best-case scenario in which our existing Dormigen stocks, including the new donations, would be sufficient. One should bear in mind, too, that the results predicted by that model had been revised steadily downward ever since we first confronted the crisis. True, we had underestimated how many people would die because they did not seek medical care. There was plenty of Dormigen at that point. Was that on us? Besides, we now had the opposite problem: perfectly healthy people streaming into emergency rooms convinced they were dying. The President believed that new developments would continue to redound to our benefit: more Dormigen donations, some progress against the virus, more effective non-Dormigen alternatives, and so on. He was wrong, obviously.

In fact, the nation's Dormigen supplies were plunging even as the President spoke. As I have noted, we all failed to recognize that the Dormigen supply was unsecured. From the moment the first *New Yorker* story suggested an imminent public health problem, Dormigen went missing—everything from trucks of the medicine stolen outright to doctors and nurses pocketing some pills at the beginning or end of a shift. I suppose the statement by Senator McDowell during the Outbreak hearings hewed closest to what was really happening on that morning: "The Dormigen supply was like an ice cube on a hot day. The administration blithely went about its business, even as that ice cube was melting away. It was an oversight of monumental proportions to assume that a shortage of a lifesaving drug would not precipitate theft and pilfering."[*] One can quibble with the metaphor, but the "melting ice cube" is a good description of what was happening. The supply was quickly secured, but that process was incomplete and ad hoc. It was as if someone suddenly directed the nation's doctors, clinics, and hospitals to implement measures to prevent the theft of ballpoint pens. How does one even begin? No one had ever thought Dormigen valuable enough to protect. To the contrary, the drug was a handy thing for doctors to keep in their pockets, for nurses to keep in the top drawer of an examining room, and so on. Even if the administration had moved more quickly to secure the supply, the pilferage might have been just as bad. The same people had the same opportunities to pocket a few pills, or steal a truckload.

---

[*]   Senator Derek McDowell, "Statement to the Outbreak Inquiry Commission," 2031.

When the President addressed the nation, he believed the nation's Dormigen stocks to be far higher than they actually were. The barn door was nailed shut eventually, but by then the "ice cube" had been sitting on a warm counter for a long time. The President and his advisers, myself included, should have anticipated that Dormigen would go missing. We should have put measures in place to prevent it; on that morning in Honolulu, the President should have been more aware of what was happening. The NIH should have reacted more quickly to the early reports of pilferage, though to be fair the NIH senior staff were busy fielding calls from foreign governments making generous new Dormigen offers. Every one of those calls—two thousand doses from Qatar; five thousand doses from South Korea; eighteen thousand from Australia—was literally a lifesaver. The irony, of course, is that the NIH was bringing new Dormigen in the front door even as it was disappearing out the back.

I should make one other non-obvious point. Stolen Dormigen was not quite as disastrous as it may first appear. There is no recreational value to Dormigen; it offers no high, not even pain relief. No one takes Dormigen if they do not have to. In theory, then, every stolen dose replaces one that would have been prescribed anyway—provided the stolen medicine goes to people who really need it. Unfortunately there were twin tragedies amplifying everything else going wrong on this front: reasonably healthy people started taking Dormigen they did not need; and many sick people ended up with counterfeit Dormigen. I can only marvel at the speed with which entrepreneurial opportunists flooded the Internet with "special deals" promising Dormigen "delivered to your doorstep." According to the Outbreak Inquiry Commission, the first of these hoaxes appeared online only ninety minutes after *The New Yorker* first made the Outbreak public.

I was simultaneously impressed and horrified by these hucksters. Each scam had its own ridiculous explanation for why an online vendor happened to have surplus lifesaving medicine while the rest of the country was in shortage: "Army surplus"; a "special unregulated supply from Costa Rica"; a "new patented method for producing the drug on demand"; and many others.* The audacity of these modern

---

*   These are all real examples gathered by the Outbreak Inquiry Commission.

snake oil peddlers was matched only by the gullibility of those on whom they preyed. Some fifteen million people rushed to the Internet to buy Dormigen; they ended up with everything from sugar pills to decongestant tablets. (There is a modicum of good news here; a reasonably high proportion of the people who bought fake medicine did not need the real stuff anyway.) Still, there were several hundred thousand people who needed Dormigen and ended up with something else entirely.

After the President finished his address, I felt the producer pulling me by the elbow out of the crowded common area. He said, "We're on in New York in ninety seconds. It's a standard interview format. You'll have about two minutes and twenty seconds. They'll try to keep you longer, but you can't. Cleveland will be queued up right when you finish." He guided me to a seat in the small soundproof room. As I put on the headphones, he hustled out of the room into the production booth on the opposite side of a soundproof glass partition. Soon I could hear his voice in my headphones: "We're on in thirty." One of the assistants had pasted a paper sign in the window that read NYC to remind me of the market to whom I was speaking. I chuckled at the notion that I would need to be reminded of that detail. Seven or eight interviews later I found myself glancing at the sign; I had new sympathy for the occasional rock band who would yell, "Hello, Dayton!" only to be greeted by stunned silence among the fans in Akron.

There was a burst of static as the producer patched me into the New York studio, at which point I could hear the program in progress: ". . . joined by the administration's top adviser on this virus. Doctor, thank you for joining us." I have a Ph.D., but I have never referred to myself as "doctor," so this left me temporarily flat-footed.

"It's my pleasure," I said.

The host began, "The President just addressed the nation, telling us the situation is under control. He made no mention of a possible terror attack. Why is that?"

"Because that's not what's happening," I said. "*Capellaviridae* is a very common virus that has turned virulent—"

"That's what we're being told, but why now? How does a common, supposedly innocuous virus suddenly become deadly?"

"We are still trying to figure that out," I said. I was not used to being interrupted midsentence.

"Then how can we be sure that this is not some kind of domestic terror attack, as is being reported elsewhere?"

"There is absolutely no evidence to substantiate those reports," I said firmly. "None."

"But you can't tell me what is happening. If you're not sure, how can you rule out terrorism?"

"This is a public health crisis; it's not a terrorist attack," I said. I immediately regretted using the word "crisis" and repeating the terrorism charge.

"Given we have a crisis on our hands, as you've said, what should our listeners be doing now?" the New York host asked.

I heard the producer's voice in my earphones: "Forty-five seconds."

I answered, "The administration is making progress on the Dormigen front—we are getting commitments from other countries, and we are also making progress on the virus—"

"So the government is going to solve this crisis?"

"There are experts—"

"Aren't these the same people who got us into this situation?"

"Well, no . . ." I stammered without any sense of where I was going with the answer.

The producer said in my earphones: "Twenty seconds and we're out."

The New York host continued, "The government is supposed to have a stockpile of Dormigen and now they don't? Am I missing something?"

"I don't think of it that way."

"I suppose you wouldn't," he said. "While we are waiting for the government to rescue us, what can individual listeners do?"

"Anyone who feels they may be ill with symptoms consistent with *Capellaviridae*—"

"Those symptoms are on our website," he interrupted.

"—should seek medical attention." I heard a click as the New York station muted my microphone, ensuring the host the last word.

He concluded the segment: "Grim news from the nation's top expert on the virus attack. Government help is on the way. If you feel ill, head to a clinic or hospital, where there probably won't be enough medicine to help you. This is criminal incompetence, people."

The station went dead in my earphones. I exhaled audibly. I heard the producer's voice, "Don't worry about it. That guy's an asshole. I'm going to connect you to Cleveland in about twenty-five seconds." The assistant took down the paper sign in the window that read NYC and replaced it with CLEVELAND. "Only thirteen more to go," the producer said.

52.

CLEVELAND WENT BETTER, OTHER THAN MY UNFORTUNATE description of *Capellaviridae* as "elegant." Nashville was another jackass host who would not let me complete a full sentence. I got steadily better at steering the conversation in the direction I wanted it to go. There was a forty-five-second break between Nashville and Chicago Public Radio. I sat back in my seat, trying to calm myself. The assistant pasted CHICAGO in the window. The producer said in my earphones, "You're doing great. Don't let these guys get to you. They're just sitting on their asses with a microphone. You're actually doing something about the problem." I nodded to acknowledge the pep talk. The producer continued, "Hey, one other thing. Bloomberg is reporting that the Chinese ambassador to the United States is going to give a news conference in Washington at two. Something about Dormigen. We're on in fifteen."

The Chicago host had seen the same Bloomberg report. After the introduction, she asked, "Do we know for certain what the size of the Dormigen gap is right now?"

I hedged: "I'm not privy to that information. I do know the number is a moving target and it's moving in the right direction. My understanding, based on the President's speech, is that we are close to closing the gap."

"And China is apparently prepared to offer whatever Dormigen the nation may need?" the Chicago host offered. "We are told that's what the Chinese ambassador is going to announce this afternoon. Can America breathe a sigh of relief?"

"I don't know any of the details regarding the Chinese offer."

"It seems fairly straightforward, no?"

"It depends what they ask in return," I said. "As you know, the President was on his way to Australia to sign the South China Sea Agreement. The Chinese government has been consistently hostile to that collective security arrangement with our allies in the region."

"So the Chinese government might ask the U.S. to scrap the South China Sea Agreement in exchange for the Dormigen?" the host asked sensibly.

"As I said, I'm not privy to the details."

The host probed more deeply: "Some officials in Beijing are saying on background that the Chinese government made this offer many days ago. Were you aware of any such offer?"

"I'm a scientist, not a diplomat."

"I understand that, but in the course of discussions about this crisis, was there any mention of an offer by China to cover the Dormigen gap?"

"Those discussions are all confidential."

This was public radio. The host was more persistent and appreciably smarter than most of the bloviaters who had been vomiting in my headphones for the past hour. She had also found her way to exactly the right question. She continued, firmly but not rudely, "What I'm left to infer is that the Chinese government is offering Dormigen with strings attached. Is it fair to say the President may be in a position where he has to trade off American lives against our future security arrangements in East Asia?"

"We'll know more about that at two," I said.

At that moment, the Secretary of State was working the phones to find out what the Chinese deal was going to look like. The Chinese Embassy in D.C. had alerted the news media that there would be "a major announcement regarding a Chinese gift of Dormigen to our American friends" but had made no formal contact with their U.S. counterparts to offer the details. When the Secretary of State reached the Chinese Ambassador, he was tight-lipped about the forthcoming announcement. "This is unprecedented," the U.S. Secretary of State shouted into the phone.

The Chinese Ambassador remained unruffled. "We would like to speak directly to the American people," he said.

"How are we supposed to react, if we don't know the terms of the deal?" the Secretary of State asked angrily.

"This is not a 'deal.' It is an act of generosity on the part of the Chinese people to cement our ongoing friendship with the American people."

"Don't insult my intelligence," the Secretary of State warned. "If I want propaganda, I'll read the *People's Daily*. When are we going to know what you want?"

"President Xing will present a new U.S.-China Friendship Agreement immediately after the press conference."

"Can you summarize for me what will be in this 'Friendship Agreement'?" the Secretary of State asked.

"As I said, we would like to speak directly to the American people."

The Secretary of State hung up without saying goodbye, much to the surprise of the National Security Adviser and the Strategist, both of whom were in the room with her. The Strategist asked, "Did you just hang up on him?"

"He'll get over it," the Secretary of State replied.

"So much for U.S.-China friendship," the Strategist said, finding a certain levity in the situation that neither the Secretary of State nor the National Security Adviser shared.

"It's clever," the National Security Adviser offered. "They're going to wave the miracle cure in front of the public and then we have to explain why we may not take it."

"We have to get out in front of it," the Secretary of State answered. "We need people to understand when they're watching that there is a price to be paid. We need people to be skeptical when they hear—"

"Maybe not," the Strategist said, almost musing to himself. The two women looked at him, waiting for him to complete the thought. "What's the first thing you think of when you hear 'U.S.-China Friendship Agreement'?" he asked.

"It's the usual Orwellian doublespeak, like reading *Pravda* back in the day," the National Security Adviser said.

"These guys are not nearly as good at propaganda as they think they are," the Strategist said. "When you can shut down newspapers and arrest critics, you tend to lose the subtle art of persuasion."

"And?" the Secretary of State asked impatiently.

"They're ham-handed," the Strategist explained. "They're amateurs when it comes to the American public. They think they're better than they are. If we let them make the first move, there is a good chance they'll overbid."*

"It's risky," the National Security Adviser said.

"Not really," the Strategist countered. "We've got no other good options. Putting out a statement when we don't know what they're going to say is like punching shadows."

Back in the studio, the balance of my interviews dealt mostly with the upcoming Chinese press conference. I got better at dodging and weaving. Also, the terrorism questions went away; there are only so many things that can be discussed in a three-minute radio interview. Between Austin and Denver, the producer spoke into my headphones. "You've got a little break here, almost seven minutes, if you want to use the bathroom or get some water or something." I stood up, just to stretch, and then I remembered Tie Guy's most recent text. I called him and he answered almost immediately. We had not spoken since the Outbreak became public. I expected him to say something about all that, but he surprised me.

"Nature fights back!" Tie Guy exclaimed.

"Yeah, that's what you texted. What?"

"Your buddy Huke is on to something. Nobody likes dust mites, right?"

"Not that I'm aware of."

"This particular subspecies of dust mite bites humans. *And the bites itch.*"

"Okay, so?"

"Check this out: *Capellaviridae* is most likely to become virulent

---

* The Strategist was, at the time, considered to be one of the top twenty competitive bridge players in the world. In bridge, players see their cards and then make a "bid" as to how well they will do in the hand. A player can mess up a hand with great cards by bidding too aggressively, or "overbidding."

in places that have been most aggressive in trying to exterminate the North American dust mite." There was a brief silence as I absorbed what he was saying. "The clusters," he added. "Remember? There are just a handful of places where the virus is common and people got sick?"

"Vaguely," I said. "How do you know about the extermination?"

"I got lucky. We don't have any data on who is trying to kill dust mites, but exterminators are licensed in a lot of states. There are pretty good records of the chemicals they use."

"I'm at a studio," I said. "I've only got about five minutes before I go back on the air."

Tie Guy continued quickly: "There is a particular kind of pyrethrin that is highly effective against dust mites and not used for much else. The few places where that insecticide has been used aggressively are also the places where *Capellaviridae* has turned virulent. The correlation is striking."

"Do you have any idea why?"

"Nobody likes to be exterminated," he said, gleeful at having finally been able to share his finding. "I need resources. You've got to help me. *The data are speaking to us.* We need to listen."

The producer was waving three fingers from the window. His assistant had pasted DENVER on the window. I gave Tie Guy the Chief of Staff's private number. "Tell her who you are and what you need."

53.

BOTH HOUSES OF CONGRESS WERE SCHEDULED TO COME BACK into session at four p.m. Senators and representatives were racing to the Capitol from across the country. The Speaker of the House had wasted no time in releasing a statement calling for a congressional investigation of all government actions related to the Outbreak. But what she had expected to be her shining moment in the spotlight— the launch of her presidential campaign, if the Strategist is to be believed—turned into a train wreck almost immediately. Back in Houston, Tony Perez, fake news author extraordinaire, was seeing a record number of views on his posts. Eyeballs are money, and he was doing his best to ride the story. Even as the President and staff were squashing the terrorism rumors at every turn, Perez was finding that the Latino separatist angle had legs. Ethnic tensions had been simmering in the country long enough that any story positing an Anglo-Hispanic rift, with a political conspiracy throw in, was bound to get clicks. In his fourth post of the day, Perez "fed" the story, a term he described as adding just enough new detail to get the original readers to come back, while attracting new ones. He did so with a "bombshell revelation": *The likely first president of the Estado Latino Nuevo would be America's most prominent and powerful Latina politician—the Speaker of the House* ("according to sources close to the Speaker").

The Speaker summoned reporters to the Capitol expecting them to bask in the glow of her leadership. She had prepared short remarks blasting the President for "turning over America's health to greedy corporations" and for his administration's "complete lack of transparency." She had rehearsed fulsome pledges to "explore every option for managing this crisis." But she would never get that far. Not long after the Speaker said, "Good afternoon," reporters began yelling questions about Latino separatism. CNN's top political reporter shouted over the din, "Have you accepted the offer to become the President of Estado Latino Nuevo?" The question was ridiculous—but devilishly so, as the layers of falsehood embedded within it were guaranteed to throw the Speaker on the defensive. No one in the mainstream media gave any credence whatsoever to the separatist story, let alone the notion that the Speaker would lead the breakaway Latino republic. But the Capitol Hill reporters were clever enough to recognize the Speaker's political ambitions. The press conference was a solid signal that she was trying to build a reputation beyond the Beltway. (The Strategist was not the only one who saw this as the beginning of her presidential campaign.) The assembled members of the press did not really want to know if the Speaker of the House was cavorting with Hispanic separatists. What they wanted to find out was how she would react when the accusation was leveled against her.

"That report is absolutely false," the Speaker said emphatically.

"Did you turn the offer down?" the CNN reporter followed up.

"There was no offer," the Speaker said.

A grizzled male reporter yelled from the back, "Would you consider such an offer?"

CNN and most other stations were covering the Speaker's press availability live, anticipating the drama. The President, the Strategist, and several other senior staff watched in the conference room on Air Force One. The Strategist chuckled maliciously. "She is so fucked. Maybe this is when she'll finally tell America that she's not even Hispanic."

A female reporter for Telemundo asked, "Would you support a separate state for America's Latino population, if the region were to vote to secede?"

The Speaker ignored the question. She said, "The reports of any terrorist attack—domestic or otherwise—are entirely false. The whole notion of some breakaway Latino nation is completely ludicrous."

A BBC reporter asked loudly, "Would you still consider yourself the most important voice for America's huge bloc of Hispanic voters?" The question was reasonable, but it tossed the Speaker into more difficult terrain, as she now had to walk a fine line between dismissing the Latino republic story and protecting a political career built on identity politics.

"My job is to represent all Americans," the Speaker said.

"That's not technically true," the BBC reporter challenged. "You were elected in a congressional district that's predominantly Hispanic, and the Democrats, who installed you as Speaker, have made repeated attempts to single out Hispanic voters—"

"I speak for all Americans."

The BBC reporter was dogged. "You have repeatedly emphasized that American Hispanics are different, apart. How does that not create fault lines in the nation?"

The Speaker said dismissively, "I think that characterization is entirely wrong."

"You gave the first ten minutes of your speech at the Democratic National Convention in Spanish," the BBC reporter said, prompting loud laughter from his media colleagues.

On Air Force One, the Strategist looked at his watch. "Five minutes in, and she's still digging out of the hole."

The President added, "She's finally learning she's not as clever as she thinks she is."

The Speaker changed the subject. "Here's what's important: Americans need to understand that there is no terrorist attack— none. Not domestic, not international. This is a common virus that has turned potentially deadly and we are seeking to understand that. In the meantime, I am working aggressively with the administration to solicit Dormigen commitments from around the world. I'm confident we can manage this crisis without loss of life."

On Air Force One, the President said, "Isn't that nice: someone gave her our talking points."

The House Speaker took one more question. Her presidential hopes may have survived but for that last question. An NPR reporter asked, "The Chinese Ambassador will be speaking shortly about the Outbreak. The expectation is that Beijing will offer the U.S. enough Dormigen to cover our shortfall in exchange for diplomatic concessions, perhaps scrapping the South China Sea Agreement. Could you please comment on that?"

The Speaker took a deep breath, nodding to acknowledge the importance of the question. "Our number one priority right now is saving American lives," she began. "If the Chinese government is offering assistance, we ought to take that offer very seriously." The comment seemed relatively anodyne in the moment. It felt entirely different when played over and over again juxtaposed against the later remarks of the Chinese Ambassador. Note to self: *Never say that an offer ought to be taken seriously before you have seen the offer.* But that was still several hours away. The House Speaker had more immediate headaches. As members of Congress arrived in Washington, they were in no mood to have her "steer" their deliberations, whether she was leader of the chamber or not. Over on the Senate side, the Majority Leader had been correct when he predicted that legislators would have to "blow off some steam" before any real business could get done.

Even after America's political realignment—with the splitting of the Republicans into the New Republicans and the Tea Party, and the President's election as an independent—the political parties were still basically tribal. The first imperative was to support one's tribe and bash the other. This had two immediate implications. First, the President, having been elected as an independent, had no tribe. Members of Congress—left, right, and center—heaped abuse on every aspect of the President's existence, from his CEO wife (which had somehow led to the Centera fraud) to Air Force One flying in circles over the Pacific. He had no legislative defenders. The Senate Majority Leader, the President's closest ally on Capitol Hill, did not pile on to the abuse, but he did not stop it, either. At one point he stepped out of the Senate chamber to call the Chief of Staff to reassure her that "tempers would soon cool." The paradox is that for all the venom heaped on the President from every political direction, he remained significantly more popular than Congress, both during and after the Outbreak. His address that morning had gone a long way toward insulating him from congressional criticism, which was perceived (rightly) as petty and self-serving.

Second, the criticism itself was neatly organized along tribal lines, as if each political party were responding to a different crisis. Members of Congress seized on the Outbreak to reinforce their preexisting political beliefs. The progressive wing of the Democratic Party hammered away at the Centera fraud, accusing the President of "privatizing American government." The Outbreak offered one more bullet to fire at corporate greed. The warehouse fire that made the Centera Dormigen necessary got nary a mention, nor did the inconvenient fact that Dormigen had been invented—$1.5 billion in private research and development spending—by the greedy private sector they were now blaming for a shortage of Dormigen.

The Tea Party, ostensibly reacting to the same crisis, blasted "yet another example of extreme government incompetence." The government had fumbled its responsibility to keep the American people safe. By this logic, responsibility for the Outbreak lay with government bureaucrats who had failed to offer adequate oversight. It was time, Tea Party leaders opined, for government to "get out of the drug business entirely." No one took the remarks seriously enough to ask if "getting out of the drug business entirely" included eliminating the government patent protection at the heart of all private investment in the pharmaceutical industry. The Tea Party proposed additional tax cuts, which would somehow induce the private sector to fix this problem that government had created.

Ironically, the far right and the far left found common ground in calling for swift and severe punishment of the Centera executives. For the progressives, this was a no-brainer. The time had come to get serious about punishing corporate malfeasance. Meanwhile, the Tea Party made a more tortured argument about how prompt prosecution would enable the private sector to reach its full potential. Really the rhetoric had the feel of frontier justice. Almost immediately after the Outbreak became public, the Texas attorney general, a Tea Party standard-bearer, issued a warrant for the arrest of the Centera CEO and CFO on capital murder charges, alleging that Goyal and Swensen had "knowingly brought about the deaths of Texas citizens." The Centera CEO and CFO were already in federal custody on numerous federal fraud charges. The Texas attorney general, a former software executive who had spent $25 million of his own money to win a special election only six months earlier, argued that the federal charges were insufficient because they did not carry the death penalty. The progressive caucus, typically staunch opponents of capital punishment, found an exception in this case and encouraged the Texas murder indictment.

It is worth pointing out—just to recognize the absurdity of what was happening—that no one had yet died from a lack of Dormigen. The supply was projected to run out, but there were still stocks readily available. People had died from *Capellaviridae* because they had failed to seek treatment. People had died because upon hearing news of the Outbreak they got in their cars and drove at high speeds to inhospitable places. And people had died because they bought dangerous counterfeit Dormigen. I do not want to minimize these casualties, but I do want to emphasize that no person—in Texas or anywhere else—had walked into a health facility suffering from an illness that could be treated effectively with Dormigen and had died because he or she was refused that Dormigen. Not one. As a result, the grand jury that was convened in Texas to issue the capital murder indictments immediately dismissed the charges. To prosecute an individual for murder, you need to show that someone was killed, even in Texas. Still, the Texas attorney general got the headlines he was looking for. Eighteen months later he was elected governor. As I write, he is being discussed as a possible presidential candidate.

The New Republicans and the centrist Democrats offered more nuanced remarks, criticizing the administration but also calling for revisions to America's system for procuring essential drugs. The senior Senator from New Jersey, a New Republican known as one of the wonkier members of the Senate,* had introduced a bill several months earlier to update the patent system and provide safeguards when government drug production was outsourced to private firms. The bill attracted only one cosponsor and never got a committee hearing. The Outbreak obviously breathed life into his proposed reforms—but just a little. Only four reporters showed up for a briefing he offered to explain the picayune details of his proposed overhaul. (The *summary* of his bill ran to eight pages, single-spaced, with five additional appendices.) Three of the reporters literally ran out of the conference room when word spread that the House Speaker was imploding elsewhere in the Capitol.

The frenetic partisanship came to a temporary halt shortly before two p.m. Eastern Time, as the Chinese Ambassador prepared to give his statement. The major American media outlets (and others around the world) covered the news conference live, giving the Beijing leadership exactly what it had hoped for: an opportunity to speak directly to the American public, without interference from America's politicians or diplomats. They would quickly learn that live news conferences in democratic countries carry risks, as well as benefits.

The President was working the phones on board Air Force One when the Chief of Staff walked into his office. "There's one more thing," she said after he hung up with the Prime Minister of New Zealand.

"You know how much I hate that phrase," he said. "What?"

"Cecelia Dodds," the Chief of Staff answered.

---

*   He had been a tenured member of the Princeton Economics Department before winning his Senate seat. At the time, he was one of only two members of Congress with a Ph.D.

"Oh, for God's sakes, what does she want? I already gave her the Medal of Freedom."

"It's more what she doesn't want," the Chief of Staff said.

"Look, I don't have time for puzzles—" He stopped as it dawned on him what Cecelia Dodds did not want. "She's sick," he said, "and she's refusing Dormigen."

The Chief of Staff nodded yes. "She's in a Seattle hospital."

"*Capellaviridae?*" the President asked.

"I don't think so," the Chief of Staff said. "It's a respiratory infection of some sort. Doesn't matter: she's refusing Dormigen that could be used to save another life."

"*But we haven't run out,*" the President insisted.

"We might," the Chief of Staff replied. "And if we do, she wants there to be one more dose for someone else."

"For real?"

"Have you forgotten the hunger strike?" the Chief of Staff asked. Cecelia Dodds had refused food to force the Senate to ratify an international agreement on climate change. The group of senators holding up the treaty vowed they would not buckle in the face of "the bullying tactics of a washed-up hippie." After seventeen days, during which global opprobrium rained down on them while Cecelia Dodds consumed only water with drops of lemon juice, that is exactly what they did.

"How old is she?" the President asked.

"Seventy-one."

He sighed. "I ran for office to make things better. *I really did.* And now I'm going to be the one who kills Cecelia Dodds." After a moment: "We can't convince her . . ." His voice trailed off because he knew the answer.

Cecelia Dodds did not compromise her principles. She had emerged in the post-Trump era as the nation's most effective voice for social change, someone with a unique ability to bring people together while simultaneously pushing them forward. She was a tiny, innocuous-looking woman with short gray hair. If you were to see her in a bus station—which you might, because she did not own a car— you would instinctively assume she was visiting grandchildren and needed help finding the right departure gate. *Oh, so many people had underestimated her.* Like the CEO of Ringlen Electronics, who made the mistake of appearing with her on a PBS news program after she announced an environmental boycott of their air-conditioning units. "I just don't understand, why can't you invest a few extra dollars per unit to minimize their climate impact?" she asked. That was part of her effectiveness—a rhetorical style that bordered on naïve. She did not yell; she did not level accusations. She buried people with her humility.

"A few dollars per unit adds up very quickly," the CEO explained.

"I have never thought of it that way," she said.

"That doesn't surprise me," the CEO said patronizingly.

"I suppose by the same logic," Cecelia Dodds said, "for just a few extra dollars per unit, consumers can buy a competitor's product that is much better for the environment."

"That's not how I look at it," the CEO replied quickly.

"That doesn't surprise me," she offered.

The exchange was legendary, and also representative of her insistence on the difference between making noise and making a difference. Ringlen stock was down 11 percent before the CEO left the studio. He was fired the following Monday. By Wednesday the company had announced plans for a new line of environmentally friendly air conditioners. And the next week—this was typical, too—she invited the fired CEO to lunch to have a discussion of why she felt so passionate about environmental issues. *It wasn't personal.* The two of them later developed a close personal friendship; the CEO (his views on climate change having evolved) served on one of her nonprofit boards. College campuses were awash with merchandise bearing Cecelia Dodds's hortatory motto: love, share, include, & improve.

When Dodds traveled to Washington, D.C., for the Presidential Medal of Freedom ceremony, she took an Amtrak train from Seattle and then rode to the White House on one of D.C.'s shared bicycles. The President described her that evening as someone who "leads by example like Mahatma Gandhi; forces change like Nelson Mandela; and holds us to account against our own values like Martin Luther King." Now she was in a Seattle hospital in serious condition suffering from an infection that could be treated successfully with a single dose of Dormigen—a dose that she would not accept.

54.

THE STRATEGIST HAD ARRANGED FOR SEVERAL FOCUS GROUPS
to watch the Chinese Ambassador's statement.* He was able to con-
vene reasonably diverse groups in five cities across the country. He
predicted, correctly it would turn out, that public reaction to the
Ambassador's talk would be extremely important in shaping the
President's response. Each of the focus group participants would have
a dial during the talk that he or she could turn to register approval
or disapproval throughout the speech. Zero represented the strongest possible negative reaction; one hundred was the most positive
response. The data were collected and averaged in real time, so the
Strategist would have instantaneous feedback to everything the
Ambassador said, from beginning to end.

The Chinese Ambassador spoke from behind a large wooden desk
at the Chinese Embassy in Washington. He was a middle-aged man
in a nondescript gray suit and blue tie. He looked like an avuncular,
undistinguished Chinese guy who could be a high school chemistry
teacher or the father of your college roommate. He stared intently
into the camera and began, "Good afternoon, people of the United
States of America."

The President was watching the address in the conference room
on Air Force One with his senior advisers. The Secretary of State
said, "Okay, we know the remarks were drafted in Beijing. That's
probably good for us." The others in the room understood her point
without further elaboration. The Chinese Ambassador had been edu-
cated in Britain; he spoke fluent English, albeit with a slight British
accent. He would never have used such an awkward introduction if
he had written the remarks himself, or even if he had had significant
latitude in editing them.

The Strategist was looking down at a laptop computer. "Wow,
they really don't like him. He's at fifteen. That's the lowest I've ever
seen anyone at the beginning of a speech."

---

* There had not been sufficient time to do this before the President's earlier
address to the nation.

"The people of China would like to extend our best wishes to Cecelia Dodds," the Chinese Ambassador continued. "We hope a speedy recovery will be possible."

"That's rich," the Secretary of State muttered. Cecelia Dodds was a persistent critic of Chinese human rights violations.

"Look at the flags," the President said. There was a Chinese flag on the Ambassador's right and a noticeably smaller American flag on his left. Many focus group participants would comment on this slight to America. In fact, it was an accident. The Chinese diplomats were not able to find a suitable American flag in the embassy that morning but felt one should be displayed during the speech, out of respect. A low-level embassy staffer was dispatched to a hardware store to buy an American flag; the fact that it was noticeably smaller than the Chinese flag—and the attendant reaction that caused among American viewers—was the result of the limited choice in flags at the Dupont Circle Ace Hardware. (If the Outbreak had occurred nearer to the Fourth of July, history might have unfolded differently.)

The Chinese Ambassador delivered banal prefatory remarks, long on rhetoric about "our two great nations." The Strategist reported, "They're warming up to him a little. But not much."

When the Ambassador reached the heart of his talk, he spoke without looking down at his prepared text: "China extends to our United States ally a hand of friendship. We are prepared to offer your great nation all the Dormigen necessary to get through this public health crisis. In exchange, we merely ask that the United States treat China with the respect a great nation deserves. The time has come for America's imperial aggressions in the Pacific region to end. The time has come for your President to *return to your country* [my italics added] and pay attention to domestic concerns, rather than meddling in the Chinese sphere of influence."

The Strategist said, "Chinese sphere of influence? I hope they will at least execute the speechwriter. This is awful."

The National Security Adviser interjected, "Did he just suggest that Hawaii is not part of the United States?" This curious feature of the talk was later dissected in minute detail. The Ambassador had clearly declared that the President should return to the United States, even as Air Force One sat in Honolulu. The officials who drafted the speech in Beijing knew that the President was in Hawaii. Even the most insular among them was aware that Hawaii is part of the United States. So what happened? The most likely explanation is a translation error—that what was intended to be "return to the mainland" or "return to the continent" was somehow mistranslated as "return to your country." We are not privy to any Chinese account of what happened. In any event, this choice of language turned out to have monumental significance, since, as the National Security Adviser realized in the moment, the speech implied that Hawaii is not part of the United States. What might have passed for an innocent mistake was perceived more menacingly because of the language about a "Chinese sphere of influence" in the Pacific. And then there is Pearl Harbor. The sad reality is that a shockingly high proportion of Americans believe that China played some role in the attack on Pearl Harbor. This point came up in four of the Strategist's five focus groups, the most common belief being that China and Japan had been allies during World War II and had collaborated to attack Pearl Harbor.

The Chinese Ambassador's speech contained no specifics in terms of what would be asked of the U.S. in exchange for the Dormigen, though Americans watching clearly perceived that the cost would be significant. The phrase "holding us hostage" came up repeatedly in the focus groups, along with "bullying" and "taking advantage of our crisis." The Chinese Ambassador concluded his remarks by saying that he would personally deliver a new "China-America Friendship Agreement" to the White House. He finished with two lines that would loom large over the next twenty-four hours. Perhaps these two sentences were a gratuitous flourish added by a speechwriter. Maybe they were dictated by President Xing, who was supposedly a huge fan of American westerns. In any event, the Chinese Ambassador stared intently into the camera and said, "Your president has a decision to make. He must refuel his plane and fly west or east."

As the speech finished, the Strategist stared at his laptop. "He never got above twenty-one. I've never seen numbers that low. Never. I worked on the defense team for a guy who shot three cops in Boston. That guy's testimony got to twenty-three. The Ambassador finished at seven. *Seven!*" Focus groups intensely disliked the final two lines of the speech because they were dismissive of the democratic process. The language was clearly drafted by someone with an autocratic mind-set. While it was technically true that the President alone could decide whether Air Force One flew on to Australia or turned back for Washington, the American public—not to mention Congress—was not keen on being told that they had no say in the matter. The whole speech was an unmitigated disaster, but the "west or east" challenge turned out to be particularly significant.

55.

THE CHIEF OF STAFF WAS TRYING TO GET THE PRESIDENT TO go to sleep, if only for a few hours. The window between the Chinese Ambassador's speech and his delivery of the so-called "Friendship Agreement" to the White House provided a short stretch during which the President might nap. However, the Australian Prime Minister had been trying to reach him since the crisis broke and she was patched through to Air Force One. The President took the call in his private cabin; the Secretary of State and the National Security Adviser joined him, along with a junior aide to take notes. "Mr. President, I am deeply sorry to hear about the public health crisis," the Australian Prime Minister began. "I appreciate the dilemma this has created for you." Her political fortunes were tied up in the South China Sea Agreement, which was extremely popular in Australia, both because of its collective security arrangements and also because it curbed Chinese overfishing and other behaviors that were harming Australian commercial interests.

"I appreciate your generous gift of Dormigen," the President said.

The obvious question, of course, was what to do about the South China Sea Agreement. The Australian Prime Minister said that there would be no problem pushing back the signing ceremony for several weeks, or even a month if necessary. She explained, "Obviously our primary concern is that the treaty remain intact with the U.S. as a signatory."

"We have every intention of honoring that agreement," the President said.

The Secretary of State added, "We fully understand how important this treaty is to the future of the Pacific region and we are doing everything we can to deal with this situation without compromising our long-term interests."

The Australian Prime Minister replied, "I think we all know the strings that will be attached to the Chinese Dormigen offer."

"Yes," the Secretary of State acknowledged.

The President said, "That bit about flying 'east or west' was a nice touch, huh?"

"How has the speech been received?" the Australian Prime Minister asked.

"So far it appears to be a complete bomb," the President said. "The Chinese Ambassador was perceived as bullying and opportunistic."

"I'm not surprised. Still, it's going to be very hard to turn down the Chinese offer if it means American lives will be lost."

"We're anticipating the Chinese will ask for the moon," the National Security Adviser interjected. "Paradoxically, that could make our decision easier."

"But you have no hint of the specifics?" the Australian Prime Minister asked.

"Not yet," the President said. In fact, the U.S. had intercepted a large volume of communications between Beijing and the Chinese Embassy in Washington, most of which suggested that China would demand a near-complete withdrawal of U.S. forces in South Korea, Japan, and elsewhere in the region.

The Australian Prime Minister said, "While respecting the delicacy of your situation, what I am hoping to hear, Mr. President, is that you are still committed to the South China Sea Agreement. Might it be possible for you to make a public statement to that effect, even if it were conditional on the contents of the China offer?"

"Let's draft something," the President said, looking to the Secretary of State, who nodded agreement.

"That's great to hear, Mr. President," the Prime Minister said. "As I said at the outset of the call, the timing of when we sign the agreement is less important than your firm commitment to it."

"Of course," the President said. "Can we speak privately for a minute?" This was not unusual. The business of the call having been accomplished, the two leaders would be able to talk without aides listening in. We know that the President and the Australian Prime Minister spoke for roughly another three minutes. There is no record of what was said, and both leaders have been strikingly reticent about the details. Based on subsequent events, however, we have a pretty good idea what the President proposed.

PART 6

NATURE FIGHTS BACK

56.

M Y MEDIA DUTIES WERE FINISHED FOR THE TIME BEING.
The NIH Director had summoned me back to the NIH offices, where
the scientific effort to understand *Capellaviridae* had been massively
bulked up once the crisis became public. Tie Guy was pursuing the
notion that efforts to eradicate the North American dust mite had
somehow created a new kind of toxicity. He had assembled a team of
organic chemists to look at whether the dust mites that survived the
pyrethrin-based insecticides might use *Capellaviridae* to metabolize
the poison in a way that makes it harmful to humans. "What do the
chemists think?" I asked him when I arrived at the NIH offices.

"They're skeptical," he said.

"Why?"

"Because there is no evidence to support the theory. The people
who get sick don't test positive for any form of pyrethrin. Also, there
is no obvious explanation for how a virus can turn a compound that
is nontoxic for humans into something deadly."

"A dead end?" I said.

"I don't think so," Tie Guy insisted. "I went back and looked
at the data again. This connection between trying to eradicate dust
mites and the virulent form of *Capellaviridae* holds up. So does that
other strange pattern we saw: when people get sick with *Capellaviridae* in areas where the North American dust mite is *not* endemic,

those people have almost always moved from a region where it is endemic."

"Moving away from an area where the virus is common is more likely to make you sick than staying there?" I said, trying to make sense of what he was saying. I was operating on relatively little sleep.

"Yeah, how weird is that?" Tie Guy said. "It's all ass-backwards. The safest place to be is an area with no North American dust mites and no *Capellaviridae*. No surprise there. But the next-best place to be is an area where dust mites and *Capellaviridae* are common and there has been no widespread extermination effort."

I tried to finish his thought: "And you are most at risk of *Capellaviridae* turning virulent if you are in an area where you try to wipe it out—"

"Where people are trying to wipe out the dust mite, the carrier, but yes."

I continued, "And someone would be at risk if they live in an area with *Capellaviridae* and then move away."

"Yes, but you're only at risk if you move to an area without it. If you move to another area where the North American dust mite and *Capellaviridae* are endemic, you'll be fine."

"How is that possible?" I asked, completely flummoxed.

"You tell me. I'm just a data guy. Ask these people," he said, motioning to the throng of activity all around us. There were easily twice as many people on the floor as there had been on my earlier visits. A frenetic pace had replaced the complacency that had been so disorienting before the Outbreak became public. Tie Guy continued, "There's something to this, right?"

"It's weird."

"Nature fights back, that's what it's telling me," he insisted.

"How so?" I asked. If I had had more sleep, maybe it would have been more obvious to me.

"Because the virus, or maybe the dust mite, or maybe both— they're saying, 'Don't get rid of me. If you do, you'll pay a price.'"

"That would be unprecedented," I said.

"So was AIDS," Tie Guy replied. "Evolution does some pretty crazy things."

"You may be right," I said. "I just don't know how or why."

Back in Hawaii, the President and his senior staff had finally found some moments of calm as they awaited the Chinese offer. Air Force One was refueled, but the President did not want to be caught airborne again if he needed to make a public statement in response to the Chinese move. The Chinese Ambassador's "high noon" challenge regarding the flight path of the President's plane, east or west, had also imbued the next takeoff with added significance. An enormous bank of cameras was parked on the runway. Before settling into his cabin for a short nap, the President phoned Cecelia Dodds in her Seattle hospital room. "I'm not taking the medicine!" she said when she picked up the phone. There was warmth in her voice but also firmness.

"That's not a battle I'm going to win," the President said honestly. "I want you to know that the Chinese are likely to offer onerous terms—"

"I understand completely," Cecelia Dodds said emphatically. "Please don't think for a minute that I'm trying to pressure you to take a bad deal. *Please, no.* It's just that I'm seventy-one, and if there is not enough Dormigen, then someone else should have it."

"Seventy-one is not that old," the President said.

"No," she agreed. "No, it's not."

"What if I were to ask you to accept the Dormigen as a personal favor to me?" the President asked sincerely.

"Mr. President, if you can promise me that we are not going to run out—that no American will die for lack of Dormigen—then of course I'll take it. I'm not trying to make this situation harder for you. I have a lot to live for . . . two beautiful granddaughters, so much work left to be done." The President did not answer. After some time, Cecelia Dodds continued, "Can you make me that promise?"

"I'm afraid I can't," the President said. Several hours later Cecelia Dodds was moved to intensive care.

There was no calm at the NIH offices. The scientists were unhappy that the President had been so sanguine in his remarks about the number of deaths if the Dormigen stocks were depleted. Not only had he focused on the lower bound of what the NIH model was predicting in terms of fatalities, but the model itself had now been revised in the other direction. Evidence of the widespread Dormigen pilferage had filtered back to the data analysts; they were putting numbers against the quantity of Dormigen that had gone missing, which included the tricky task of trying to figure out where the stolen Dormigen would ultimately end up (wasted or helping people who needed it). The best-case scenario for incremental fatalities no longer included "zero." It had climbed to forty-five thousand. Meanwhile, the added uncertainty had broadened the range of possible outcomes, so the worst-case scenario was now a hundred and ninety-five thousand deaths. The NIH staff had watched the Chinese Ambassador's remarks; they were feeling the weight of the President's dilemma.

I apologized to the NIH Director for being late. "Don't worry about it. I think you're going to be impressed," she said, ushering me into a small conference room, where five binders of different colors were laid out neatly on the table. "This can be your workspace." She pointed at the colored binders. "Those are summaries of the work done so far by each of the working groups: *Capellaviridae*; the North American dust mite; possible antidotes; alternative treatments to Dormigen. The organic chemists put together the red one, but they've just started." The work product was impressive. Once again I found myself wondering if we had made an egregious error in keeping the Outbreak secret. If the great minds here had spent less time eating cupcakes in those early days, might we now be a week ahead? "I'll let you peruse those," the NIH Director said. "Each one has a summary, so you don't have to wade into the details. We have a meeting of all the teams in the big conference room in about forty-five minutes. We're trying to meet every six hours, around the clock."

The Director left me to the colored binders. I sat down and picked up the one closest to me: green. The summary described the recommended protocol for treating *Capellaviridae* in the absence of Dormigen: fluids, rest, conventional antibiotics to deal with any secondary infection. I had little to add in this realm, so I set the binder aside. I picked up the blue binder next: *Capellaviridae*. The report documented everything the team had learned about the virus, which was an impressive amount in such a short time. The summary included three lines in bold text that caught my eye: **Capellaviridae bears a striking resemblance to strains of the influenza virus. Some of our scientists, unaware of what they were looking at, assumed they** were examining a historic strain of influenza. Not surprisingly, *Capellaviridae* acts on the body in nearly identical fashion to the more virulent strains of influenza. This explained what I had just read in the green binder, namely that without Dormigen *Capellaviridae* should be treated like a bad case of the flu. It also explained the likely fatality rate (broadly comparable to a serious flu). Creating a vaccine specific to *Capellaviridae* would be a straightforward task, but like Dormigen, a flu-type vaccine takes time to cultivate. Time was the one thing we did not have.

Okay, I thought, Capellaviridae *is really just a nasty form of the flu that is somehow, and for some reason, passed to humans by the bite of a dust mite.* I picked up the yellow binder: everything we now knew about *Dermatophagoides mensfarinae*, the North American dust mite. There was even a highly magnified photo of the nasty-looking critter on the cover page. Again, I perused the summary. The North American dust mite is different from other common dust mites primarily in that it bites humans. Other mites feed off human detritus, such as dead skin that has been sloughed off. The North American dust mite feeds off live skin and blood, making a tiny, painless bite that causes a modest allergic reaction in some people. The *Dermatophagoides mensfarinae* research group was operating on the assumption that there is some evolutionary advantage to being able to feed on live skin and blood. They estimated that this mutation in the species had taken place eight thousand to ten thousand years earlier, coinciding with the first modestly dense human settlements in North America.

That made sense. When humans started living in closer proximity to one another, this particular dust mite developed an ability to feed directly off skin and blood, rather than waiting around for discarded dead cells. I was about to pick up the black binder when the door to the conference room opened and a young woman about my age looked into the room. She was petite, with straight brown hair that hung to her shoulders. "Sorry," she said sheepishly. I looked up, waiting for some explanation. She said nothing but continued to linger in the doorway, as if deciding what to do next.

"Can I help you?" I asked, genuinely perplexed.

"Someone told me you had Professor Huke," she said. "I'm really sorry to bother you, with all that's going on."

"How do you know Professor Huke?" I asked. And then: "Please come in."

She came into the conference room and stood on the other side of the table. I motioned to a seat, but she remained standing. "I took his class at Dartmouth," she said. "Two of his classes, actually."

"And what are you doing now?" I asked.

"I just finished a graduate program in public health. I'm doing a fellowship at the CDC. They sent me over here when the crisis broke—an all-hands-on-deck kind of thing."

"I went to see him—Huke," I said. "I went back to Hanover to ask him about this."

"What did he say?"

"It was before everything was public, so he thought I was just working on some academic puzzle. He told me to pretend it was a question on a midterm exam."

"Seems like it should at least be the final exam," she said.

I laughed. "Yes, that's true. He said the usual things: think like a virus, figure out the evolutionary advantage, that kind of stuff."

"And?"

"And it doesn't make any sense. We have a relatively benign virus that kills its host to no obvious advantage."

"I really didn't mean to bother you," she said, turning to go. "It just seemed too crazy: two Huke grads in the middle of this virus crisis. I'll let you get back to what you were doing."

"If you really want to help," I said, causing her to pause in the doorway, "work through this with me." I pointed at the binders. "It's not crazy to think of this like a Huke final exam. I feel like everything I need to know is right there. I just can't make sense of it. My brain's in a fog."

"When was the last time you slept?" she asked, looking at me in a way that reminded me of the toll the morning had taken. My suit was still wrinkled from the rain. I had the remnants of television makeup on my neck and collar.

"A couple hours last night," I offered.

"You know what the research says."

"The research on what?"

"On how the brain works," she said. "You can stare at that table all afternoon. You'd be better off taking a walk and not thinking about it for a while."

"Now's not really a great time for a walk," I said with a hint of impatience.

She came right back at me. "Well, do you want people to think you're working hard in this little room, or do you want to figure out the puzzle?"

Her name was Jenna. She had her Ph.D. from the Harvard School of Public Health and we did end up going for a walk. Jenna was thoughtful and smart. I have often wondered what would have happened if the loaner employee from the CDC who opened the door and said he had taken Huke's course had been some overweight guy with a poorly trimmed beard and bad teeth. "That's really cool," I would have said, "but now is not a great time." Instead, I was instantly attracted to Jenna and I wanted her to sit down in that conference room with me. I will spare you the rest of our origin story, but it does play a role in this larger narrative. What if Jenna were not so cute? I still ask her that sometimes: "What if you were a hairy guy who smelled bad? What if we had not gone on that walk?"

57.

THE CHINESE AMBASSADOR LEFT THE EMBASSY FOR THE White House shortly after two Eastern Time. The Washington police offered his black sedan an escort. The press corps, who had been camped outside the embassy, scrambled into vehicles to follow him, creating a train of vehicles that looked like a funeral procession. The President and senior advisers watched the live coverage from the conference room on Air Force One. As the Ambassador's sedan made its way slowly through Washington traffic, the Strategist said, "He could have just e-mailed the fucking thing."

The U.S. intelligence agencies had gathered a great deal of raw information on the Chinese deliberations around their proposal. There were sharp disagreements within the Chinese leadership over what the offer ought to be, making it difficult for U.S. analysts to discern which faction would prevail. As Yale historian Mason Freeman has explained in his excellent book on the subject, the Outbreak came at a time of political intrigue within the Chinese leadership. President Xing was being challenged from within by a group of hard-liners, including some of the top military leaders, who were urging him to take a more aggressive stance in Southeast Asia. (The use of the phrase "sphere of influence" in the Ambassador's remarks, however inelegant it may have felt to the American audience, was meant for Beijing listeners.) The hard-liners considered the Outbreak a heaven-sent opportunity for China to cement its role as a superpower on par with the United States—a role that would be severely hampered by the South China Sea Agreement.

A separate faction within the Chinese leadership, the "pragmatists," as U.S. intelligence analysts would come to call them, were worried that if the Dormigen terms were too onerous, the U.S. leadership would balk at the deal. (When the President had declared in his speech that morning that the nation might get through the Outbreak without any incremental deaths, it had seriously strengthened the hand of the pragmatists.) Many of the pragmatists had spent significant time in the United States, often as university students. They recognized the likely backlash that would result from any diplomatic offer that felt extortionate to the American public. Nobody likes to be charged $25 for a bottle of water, even in the desert. A cursory search of the psychology literature would have alerted the Beijing bureaucrats to the fact that humans have a profound aversion to deals they perceive to be grossly unfair, and Americans can be a sanctimonious bunch—even relative to other humans on the planet.

Chinese intelligence operatives were reporting back to Beijing that the American President's senior foreign policy advisers were pressuring him to stick with the South China Sea Agreement. Much of this information was deliberately leaked to the Chinese. The American intelligence agencies did not know about the power struggle going on around President Xing. However, they did assume, correctly it would turn out, that making the U.S. President appear willing to accept large numbers of American casualties would strengthen his bargaining position with the Chinese government.

In the end, the hard-liners in Beijing won out, mostly for reasons to do with Chinese domestic politics. President Xing was acutely aware of the backlash that the whiff of Chinese opportunism might create among the American public. (Because of his fondness for American westerns, he considered himself somewhat of an expert on the American psyche.) He had also spent more than five years in the U.S. getting his doctorate in engineering at MIT. His understanding of American public opinion was far more sophisticated than that of the generals urging him to take maximum advantage of the Dormigen shortage. But Xing did not feel he had a sufficiently strong grasp on power to face down the military establishment, who were united on this issue. Although President Xing has never spoken publicly about his decision regarding the contents of the "Friendship Agreement," some advisers have since intimated that he knew it was likely to be rejected. To solidify his grasp on power, President Xing gave the military hard-liners what they wanted, even as he knew they were making a major strategic blunder.

The Chinese Ambassador's black sedan pulled into the West Gate of the White House. On the U.S. end, there had been a scramble to determine who would receive the document. The Secretary of State and the National Security Adviser were in Hawaii with the President. The Vice President was ultimately designated to meet the Ambassador as he arrived. There was a brief handshake, after which the Chinese Ambassador handed over a black binder. The Vice President turned abruptly and walked back into the White House, leaving the Chinese Ambassador standing somewhat awkwardly near his car. There was no deliberate snub intended. Rather, the Vice President was under strict instructions to have the document scanned and distributed as quickly as possible. As the Strategist had sardonically observed, it would have been much easier if the Chinese had e-mailed an electronic version.

On Air Force One, the President and his senior advisers waited anxiously as the Chinese proposal was printed and copied. Only a few minutes after the awkward handoff at the White House, a State Department aide hustled into the conference room with multiple copies, still warm. She passed them around the table; the principals began to read. The Strategist was the first to speak, to no one in particular: "You've got to be kidding me."

The Secretary of State said, "This is good. This is good for us."

"It does make the decision easier," the President replied. After just a few pages, it was clear that the Chinese "Friendship Agreement" sought to neuter the entire American presence in East Asia. There were several fluffy paragraphs about providing Dormigen in America's time of need, but then the document changed tone entirely, listing demand after demand. The United States would have to withdraw immediately from the South China Sea Agreement and "disavow any such aggressive collective agreements in the region for a period of twenty years."

"We knew they were going to make us scrap South China Sea," the Chief of Staff said.

"Keep reading," the President said. The agreement demanded that the United States withdraw all troops from South Korea and Japan within eighteen months. The U.S. would have to pledge "not to meddle in domestic Chinese decisions affecting economic development."

"I don't even know what that means. What does that mean?" the Communications Director asked.

The President answered, "That means no environmental restrictions, no leaning on them for trading in endangered species. It's a catch-all for anytime we try to make them behave like responsible members of the global community."

"Should I start drafting a statement?" the Communications Director asked.

"Let me finish reading," the President said.

The Strategist blurted out, "Oh, my God, this is gold. Check out page thirteen, last paragraph."

The Communications Director flipped several pages ahead and began to read: "'The United States will double the number of diplomatic license plates granted to the Chinese mission at the United Nations . . .'" He paused, incredulous. "They're asking for more parking permits?"

In fact, yes. As Mason Freeman's research has subsequently uncovered, the Chinese leadership in Beijing settled their disagreements over the contents of the document by including everything—not just parking issues at the UN, but also student visas, banking regulations, and even two paragraphs on the price American zoos would have to pay to breed Chinese pandas. Every diplomatic grievance the Chinese government had broached in the previous decade found its way into the "Friendship Agreement."

"Is this serious?" the Chief of Staff asked.

The President replied, "They think they're holding all the cards. They've gone all in."

"But parking permits?" the Strategist said.

The Secretary of State offered the best analysis of the situation in that moment. She explained, "They perceive democracy to be a weakness. They can't imagine that we'll say no. They feel democracy forces leaders to make shortsighted decisions, that we have no choice but to do whatever it takes to get the Dormigen. When you have maximum leverage, why not ask for the moon? Worst case, we negotiate and they get most of what they want."

"They don't think we'll let anyone die," the President said.

"And?" the Strategist asked, inviting the President to verbalize what everyone in the room knew was going to be his decision.

"We can't sign this," the President said emphatically.

"I'll draft a statement," the Communications Director said.

"We should reflect on this," the Chief of Staff said. "Let's take a few minutes just to consider our options."

"There's nothing to think about," the President said.

"Still," the Chief of Staff implored. "Maybe we should go around the table?"

"I agree," the Secretary of State said. "I'll go first. Mr. President, I appreciate what we are asking you to do here. I don't take that lightly. I think we need to reframe our thinking. As awful as it is that we may come up short on Dormigen   and that lives may be lost as a result—I would ask you to think about this situation differently. If China made this declaration unilaterally, if they took actions to expel us from East Asia, we would not let those actions stand. We would respond militarily, if necessary."

"Probably not to the parking thing," the Strategist said. The Secretary of State stared at him malevolently, furious at the interruption (and relatively unaccustomed to his attempts at irreverent humor). Others in the room suppressed smiles.

The Secretary of State continued, "If the military came to you and said, 'We think we can repel this aggression successfully, but here are the projections for casualties,' you would find the numbers we are looking at to be an acceptable cost for defending our vital interests."

"I understand the logic," the President said noncommittally. He looked to the National Security Adviser.

"I agree with the Secretary," the National Security Adviser said. "If they asked only that we walk away from the South China Sea Agreement, or postpone it, then maybe it would be a harder decision, though if I'm being honest, even that would be a dangerous capitulation. But withdrawing all troops from East Asia? From a national security standpoint, I think there is only one defensible course of action here."

"What's the most appropriate historical comparison?" the President asked. "Because this is not Pearl Harbor. There is no obvious aggression here that I'm asking Americans to repel."

"Probably Kennedy and West Berlin," the National Security Adviser offered. "The East Germans started building the Wall. If Kennedy didn't save West Berlin with the airlift, it would have been a major capitulation to the Soviets."

"There wouldn't have been major casualties, even if it went wrong," the President said. "He wasn't asking Americans to accept thousands and thousands of lost lives."

"That's right," the National Security Adviser said. "The Cuban Missile Crisis might be more apt. Kennedy had to decide if the U.S. could tolerate Soviet missiles in Cuba. In facing down the Soviets, he was risking war. Maybe nuclear war."

The President nodded in agreement. "What's the best case for accepting the agreement?" he asked the room.

"For taking the Chinese Dormigen?" the Chief of Staff asked, trying to clarify what he was asking.

The Strategist, always keen to take any side of any issue, said, "A lot of Americans may die. You have access to the medicine that will save them. That's your first responsibility, to protect the country."

"Isn't that what Cecelia Dodds is telling us?" the President asked. "It's hard to watch people die when they could be saved. There's something particularly terrible about that."

"Yes," the Chief of Staff agreed softly. "But she did tell you to stand firm with the Chinese."

"While simultaneously reminding us of the price we'll pay," the President replied. "Maybe thousands and thousands of times over. All preventable."

The National Security Adviser said, "Well, if I'm playing devil's advocate, I would argue that America could tolerate a lower profile in East Asia. We could cede that sphere of influence to China without meaningfully impacting our quality of life. The are a lot of costs associated with being the world's only democratic superpower."

The President nodded to acknowledge the thought without betraying any obvious reaction. "Britain gave up its empire," he said.

The Secretary of State interjected, "But not to the Soviet Union. Or to China. There's a difference between acceding to independence movements and acceding to the demands of a nondemocratic power whose interests are very different from our own."

"There are costs to leaving the world without a democratic super-power," the President said.

"That's right," the Secretary of State agreed.

The Chief of Staff asked, "Who's to say we can't take the Dormigen and then ignore the agreement? Once we have the Dormigen, we don't have to withdraw our troops from South Korea and Japan. Yes, they have the leverage now, but once we have the Dormigen that leverage goes away. Besides, an agreement made under duress, which this clearly is, is not legally binding."

"You didn't read page nineteen," the Strategist said.

The Chief of Staff flipped through the document in front of her. After a moment she said, "Clearly I was not the only person who had that thought." The Agreement stipulated that the U.S. would post a bond of some sort—nearly $500 billion in Treasury securities, along with the "deed" to assorted U.S. possessions in the Pacific, including Guam.

The Strategist said, "If we go back on our word, they get Guam. It's not exactly Pearl Harbor, but close."

The President, ignoring the comment, said, "Technically this is not duress. The Chinese government is offering us something that we are free to refuse. We can always walk away from the agreement."

"This is just their opening offer," the National Security Adviser offered.

"We don't have a lot of time," the President replied. "In any event, it doesn't change our response if we think this is a bad deal. The more forcefully we repudiate what's on the table, the more leverage we have to negotiate something better."

"Is there any part of this, other than the UN parking, that we would be likely to agree to?" the Secretary of State asked the room.

The Communications Director interjected, "We probably don't have too long before the document gets leaked to the press. Shall I draft a statement? Even if we haven't come to agreement here, I can say something about how we are weighing—"

"No," the President said sharply.

"No statement, or no to the idea of being noncommittal?" the Communications Director asked.

"No statement. I'd like to speak with the Majority Leader," the President instructed. "As soon as he's on the line, I want the room." The advisers began filing out of the conference room so that the President could speak with the Majority Leader in private. "We should just release the agreement," the President added.

"Leak it?" the Communications Director asked.

"Just release it to the press."

"And what kind of statement should we make?"

"None."

"I don't understand," the Communications Director said.

"Just make the agreement public," the President said firmly. "Release it to the press. The American people should know what the Chinese government is asking in exchange for the Dormigen."

"With respect, sir, we should try to put our own spin on this."

"What is there to spin? It speaks for itself."

The Communications Director looked around the room, hoping to find some nonverbal support for his case. Like all the President's senior advisers, he was expected to walk a fine line between offering candid advice and carrying out the President's orders. "This is our only chance to frame the story," he said.

"Take the document to the back of the plane and hand it to a reporter," the President said.

The Communications Director picked up a spare copy of the agreement from the conference table but did not move toward the door, prompting the Strategist to interject, "The reporters are the cranky, poorly dressed people in the last cabin."

The Chief of Staff, seeking to ameliorate the tension, said, "Give it to the AP correspondent. She'll share it with the press pool."

The Communications Director continued to plead his case: "Maybe we do a photo op of some sort, with the President reading the document—"

"Just release it," the President said angrily. "Don't make me walk it back there myself."

One can second-guess a lot of the decisions made during the Outbreak, from the President on down, but this moment suggests to me that there is such a thing as political talent—just like athletic talent, or entrepreneurial instinct, or acting ability. I do not know if people are born with political talent, or if they acquire it through hard work and experience, or perhaps both. I do know that the President was elected student body president when he was in high school. He was elected editor of the *Law Review* at the University of Virginia. If one counts every election and reelection he participated in—from high school to the White House—there were sixteen times when he got more votes than the next man or woman (and two times when he did not, which might teach the more valuable lessons). As much as we despise politicians, the President had something that his Chinese counterparts did not: a feel for voters.

58.

IT TOOK A FEW MINUTES TO CONNECT THE PRESIDENT WITH the Senate Majority Leader, who had been given a copy of the "Friendship Agreement" immediately after the Chinese Ambassador delivered it. "How are you doing, Mr. President?" the Majority Leader asked.

"I've had more enjoyable trips to Hawaii," the President said. "What do you think of the Chinese offer?"

"I'm in shock," the Majority Leader said. "Do they really expect us to accept this?"

"It's an opening bid," the President replied.

"Yes, but they've completely ceded the moral high ground. Did you see that thing about the UN parking? They come across as completely opportunistic, predatory even."

"That was my reaction," the President said.

"Are you going to make a counteroffer?" the Majority Leader asked.

"What do you think?"

"I don't think there is a deal to be had. Never mind troops in Korea and Japan, at a minimum they are going to ask us to walk away from the South China Sea Agreement."

"Yes," the President agreed.

"That leaves us in a tough spot."

"The NIH has raised their fatality projections because of all the Dormigen that's gone missing," the President reminded him.

"If you turn away the Chinese offer, you'll have my complete support," the Majority Leader assured him. "I want you to know that. I'm confident I can get the Senate behind whatever you decide."

"I don't care about the Senate, to be honest," the President replied. "Could you sell it to a Rotary Club?" The President had enormous respect for the Majority Leader's emotional connection to Main Street. The President's senior advisers could speak compellingly of the Berlin Airlift and the Cuban Missile Crisis. The Majority Leader could connect with Americans who had never heard of the Berlin Airlift and had only a vague sense of how the Cuban Missile Crisis played out. That was why the President called him first.

There was a pause as the Majority Leader considered the question. "This situation with Cecelia Dodds, that makes it harder. They moved her to intensive care, you know."

"Yes," the President acknowledged.

"It reminds people of the reality. If we have to go to some kind of rationing . . . shit. A lot of people are imagining someone they love in that ICU, not able to get the pill that would send them home healthy." There was a brief silence during which the President did not respond. The Majority Leader continued, "On the other hand, I think the Chinese have made it easier for us. This offer they've made says a lot about their designs in the region. If you were to give in to them, it would feel like appeasement."

"Yes, but when people start dying in hospitals because there's no

Dormigen, is anyone going to care about troops in South Korea?" the President asked.

"I don't think that's the right way of looking at this," the Majority Leader said. "You can't make it about South Korea or carbon emissions or overfishing or any of that other wonky stuff. I can't sell any of that at a Rotary meeting. I can't justify Americans dying because we're trying to play policeman around the world."

"Okay," the President said, inviting him to continue.

"But nobody likes a bully. Nobody likes to be taken advantage of. Most Americans know enough history to appreciate that there are good guys and there are bad guys and that you can't let the bad guys get away with doing bad things. You've got to stand up to them."

"I need to make this about standing up to China," the President said.

"I think that's right," the Majority Leader affirmed. "When the United States needed medical help, the Chinese leadership made a grab for power. It's like someone who knows you're at the hospital visiting your sick wife, so they break into your house."

"But they haven't violated any laws," the President pointed out. "They're not actually doing anything wrong, other than driving a hard bargain. Isn't that what diplomacy is about? I don't think the analogy works."

"Then find a different one," the Majority Leader said quickly. "How about this: You need heart medicine to keep you alive. One week you come up a little short and you can't afford it. Your rich neighbor comes over to your house and says, 'Sure, I'll spot you the money for your medicine. Just let me fuck your wife.' How about that?"

"I'm not sure that would work with a Rotary Club."

"If you fix the language, it would work real well. People get that."

"Did you watch the Chinese Ambassador's remarks?" the President asked.

"Yes. He made the whole situation seem like some kind of showdown—that whole flying east or west thing."

"That language came from Beijing."

"I assumed as much."

The President said, "I spoke to the Australian Prime Minister. She's worried we'll ditch our commitments to the region."

"Of course she is."

There was a long silence. As the Majority Leader would later describe it, he waited patiently for the President to steer the conversation. Eventually the President said, "Let me bounce an idea off you."

59.

JENNA PERSUADED ME TO TAKE A WALK, TO GET OUT OF THE NIH building and clear my head. I had been awake since before dawn; I had not had enough sleep in the week before that. "Let's see a movie," she offered.

"I can't do that," I said quickly. "It feels totally wrong."

"You're not going to figure this out by grinding away," she implored. "That's not how inspiration works. What you should do is go home and sleep for twelve hours."

It was late afternoon and the spring day was turning cool. We did not plan where we would walk, but we headed toward the Capitol Mall, which felt like a logical place to go. The cherry blossoms were past their peak—they came early that year—but the view was still beautiful. Even in my most cynical moments, I appreciated the majesty of the Capitol, the White House, and the monuments in between. I had never taken the time to explore the city properly as a tourist, but I did pause on occasion to reflect on whatever monument or historical site I happened to wander past. Even on my busiest, most self-absorbed days, I could not rush by the Vietnam Memorial without giving some thought to the names on the wall, and, by extension, to the decisions that got them there. I was always affected by the mementos left at the base of the wall: a single boot, or a can of Pabst beer, or a Chicago Cubs hat—mundane objects that clearly had enormous significance for those who had taken the time to leave them behind.

One day some months earlier I had accidentally shown up for a meeting at a Starbucks near the Mall an hour early. There was no sense in heading back to my office, so I took advantage of the found time to walk through the Roosevelt Memorial, wondering how the man was able to confront the unique challenges of the Great Depression and World War II. How might the U.S. have fared with lesser leadership? With someone who lacked FDR's remarkable ability to reach and persuade the American people? Sometimes I wondered if the tourists—guidebooks in hand, checking off site after site— were really processing what they were seeing. Never mind the dates or the height of the sculpture or the other details that can get in the way of really thinking about FDR. The whole system had been under assault. Some really smart people had given up on capitalism, attracted by the false allure of communism. Another group of smart people were ready to ditch the untidiness of democracy for the efficiency they were seeing in Italy and Germany. How did FDR get out of bed in the morning? And by that, I do not mean anything to do with his paralysis, because to focus too much on the fact that he was in a wheelchair is to miss the essence of what really made him so extraordinary.

Jenna and I sat on a bench in the shade with a nice view of the Washington Monument. I was struck by the sense of normalcy that was returning to the city, barely twelve hours after the first news of the Outbreak had gone public. It was as if the public, unable to see any obvious manifestation of a crisis, began to assume that things must not be so bad. Shortly after we sat down, a Chinese tour group walked loudly by, following a guide carrying a large orange umbrella. Even in the moment, I appreciated the irony. I looked at my phone, where the first details of the Chinese offer were being reported. Jenna said, "Twenty minutes."

"Twenty minutes what?" I asked.

"You've got twenty minutes to think and talk about *Capellaviridae*. After that, give your mind a break."

"The White House just released the details of the Chinese Dormigen offer," I said.

"And?"

"It's even more unreasonable than we expected," I said, reading the first stories as they appeared. News organizations were rushing to get out their own versions of the story, but the "Friendship Agreement" was long enough that it required time to read and digest thoroughly. As a result, minutes after the Communications Director walked copies of the document to the back of Air Force One, media outlets began releasing details in bursts. The Associated Press was first, just three minutes after getting the report, posting: "Chinese Government Issues Demands for Dormigen." Bloomberg followed shortly thereafter with more specifics: "Beijing: Ditch South China Sea Agreement, Withdraw from 'Chinese Sphere of Influence.'" The *New York Times* and other publications posted the whole agreement to their sites. The public immediately fixated on the incongruity of Beijing demanding a complete withdrawal of U.S. troops from the region *and* more parking permits at the UN. The pettiness of the latter somehow threw the sacrifice of the former into sharper relief.

Jenna was reading from my screen. "I assume the President's not going to accept that," she said.

"He's going to make a statement in forty-five minutes."

"Okay, then you get an hour to think about *Capellaviridae*."

"How about if I think about it for the rest of the day, if I promise to get ten hours of sleep?" I pleaded.

"That's probably better."

"So here's what I'm thinking," I began. "The places where people are getting sick from *Capellaviridae* are the places where there have been intensive efforts to get rid of the North American dust mite."

"Right."

"And *Capellaviridae* is also prone to turn virulent when people move away from a region where dust mites are endemic to one where they are not."

"Yes."

"That's odd, right?" I asked. Jenna nodded and I continued. "If you strip away everything else we think we know, that's the bit that feels strangest. The dust mite is the vector, but for some reason once you are carrying *Capellaviridae*, you are better off if there are still dust mites around."

"It could be just some kind of statistical aberration," Jenna offered.

"Maybe," I said skeptically, my voice trailing off as ideas bounced around. "Okay, there are three crazy things about lurking viruses that we can't explain."

"And they are?"

"First, the virus infects humans for no particular reason. Humans don't spread it, so there is no obvious advantage to the virus from infecting humans."

"Okay."

"Second, the virus is benign most of the time, then suddenly virulent, for no obvious reason."

"Right. And third?"

"The virus is somehow more likely to be benign when the vector—the dust mite—is still present."

"None of it makes any sense," Jenna said.

"Maybe they make sense together," I suggested. "That's the Huke final exam question: How do these things make sense together?"

Jenna laughed. "Except we never got the required reading."

"Then we'll just have to figure it out," I said.

We began tossing around ideas and theories. Eventually the time drew near for the President's statement.

"Shall I stream it?" I asked.

60.

THE COMMUNICATIONS DIRECTOR HAD ISSUED SPECIFIC instructions to the traveling press corps: a handful of print reporters were to stay on board Air Force One; the cameras were to be on the tarmac, presumably because the President would be making his statement from the stairs of the plane, or on the tarmac. The print reporters balked at being told to stay on the plane. The Home Depot Media correspondent demanded to get off. "You can do whatever you want," the Communications Director told him. "But if you get off the plane, you're not getting back on. Anything the President says will be piped back here in the cabin, so you'll hear it in real time. Trust me on this one." By and large the press corps did trust him, something he had earned over time. The Communications Director could parry and obfuscate with the best of them, but he was never overtly dishonest. He had been a political reporter and an international correspondent for nearly twenty years, mostly television, before the President had tapped him to cross to the "dark side." Reporters were always skeptical of paid flacks, but at least the Communications Director was a former member of their guild.

The television cameras were lined up on the tarmac, awaiting the President's appearance. The front door to Air Force One remained closed. There was no staircase in place. "Why isn't the front door open?" a CNN cameraman asked a low-level staffer who'd been left behind on the tarmac with the cranky reporters.

"There will be a statement in ten minutes," the staffer answered. Shortly after that, the staircase at the rear of the plane was wheeled away and the door was closed.

"You better not screw us on this," the CNN cameraman growled. The other members of the press were growing similarly concerned.

"Just make sure you're recording," the staffer said loud enough for all the camera crews arrayed on the tarmac to hear. "I promise you will get what you want." There was a whir as the engines on Air Force One came to life and the plane began to move forward. On board, the Captain instructed the passengers to fasten their seat belts. The press corps began texting and calling one another frantically, trying to assess what was happening. What about the President's statement? A Reuters reporter on the tarmac threw his headphones to the ground in fury, screaming about the perfidy of the Communications Director, the President, the pilot, and everyone else associated with this dirty trick.

"I promise you that if you stand here and pay attention, you're going to get the story," the staffer said calmly. He was convincing enough that most of the reporters turned their attention back to Air Force One, which was taxiing steadily away from them.

"I've got plenty of stock footage of Air Force One taking off," the CNN cameraman said angrily. "Now how the hell am I supposed to get back to Washington?" The staffer ignored the chorus of complaints. When Air Force One reached the end of the runway, the plane turned slowly, preparing to take off past the reporters into a gentle breeze. The camera crews focused on the plane, trying to make the best of what little they were being offered. The 747 accelerated steadily, the front wheels leaving the ground right as the plane passed the press corps arrayed on the tarmac. Seconds later, Air Force One was aloft.

"Whooptie-fucking-doo," a Home Depot Media camerawoman yelled.

"Don't stop filming," the staffer said. Once again, something about his tone was convincing. The camera operators focused on the plane as it ascended away from the airport. Roughly ten seconds later, Air Force One banked sharply and began a slow 180-degree turn back toward the airport. The plane, still flying relatively low, passed over the assembled press corps, who stared at the hulking jet in confusion. As the plane flew overhead, ostentatiously low, an AP reporter suddenly grasped what was happening. "Which way is west?" she yelled to no one in particular. "Which way is west!"

The camera operators looked to the staffer, who pointed toward Air Force One as it flew away from them. "That way is west."

"Holy fuck!" the CNN cameraman yelled. "He's flying west! He's flying west!" As the cameras focused on Air Force One, the plane climbed steeply, the roar of the engines drowning out the yells of the reporters capturing the moment.

On board Air Force One, the Captain made his now-famous announcement, "Ladies and gentlemen, please make yourselves comfortable. We will be touching down in Canberra, Australia, in approximately ten hours." The effect was electric as reporters scrambled to report what was happening. In Washington, where I was watching all of this on my phone from a bench on the Capitol Mall, it was opening day for the Washington Nationals, who were playing the Atlanta Braves. There were two outs in the bottom of the third inning (the Nationals at bat), when the game was halted temporarily. The home plate umpire signaled a pause; the Braves pitcher stepped off the mound, perplexed.

The stadium's PA system boomed to life with the familiar voice of the Nationals' home announcer: "Ladies and gentlemen, please excuse this interruption." There was a scattering of boos as fans protested the break in the action. "We have just been informed that three minutes ago the President of the United States took off from Honolulu . . ." The announcer paused slightly for dramatic effect, after which he articulated each word slowly and forcefully. "*Air Force One is currently westbound, headed for Canberra, Australia.*" There was a short silence as the crowd processed what they had been told, and then a sustained, visceral cheer. In a gesture that has now become synonymous with the moment, the Braves pitcher turned slowly toward center field and pointed at the American flag.

In Seattle, where hundreds of people had gathered outside the hospital where Cecelia Dodds now lay in intensive care, a murmur went through the crowd. Most had not gathered in protest, but rather to honor her life and acknowledge her sacrifice. Still, when the news of Air Force One's westward departure spread quickly through the crowd, there were cries of shock. "He just pulled the plug on her!" someone yelled. That was not an accurate description of what had happened—but it was not wholly inaccurate, either. Time was running out: for Cecelia Dodds and for thousands of others.

We have no information on the reaction in Beijing, but one can easily infer that President Xing had seen enough westerns to know what had just happened to him.

PART 7

OKAY, NOW WHAT?

61.

FELT THE SAME IRRATIONAL SURGE OF NATIONAL PRIDE AS everyone else, only mine was mingled with dread. I watched video clips on my phone of Cecelia Dodd's family leaving the hospital after a visit. Cecelia's daughter and her husband walked out with their twin daughters, no more than three or four years old. Each little girl was clinging happily to a large stuffed animal, as if it had been just another visit to see Grandma. The look on their parents' faces, the puffy eyes and the tear-stained cheeks, told a different story. Neither Cecelia Dodds nor her family ever commented publicly on the political drama unfolding around them, but that night her daughter did stop to address a cluster of reporters. She had one arm draped over each daughter. "I want her to see them grow up," she said. "My mother deserves that." Whether she meant it or not, the message was clear to me: *A lot of people are going to miss a lot of graduations and weddings.*

If the China offer was really off the table, our best hope was to make more progress on the virus side. The NIH fatality projections were bouncing all over the place. The last time the President had spoken to the nation about *Capellaviridae*, he had suggested we could weather the Outbreak without any incremental deaths. That was an optimistic statement at the time; as I sat there on a bench looking out on the Capitol Mall, it was impossible. The Atlanta Braves pitcher was not likely to point at the flag when people started dying in Atlanta hospitals from diseases that should have been easily treatable.

The President had no long-term plan. He later admitted as much. The flight to Canberra was an impulsive political gesture. He could have declined the Chinese offer from Washington. The other signatory nations of the South China Sea Agreement were all comfortable postponing the signing ceremony. There was no logical reason for the President to order Air Force One to make that low, flamboyant loop over the runway before accelerating "west." The President's critics on the far left were merciless, blasting everything from his jingoism to the wasted fuel. They were right—and utterly wrong. True, there was no reason to fly Air Force One across the Pacific. What that misses, however, is how the President was constructing an edifice of political support for whatever he would have to do next, even without a political party to depend on. The Senate Majority Leader, a dependable ally to begin with, was complicit in the decision to fly to Canberra and was now even more firmly bound to the President.

Meanwhile, the Speaker of the House was continuing her self-immolation. As soon as the U.S.-China Friendship Agreement became public, her comment that we should "take seriously" what the Chinese have to offer was played over and over again, juxtaposed against the most egregious and the pettiest of the Chinese demands. This was totally unfair, of course, as the Speaker had made her comments before the terms of the agreement were known. No one seemed to care about the finer points of context in this case, however. The Speaker's ascent had been built on self-interest, calculation, and power; those who crossed her over the years found themselves stripped of committee assignments or facing a well-financed primary opponent. Unlike the Senate Majority Leader, she had no deep pool of goodwill to draw upon during a rough patch. Machiavelli may have written that it is better to be feared than loved—the Speaker was definitely feared and unloved by the House rank and file—but that assumes one can hang on to power. Machiavelli did not live through the early 1990s when Eastern Europe Communist despots were toppled and citizens rushed through the streets knocking over their statues. (The leaders themselves typically fared worse than the statues.) The Speaker was no East European dictator, but the larger point still holds. Her power had been kicked from beneath her, at least temporarily. Meanwhile, the President's support had surged to over 90 percent after the Air Force One show; most House members (never that popular) rushed to pledge their public support to the White House.

So yes, when Leonard Creelman went on *This Week* and pointed out that the President had used seventy thousand gallons of jet fuel ("an abhorrent carbon footprint") just so he could "impress people eating hot dogs at baseball games," he was absolutely correct. It is also true that a solid majority of Americans felt a powerful urge to punch Leonard Creelman in the face. (Even 53 percent of self-described progressives "supported" or "strongly supported" the President during the Outbreak, up from less than 20 percent during most of his tenure.) Meanwhile, the Tea Party, normally eager to lambaste the President for every nickel of public money he spent (that jet fuel is not free), was eager to have yet one more reason to blame China for America's problems.

It is crucial to recognize two things. First, in just a matter of hours, the President had fortified his political position and gained the support of most Americans for whatever he would do next. Second, he had no idea what he was going to do next.

62.

THE PRESS WAS ALWAYS A STEP AHEAD OF THE PUBLIC, AT least the print reporters were. While the video of Air Force One doing a loop over the Honolulu base and accelerating west was played repeatedly on tablets, and watches and eyeglasses, the more enterprising reporters grasped what must inevitably come next: we were going to run out of Dormigen. The NIH projections had never been public, but any reasonably intelligent person could connect the dots. We had a shortage of Dormigen; the Chinese offer was off the table; at some point "the constraint would become binding," as the scientists like to say. And then what? The media was aware that the White House had "a number" with regard to likely deaths, and enterprising reporters redoubled their efforts to get it. As usual, the Internet was awash with bogus projections and reports.

On board Air Force One, the President basked briefly in the glow of his dramatic takeoff before confronting the same reality I was contemplating on the park bench. What now? The Dormigen supply across the country had finally been secured, though it was still uncertain where the stolen drugs would end up. As the President flew toward Canberra, the NIH projections were showing a range of likely fatalities from forty thousand to a hundred thousand. There was no full-blown Dormigen rationing in place yet. In theory, everyone who really needed the drug was still getting it, but the protocols for prescribing Dormigen had been tightened sharply to help make the existing stock go further: no prescriptions when another antibiotic might work; no prescriptions for non-fatal infections likely to heal on their own; no prescriptions for secondary infections among terminal patients; and so on. The video communications equipment on board Air Force One had been repaired during the long stop in Honolulu. (This was one small factor in the President's decision to fly toward Australia; he was now as well equipped on the plane as he would have been in the Oval Office.) The Communications Director was urging the President to make another address to the nation, seizing on his surge in popularity to prepare the country for the possibility of fatalities. The President was noncommittal, presumably still hoping that those of us in the scientific community would pull an antidote out of a hat.

In fact, the first preventable fatalities had already happened. While all eyes were on a weakening Cecelia Dodds, other people were dying. An eighty-three-year-old man had been admitted to a hospital in Tucson with a severe case of pneumonia. He would normally have been prescribed Dormigen on admittance, but with the new protocols in place the emergency room physician prescribed a traditional antibiotic as a first line of treatment instead. The man's condition worsened almost immediately and he died before he could be switched to Dormigen. In Atlanta, a much younger man, African-American, died in an emergency room after being denied Dormigen when he arrived unconscious in an ambulance. His mother gave a tearful press conference in which she alleged that her son had been denied the lifesaving drug because he was a young black male. The controversial civil rights leader Latisha Andrews rushed to Atlanta, where she planned to organize a protest against "Dormigen discrimination," but before she had even landed at the airport it was widely publicized that the young man had suffered a massive stroke, not any kind of infection, and would not have benefited from Dormigen.

And then there was Larry Rowen, the smarmy Los Angeles nurse who inadvertently set in motion a massive law enforcement dragnet that would recover over twenty thousand doses of stolen Dormigen. Rowen was an aspiring actor who had moved to Los Angeles ten years earlier from Moline, Illinois, hoping to capitalize on his nursing background by getting himself cast in a medical drama. He was short and pudgy, with thinning reddish brown hair, a wispy little mustache, and a severe wandering eye. Rowen learned quickly that he did not have the looks to thrive in Los Angeles; he was further disappointed to discover that his nursing background offered no casting advantage in medical dramas. (As the balance of this incident will demonstrate, Larry was no genius.) Rowen supported himself in Hollywood by working at an exclusive plastic surgery practice in Brentwood and doing two night shifts a month at a twenty-four-hour clinic in Pasadena. It was in the former that Rowen developed a deep antipathy for the stars and starlets coming in to have their breasts, lips, calves, chins, and butts improved. And it was in the latter where he had access to Dormigen during the stretch when the supply was still unsecured.

Having stolen a thousand doses of a drug that was potentially more valuable than heroin, Rowen soon realized that he had a problem: he had no distribution network. There is a reason that drug kingpins offer a big cut to the street gangs that push their stuff; one cannot sell heroin (or stolen Dormigen) without finding customers, and it is hard to find customers when the product is illegal. Rowen had two additional challenges. First, the window during which his stolen Dormigen stash would be valuable was very small (and could close, if the government found some fix for the crisis). Second, as noted earlier, the man was no genius. He may have had a social conscience on par with the typical drug dealer, but he was not nearly so clever. Rowen—who remains fodder for late-night comedians—envisioned a scenario in which he could strike back at the Hollywood establishment while simultaneously enriching himself.

Yes, Larry Rowen sought to trade his stolen Dormigen for cash (from rich men) and sexual favors (from beautiful women). "I wanted them to respect me," he explained at his arraignment. Rowen's advertisement in the *Hollywood Reporter* intimated as much: *Safe, plentiful supply of Dormigen. Only the rich and beautiful need apply.* Yes, he really ran that ad. And yes, FBI agents arrested him one day after it appeared. According to court documents, however, he had already sold six doses of Dormigen and at least two of the buyers were women. The identities of the buyers were kept confidential—sealed by the court. Anyone who really needed Dormigen at that point could still get it. We had not run out yet. The good news is that Rowen's clumsy sales effort inspired law enforcement to mount a nationwide sting operation. It was not terribly difficult to pose as buyers, track the Dormigen back to its illicit source, and arrest the dirtbags like Larry Rowen who were selling it.

As the President flew toward Canberra, I became involved in an unfortunate communications snafu. Jenna and I did not see a movie, but we did continue our walk, still trying to piece together the mysteries of the colored binders. Jenna graciously invited me back to her apartment, where we continued our conversation. It was clear to both of us that I needed sleep more than anything else. I had been awake for fifteen hours. The radio and television interviews had been exhausting. My mind was moving at three-quarters speed. I took a nap and made the unwise decision to turn off my assorted communications devices, thinking it would just be a short power nap, fifteen or twenty minutes. The timing could not have been worse; several members of Congress showed up at the NIH office and demanded a personal briefing from the Director and me. There are a hundred reasons why members of Congress should not show up in the middle of a crisis and expect answers, not least because it wastes valuable scientific time. Still, there they were, sitting in the Director's office, expecting answers from those of us whose time would be better spent generating those answers.

The Director tried to reach me while I was sleeping. Tie Guy filled in for me and answered the basic questions. The important thing to recognize is that nothing about this unfortunate incident affected our scientific approach to the Outbreak. No time was lost. If I had not carved out some hours to refresh myself, I would have been answering basic questions for some of the Speaker's congressional minions. Their pride was wounded—this I understand—and I was remiss in turning off my devices. But the finding by the Outbreak Inquiry Commission that "the top NIH adviser went AWOL at the peak of the crisis" is just political hyperbole.

In fact, I stepped out of the shower reinvigorated and with a plan for moving forward. I turned on my secure phone and saw the series of frantic messages from Tie Guy and the Director. I was still wrapped in a towel when I called Tie Guy back. "Where the hell are you?" he answered.

"I just needed some sleep," I said truthfully. "And I have an idea."

"Well, if you want to explain it to six members of Congress, they just left."

"That's a waste of our time right now," I said.

"Not yours," Tie Guy answered angrily, though he was already starting to simmer down.

I shared my unorthodox thought: "Maybe we just need to expose these people to the dust mite. Have you thought about that? Right? If the pattern is—"

"Of course I thought of that," he interrupted. "How could I not think of that?"

I ignored him and continued. "*Capellaviridae* turns virulent when people with the virus are no longer exposed to the dust mite that carries it. So maybe the dust mite is preventive somehow?"

"Yeah, that's one possibility," Tie Guy agreed. "But how? And why? I sent that idea up the chain yesterday afternoon but I can't get anyone to bite." Tie Guy had been curt before, even rude, but this was the first time he sounded patronizing, or maybe just angry.

"What's the harm of trying the dust mites?" I asked.

"That's what I said," Tie Guy replied, still peeved. "But think about it. If someone has the virulent form of *Capellaviridae*, they can still be treated successfully with Dormigen. Who would want to forgo that for some experiment with dust mites?"

"But what's the worst thing that could happen if we try?"

"The worst thing that could happen is that the dust mites have no effect and people get sick enough so that Dormigen is no longer effective and then they die." He changed his voice slightly, imitating the NIH bureaucrats with whom he had obviously discussed this: "The NIH will not do a human trial when a safe, proven alternative exists and we have no theory or evidence to suggest the alternative treatment will be effective."

"You asked yesterday?"

"Yeah, right after I saw the data on who is becoming sick," Tie Guy explained.

"But that was before they knew about the Dormigen shortage," I pointed out. "Everything is different now. We have a safe treatment, but it's going to run out. What's the harm in testing something that might work?"

"That's true," Tie Guy conceded. "But we still need a theory. We have to have some explanation for what's happening here. Why would people get sick from *Capellaviridae* when they are no longer around dust mites? And why would reintroducing dust mites make them healthy?"

"If it works, we can figure out the theory later," I said.

"We don't have time to do any meaningful trial," Tie Guy declared. "*Capellaviridae* is not fatal most of the time anyway, so it would take a long time to figure out if the dust mites have any real impact. Besides, I think it's a dead end. There's a confounding variable out there that we haven't figured out. *The data are right, but we're not hearing what they are telling us.*"

"Why can't we just test the dust mites?" I insisted. "We need a Jonas Salk."

Tie Guy's tone turned caustic. "Really? Tell me how that would work."

My mind worked slowly as I tried to figure out why Tie Guy sounded so dismissive. Salk was the inventor of a polio vaccine. Like other successful vaccines, it works by introducing a weakened form of the virus to the subject, whose body then creates antibodies to fend off the full-strength version of the disease. Salk offered himself and his family as test subjects. As my mind ground away slowly, Tie Guy continued, "Why don't you give yourself the virulent form of *Capellaviridae* and then try the dust mite cure?"

My mind caught up to him: We still had no understanding of when or why the virus turned virulent, so even the notion of exposing someone to the harmful form of the virus was beyond us. I couldn't test the dust mite cure on myself because I did not know how to make myself sick with the virulent form of *Capellaviridae* in the first place. "I'm a little worn down," I said.

"The media stuff looks awful," Tie Guy said, finally betraying some sympathy. There was a brief pause and then he asked, "Don't you think the Chinese are going to pony up the Dormigen in the end?"

He had never asked me about any deliberations beyond the science. At that point, I had not been privy to the discussions on Air Force One, but I had heard enough at the White House to know that the President would likely refuse any offer that required abandoning the South China Sea Agreement. I took a seminar on negotiations in graduate school, a class where we broke down in pairs and did mock exercises. One of the things I learned is that sometimes there is not a deal to be had. Fifteen different pairs of negotiators read a set of secret instructions—half of us were banana plantation owners and the other half were fishermen—and somehow we were supposed to figure out how to split limited water resources in our village. All fifteen teams returned to the classroom ninety minutes later, and not one of us had managed to come to agreement. There just wasn't enough water. That was what we were supposed to learn from the exercise.

Tie Guy's question was instructive to me. He was a hardheaded analyst if there ever was one, and here he was assuming optimistically that everything would work out okay. That may be a unique American gift, this ongoing optimism. *It all works out in the end.* How else can one explain what happened at that Washington Nationals game? The President of the United States gives the middle finger to the country offering us the Dormigen that would get us through the crisis, leaving us in a situation where thousands of people might die unnecessarily. The Atlanta Braves pitcher points at the flag, causing people to get to their feet and cheer for nearly five minutes. Why? Because they believed it would work out okay.

There are two things I do not understand about that baseball game moment, even now as I write. First, Americans despise politicians. Faith in government has been trending down for forty years. The approval rating for Congress is routinely in single digits. Even politicians can get an easy laugh by bashing politicians, or better yet "government bureaucrats." Our funding at NIH had survived more or less intact because we did work with counterterrorism implications, but my colleagues working on dementia or diabetes or heart disease had no such luck. Their budgets were all lower than they had been back at the turn of the millennium. Who did all these folks eating hot dogs at the Nationals game think was going to bail them out? Should I go back to the NIH, where teams were working around the clock, and yell, "Hey, everybody, it's after five! Time to go home. This is government work"? What little we did know about lurking viruses came from research mostly funded by government grants. Who else cares about a lurking virus until it's too late? When I told people I was a government scientist—at a party or my college reunion or among my parents' friends—they would often make a wisecrack about studying the mating habits of potbellied pigs, intimating that my work was a waste of their hard-earned tax dollars. This, by the way, was often coming from someone who was marketing dandruff shampoo or doing research for a hedge fund, as if fighting bad hair or further enriching rich people were some kind of high calling. (Yes, that is a bit of a rant, but given my role in this whole debacle, I am entitled to some venting.)

Second, *things do not always work out okay.* That is just an objective historical fact. Have these people not read about the Civil War? I am no historian, but I know enough to recognize that Americans could see that crisis coming for forty years before the shooting started at Fort Sumter. There are historical examples of when politicians did things that caused needless deaths and suffering (World War I, Vietnam). There are historical examples of when politicians did not cause the problem but were unable to stop the devastation (the Spanish flu pandemic, the opioid crisis). There are examples of when politicians were heroic and successful but the social cost was still enormous (World War II). In any event, I do not understand how anyone could make even a cursory examination of American history and just assume that the Outbreak was going to turn out okay. As I stood wrapped in a towel in Jenna's apartment, I did not believe the President and the Chinese were going to come to a deal. In some ways, the President had backed himself into a corner with his cowboy-like takeoff from Honolulu. For their part, the Chinese would lose face (and all the diplomatic prestige that came with it) if they walked away from most of the bold demands in the "Friendship Agreement." The two parties might have reached some agreement if the negotiations had been conducted in private, but that ship had sailed. (Or, to keep the metaphor correct, that plane had flown west.) The likelihood of some scientific breakthrough was getting less likely by the hour. Tie Guy was correct: we had run out of time to do even a simple clinical trial.

I dressed and sat down next to Jenna on the couch in her tiny sublet apartment. I had known her for a mere three hours. It was clear that there was some connection between the two of us, though I had not told her I was still living with Ellen. I could try to explain that my relationship with Ellen was already over but that would make me sound like a lecherous sixty-year-old telling some young thing that his marriage had been "dead for a long time." The fact is that I felt much better with Jenna sitting next to me on that couch. Not coincidentally, her instincts regarding *Capellaviridae* were good. I appreciated having a fellow Huke acolyte to share ideas with. In the back of my mind—lurking there, if you will—I was convinced that his approach was fundamentally correct. Our best hope was to "think like the virus." There had to be some reason for the pattern we were seeing—some reason that *Capellaviridae* or the dust mite benefited in the long run from making people sick. As Huke told us repeatedly, "It's all about evolutionary advantage." So why couldn't I figure that out? What organism was getting what advantage from this bizarre pattern we were seeing?

I decided to walk home, in part to clear my head. Jenna offered to walk with me. I demurred, in part to avoid having to explain: (1) to Ellen, why I had invited a coworker up to our apartment; and (2) to Jenna, why I could not invite her inside for a drink of water after she had walked twenty blocks with me.

63.

I WALKED ALONE, MY MIND STILL IN A FOG. BY THE TIME I reached home, the sun had gone down and my neighbors were returning from work. I said hello to the older woman who lived in the unit above us; I could never remember her name, but I did recall that she did something for United Airlines. As I exchanged small talk with her, it dawned on me that I had left the apartment that morning without my keys. I buzzed my own apartment, hoping Ellen was home, while also kind of hoping she was not.

Ellen buzzed me up. When I got to the door of our apartment, she was standing in the doorway waiting for me. "Oh, my goodness, how are you doing?" she asked. This was the first time we had spoken since I had run out of the apartment before dawn with no explanation. Once the news of the Outbreak became public, the late nights and cryptic comments over the previous days finally made sense to her.

"I'm okay," I said unconvincingly.

"What's going to happen?"

"I have no idea," I said with much more conviction.

"Did you see the news about Cecelia Dodds?" she asked.

"Of course."

"I did a term paper on her in high school," she offered.

"You and a lot of other people," I said.

"It's horrible."

"Yes."

"Do you want something to eat?" she asked.

"I just need to think." I turned on the television and was surprised to see that the Outbreak was not the top story on *Headline News*. The President was still flying westward, so there was nothing new to report there. Two things had happened that afternoon to distract attention, if only for a few hours, from *Capellaviridae*. First, the country music star Tigue McBride (remarkably, the name he was born with) died in a fiery car crash somewhere in West Texas. I am no country music fan, but even I knew that Tigue McBride was a known "bad boy" with a history of substance abuse and broken relationships. He ran his pickup truck into a tree with a seventeen-year-old girl (unnamed because she was a minor) in the front seat. Tigue (thirty-eight years old and married to the B-actress Rhyme Marr— not her born name) was killed on impact; the unnamed minor was in critical condition. Country music fans were scandalized and devastated; everyone else saw the irony in the fact that McBride had died in circumstances that sounded like one of his songs. The news was full of speculation about whether McBride was drunk (yes, it would turn out) and why he was driving on the back roads of Texas with a seventeen-year-old girl who was not his daughter (still not clear).

The second story sucking up airtime was a bizarre kidnapping in Germany. An aggrieved scientist with some serious mental health issues had stormed the podium at a political rally near Munich. Before anyone knew what was happening, the guy jumped up onstage with what looked like a small syringe. There was video of all this, which explained part of the appeal of the story. The crazed scientist, who had been fired from his university post some years before, had a long white beard and frantic eyes. As the startled crowd looked on, the scientist poked the speaker, the CEO of a major agribusiness company, with the small syringe, jamming the pointed end through the man's suit into his upper arm. The CEO looked more perplexed than pained after he had been poked in the arm. There was no shooting or gore. Local police stormed on the stage and the wild professor left willingly with them.

That, however, was when the story took a turn for the bizarre, as all the news channels were reporting. Once in custody, the scientist explained that he had injected the CEO with a slow-acting toxin of some sort for which only he would be able to provide the antidote. The mad scientist reportedly sat calmly in the police station, explaining to officers that if they wanted the CEO to live, they would have to honor his demands. The former professor had been in the chemistry department at a university in Berlin; there was no doubt that he had the expertise to concoct some fatal formula. Experts had no idea what it might be, however. The scientist intimated that he had used some combination of snake venoms. The CEO was rushed to a hospital, where he developed nausea and a mild fever. Needless to say, he was frantically urging authorities to do whatever it would take to procure the antidote.

The scientist, sitting in the police station, made what he said would be the first of several demands: He wanted an ice-cream cone—a strawberry ice-cream cone, to be more precise. And he wanted to walk freely with police officers to get it. He did not want them to bring his ice-cream cone to the station, and he did not want to walk to the ice-cream parlor in handcuffs. This demand set off a wave of protest and debate in the law enforcement community, not just in Germany but around the world. Germany had a strict policy against publicly negotiating with terrorists; the mad professor's act had been declared terrorism, mostly for the lack of a more appropriate description of his bizarre behavior. Would it violate Germany's policy to give the guy his strawberry ice cream? German police officers argued that giving their suspect ice cream was not radically different than giving a suspect a cup of coffee or a cigarette to encourage cooperation.

Right-wing pundits everywhere argued that acceding to the ice-cream demand would encourage the "terrorist" to make more outrageous demands. This prompted the FBI Director's now-famous retort, "If we give him an ice-cream cone now, we can always say no if he asks for the release of one hundred Hamas prisoners in the future." There was a robust debate in the media over whether torture would be appropriate in this kind of situation—the poison equivalent of the "ticking bomb" that U.S. presidential candidates are always asked about—but Germany forbade torture under any circumstances, so as a practical matter this was a nonstarter. Meanwhile, the CEO, growing more ill by the minute, was apoplectic that he might expire for lack of a strawberry ice-cream cone.

The story was packaged beautifully for global attention: the mad scientist perpetrator; the privileged CEO victim, waiting anxiously for the antidote; the bizarre ice-cream cone request. The situation grew weirder still when authorities realized that strawberries were not yet in season and none of the ice-cream shops in the neighborhood had strawberry ice cream. When informed of this snafu, the scientist apologized for being difficult and said that chocolate almond would be fine. CNN's Jake Tapper would later say this was the single most bizarre news development he had ever reported on air. Camera crews followed the scientist and police as they strolled several blocks to a small ice-cream shop, where a terribly nervous young girl with bad skin stood behind the counter. (All of the customers had been cleared out.) The police commissioner asked her for a scoop of chocolate almond ice cream.

"Might I have two scoops?" the scientist interjected.

"Of course," the police commissioner replied. (Even this decision would be debated later, with one semi-hinged Fox pundit declaring that it validated his assertion that giving in to the ice-cream request would lead to escalating demands.) The poor young ice-cream clerk stood there paralyzed. The police commissioner said more emphatically, "Two scoops of chocolate almond, please."

The young girl stammered, "In a cone or a cup?"

"A cone, please," the scientist answered politely. As she scooped, her arm trembling visibly and with millions of people watching live around the globe, the scientist reached into his pocket and put a one-euro coin in the tip jar. By this time, his family had contacted authorities to inform them what they were already beginning to suspect, namely that the man was unbalanced but harmless. The syringe had been rushed off to a laboratory for analysis, and just as the mad scientist was finishing the last of his sugar cone, a laboratory official called police to tell them it contained nothing more than saline. The CEO's nausea (he had been vomiting repeatedly) was entirely psychosomatic, which one can understand given the circumstances.

The mad scientist was transfixing. The video clip of him ordering ice cream was viewed over twenty million times. The phrase "Might I have two scoops?" entered the lexicon; young people used it in an ironic way in all kinds of circumstances. There was even a temporary surge in the popularity of chocolate almond ice cream. More serious people recognized the cleverness of the scientist's fake scheme: infecting a victim (or millions of victims) and then using the antidote as leverage. The press clamored for evidence that the *Capellaviridae* was not a similar terrorist plot, leaving the Communications Director with the impossible task of proving a negative. "We have no evidence whatsoever that any human actors are involved in any criminal actions related to *Capellaviridae*," he declared at an impromptu press briefing at the rear of Air Force One. "None. No ransom request, no biological evidence—nothing."

"But it's possible?" a Fox reporter asked.

The Communications Director, who had been sleeping even less than the President, snarled back, "Look, it's possible this virus came to earth on a secret spaceship from Mars. I can't prove it didn't."

Upon reading this exchange, a new and very young Ukrainian correspondent failed to recognize the Communication Director's use of satire to make his point and reported earnestly back to her national news wire that the White House now believed it was possible that aliens may have introduced *Capellaviridae* to our planet. Several Ukrainian radio stations reported the story before the State Department set them straight. Meanwhile, the *Onion*—still the best source for real fake news—found dark humor in the Outbreak. The headline of the most recent issue proclaimed, "God Says *Capellaviridae* Is Punishment for Bears Not Winning Super Bowl." The Bears had lost to the Broncos in a Super Bowl blowout a few months earlier; the Bears coach was a very religious man who wore that religion on both sleeves. Before the game, not only did he lead his team in prayer on the sidelines, but he told reporters, "I am certain that the Man Upstairs will lead us to victory." In fact, God allowed the Bears defense to give up over five hundred passing yards and forty-one points. The *Onion* had been mining this humor trove for some time, beginning with the first headline after the game: "Man Upstairs Apologizes to Bears Fans for Crappy Pass Rush."

Ellen was understandably eager to talk about what was happening. She was curious about the work I had been doing, and, like everybody else, she wanted to know how worried she should be about *Capellaviridae*. "I get it now," she said, which I took to be an all-purpose apology for our squabbles in recent days, most of which had to do with my absences and general lack of attention. I wanted to sleep more than anything else, but I realized I owed Ellen at least a cursory discussion of the situation. "You met the President?" she asked.

"Just about every day," I said.

"What's he like?" she asked. I did my best to describe the President and the other senior officials with whom I had been interacting. Ellen had relatively little curiosity about my work but great interest in the people I had been doing it with. If I had been less exhausted I might have been more charitable, but I remember wondering if Ellen was going to have me describe their outfits, including the designers.

At about this time, I got a short text from Jenna: "Did you see the ice cream cone thing?"

"Sorry," I said to Ellen. "I have to reply to this." I felt awful in that moment, knowing I had exploited the situation to flirt with someone I had known for less than twelve hours. At the same time, I realized—and Jenna would later tell me that she had realized—that those three hours beginning on the bench were more than just three hours on a bench. Jenna was the person I wanted to be speaking to at that moment. I texted back: "Amusing but also a reminder that the guy with antivenom gets the ice-cream cone!" In hindsight, this was not as clever as I thought it was. (I have no future career with the *Onion*.) I went to bed thinking about Jenna and knowing that I should have been thinking about Ellen. But that is not the larger point here. I also went to bed with the German mad scientist on my mind. I remember thinking, *The guy with the antivenom gets the ice-cream cone!* was the kind of chippy thing Professor Huke would say.

In fact, it was exactly the kind of thing that Huke would say. Because it finally got me thinking like a virus (after eleven more hours of sleep).

64.

THE PRESIDENT AWOKE SHORTLY BEFORE AIR FORCE ONE touched down in Canberra. The exuberance of his exciting take-off to the west had dissipated; the senior staff realized there was no plan once they arrived in Australia. As expected, the Chinese had made a new offer via the U.S. Embassy in Beijing, but they were still demanding that the U.S. walk away from the South China Sea Agreement, as well as an array of other unacceptable concessions. The press—both on board Air Force One and back home—had moved beyond the U.S.-China showdown and were asking the right questions: When would the Dormigen supply be exhausted? Who would be given priority as the supply ran out? And what would be the public health implications? The President asked for basically the same information upon landing. The Chief of Staff gave him a short briefing. "The Dormigen supplies have been secured," she said, consulting the notes on her yellow legal pad. "We have tightened the prescription criteria so that no one is getting Dormigen who does not absolutely need it. That seems to be working okay."

"Cecelia Dodds?" he asked.

"She's still in intensive care. It's a nasty infection. She's tough and they're doing what they can."

"Tell me if she gets worse."

"I will."

"What about this high school principal in Arkansas?" the President asked, waving a copy of his daily press clips (a compilation of news stories from around the world that the White House Press Office felt would be of interest to the President). The *Washington Post–USA Today* had run a front-page story about a fifty-three-year-old man who arrived at a hospital with failing kidneys. He was correctly diagnosed with a raging kidney infection. He also had a serious heart condition that got less attention. Per the new guidelines, he was started on a traditional antibiotic rather than Dormigen. The infection responded to the antibiotic, as doctors had hoped, but his failing kidneys put unexpected strain on his heart and he died of a heart attack. The man, Paul Gannett, was a prominent member of the local community and his death had been a shock. Hence the national news story.

"He should have gotten Dormigen. It's going to happen," the Chief of Staff said. "Even that may not have saved him." The President nodded in acknowledgment and she continued. "At the current run rate, the Dormigen supply will be exhausted in about five days."

"How many deaths?" the President asked.

"The low end of the projection is now forty-five thousand."

"What's the top end?"

"A hundred and fifty."

"Jesus."

The Communications Director had been sitting in on the meeting. He interjected, "The NIH has been working up some new numbers. There is a way to dress up the figures—"

"They're dead. How do you dress that up?" the President snapped.

The Communications Director, impervious to the President's

tone, continued. "Most of the projected deaths are people who are already old or ill."

"So they don't count?"

"Kind of. I was talking to one of the senior guys at NIH. He explained something to me that's kind of intuitive, if you think about it. Most of these people were going to die anyway, right?"

"Get to the point," the President said wearily.

"If we measure incremental deaths over a longer period of time, say a year or two, the number is going to be a lot lower." The President frowned, took a bite of toast, and said nothing. The Communications Director continued, "The number of deaths will spike when we run out of Dormigen, but then the death rate will be below average for the next three to six months. That means over the next year, the number of incremental deaths will be much, much lower—close to zero."

"People aren't really being killed by the epidemic, they're just dying early," the President said sarcastically. "Why don't you call Cecelia Dodds's grandchildren and explain that to them? 'She won't be at your wedding because she died early.'"

"This is straight from the NIH," the Communications Director said defensively.

The Chief of Staff said, "People are going to go to the hospital, they're going to be denied Dormigen, and they're going to die. It doesn't matter how we tally the deaths, that reality is not going away."

The President added, "Maybe Hallmark can do a new card: 'Sorry for your loss, but she was going to die in the next twelve to eighteen months anyway.' I can send one to the Dodds family."

"I'm just trying to get through today," the Communications Director said, displaying some impatience of his own.

The cable news stations had developed fancy graphics and names for the crisis: the Dormigen Countdown; the Dormigen Debacle; and so on. The new NIH projections had not leaked, but some of the old ones had. The media had a decent idea of when the Dormigen supplies would run out, as well as a crude projection for the virulence of *Capellaviridae*. Overall, their estimates were not wildly wrong, no doubt because some of the concerned scientists on our team were feeding information to the press. The President also suspected the Speaker had been strategically leaking information to create support for the China option before that deal blew up and made her collateral damage. In any event, the public would soon have a more refined sense of the situation. Congress had (rightfully) demanded a full briefing on the situation. With the President in Australia, the Acting HHS Commissioner was tapped to do the congressional briefing. That briefing would be private, but anything said in there would leak immediately. The Communications Director recognized the White House needed to get out in front of the leaks to put its own spin on the situation. (Hence his reference to just getting through the day.) The President would do a national television address immediately after the "closed" congressional briefing.

The President's senior advisers were feeling the same sense of doom that had descended on me the day before. At previous junctures in the crisis, we could imagine developments that would bail us out: Dormigen from allies; China; a scientific breakthrough on the virus. Each of those options was now gone, or dwindling away. The bravado of the takeoff to Australia had bought some political breathing space, but it had done nothing to improve Cecelia Dodds's condition. The hourly update from that Seattle hospital now became a barometer of the nation's future. Meanwhile, the press had begun to ask what the President could accomplish in Australia. And whatever goodwill the President had amassed by standing up to China would dissipate immediately as Americans began dying in serious numbers. The Chief of Staff would later describe the mood as "an oppressive anxiety as we internalized the reality of what was likely to happen."

"I need to draft remarks for the congressional briefing," the Communications Director said. He looked around the room for some general guidance to get him started. Curiously, the Strategist had gone missing. The President's more substantive advisers typically considered the Strategist an irritant, not just because of his irreverent demeanor, but also because he was a constant reminder of the messiness and tawdriness of politics. He was the one who explained impatiently why high-minded policies would have "absolutely no fucking support" in most of the Midwest, or how information could be cleverly spun to obscure, confuse, or persuade. He had famously called

the Secretary of Energy a "total moron" for using the word "tax" to describe the administration's carbon tax proposal. One might assume that the word "tax" was an accurate and efficient way to describe a policy that was, in fact, a tax on carbon emissions. "It's a pollution fee," the Strategist yelled during a staff meeting. "Tell the jackasses at the EPA to stop calling it a tax."

"Which part of it is not a tax?" a young economist from the Council of Economic Advisers had made the mistake of asking. The Strategist had literally thrown a bundle of papers across the conference table at him.

"Read that, you smug prick!" the Strategist screamed. Behavior aside, the public opinion data he had thrown across the table confirmed his point. Only 23 percent of the American public supported a carbon tax. But when the exact same policy was described as a "fee on polluters," support climbed to 68 percent. "If you want to sit alone in your office doing mental masturbation, go back to Harvard," the Strategist told the young economist (who was from Stanford). "If you want to improve American energy policy, don't use the word 'tax.' *Not fucking ever.*"

The more cerebral members of the President's team bristled at the manipulation, clinging to the politically naïve notion that a policy was just a policy, regardless of the words one used to describe it. They would appear on the Sunday morning talk shows, awkwardly trying to explain how the President's proposed tax on carbon was not a tax. The host would probe relentlessly: "If the government imposes a charge on the emission of carbon, how is that not a carbon *tax?*"

The Secretary of Energy or the Chair of the Council of Economic Advisers or the head of the EPA would parry uncomfortably: "What we are proposing is a *fee* on polluters."

"What's the difference between a *tax* and a *fee?*"

"A fee is a charge levied on some activity, such as registering a car. The most elegant part of the President's proposal is that the biggest polluters will pay the largest fees."

"How is that any different than the income tax, where those with the highest incomes pay the most in taxes?"

"Because this is a fee, not a tax."

And so it would continue. The cerebral advisers would apologize

to their erstwhile academic colleagues for such silliness. The fact that the Strategist was generally right on these matters was no salve for wounded academic dignity. Congress eventually passed a modified version of the "carbon emissions fee," with many members declaring to their constituents that they were supporting it because it was not a tax.

Now, with the Communications Director trying to put a positive spin on a minimum of forty-five thousand deaths, the senior advisers were looking for some guidance from the Strategist. "He needed some rest," the President said, explaining the absence unconvincingly.

"We all need some sleep," the Communications Director said. "Can we at least test the language?"

The Chief of Staff, sitting nearby but not following the conversation, said to no one in particular, "It's my daughter's birthday."

The President ignored her. "Just draft a straightforward statement," he instructed the Communications Director.

"Excuse me," the Chief of Staff said as she got up and walked out of the cabin.

The Communications Director looked around the room. "We're talking about a minimum of forty-five thousand premature deaths. What am I supposed to say?"

"We need to prepare the country for the worst," the President replied. He outlined a rough plan. The Acting HHS Secretary would brief Congress on the basic details: the state of our Dormigen supplies; the nature of *Capellaviridae*; the steps that had been taken to minimize the adverse effects of the Outbreak. Those details would be released to the public immediately following the briefing and the President would address the nation after that. "This is the reality of the situation," the President stated. "We shouldn't try to sugarcoat it."

He was right, of course. How could one put a positive spin on an outbreak that might kill over a hundred thousand people—however weak, old, or sick those people may be? The advisers who had been working around the clock to avert this moment were loath to concede that their efforts had been fruitless. "I still think we need to pay attention to how we explain this," the Communications Director said, implicitly probing the Strategist's absence.

"He's not here," the President said tersely. "Just do your job."

The Secretary of State had also gone missing, but her absence would not be noted for some time.

65.

I AWOKE FEELING DIFFERENT THAN I HAD IN DAYS. I COULD remember my dreams, one of which had been about a giant chocolate almond ice-cream cone. If I had been in a soap commercial, I would have danced around the bedroom singing about how refreshed I felt. I reached for my phone on the bedstand; there were eighteen texts from various people at the NIH headquarters. I had told the NIH Director that I needed a morning to sleep and think. She agreed it was a good idea, but as the Dormigen deadline drew nearer without any meaningful progress on our part, the staff had begun to confuse motion for progress. Only one of the texts required any real input from me; the others either boasted of some new activity or posed questions with answers that were self-evident. Ellen had already gone to work. She left a note at the foot of the bed wishing me a good day and telling me that she had made an omelet that I could heat up in the microwave. "Sorry if I have not been as supportive as I should be!" it concluded, with a little smiley face. That just made me feel bad, particularly as I texted Jenna before leaving the apartment.

I put the omelet in the microwave and wandered over to the window while it heated up. We lived on the fourth floor, high enough to get a decent sense of the activity below. Three boys in Catholic school uniforms hustled along the sidewalk. They had to be late, I thought. Across the street, a bakery truck was double-parked as two guys unloaded trays of bread onto a trolley and wheeled it into a small convenience store. The initial panic of the Outbreak had given way to normalcy, mostly because people could not see anyone getting sick around them. This stiff upper lip was less about resolve in the face of adversity and more about a failure to imagine how bad things could get when the Dormigen supply was depleted, a contingency that most people now did not think was going to happen. The White House had also worked aggressively to make *Capellaviridae* seem less scary. Acting on the recommendation of the Strategist, senior officials had compared *Capellaviridae* to influenza at every possible turn. (To be more accurate, they compared it to "the flu," which focus groups found far less scary than "influenza.") For example, the day before, with the press clamoring for projections and details, the Communications Director had declared during an interview, "It is crucial to remember that even if untreated, *Capellaviridae* is no more harmful than a serious case of the flu."

This statement was both technically accurate and entirely misleading. The public had no conception of how serious a bad strain of influenza could be. Before the advent of Dormigen, a nasty global influenza outbreak could kill a million people, including tens of thousands in the United States. There were a few media references to the Spanish flu outbreak of 1918, one of the worst pandemics in modern history, but "the flu" was the image cemented in most minds. Ironically, most Americans still believed that *Capellaviridae* could be contracted via contact with other humans (like the flu), but the initial panic over the disease had subsided. Schools were open again and attendance at public events was drifting back toward normal. (The Washington Nationals stadium had been only about a quarter full during the spontaneous burst of patriotism in response to the President's takeoff from Honolulu.) I watched the guys unloading bread for a few minutes and then retrieved my omelet when the microwave made its loud, annoying beep.

I do not want to overdramatize what happened next. I was hungry enough that I made short work of the omelet. I was getting up to make some toast when I got a text from Jenna. "Good sleep?" it said. I was elated to hear from her, and like anyone who has ever flirted by text, I carefully crafted my reply: "Excellent. Ice-cream cone later?"

I waited nervously for the response: "Definitely. See you at NIH?"

Jenna's text had pushed that crazy German terrorist incident to the front of my mind. The ice-cream cone is what had made it so bizarre. What I realized explicitly as I sat at the dining room table was that the eccentric scientist was entirely protected as long as he was the only one who could procure the antidote. That was his innovation.

Other terrorists plant bombs and demand ransom, but the strategy has limitations. The bombs must be in a population center, which increases the likelihood that they are detected and defused.

Or the area can be evacuated, rendering the bomb harmless (to people). Meanwhile, the terrorist is always at risk of being killed by the authorities; they do not need him alive to deactivate his explosive device. By introducing an unknown pathogen, however, the perpetrator guarantees his safety, particularly if the antidote is not commonly known. What was so surreal about the German scientist asking for his double-scoop ice-cream cone was his certainty that the authorities would not harm him. He could stash the antidote anywhere—in a safe-deposit box or buried in a public park—and the authorities would likely never find it if he were killed. In fact, we now know that the CEO, feverish and throwing up from his psychosomatic illness, was pleading with German authorities: "Do not kill him! I need him alive!"

These thoughts rushed through my mind as I sat at the dining room table. One can quibble with my analysis of terrorism, but that is not the point. My mind turned almost immediately to *Capellaviridae* and the North American dust mite. The most perfectly adapted species find some way to make themselves valuable to the broader ecosystem, thereby helping to ensure their own survival. Think about those little birds that perch inside the mouths of crocodiles and clean their huge, dangerous teeth. *Everybody leaves happy.* Evolution has a way of creating these synergistic relationships: bizarre creatures that interact in mutually beneficial ways. But what if nature had served up something different in the case of the dust mite, *Capellaviridae*, and humans? What if their relationship was something more akin to that of the German CEO and the mad scientist: extortion? Wouldn't it be possible—and entirely consistent with everything we know about evolution—for one species to essentially hold another hostage? *You continue to provide for my basic needs or I will kill you.* Nature offers up innumerable examples of toxins and venoms wielded by bizarre creatures either to hunt prey or to protect themselves from predators. Couldn't such weapons be wielded more creatively?

This rush of thoughts was not as clearly articulated as I have described them here. Rather, it felt like a half-formed idea engulfing my brain, like seeing an exam question that you know you can do but have not yet figured out. Or encountering a person you recognize in the street and searching your mind for her name. *You know it's com-*

ing. "It's on the tip of my tongue!" my grandmother used to say (more and more as she got older, sadly). I was certain in that moment that the key to understanding lurking viruses was lodged in my subconscious, working its way toward somewhere else in my brain where I could put some form around it. I did have two concrete thoughts in the moment, however.

First, I had an example—admittedly hypothetical—that I would use repeatedly in the coming hours to make myself understandable. Imagine there is a venomous snake, I would tell the Chief of Staff and others. This snake leaves its hole in the ground in the day or night to hunt lizards, which it paralyzes with venom. But the danger of leaving the hole is that the snake exposes itself to predators, such as a hawk that can swoop down and grab the exposed serpent in its talons. There is a trade-off: the snake needs to hunt, but it exposes itself in doing so. This is standard Discovery Channel stuff.

Now let's suppose that over the course of thousands of years, nature serves up a variation of that snake, a more "clever" species (if we are going to be anthropomorphic about it). This snake slithers into the hole of its prey, where scores of lizard eggs have just hatched. The "old" edition of this snake, the less "clever" one, would gobble up the baby lizards, enjoying one very fulfilling meal. Next week it will have to hunt all over again, once again exposing itself to all the predators aboveground. But the "clever" snake—again, somehow evolved over tens of thousands of years, maybe longer—finds a strategy that is nature's equivalent of room service. Rather than eating the baby lizards in one glorious meal, the "clever" snake uses them to eat for a lifetime (or at least a couple of weeks); it holds them hostage, doing no harm as long as the adult lizards bring it food. This is nature's equivalent of a guy who moves into your house, puts a gun to the dog's head, and says, "No one gets hurt as long as you feed me well and do my laundry. Also, we're going to need to order the premium cable channels." (Remember, nature has no 911.) In my hypothetical "clever" snake example, both species derive an evolutionary advantage. The snake obviously benefits from getting fed without having to expose itself to predators; the lizards are also more successful as a species in the long run because: (1) the baby lizards do not get eaten; and (2) the snake interloper scares off other predators (e.g., other snakes).

As I have mentioned repeatedly, this example was entirely hypothetical. (When some jackass staffer at the National Security Council started asking me questions about whether lizards really live in holes, he was obviously missing the big picture.) The point is that I had developed a theory that could potentially explain the behavior of lurking viruses in a way that was entirely consistent with evolution. Why and how could the same virus live harmoniously with its host in some cases while causing serious illness or death in others? Perhaps it depends on whether the host is delivering what the virus needs to thrive. And if not . . . well, every once in a while you have to shoot a hostage to keep everyone in line. Or, in my hypothetical "clever" snake example, if the adult lizards stop bringing food, the baby lizards become dinner.

My second concrete thought as this amorphous theory surfaced in my brain was that I had to call Professor Huke. I was finally "thinking like a virus." I was reasonably sure I had an answer worthy of one of his final exams, but I wanted to be sure before sending it up the scientific chain of command, let alone passing it along to the President of the United States. I found Huke's home number in my phone and dialed. His wife answered promptly. "He's off running errands," she said.

"Do you have a sense of when he'll be back?" I asked, trying to steer a path between urgency and rudeness.

"He was going to Home Depot, but usually that means he's going to stop at the driving range," she said. I remembered the driving range, a decrepit little place with mats and nets at the end of a huge strip mall (near the Home Depot). There was a soft-serve ice-cream cart in the parking lot that was popular with Dartmouth students.

"Does he carry a cell phone?" I asked.

"May I ask who's calling?" she replied, more curious than suspicious. I apologized and explained as briefly as I could why I needed to reach her husband. "Oh, yes, you visited us," she said. "Richard really enjoyed speaking with you. He does have a mobile phone, but I can see it right here on the dining room table. I keep telling him there's no point in having a mobile phone if all he's going to do is leave it at home."

Huke called back about a half hour later. "I went to the driving range. The course opens this weekend," he said, as if he needed to explain his whereabouts. "So how bad is this *Capellaviridae*?"

"Not terrible in the grand scheme of things," I said truthfully. "It acts like a virulent strain of influenza."

"That can be pretty bad," he said.

"True, but the Dormigen gap is not that big. We're only looking at about a week without it."

"Yes, I've read about how they are trying to stretch out what they've got."

"I'm calling because I want to bounce a hypothesis off of you," I said. "A theory of how lurking viruses might work."

"Very exciting! Okay, I'm listening," he said. I explained the thoughts that had been percolating through my brain that morning, including the example of the venomous snake and the baby lizards. I also explained some of the patterns that Tie Guy had observed, such as the fact that *Capellaviridae* was most likely to turn virulent in areas where there had been the most aggressive efforts to eradicate the North American dust mite.

"That's certainly enough to get you a plump research grant," he answered, "but there are still a lot of things to be worked out, even if you're right." And then, after a moment: "How long do you have?"

"Days," I said. "Not even a week." Huke did not answer right away. His silence signaled the obvious: we needed years, or at least months, to turn this thought into anything practical—and even that assumed I was racing along the right track. "Here's what I'm thinking," I continued. "When people become sick with the virulent form of *Capellaviridae*, we need to reintroduce them to the North American dust mite."

"Hmm." Huke was silent as he tried to follow my line of thinking. Eventually he said, "You are thinking that this dust mite fights back somehow, using *Capellaviridae*?"

"Yes."

"But you don't know how. Just that *Capellaviridae* turns virulent when the dust mite disappears," he said.

"Yes. Either because the dust mite gets exterminated, or because people move from an area where the dust mite is endemic to a place where it's not. In both cases, when there are no North American dust mites, the virus can turn virulent."

"There's no harm in testing it, is there?" Huke asked.

"Well, it might be hard to persuade people who are sick with *Capellaviridae* that the cure involves letting them get bit by the same dust mite that gave them the virus in the first place."

Huke laughed. "Do you think it was easy persuading people that injecting them with a weakened polio virus would protect them from polio?"

66.

THE PRESIDENT WAS OPENLY AND SHOCKINGLY DISMISSIVE OF many members of Congress. Part of that stemmed from his animus toward the Speaker, which had only deepened since the beginning of the Outbreak. "You don't have to be a genius to win an election," the President told me once after I had expressed amazement when a congresswoman from Arizona declared that it was still an "open question" as to whether germs cause disease. "That's not the craziest thing I've heard," he said, turning to the Chief of Staff. "What's the name of that guy from Tennessee who kept introducing bills to ban witchcraft in schools?"

"I don't remember his name, but he served eight or ten terms," the Chief of Staff said.

"Then he got arrested for sexual assault."

"No," the Chief of Staff corrected him. "That was the guy from Kentucky."

"With the wooden leg."

"I don't think it was wooden, but yes, he had a prosthetic leg."

The President turned to me and explained, "He ran a campaign saying he'd lost his leg to an IED in Afghanistan. Turns out he was never in the Army. He lost his leg in a drunk-driving accident on a motorcycle."

"He still got elected," the Chief of Staff added.

"He served a bunch of terms. Didn't he get reelected after he was arrested?"

"I think so," the Chief of Staff said. "He had to give up the seat when he was sentenced. There was a special election."

"That's right," the President said.

"How does someone get elected with a fake war record and then reelected after being arrested for sexual assault?" I asked.

The President waved his hand dismissively, suggesting my question was as naïve as I felt it to be. "He blamed the press. Said it was fake news. All the usual crap." Then he turned more serious. "People aren't paying attention. That's really it. Americans are busy driving their kids to soccer practice and designing iPhone apps and bashing government—until something like this happens, then everyone wants to know who's going to fix the mess. Is there an iPhone app for this?" He picked the Chief of Staff's phone up off the table in front of us. "Which button do I push to get more Dormigen? Is there an app to fix the Middle East? How about getting Newark schoolkids to read at grade level? Has Silicon Valley figured that one out yet?" An uncomfortable silence settled over the room. Then the President said, "They elected him again, didn't they?"

"Who?" the Chief of Staff asked.

"The guy with the prosthetic leg who got arrested for sexual assault."

"Yes, I think so. He ran when he got out of prison."

The President threw up his arms, as if to say, "See!" And then after a moment, more seriously: "You can't systematically ignore governance and then expect it to work well."

I remember passing the Chief of Staff in the corridor hours later. She pulled me aside and said, "He's tired." I knew immediately what she was referring to.

"That doesn't make him wrong," I replied.

"No."

Congress had certainly not distinguished itself in the hours since the Outbreak had become public. There had been a flurry of legislation introduced to nail the barn door shut: a bill to ban the outsourcing of Dormigen production; a bill declaring access to Dormigen "a basic American right"; a bill formally censuring Centera; and many others that had no chance of passing and would not have helped the situation even if they had. Then there was the bill demanding an investigation into Israeli involvement in the Dormigen shortage (introduced by the avowedly anti-Semitic "white Christian caucus"). This was the "teakettle" activity that the Senate Majority Leader had predicted at the beginning of the crisis—legislators presenting the illusion of action for constituents who did not know, or did not care, that introducing a bill is different than passing a law.

The President was not, however, dismissive of Congress the institution. He had a group of legislators whom he and the Chief of Staff referred to as "the adults." Every once in a while, he would turn to her and say, "Let's run it by the adults." As best as I could infer, this was a group of ten or twelve senators and thirty or forty House members whom the President respected a great deal. The group, which studiously avoided publicity, had coalesced near the end of the Trump presidency when a handful of serious legislators across parties began to believe that American governance had become dangerously unhinged. Some of the more impressive legislators in each chamber—former governors and Rhodes Scholars and CEOs and even a Ph.D.—began meeting informally after yet one more threatened government shutdown. There was no formal membership, just a series of relationships among serious people who sought to transcend the rancor and futility that had engulfed Washington. There was no ideological litmus test; the group included several committed progressives and one hard-core libertarian. What the participants had in common was a genuine commitment to civility and an aspiration to govern. In that spirit, they called themselves the "Conventioneers," after the delegates to the Constitutional Convention, the group of Americans who came to Philadelphia in 1787 representing an array of regions, interests, and ideologies and, over the course of a long, hot, arduous summer, managed to compromise their way to one of the greatest political documents ever written. No one ever told me why the President called them the "adults" rather than the "Conventioneers." I do know that the Congressman from Kentucky with the prosthetic leg was not one of them.

The "adults" were not powerful enough to pass legislation by themselves. Too much of what had to be done in Washington involved medicine the country was not prepared to take. They could, however, derail the very worst ideas. They could also generate momentum for an idea whose time had come. The press and the nation's opinion leaders respected their collective wisdom. Most of the members were sought-after guests on news programs, not because they yearned for the spotlight (many were openly disdainful of it) but because media outlets were keen to have guests who could offer a modicum of depth. (Ironically, the legislators most eager to get on such programs were typically the least-favored guests.) The Conventioneers were not miracle workers; they had to win elections like everyone else. Then again, so did the delegates to the Constitutional Convention. The President's informal liaison with the "adults" in the Senate was the Majority Leader, who had earned that position because of his decades-long reputation as a legislative workhorse. In the House, the President typically called Gail Steans, a particle physicist who had run for her first term in Congress when she was well into her fifties.

The President reached out to the adults before his formal briefing to Congress, both to ensure their support and to get feedback on his proposed remarks. He contacted Representative Steans first. She was a feisty woman, short and wiry, with a husky voice, who seemed perpetually annoyed that human beings did not act as predictably as other elements in the universe. She had been elected as a Democrat but left the party and became independent when the Speaker started trying to tell her what to do. (After the President was elected as an independent, it gave cover to a small but influential group of legislators to ditch their party affiliations. Three senators and eleven representatives had also been elected as independents.) The scuttlebutt in the capital was that Representative Steans did not "play nice" with her Washington colleagues. That was misleading, as she was a delightful and courteous person who happened to have zero patience for political nonsense. "I'm too old for that crap," she would often remark. In fact, she was well liked by her fellow Conventioneers, who often looked to her for guidance on scientific matters.

"How are you holding up, Mr. President?" Representative Steans asked when the President called her on the way to a town hall meeting in her home state of Maryland.

"I've had better stretches."

"You wanted the job," she said. This was a statement of the obvious and could pass for small talk, but there was a slight edge in the remark, as if to remind him that others in his seat had faced worse. "What's the latest?" she asked. The President walked her through the situation: the amount of Dormigen left, the fatality projections, and so on.

"First thing," Steans said, "you need to get yourself back to D.C. This whole flying west stunt has played itself out."

"We'll be wheels-up right after I give my address," the President replied. He had met with the Australian Prime Minister and other Asian leaders while on the ground in Canberra. They had recommitted themselves to the South China Sea Agreement before posing for a group photo, fourteen heads of state effectively facing down Chinese hegemony in the region. The President did not land on an aircraft carrier—it felt wrong in light of developments stateside—but the group photo had been taken on one of the disputed South China Sea islands, which broadcast the same message to Beijing.

"Why don't you speak from Air Force One in flight?" Representative Steans asked. "That will give you some extra drama. Very presidential." Her tone was not facetious. Rather, she acknowledged the effectiveness of these political gestures even as she wished they were unnecessary.

"We had some problems with the broadcasting technology, but yes, I think I can do that now," the President said. "What's the tenor on the Hill?"

"A lot of noise, mostly. The Tea Party jackasses are talking about impeachment."

"On what grounds?"

"Who knows, who cares?" Steans said dismissively.

"They all voted against any public funding for Dormigen in the first place," the President complained.

"Of course they did. Government is the problem for those morons until they call 911 and no one answers. Ignore them. That's a sideshow."

"And elsewhere?"

"I think you've got decent support on Capitol Hill in the places where you need it," Representative Steans said thoughtfully. "Other than the Speaker and her minions, I don't think anybody thinks we should kowtow to the Chinese. We'll see how that sentiment holds up when people start dying . . . Is there no better deal to be struck there?"

"We've been working that one hard," the President answered. "They've come back with some better offers, but they all involve walking away from the South China Sea Agreement. I just don't see them dropping that condition."

"What about postponing it? President Xing could save face and we'd still get the agreement."

"We tried that. No go."

"What a waste," Representative Steans said, sighing audibly. "People are going to start dying here and they'll have warehouses full of Dormigen there."

"World War I was a waste, too," the President said. "If you think about the big picture, we need to push China toward becoming a more responsible global power. That's why the South China Sea Agreement is so important. It's like Germany and Japan after World War II. We need China as a force for good."

"Hmm, I suppose that's right."

"We do have one more potential diplomatic option," the President offered.

"Yes?"

"I can't say anything more, but I'm cautiously optimistic." Representative Steans knew better than to pry; the President was not one to play coy. After a brief silence, he offered, "We may have a breakthrough on the virus front, too."

"What's that?"

"The NIH folks can brief you better than I. My understanding is that they have some new insight into why the virus turns virulent."*

"I wouldn't expect too much on that front," Representative Steans warned.

"Why is that?"

"We have, what, a handful of days until the Dormigen supplies run out?"

---

* The NIH Director had briefed the President on my hypothesis.

"My understanding is the scientists may be able to come up with some kind of antidote."

"I'm skeptical," Representative Steans said. "Scientific breakthroughs don't happen in days. I certainly would not say anything about that in your remarks. What you need to be doing now is setting expectations for how bad it could be."

"Cecelia Dodds is helping us with that," the President said.

"What a needless tragedy," Representative Steans said. "There's nothing you can do?"

"I've tried."

Representative Steans exhaled audibly. "That's what we're facing on a massive scale," she said. "You don't want to create panic, but complacency might be just as dangerous."

"I understand."

The President took her advice (reiterated by many others) that he should address the nation from Air Force One on his way back to D.C. The technology on board had been fixed and double-checked (and triple-checked after the President growled at the Chief of Staff, "It better fucking work"). The word went out that Air Force One would be departing shortly. As the last supplies were loaded on board and the doors were closed, the Strategist had not boarded. The Secretary of State had gone missing as well.

67.

THE NIH WORKING GROUPS WERE ENERGIZED BY MY THEORY of how lurking viruses might work, but the response was still less robust than one might think. The working hypothesis was that proximity to the dust mite was somehow protective against the virulent form of *Capellaviridae*. To stick with the earlier analogy, the dust mite is the extortionist; humans are the hostages; and somehow *Capellaviridae* is the weapon the dust mite uses to advance its own interests. One can imagine the dust mite holding the *Capellaviridae* "gun" to the head of its human host, saying, "As long as I stay fed and comfortable, nobody gets hurt." If humans start to wipe out the pesky dust mite, however, things would turn ugly. (My hypothesis was that moving away from an area with dust mites to one without them somehow sent the signal that the dust mite was under siege, kind of like the protagonist in a western saying, "If I'm not back safely in an hour, kill them all.")

"I understand all that," the NIH Director told me, "but I need you to understand that it takes time to test a hypothesis that is still only half-baked."

"Half-baked?" I asked incredulously. "Have we got any ideas that are fully baked?"

"I'm sorry, that was a poor choice of words," she said. "I've been talking to people at the FDA all morning. A clinical trial typically takes months, if not years. You're asking me to do something in days that usually takes years, and to be honest, it's not even clear what we're testing."

I paused for a moment before responding. For most people, that involves some kind of cooling-off process. Unfortunately, I was heating up. "First of all," I began, trying to project anger and seriousness without any hint of hysteria, "I'm not asking you to do anything. The people who are likely to die from *Capellaviridae* are asking you to do something. Second of all, what we're testing here is really simple. Just expose people who've become sick to the North American dust mite. The hypothesis is that somehow repeated exposure to the dust mite protects against *Capellaviridae* turning virulent. I can't tell you how or why that will work, and frankly we shouldn't care at this point. We can figure that out five years from now and we'll all share the Nobel Prize. We just need to try this very simple fix because we have nothing else."

Now it was her turn to pause and sigh. "It's not that simple," she said in a tone that suggested I probably would not get it anyway, like a high school girlfriend who says pityingly, "Oh, you'll never understand . . ."

"Which part of just letting people get bit by dust mites is not simple?" I asked angrily.

"Let's start with 'who,'" she said. "Who is in this trial? We have no federal protocol for this kind of situation. We have a treatment that is one hundred percent effective—Dormigen. Anyone who is sick now or becomes sick in the next few days will receive Dormigen. Meanwhile, we have a completely untested theory that involves exposure to biting insects—something that hasn't even been tested on rats. Would you volunteer for that clinical trial? Would you enroll your children? 'Oh, no, Bobby doesn't need Dormigen, let's try the biting-bug cure.'"

"That's not fair—"

"I'm not done yet," she snapped. "We can't test this on people without their knowledge, obviously." I was being reminded that the Director was tough and smart; one does not get to be the head of a federal agency without heavy dollops of both of those attributes. Also, she had had as little sleep as the rest of us, maybe less. "Now let's talk about 'how,'" she continued. "Even when *Capellaviridae* becomes virulent, the body fights it off about ninety-nine percent of the time. So to determine if a treatment is effective with any degree of statistical confidence, we need a huge sample. And I just finished telling you that we're having some trouble finding *anyone* who would be in that sample."

"I'm sorry," I said, raising the white flag. "We're on the same team here."

"Then stop telling me how to do my job," she said angrily. My apology worked to soften her tone, but she needed to wind down, like an engine that continues to run for a few seconds after the ignition has been turned off. "Also, I have to deal with that French asshole."

"Giscard?" I asked.

"Yeah, he's here."

"Like in D.C.?"*

"Yeah, he took it upon himself to fly over when he heard the news," she offered. "He got in last night."

Lionel Giscard was—by science standards—a global celebrity. He was the lead author on not just one, but two of the key papers that led to the development of Dormigen. He had won about every major science award and was dusting off a place for the Nobel Prize medal

---

*   In her accounts of this conversation, the NIH Director has maintained repeatedly that I asked her, "Who invited Giscard?" That is not what I said. I do not like Giscard personally, and our feud is now public, but I would never have spoken in a way that suggested a scientist of his caliber should be excluded from our efforts to deal with the Outbreak.

(which is typically awarded near the end of one's career). Within the scientific community, Giscard was considered a lecherous ass-hole, for lack of a politer way of saying it. He had been married four times; after his most recent divorce, he was photographed cavorting with a former graduate student of his who was younger than all of his children. His starter wife was a doctor; they had met at university. Each subsequent relationship involved a search-and-replace process in which he sought out the most attractive graduate student and made her the new Madam Giscard. He stunned a conference of microbiologists—I mean, left a room of two hundred just stone-silent—when he opened a talk on cell longevity by saying, "I must have found the key to eternal youth, because the woman I am married to never seems to get any older."* There was not even uncomfortable laughter.

Giscard eventually found his way to Harvard, where the university built and funded a laboratory for him. This became a cause célèbre on campus, as Giscard's pattern of behavior was already well established before Harvard recruited him. (Yes, he had married some of his protégés, but most of the attractive graduate students who had been the recipients of his amorous advances had no interest in becoming the next Madam Giscard.) He made it barely four months in Cambridge before a laboratory assistant alleged that he had pressed his body up against her and smelled her hair while she was looking at a microscope. This was a tough case to make, as people do bump into one another in close quarters, and sniffing hair (wildly parodied in the *Harvard Lampoon*) is not generally a firing offense. Still, Harvard's president decided this was not a work environment that should be encouraged. Perhaps more important to the resolution of the situation, Giscard decided he was not happy at Harvard, either. In a remarkably telling comment, he told a reporter at the *Harvard Crimson*, "No one has ever complained before."

There were no quibbles over Giscard's scientific talent. He was

---

* You can watch the YouTube clip, which includes not just the remark (in French) but also about five seconds of audience reaction during which the scientists look around in shock.

not a brilliant theorist; rather, he had a brilliant ability—and I am not using the word "brilliant" lightly—to absorb a theory and digest it into smaller, more actionable pieces. This was his contribution several times over in the development of Dormigen. On the other hand, Giscard's colleagues did quibble—more than quibble, actually—about his prodigious ability to appropriate credit for major breakthroughs. When teams of researchers were tackling similar problems at different universities, as is often the case in academe, Giscard's papers always seemed to get published first, often with the results advertised to the press before the peer review process was complete. And when those papers were published, he always demanded to be first author, regardless of his actual contribution. It was not negotiable.

I would see all of this play itself out—every single one of Giscard's extreme personality traits—over the next thirty-six hours.

68.

THE U.S. AMBASSADOR TO INDIA IS ONE OF THE UNSUNG heroes of the Outbreak. Early in the crisis, our request to the Indian government to "borrow" any excess Dormigen had been firmly rebuffed. The Indian Prime Minister was a prickly populist, keenly sensitive to being perceived as the junior partner in the U.S.-India relationship. He was facing an impending parliamentary election and feared that sending Dormigen to the U.S. would be perceived by the Indian masses as putting U.S. health interests ahead of India's own massive challenges. Hence, the Indian Prime Minister had offered to sell Dormigen to the U.S. only for a ridiculous sum. Subsequent discussions had gone nowhere productive; State Department diplomats reckoned that India was not a likely source of Dormigen as long as: (1) the Indian Prime Minister was concerned primarily about his party's electoral prospects; and (2) he believed that any assistance to the U.S. would be perceived by Indian voters as bad for India.

Once the Outbreak became public, however, American diplomats on the ground in New Delhi noticed a subtle undercurrent in

Indian public opinion that presented an opportunity. It began with a newspaper column by a prominent journalist. If China is exploiting America's desperate situation, the columnist asked, does this not represent an opportunity for India to transform its relationship with the United States? India and China, the world's two most populous countries, had been eyeing each other warily for decades. They were each trying to lift hundreds of millions of people out of poverty, albeit with radically different approaches to governance and development. They had gone to war once, just a month-long conflict in 1962, but the border dispute that had precipitated the shooting remained unresolved. Three years before that, India had welcomed the Dalai Lama when he fled from Tibet; he has resided in northern India ever since—a constant source of irritation for Beijing. Over time, the India-China rivalry had morphed into an ideological battle: Democracy or autocracy? And, like two needy siblings competing for parental affection, each jockeyed on the world stage to gain a strategic advantage via its relationship with the United States. There was a strain of thinking in New Delhi—perhaps oversimplified but not necessarily incorrect—that China's loss must be India's gain. While China was being demonized in Washington for clumsily exploiting the crisis, would this not be a natural opportunity for India, the world's largest democracy, to deepen its ties with the U.S., the world's most powerful democracy?

These were the thoughts that Indian intellectuals had begun to bandy about. The Prime Minister was never confused with the intellectuals. He did, however, have a brilliant sense of which way the intellectual winds were blowing. The U.S. Ambassador to India, a former senator from New Hampshire, was a keen enough observer of Indian politics to spot an opportunity in all this. We should be thankful that the Ambassador was not one of those political hacks who make huge contributions to a presidential campaign and then find themselves ambassador to a country that they cannot find on a map. Rather, the Ambassador had started his career in the Foreign Service and had been a member of the Foreign Affairs Committee in the Senate. The President had offered him the post as a consolation after he was beaten unexpectedly in a Democratic primary. He knew politics. He knew diplomacy. And he understood the needs and wants of the Indian Prime Minister. As the South China Sea Agreement drama was unfolding, the Ambassador passed an urgent message along to the Secretary of State: If we play our cards right, India might be the solution here.

When the Secretary of State and the U.S. Ambassador were finally able to speak, shortly after Air Force One had touched down in Australia, the Ambassador laid out his thinking: "If we can create a political win for the Indian Prime Minister, he'll give us whatever Dormigen we need."

"He turned down our earlier inquiries without a second thought," the Secretary of State said skeptically.

"That was then. This is now," the Ambassador explained. "There are murmurings in the press and elsewhere that this could be India's shining moment on the world stage, the perfect opportunity to poke a finger in China's eye."

"Do they have enough Dormigen?" the Secretary of State asked.

"Yes," the Ambassador answered confidently. The Secretary of State did not ask how the Ambassador would know something like this. She assumed that the resident spooks in New Delhi had done their homework.

"Okay, then, I think we should pursue a conversation," the Secretary of State said.

"Yes, well, there's one caveat," the Ambassador said.

"Of course there is. What?" the Secretary of State asked.

"The Prime Minister is going to have to think this is his idea. If we ask again for the Dormigen, we're not going to get it. He needs to offer it to us. It has to be his shining idea, and Indian voters need to know that."

"Really?" the Secretary of State asked. She was intolerant of the exigencies of politics in the best of times. Now, having slept little and facing a deadly deadline, the Secretary of State was even less patient with such silliness. "Really? We're facing down a hundred thousand deaths, and he needs to feel this is his idea? Are we dealing with a teenager?"

The Ambassador laughed. "That would not be a bad guide for the negotiations. But if I'm being more charitable, I'd say that one does not become prime minister in a country of a billion people, many of them illiterate, without some rather coarse political calculations."

"Okay, fine. How do we make this his idea?" the Secretary asked.

"I was hoping you would have a suggestion," the Ambassador answered.

The Secretary of State relayed the conversation to the President, who seized on the possibility eagerly. "It can't be too hard to feed this idea to the Prime Minister," the President said. "I don't care who gets the credit."

"Washington is full of people who think they've come up with other people's brilliant ideas," the Strategist offered.

"Exactly," the President agreed. "Can't we do a poll, something that shows that Indian voters want to come to the rescue here?"

"There's not enough time," the Strategist said. "We need three or four days to do a decent poll. And that's in the U.S.; India is even more complicated."

"Give me something here," the President said in exasperation. "I'm tired of people telling me what I can't do."

"Poll results, on the other hand—I could do that in about five minutes," the Strategist said.

"What's that supposed to mean?" the Secretary of State asked suspiciously.

"It means we create the results we want and leak them to an influential Indian news source," the Strategist explained.

"Oh, for God's sake, that's exactly the kind of thing that will make people around the world even more paranoid about American meddling," the Secretary of State said.

"Let's worry about that next week, when people aren't dying of *Capellaviridae*," the President said.

"With all due respect, sir, we should think very carefully—"

"I just did," the President said sharply. "Make it happen. The two of you. I want the Indian Prime Minister to wake up tomorrow and think that his entire political future depends on shipping huge quantities of Dormigen to the United States. How you make that happen—that's your job."

69.

LIONEL GISCARD ARRIVED AT THE NIH OFFICES WITH GREAT fanfare. He had long gray hair and a carefully manicured goatee. He wore a blue suit with a florid purple shirt and a paisley silk scarf around his neck that he wrapped and unwrapped frequently, almost like a nervous tic. Giscard was stylish for a fifty-year-old man; by NIH standards he looked like a fashion model (with a great accent). Giscard's arrival caused a frisson of excitement. Those who knew him greeted him effusively. Others waited to be introduced. I was surprised by how all the charges of bad behavior melted away in his presence—scientific celebrity. I also recognized that celebrity can be relative. As soon as Giscard stepped out of our scientific den onto the street, he became just another old guy with a goofy-looking scarf.

The NIH Director ushered Giscard into a conference room, where the *Capellaviridae* team was assembling. I was seated at the table; the Director introduced me as the resident *Capellaviridae* expert. "Okay, yes," Giscard said. "But I am not familiar with your work. You publish on *Capellaviridae*, yes?"

"I did my doctoral work on it," I said.

"And since?"

"I work on the staff here."

"Ah, yes, I see." His tone could not have been more dismissive. He immediately turned and looked around the room. His gaze settled on Jenna, who was seated in the back of the room in one of the chairs reserved for junior staff.

"Good to meet you," I said sarcastically as Giscard made a beeline for Jenna, like a wolf that has spotted a baby rabbit limping in the grass. From across the room I watched as Giscard shook Jenna's hand, placing his other hand lightly on her arm. She laughed at something he said. Some of the senior scientists waited patiently to meet Giscard while he finished his flirtation.

The NIH Director called the room to order. She introduced Giscard to the senior staff and gave a brief overview of our progress to date, including a summary of my "hostage hypothesis." "But of course," Giscard said. "This makes perfect sense. I have been working on a paper to this effect. In French, we say 'preneur d'otages,' the taker of hostages." Like so much else with Giscard, it is hard to know if this was the truth, an exaggeration, or a complete falsehood. He claimed he was working on a paper with a theory of lurking viruses similar to what I had proposed. "You were invited to the conference in Toronto, yes?" he asked me.

"I wasn't able to attend," I said. That was technically true. If one is not invited, it is difficult to attend. Also, I had no idea what Toronto conference he was referring to.

When the Director finished her briefing, the room fell silent. All eyes turned to Giscard for some pearl of wisdom. He swept the paisley scarf around his neck with even more care than usual. "Mais oui," he said, drawing the attention of the few people in the room who had not been looking at him. He struck a pensive tone, deliberately unfurling the scarf. At last: "I think that if a vector can spread a virus, then it can also spread an antibody, yes?" He had a prodigious ability to appear profound while repeating what he had just been told.

"That is the hypothesis we are now exploring," the Director said.

"By this thinking, the small bug—how does one say it?"

"The North American dust mite," the Director offered.

"Yes, the dust mite. The dust mite becomes valuable to its host, the human, because it somehow introduces the antidote for *Capella-viridae*. Yes?"

A scientist at the conference table interjected, "We've not found any sign of an antibody. That was one of the first things we checked for. We cannot find any antibodies in those who are not affected—"

"Yes, yes, okay," Giscard said, cutting him off and, at least from my perspective, dismissing him with what looked like a wave of the scarf. "I assume as much, or I would not be here. This is not your typical potato, right?" Remarkably, people throughout the room, including most of the senior scientists, laughed at this bizarre potato comment. Giscard continued, "But somehow the ongoing presence of this small bug—"

"The dust mite," a scientist sitting opposite Giscard offered.

"Yes, okay, the presence of the dust mite is somehow affecting *Capellaviridae* so it does not turn dangerous."

Tie Guy, who was sitting in a chair against the wall, interjected confidently, "We have nothing to show causality here—no biological evidence whatsoever—just a robust inverse correlation. When people are exposed constantly to the dust mite, they do not get sick. When that exposure is interrupted, either because the dust mite is successfully exterminated, or because a person moves to an area where there are no dust mites, *Capellaviridae* is prone to turn virulent."

"Yes, yes, like the Director said," Giscard agreed. "And when you expose people who are sick with *Capellaviridae* to the dust bug, they get better?"

"It's been very hard to test," I offered. "Most people get better on their own, so we'd need a huge trial to prove effectiveness. We don't have the time and we don't have the volunteers."

Giscard gave the scarf one final furl around his neck. He leaned back in his chair and put his fingertips together, making sure that the whole room recognized that he was now engaged in deep contemplation. "And so here we are," he said.

"This is where we've been since I proposed the hypothesis," I said with more than a little irritation.

"Can we break for a coffee?" Giscard asked. "I think this situation is very manageable."

"It's not feeling manageable," the Director said. "We have very little time."

"Let's have a coffee," Giscard insisted. "I have some ideas." The Director was nonplussed at having the meeting interrupted for a coffee break. (There were urns of coffee in the conference room.) Giscard was disrupting the protocol: reports to be presented, assignments to be made, and so on. The guy had no official role, and now here he was proposing a coffee break eighteen minutes into our official daily briefing.

"We have a lot of business to get through," the NIH Director said.

Giscard waved dismissively at the crowded conference table. "But this is not how science happens, with bureaucratic meetings. We need to think—how do you say it, brainstorm. We do not need the accountants in the room." Obviously there were no accountants in the room, and Giscard had now managed to annoy much of the staff, but he was not entirely wrong. The NIH meetings had become increasingly mechanistic and process-oriented. The time spent in meetings like this drowned out some of the casual conversations among researchers that could often lead to breakthroughs.

"We have some important things to get through," the Director said. "Then perhaps we can do a smaller session a little later with no agenda. Please understand that we are keen to take advantage of your expertise, Dr. Giscard."

"As you like," Giscard said with a twirl of the scarf. "I am here because there is a crisis."

The Director moved through business quickly, after which a group of us on the science side retired to a small windowless conference room with whiteboards on three walls. As we filed into the room, Giscard spotted Jenna speaking with the Director. Once again, he made a beeline for her. "Will that room be okay, Dr. Giscard?" the Director asked as he approached.

"Yes, yes," he assured her as he turned to Jenna. "But you will join us?"

"Me?" Jenna asked, apparently oblivious to the fact that Giscard was stalking her. "I'm just an extra pair of hands around here."

The Director, no naïf when it came to predatory scientists with huge egos, said quickly, "Jenna has some things to do for me. She's not part of the virus working group."

Giscard touched Jenna lightly on the shoulder: "We will talk later."

"That would be great," Jenna said.

With the flirtation out of the way (for the time being), a group of six or seven of us retired to our small windowless room. Tie Guy spoke first, outlining his statistical findings. A scientist from the CDC summarized what we had learned about *Capellaviridae*, including its similarity to the influenza virus. Giscard behaved differently in this environment—more scientist and less French showman. It may have been my imagination, but I think he even twirled his scarf less often. Moments earlier I had felt a strong urge to strangle him with the scarf, but now I could not help admiring how his mind worked. I presented my theory that the North American dust mite was somehow using *Capellaviridae* to gain an evolutionary advantage. "I suspect this virus has an on-off switch—somewhere, somehow," I said. "The dust mite controls that switch and benefits as a result."

"Yes, this is right," Giscard said confidently.

"We can't find any evidence of that," a CDC scientist objected. "The virulent and dormant forms of the virus are identical."

"That's not right," Giscard said dismissively. "One form of the virus makes you sick, one does not. Those are not the same. They cannot be the same."

"They have the same DNA," the scientist replied.

Giscard grew even more dismissive, something I did not think possible. He made a strange *pffff* sound, blowing air out his pursed lips. He pointed at a young CDC scientist sitting next to him. "You have DNA. I hit you with a mallet. Your DNA does not change. But now you are different because your brain is on the floor." He paused as we digested and recoiled from his analogy, not least the scientist whose hypothetical brain was now lying on the floor. Giscard continued, "If you people start with the assumption that the virulent form of the virus is no different than the dormant virus, then of course you will miss the difference!" I watched the body language of the scientists around the table as this French interloper chided them for their sloppy work. There were a few sets of rolled eyes, but I suspect most in the room were feeling some variation of what I was feeling, namely that Giscard was a complete asshole who was probably right.

"Healthy people carrying *Capellaviridae* have no antibodies," I offered. "It's not that their bodies are fighting it off. There is nothing to fight off. It's innocuous—until it's not."

"Okay, yes," Giscard said, encouraging this line of thought. I felt like an elementary school student who has answered a math problem correctly, basking in the admiration of my teacher. I hated myself for it, but I wanted Giscard to appreciate my input.

"So what's happening is not a difference in reaction to the virus," I continued. "It's not that some people fight it off and others don't.

The virus itself appears to be behaving differently. Maybe there is a difference at the molecular level.”*

"Exactly," Giscard said.

"The President is going to speak in about twenty-five minutes," Tie Guy said.

Giscard turned to him, seemingly annoyed by the interruption. "The President is not going to help us understand the virus," he said.

"I'd like to watch," one of the CDC scientists said with a hint of hostility.

"We have time to waste?" Giscard asked.

"I'll stream it on my laptop," I said. "We don't have to interrupt what we're doing."

The rest of the meeting is the subject of what might generously be called "competing memories" (which have in turn generated competing news accounts, competing lawsuits, competing memoirs, and even one pathetically inaccurate French documentary, *The Hero in the Room*). Here is what we do know: (1) the biochemists began comparing the molecular structures of the dormant and virulent *Capellaviridae* viruses; (2) we proposed a hypothesis whereby *Capellaviridae* is rendered indolent by the disruption of a key protein; and (3) we further hypothesized that the North American dust mite transfers an enzyme to humans that renders *Capellaviridae* harmless. Our theory left some crucial questions unanswered (e.g., Why did this effect appear to be only temporary?). But for the first time, we had an elegant and testable hypothesis that could explain not just *Capellaviridae*, but potentially all lurking viruses. Most important, if we were correct, we would in theory have an antidote for the virulent form of *Capellaviridae*: the mystery enzyme.

The biochemists immediately reached out to their colleagues at

---

* I am certain that I was the first person in the room to suggest that the virulent form of *Capellaviridae* was different than the benign form at the molecular level. Several people who were in the room have affirmed this. Giscard, however, maintains that he had always believed this might be the case and that he had traveled to the U.S. to share this hypothesis with us. From this point on, as I will subsequently note in the text, most of the important details from this meeting—in terms of who said what—are still in dispute.

the NIH and in academe to begin examining the protein structures of the virulent and indolent *Capellaviridae* viruses. I briefed the NIH Director on our progress. She in turn called the Chief of Staff to report the potential breakthrough. And Lionel Giscard, as best as I can tell, immediately set to work claiming credit for all the important work we had done.

PART 8

THE
HYPOTHESIS
AND THE EGO

70.

THE PRESIDENT WOULD SPEAK FROM AIR FORCE ONE immediately after the Acting HHS Secretary gave his briefing to Congress. The Communications Director was adamant that there be as little time as possible between the congressional briefing and the beginning of the President's speech. "I don't want them to have time to make a single tweet—not even two hundred and eighty characters," he told the Acting HHS Secretary. "And keep it simple: here's what's happening, here's what we're doing, and here is our plan in the unlikely event that we encounter a temporary shortage of Dormigen."

"Is that still an unlikely event?" the Acting Secretary asked. "I thought the whole point of the briefing was to make people aware of the seriousness of the situation."

"Okay, don't say 'unlikely.'" the Communications Director conceded. "But I want it clear that we are still pursuing multiple options to forestall a shortage."

"How about I just say that?" the Acting Secretary asked.

"Fine," the Communications Director said. "But whatever you do, don't use the word 'ration.'"

"We are going to prioritize who gets Dormigen in the event of a shortage," the Acting Secretary suggested.

"Perfect."

"Because that's not rationing."

"No one in this administration is going to use that word," the Communications Director declared.

"And what about Cecelia Dodds?" the Acting Secretary asked.

"What about her?" the Communications Director asked impatiently.

"It's hard to say everything is going to be okay as she drifts in and out of consciousness." That was the latest update from the hospital. Cecelia Dodds was being treated with an experimental German antibiotic that had proven effective against respiratory infections. So far, she had not responded positively.

"We can say something about the German drug," the Communications Director offered. "That's the kind of thing we'll do in the absence of Dormigen."

"And if she dies while I'm giving my briefing—"

"*I don't know what the fuck we should say!*" the Communications Director exploded. He composed himself and continued. "I think maybe we just don't say anything."

The administration had vowed not to use the word "ration." The Speaker of the House was intent on using that word as frequently as possible. She had taken a beating for her position on the South China Sea Agreement and as the putative leader of a Hispanic separatist movement before that. Those news cycles were now past. One does not get to be Speaker of the House, let alone a credible presidential candidate, without taking a few punches to the gut. The Speaker had arranged a press briefing in the Capitol forty-five minutes before the Acting HHS Secretary was scheduled to brief Congress. "How is she going to react to the briefing before the briefing?" the Chief of Staff asked sarcastically upon learning of the Speaker's plans.

"Call her," the President directed. "Tell her we all need to be on the same page." The Chief of Staff phoned the Speaker, who was unavailable, according to the young staffer who answered the Speaker's cell phone. "Tell her that if she doesn't become available, I'm going to take away her plane," the President growled in the background, loud enough for the staffer to hear.* Miraculously, the Speaker became available.

* At the beginning of the administration, some observers had suggested— presciently, it would appear—that the President had passed out the military planes

"The President would like to know what you plan to say at your press briefing," the Chief of Staff said. There were no pleasantries exchanged.

"May I speak with the President, please?" the Speaker asked. The President, who could overhear the conversation, shook his head no.

"He's working on his remarks," the Chief of Staff said. "We all need to be on the same page here."

"Of course," the Speaker agreed.

"Then why are you doing a media availability before we brief Congress?" the Chief of Staff asked.

"I have a pretty good idea what you're going to say," the Speaker replied. It was true that the President had done an informal briefing for the Senate Majority Leader and for many of the Conventioneers. There was no doubt that the content of these conversations had been leaked to the Speaker, if not more broadly. "Congress is a coequal branch here," the Speaker said. "I want the public to understand that we are a partner in dealing with this crisis."

"So you're calling the press to the Capitol to give them a civics lesson?" the Chief of Staff asked facetiously. "I don't believe that." In the background, the President was shaking his head in anger and frustration. Before the Speaker could answer, the Chief of Staff continued, "Could you just support us here for five minutes?"

"If you are going to cut me out of the loop, I have no choice but to reassert congressional prerogative," the Speaker said insolently.

"We involved you from the very beginning," the Chief of Staff said. "You decided to freelance on the South China Sea Agreement and you got burned. That's on you."

The Speaker was in no mood to back down. "I'd like to know what the President plans to say," she declared.

"That's why we're doing the congressional briefing before the speech," the Chief of Staff said.

The Speaker gave a short, mirthless laugh. "The President has been calling people all over Washington. Everybody knows the situation."

---

to legislative leaders so that he could threaten to take them away, not unlike giving a teenager a car and then using it as leverage.

"Then you don't need the briefing, apparently."

"As a courtesy, I would appreciate hearing directly from the President," the Speaker said. In the background, the President motioned for the phone; the Chief of Staff handed it to him.

"Madam Speaker," the President said, "I am telling you not to address the press before we do our congressional briefing."

"Cecelia Dodds has lost consciousness," the Speaker said. "You know that, don't you?"

"I didn't realize the two of you were close," the President replied. They were not, of course. Cecelia Dodds had criticized the Speaker on several occasions for her divisive tactics. The Speaker had declined to attend the ceremony at which Dodds was presented the Presidential Medal of Freedom.

"She's a national treasure," the Speaker said. "This will be your legacy."

"One has to admire her selflessness," the President said honestly.

"Let's cut to the chase, Mr. President, you can't *tell* me when to meet with the press."

"Okay, then I'm asking. I'm asking you to be a team player here."

"It's always about your team. It's your team or no team," the Speaker said.

"What?" the President asked in genuine amazement. "I think we're done here. You do what you have to do."

Eager to have the last word, the Speaker said, "And by the way, Mr. President, you can have the plane. American taxpayers shouldn't have to bear that expense."

The President hung up without reply. "She's running for president," he told the Chief of Staff. "Her donors are going to give her a nice big campaign plane. That's what that means."

Two other things of note were happening at roughly the same time. In Riyadh, Saudi Arabia, a small group of armed Sunni extremists burst into an international school, overwhelmed a night security guard, and took a hundred and twelve students and faculty hostage. There were twenty-seven American students and two teachers among the hostages. The terrorists' grievances were nothing new. They demanded a withdrawal of U.S. forces from Saudi Arabia and the other Gulf nations; the end of U.S. support for the Saudi monarchy; and assorted other such things. What was new, however, was the method to their madness. The hostage takers identified the American students with parents who worked for either the American military or the U.S. Embassy; the others were released unharmed. The kidnappers then demanded that the parents—the military and embassy officials—exchange themselves for their children. They had twelve hours to present themselves. When a parent walked into the school gymnasium, their child would be released; if that did not happen in twelve hours, the child would be shot. The terrorists had found and exploited the underbelly of the heavily fortified American presence in Saudi Arabia. Our military facilities and the embassy were impregnable; the international school, less so. The rest of this story is familiar to anyone who lived through it. I mention it merely to draw attention to the timing. The President received word of the terrorist assault just before his address to the nation.

Meanwhile, the Secretary of State and the Strategist were on their way to Bahrain. They had not boarded Air Force One for the flight back to the U.S., as staffers had realized. The President had instructed them to reexamine the possibility of India as a Dormigen donor, but the delicate nature of that situation was such that they could not fly to India unless and until the Indian Prime Minister invited them to do so. The Secretary of State chose Bahrain as a logical intermediate destination: a place where they might plausibly have diplomatic business that was close enough to India to allow them to get there quickly should the Prime Minister summon them. Just as the two of them were touching down at Naval Support Activity Bahrain, several prominent Indian newspapers were reporting on a "new poll" from the Indian Institute for Future Security showing that 68 percent of Indian voters believed that India had an obligation to help the U.S. during the Outbreak; 73 percent agreed that "India would benefit from closer ties to the United States." The details surrounding the poll—and the origins and funding of the Indian Institute for Future Security—remain shrouded in mystery. In a later moment of indiscretion, the Strategist did tell an audience at the Council of Foreign Relations in New York: "The Soviets taught us that no one ever wins an election with ninety-nine percent. To be credible, your fake results need to be in the sixty to seventy percent range. Even eighty percent strains credulity."

The Secretary of State and the Strategist stepped off the small Air Force jet in Bahrain and were immediately belted with a blast of hot, dry desert air, like opening a hot oven. An officious two-star general met them on the tarmac, eager to be of assistance and excited to be involved in whatever was happening. One did not need to be a rocket scientist—though, coincidentally, the general in question *was* an aeronautical engineer—to recognize that the Secretary of State does not show up on short notice with the President's chief strategist unless something interesting is afoot. The Secretary of State was traveling without a staff, which was also highly unusual. "We're honored to have you here, Madam Secretary," the General said earnestly. He ushered her and the Strategist toward a terminal where a handful of other officers were waiting awkwardly with cold drinks.

"Now what do we do?" the Secretary of State asked the Strategist under her breath.

"We know the Prime Minister is going to read the papers. We just wait for the phone to ring," the Strategist answered.

The General said, "I know you have meetings with Bahraini officials, but might I be able to offer you a tour of the base?"

"That would be excellent," the Strategist replied.

71.

THE SPEAKER OF THE HOUSE STEPPED TO A PODIUM BENEATH the rotunda of the Capitol, the very same place where she had advocated strenuously for "the China option." The Washington press corps recognized that the Speaker was violating protocol by making a statement before the President's address. The bad chemistry between the President and the Speaker always made for good copy, especially now that the Outbreak had raised the stakes in their pissing match. "I will be brief," the Speaker began. "Today I will introduce legislation guaranteeing every American access to Dormigen, irrespective of gender, religion, race, sexual orientation, or, most important, age.

We do not live in a society where lifesaving drugs should be rationed. We should not have to pass legislation to guarantee such a basic right, and yet here we are. In less than an hour, the President, having failed to provide the nation with sufficient Dormigen, will announce a plan to deny that lifesaving drug to some of the most vulnerable members of society: the old and the infirm—the very people who need the nurturing hand of government most."

The President and Chief of Staff were watching the statement in the conference room on Air Force One. "For fuck sake," the President muttered. "Please tell me this is not happening."

"It doesn't make any sense," the Chief of Staff said, genuinely perplexed. "We don't have enough Dormigen. She's not an idiot. What does she think we're going to do? You can't promise what you don't have—"

"She thinks we're going to avert the crisis," the President said with a sardonic laugh. "It's a backhanded compliment, actually."

"I don't follow," the Chief of Staff said.

"You have to give her credit for creativity, if nothing else," the President answered. "She thinks we're going to come up with the Dormigen, or figure out the virus, or something. She doesn't think we're going to have to ration anything. So she introduces her grandiose bill—protecting the old, the infirm, the left-handed, and everyone else—right before we lay out our rationing plan. Then, when the crisis is averted, she's the one who promised Dormigen to everyone and we're the ones who planned to let old people die."

"And if things don't turn out all hunky-dory?"

"Then it doesn't matter anyway," the President explained. "We can't give out Dormigen we don't have. She's taking a gamble here."

"Unbelievable."

"You don't win the presidency without taking some risks," the President said with what his Chief of Staff would later describe as "an admixture of respect and disgust."

The Speaker finished her statement: "The President will soon tell the nation who will be excluded, who is too sick or too old to be saved. Congress cannot allow that to happen. I will not live in a country that turns its back on the most vulnerable. *In my America, there is Dormigen for every one of us.*"

She did not take questions. There was no way she could. The statement made no sense given the reality of what was going on; some members of the media were openly snickering. We had crowded around my laptop to watch the talk in the NIH conference room, which had grown warm and stuffy. "Is that woman crazy?" Giscard asked without a hint of sarcasm or irony. "I mean, really, does she understand what is happening?"

"She's a politician," one of the CDC scientists said.

"Yes, okay, I understand, but still: How can one promise Dormigen for all when there is no Dormigen?" Giscard asked, genuinely flummoxed. Several of us shrugged by way of reply. The Speaker clearly had better political antennae than the rest of us, because almost immediately social media exploded with what would become the #norationing campaign. Progressives organized rallies in D.C. and other big cities. One influential lefty blogger compared the President to a concentration camp guard who met the trains and sent prisoners "left or right."

The President called the Acting Secretary of HHS just before he was scheduled to do the congressional briefing. "Thank you for doing this," the President said.

"I'm too old for this shit," the Acting Secretary said. "What was she thinking?"

"About the 2032 race," the President said.

"Apparently. How should I respond?"

"Don't. Just lay out our plan. Stick to the briefing materials. The important thing is that people realize how serious the situation might become. That's our responsibility here. Everything else is just noise."

"What about Q and A?" the Acting Secretary asked.

"You have to answer questions. It's Congress. But you know the drill: act professional and say as little as possible, no matter what they throw at you. It's like a congressional hearing; you've done it a hundred times," the President assured him.

"Except this time it's *all* of Congress and we've just been compared to concentration camp guards."

"Right. Good luck with that," the President replied. And then, after a pause, "Seriously, thank you for carrying the water on this one."

"It's an honor to do what I can, Mr. President."

"Okay, then, good luck. I'm on right after you."

In New Delhi, the phone rang—the phone call the U.S. Ambassador had been hoping for, or at least a step in that direction. A functionary in the Indian Ministry of Health called the U.S. Embassy, asking if perhaps the U.S. Ambassador would have time for a short chat with someone in the Prime Minister's office regarding the American Dormigen shortage. As soon as possible.

72.

THE U.S. AMBASSADOR IMMEDIATELY RELAYED THE NEWS TO the Secretary of State and the Strategist, who cut their tour of the Bahraini base short and ensconced themselves in a small secure conference room. "I assume I call him back?" the U.S. Ambassador asked.

"Give it at least a half an hour," the Strategist advised. "The Indian PM is a rug merchant—"

"Can we show some respect, please?" the Secretary of State interrupted, casting an exasperated look across the table.

The Strategist, not one to back down when he believed himself to be right, said, "Isn't that literally true? His family traded carpets. Wasn't his family in the carpet business?" the Strategist asked the U.S. Ambassador.

The Ambassador replied uncomfortably, "I do believe his mother's family exported carpets from Kashmir."

"He wrote about it in his autobiography," the Strategist explained.

"Fine, but for my benefit, can we please not call him a rug merchant?" the Secretary of State said. (In her memoir, she would describe herself as "horrified" by the Strategist's manners but "simultaneously impressed" by his depth of knowledge on myriad topics.)

The Strategist, taking no offense, replied, "I don't care what we call him. The point is that he sees the world as a zero-sum game—everything. If we win, he loses, and vice versa."

"I would agree," the Ambassador offered. "He's hard to deal with that way."

"We need to make him think he's getting a huge win and that we're somehow losing," the Strategist said.

"That seems difficult, given the circumstances," the Ambassador said earnestly. "How does the U.S. lose by getting Dormigen that's going to save thousands of lives?"

"We suggest that we can't give him what he most wants," the Strategist said.

"Publicity," the Secretary of State offered.

"Exactly," the Strategist said, impressed his pupils were keeping up with him. "The PM wants a political win, domestically and on the international stage. We tell him that won't be possible. We appreciate his Dormigen offer, but the President is not comfortable appearing dependent on a developing country to protect—"

"Do not refer to India as a developing country," the Ambassador said firmly. "He will be very sensitive to that."

"Of course he will!" the Strategist blurted out, now exasperated that one of his pupils was falling behind. "Not that people tend to confuse India with Switzerland, but still, you're correct, so we need to exploit that sensitivity. What better way for India to signal its economic progress than to bail out the richest country on the planet?"

"I agree," the Secretary of State said.

"Okay, so what next?" the U.S. Ambassador asked.

"You need to set up a meeting with someone in the Prime Minister's office," the Strategist instructed the Ambassador. "Tell them it needs to be confidential. Request to meet in a shopping mall, or a restaurant, or someplace like that. Tell them the President is very sensitive to appearing as a supplicant—yes, use that word, 'supplicant.'"

The Secretary of State added, "Especially after the polling data showing what a huge political win this would be for the PM."

"Yes, exactly! Good," the Strategist said. "And then when they hint at a Dormigen offer, which they will, you must make clear that the President would be willing to accept the Dormigen, but the deal would have to be confidential, or at least very low-key."

"And how does the President really feel?" the Ambassador asked.

"What do you think?" the Strategist answered impatiently. "The President just wants the Dormigen. The Indian PM can ride it down Fifth Avenue on a white horse, if that's what he wants."

"This feels like a long shot," the U.S. Ambassador said. "We're treating a head of state like Br'er Rabbit."

"First of all," the Strategist said, "Br'er Rabbit was the one who got thrown in the briar patch, so technically we're treating the PM like the fox. Second, we've got no other fucking options. And third, I'll bet you my left testicle it works."*

73.

THE CONGRESSIONAL BRIEFING BY THE ACTING HHS SECRE-tary was somewhat anticlimactic after the Speaker's press conference. The President had already spoken at length with the Senate Majority Leader and many of the Conventioneers. The Communications Director had released the key points of the briefing five minutes before the Acting Director began speaking, creating an odd situation in which members of Congress were getting texts from their staffs giving them the key points of the briefing they were waiting to receive. The Speaker tweeted that this was "beyond insulting," prompting the Communications Director to tweet back (publicly, of course), "Key 4 America should be content of briefing, not who gets it when," at which point the Chief of Staff ordered him to disengage.

For those of us working on the Outbreak from the beginning, the congressional briefing was old news. The Acting Secretary walked through the details of how we got to this point (including the arrest and indictment of the Centera Pharmaceutical executives); the efforts the administration was making to gather Dormigen from other countries; the scientific advances that had been made with regard to the virus. The chamber was loud and unruly, as staffers scurried about and members studied their devices for details of what the Acting Secretary was about to tell them. After a few minutes of what felt like prefatory remarks, the Acting Secretary turned to the essence of the briefing, the "what now" part, and although nearly everyone in the chamber knew what was coming, the noise dissipated and most eyes turned to the Acting Secretary as he stood in the well of the House. "As you are well aware," he intoned, "even with all of the efforts I

---

* We know this was the exact language the Strategist used, as the Secretary of State devoted a page and a half to this conversation in her memoir.

have just described, it is increasingly likely that we will find ourselves with an insufficient supply of Dormigen to meet our basic needs."

There were hisses and catcalls in the chamber. "Not in America!" someone yelled from the Acting Secretary's left. "No rationing!" came another cry. The outbursts felt choreographed, as they probably were. Someone who heard only the audio, as opposed to sitting in the august House chamber, might assume they were listening to a high school principal lecturing unruly students. Of course, if I am being honest, the briefing itself was mostly theater, too. The President had instructed the Communications Director, "Just tell them enough to keep them busy." Still, it was the public's first official glance at what lay ahead as the Dormigen stocks were depleted.

The Acting HHS Secretary continued: "Despite our best efforts to conserve Dormigen in recent days, we are now projecting a short-fall for several days before plentiful new supplies of Dormigen can be produced. This is a short window, not quite four days according to our most recent calculations, but during that period we anticipate that not every patient who would normally benefit from Dormigen will have access the drug." There was more hissing and jeering, but the Acting Secretary's calm, avuncular tone took some of the negative energy out of the chamber. He continued: "In consultation with physicians and medical ethicists, we have developed a contingency plan—a plan, by the way, that we still hope will not be necessary— to allocate the available Dormigen supplies in a way that will offer the greatest possible health benefits. The available Dormigen will be prescribed where it can do the most good, and doctors will be dis-couraged from using the drug when the benefits are likely to have the least impact." This last bit had been run past focus groups repeatedly, despite the confidential nature of the plan. The Strategist had been able to get groups to respond to a "hypothetical situation" in which the captain of a cruise ship adrift at sea had to explain how the dwin-dling food supplies would be allocated among the passengers. "The exact details of our plan are explained in the briefing packet that we have distributed," the Acting Secretary said.

"Old people to the right!" someone yelled from the floor.

"Rich people to the left!" a different voice responded.

The Acting Secretary seized on a momentary pause to interject, "I will now answer any questions you may have." The exact details of the Dormigen rationing were laid out in small print in the documents distributed in the congressional briefing packets: the age cutoff; the kinds of illnesses that would render patients ineligible for Dormigen; the penalties for physicians who did not comply with the protocol; and, of course, "a range of estimated incremental preventable fatalities"—right there, two-thirds of the way down page eleven. Many of the members of Congress scurried out of chamber, eager to get on camera or to push their inspired thoughts out on social media. Predictably, these missives were long on vitriolic criticism of the "White House rationing scheme"* and short on alternative suggestions. The Acting Secretary patiently answered questions from the members of Congress and staff who remained behind, but it soon became apparent that most of the questions were not really questions ("Isn't it true that . . ."). Nor were most of the Acting Secretary's answers really answers. He showed remarkable discipline, repeatedly referring questioners to "the briefing document you have received" and answering even the most asinine suggestions with, "We will take that under advisement."

The Communications Director had forbidden most of us from speaking to the media: "I don't even want you to say, 'No comment.' That's too much talking. Just shake your head no. Your lips should not be moving!" For those who would be speaking in public, beginning obviously with the Acting Secretary, he was equally emphatic: "Do not, under any circumstances, say anything specific about who gets Dormigen and who does not. *It's in the briefing document.* Refer to the briefing document. If someone asks, 'My grandfather is a hundred and nine and has emphysema. If he were hit by a bus, would he be eligible for Dormigen?' you say, 'The specifics of the plan are in the briefing document.' Is that clear? I don't want to see anyone on camera saying anything remotely newsworthy about who gets Dormigen and who does not. They're going to have to get their sound bites about Grandpa from somewhere else."

The Communications Director distributed a press release in which

---

* Language worked out in the progressive caucus that the Tea Party subsequently adopted as well.

he tried to find a kinder, gentler way to point out that most of the people who would be denied Dormigen were going to die soon anyway. He quoted an NIH epidemiologist: "The temporary shortage of Dormigen will have only a modest impact on the two-year mortality rate." (More accurately, the Communications Director wrote that sentence and then called the NIH epidemiologist to tell him how he would be quoted in the press release.) The release offered several other euphemisms for "they were going to die anyway." Only NPR figured this out at first, with a story that included the following exchange:

PUBLIC HEALTH EXPERT: "I don't mean to be insensitive, but most of these people are very old or very ill, so their life expectancy is limited, even if they were to receive Dormigen."

MORNING EDITION HOST: "So you're saying they were going to die soon anyway."

PUBLIC HEALTH EXPERT: "Obviously each one of these cases is difficult—we are denying a lifesaving drug, after all—but yes, that is the essence of what would happen if we were forced to ration the Dormigen as the administration has described."

MORNING EDITION HOST: "And do you agree with that plan?"

PUBLIC HEALTH EXPERT: "Obviously as a physician I am very uncomfortable denying lifesaving drugs to anyone—"

MORNING EDITION HOST: "Yes, of course, but do you see a better option here?"

PUBLIC HEALTH EXPERT (after an uncomfortably long pause for radio): "Given the horrible circumstances, I would be hard-pressed to come up with a better option. Obviously, I hope we don't get to that point."

Our efforts to calm the public kept running smack into the reality of what was happening in the Seattle intensive care unit. Cecelia Dodds was taken off the experimental German medicine because it was harming her kidneys. Doctors put her in an induced coma in a last-ditch effort to help her body fight off the infection. As the Acting Secretary was answering questions in the Capitol, Cecelia Dodds's daughter gave a short briefing in front of the hospital. "I spoke to my mother this morning," she began. "There was about half an hour when she was lucid and comfortable and we were able to talk." Her twin daughters—Cecelia Dodds's granddaughters—were clinging to her legs, one on each side. "My mother is a strong woman and I have every hope she will pull through. She asked me to thank all of you for your love and support. And she asked me to convey to you . . ." The daughter paused to compose herself. Her children gripped her legs more tightly. They no longer had the care-free jauntiness of little girls; they either intuited the seriousness of the situation, or someone had explained it to them.

Cecelia Dodds's daughter continued, "My mother asked me to convey to you, to the nation, that whatever lies ahead in the coming days . . . that each of us should aspire to be as brave and magnanimous and selfless as we can—as she has been. Let's aspire to be the best of America . . ." Her voice choked up and she paused. After a moment: "Love, share, include, and improve. Thank you so much." This was not exactly the nightmare scenario that the Acting Secretary had feared—that Cecelia Dodds would die while he was explaining to Congress that things would not be so bad, but it was close. As the President began to speak from Air Force One, many media outlets ran a split screen: the President on one side and the large crowd gathered in front of the Seattle hospital on the other.

The Communications Director had drafted a speech for the President that was long on language putting the Outbreak in historical perspective and short on Dormigen rationing details. The President urged the nation to face the challenge with the same vigor and bravery with which Americans had faced other adversities—and so on, and so forth. He reminded the country that his administration was still working around the clock to "beat this virus" (true) and, if that were not successful, to procure additional Dormigen stocks (also true). The President looked tired and drawn, almost grim, as he delivered the eight-minute talk. Anyone watching his speech would assume the Outbreak had taken a heavy toll on him. While this was undoubtedly true, the more immediate explanation (we now know) was that he had just spent two hours speaking to his national security staff, most of whom were sequestered in the situation room back at the White House, to devise a response to the hostage situation in Saudi Arabia. Any kidnapping situation is difficult, but this one—in which parents were being told by the terrorists to swap places with their children—was particularly fraught with ethical and strategic challenges.*

Near the end of the President's talk, the Strategist and the Secretary of State had inserted a paragraph (drafted as they stalled before returning the call from the Indian Prime Minister's office): "The people of the United States are deeply thankful for the contributions of Dormigen that have poured in from around the world. But for that generosity, this crisis would be far more devastating. We have been taught, yet once again, the role the world's great democracies must play in fighting our collective global challenges." This was more bait for the Indian Prime Minister—a big, bloody decapitated tuna being towed slowly behind the boat.

India, of course, is the world's largest democracy. That paragraph had been drafted explicitly to suggest that by shirking its Dormigen duty now, India was putting its claim to global leadership at risk in the future. "Too subtle?" the Strategist had asked as the two of them polished the prose.

"Just right," the Secretary of State assured him. "Even a hint that India is not one of the 'world's great democracies' will send him into hysterics." We have no account of what was happening on the India end of this. We do know there was a second phone call from the Prime Minister's office to the U.S. Embassy (where the U.S. Ambassador was still waiting to return the first call, like a teenage girl playing hard to get). A senior American diplomat fielded this call, and a meeting was fixed at a California Pizza Kitchen in a large mall on the outskirts of Delhi. "This better be important," the American diplomat warned his Indian counterpart. "Because we've got a lot going on right now."

---

* As most readers will recall, the strange feature of this kidnapping—children being released as their parents turned themselves in—provided an opportunity for U.S. and Saudi Special Forces to sneak a soldier into the compound. The still-unnamed female Army Ranger, who posed as the U.S. Deputy Counsel General, was given only a cursory search by the male kidnappers, as the U.S. officials had anticipated. Six of the ten kidnappers were killed; all but two of the hostages were rescued safely. The fact that a woman had foiled a fundamentalist terrorist group with Stone Age views toward women was, of course, a profound irony.

74.

I WATCHED THE PRESIDENT'S SPEECH ON MY LAPTOP AT THE NIH headquarters, along with Giscard and the rest of our impromptu team. After a flurry of activity, our work was temporarily stalled while the biochemists at the CDC examined the protein structure of the dormant and virulent forms of *Capellaviridae*. As we waited for those results, we confronted yet another theoretical conundrum: Suppose the dust mite did somehow deliver an antibody for *Capellaviridae* to its human host—then why was this effect not permanent? Antibodies typically last a long time, if not a lifetime, which is why a childhood immunization (or bout of the disease) is usually sufficient to provide immunity well into adulthood. This is where our dust mite theory collided with biological reality. We hypothesized that *Capellaviridae*—all lurking viruses, for that matter—bestowed some evolutionary advantage on the vectors that spread them, the North American dust mite in this case. Humans do not like having dust mites around; their bites are itchy and annoying. But *Capellaviridae* turns the North American dust mite into a lifesaver, literally. The dust mite somehow renders *Capellaviridae* impotent, making it nice to have around, all things considered.

Yes, we had some crucial details to figure out, but the theory was at least consistent with evolution—elegantly so. The three species were poised in a symbiotic relationship. Humans are more apt to thrive when the North American dust mite is present. The dust mite is more successful as a species because of the existence of *Capellaviridae*. And *Capellaviridae* thrives (in its benign form) when humans and dust mites live in proximity to one another. This is how nature is supposed to work.

So far, so good. But we were still missing the last twenty points on that Huke final exam. The only protection against viruses we were aware of consisted of antibodies, and antibodies are long-lasting—*rendering the dust mite no longer relevant.* "At that point, our theory consumes itself," Giscard said dramatically as he tried to explain our theoretical conundrum to the NIH Director.

"I have no idea what you are talking about," she said impatiently.

One of the biochemists followed up with less dramatic flair. "We've reached a contradiction," he said. "Our hypothesis is that the North American dust mite makes itself valuable to humans by providing protection against *Capellaviridae*."

"The dust mite spreads *Capellaviridae*," the NIH Director interrupted.

"Exactly," I said. "And the dust mite also *protects* against *Capellaviridae* turning virulent. That's what makes this situation so biologically interesting." We had developed more and more analogies to explain this "hostage" relationship. I offered up one of them: "A guy walks into a shopping mall with a bomb. He says, 'I have a code that will prevent the bomb from detonating as long as I enter it every fifteen minutes. I will be perfectly happy to do that as long as you bring me food.' Obviously if anything happens to the guy—"

"Really, it would be many, many guys with many bombs," Giscard said.

"Yes, okay," I agreed. "But the point is that everybody needs this guy—all of these guys—to stay alive. If anything happens to them, the whole place goes boom."

"I already understand this," the Director said.

"Of course you do," Giscard said with what felt like excessive deference. Once again I was feeling the urge to harm him.

"Here's the problem," the biochemist explained. "That's not how antibodies work—"

"They defuse the bomb," Giscard interrupted. "The antibody team comes to the shopping place, they defuse the bomb, and then there is no need—"

"Enough with the bomb analogy," the Director snapped. Various officials in the White House had been phoning her repeatedly for updates on the virus front. At one point she had angrily told the Chief of Staff, "Nothing since you called fifteen minutes ago." I suspect the President was leaning on all the staff for some glimmer of hope that science might ward off the impending crisis.

I continued with our explanation to the Director: "Our whole theory revolves around the idea that the dust mite has somehow created a strategy to make itself valuable to humans—presumably by preventing *Capellaviridae* from turning virulent."

"That's what the data show," Tie Guy said. "When the dust mite gets wiped out—"

"Yes, I know what the data show," the Director said sharply. And then, more calmly, she summarized our dilemma more succinctly than we had ourselves: "The easiest way for the dust mite to protect against *Capellaviridae* turning virulent would be to introduce an antibody into the human host. But if that were the case, then there is no ongoing advantage to the humans from protecting the dust mite."

"Exactly," Giscard said, with what I felt to be a hint of surprise that the Director had so easily grasped the situation.

There was a brief silence as the Director reflected on what we had told her. "Well, I trust you'll figure it out," she said brusquely. With that, she turned and left the conference room. Giscard made a rude comment about female scientists and then retreated to his computer at the far end of the conference table. It never dawned on us that he was sharing our conversations with some of his French colleagues, in violation of our explicit orders. The pathetic irony is that he received credit for many of the ideas that emanated from our working group, not because he provided the intellectual spark for those breakthroughs (though that was occasionally the case) but because he disregarded our most important security protocols and wrote about them first.

75.

SHORTLY BEFORE NOON IN DELHI, JUST ABOUT THE TIME AIR Force One entered American airspace, the U.S. Ambassador walked discreetly out the back of the Embassy compound and hailed a taxi. He normally traveled in an armored Cadillac with a security detail, but that entourage was inimical to what he was trying to do: somehow persuade the Indian Prime Minister that he would be fortunate to have the United States accept his offer of lifesaving Dormigen. "That just doesn't make any sense," the Ambassador complained as the Strategist gave him his final marching orders. "We have no leverage here. The Indian PM is perfectly aware of what's happening in the United States. People are going to die. And you expect me to somehow persuade him that we are doing *him* a favor by letting him give us Dormigen?"

"No," the Strategist said patiently. "Forget about the Dormigen. That's not relevant here."

"Of course it's not," the Ambassador said facetiously.

"Really, it's not. What's important is the publicity around the donation. We have to make him want that recognition more than he thinks we want the Dormigen."

"That's a tall order," the Ambassador said.

"He's got an election coming up. There are corruption investigations coming at him from every direction. Now he's got an opportunity to transform India's place in the world, to join the elite club of the world's most important democracies—"

"Yes, I like that language," the Ambassador offered.

"Who was that douchebag from New Mexico when you were in the Senate?" the Strategist asked.

"Pardon?" the Ambassador asked.

"The senator from New Mexico. Remember, 'Never get between a television camera and'—what was his name?"

"Luvardnik," the Ambassador answered.

"Yes. Remember how easy that guy was to deal with? He had no ideological convictions whatsoever. As long as you could assure him some political benefit, he was with you."

"I remember. I'm not sure the Indian PM is as bad as that," the Ambassador said.

"No, but he certainly doesn't care whether eighty-five-year-olds in the U.S. die because they can't get Dormigen," the Strategist pointed out. "This is all about him, so make him a hero in India."

"Luvardnik really was an asshole, wasn't he?" the Ambassador reflected.

"You know the drill," the Strategist said.

"Twelve years in the Senate did teach me a few things."

"Then go get us some Dormigen." And then the strategist added, "And don't pay the bill."

"We're meeting at a pizza parlor," the Ambassador pointed out.

"I don't care if it's three dollars. You're doing him a favor, so he pays the bill. That's really important."

"Okay, maybe I'll order dessert," the Ambassador said jokingly.

"Even better," the Strategist answered, not joking at all.

The California Pizza Kitchen was deep in the New India Mall, past every manner of Western shop and up an escalator that passed over a garish fountain in which an elephant was shooting water from its trunk. The mall was busy with shoppers—an occasional tourist but mostly locals seeking out a clean, orderly place to shop for the same reason Americans do. The Ambassador had never been to the mall before, though the head of the embassy's Economic Section often used it as an example of India's growing middle class. The Ambassador made his way to the food court before recognizing that the restaurants were scattered elsewhere. By the time he reached the California Pizza Kitchen, he was several minutes late. The Ambassador recognized Sumer Patel, one of the Prime Minister's trusted lieutenants (albeit with an ambiguous official portfolio), sitting at a table near the door looking somewhat impatient. The Strategist would be proud of him for keeping Patel waiting, the Ambassador thought, even if it was an accident. The Ambassador and Patel had met several times before; they reintroduced themselves and exchanged pleasantries. Eventually Patel broached the substance of the meeting: "I watched the President's speech."

"We've got ourselves in a bit of a pickle," the Ambassador said. Patel had attended university in the U.S. and was familiar with the idioms and slang.

"The Prime Minister feels this may be an opportunity to take the U.S.-India relationship to a new level," Patel said.

"How so?" the Ambassador asked solicitously.

"The Prime Minister is now confident we will have excess Dormigen over the next week."

The Ambassador raised an eyebrow, suggesting surprise and interest. "On what scale?"

"Perhaps enough to close your gap."

"There are a lot of lives at stake," the Ambassador said. At that moment, a male waiter approached the table to take drink orders. Patel waved him away angrily, telling him in Hindi to come back later.

"The Prime Minister recognizes the gravity of what is happening," Patel said.

The Ambassador replied, "As you may or may not know, we made an overture earlier and it was not well received. If I recall correctly—"

Patel waved his hand dismissively. "The circumstances have changed."

"They have," the Ambassador agreed. "With China, in particular."

"That was a terrible embarrassment," Patel said, shaking his head.

"An embarrassment?" the Ambassador asked with concern. "An embarrassment for . . ."

"China," Patel said emphatically. The waiter returned, once again drawing an angry look from Patel.

"Maybe we should just order," the Ambassador said.

"I'll have a Coke Zero and a pizza," Patel said sharply.

"Sir, we have many kinds of pizza," the waiter replied.

"Veggie."

"Yes, sir, one veggie pizza," the waiter said.

"I'll have the same," the Ambassador said.

"With Coke Zero?" the waiter asked.

"Yes," the Ambassador said. The waiter acknowledged the order with a slight nod of his head. As he walked away, the Ambassador continued to Patel, "Please tell the Prime Minister that we are prepared to make some serious gestures to express our gratitude—to take our bilateral relationship to a new level, as you say." The Ambassador listed several diplomatic issues the Americans and Indians had been wrangling over in recent years: cooperation on India's civil nuclear program; more aggressive intelligence-sharing regarding Pakistan; raising the U.S. cap on H-1B visas for skilled workers. Patel nodded in approval as the Ambassador ticked off the list, all of which happened to be initiatives he had been pushing the State Department and the White House to act on anyway. "We can create a political win here for the Prime Minister," the Ambassador assured Patel.

"Yes, these are significant gestures," Patel agreed. "The White House has signed off on all of this?"

"Of course," the Ambassador assured him. There was a brief silence as Patel absorbed the offer on the table. The Ambassador continued, "One thing to appreciate here is that China is trying to exploit our crisis in the U.S. The things they are asking for would make us weaker. It's predatory. The things you and I are discussing here, on the other hand, are measures that would strengthen the U.S.-India relationship. The world's two most important democracies, working together."

"Yes, of course," Patel agreed. Silence settled over the table as Patel contemplated the situation. The Ambassador had a strong sense of what direction the conversation would likely turn. They were approaching the money moment. The next minute or so would likely determine whether the Strategist would lose a testicle or not. The waiter appeared with drinks, giving Patel more time to cogitate on the situation. As the waiter walked out of earshot, Patel said, "The world's two most important democracies, but India is very much the junior partner."

"India has three times the population of the United States," the Ambassador replied.

"Exactly, and yet . . ." Patel let the dissatisfaction with the relationship just kind of hang there.

"The President would be very happy to publicly thank the Prime Minister and the country for their generosity," the Ambassador said.

"Yes?" Patel replied, his face brightening.

The Ambassador continued: "We will have to work on the scheduling, but the PM could do a state visit, perhaps at the beginning of next year. We could use the visit as an opportunity to announce all these agreements."

Patel's excitement dissipated immediately. The pizzas arrived. "May I get you anything else?" the waiter asked in English with a pleasant, lilting accent. Patel told him brusquely in Hindi to go away and the two men ate in silence.

Eventually Patel asked, "May I speak candidly?"

"Of course."

"The Prime Minister has an election coming up."

"His party is in a spot of political trouble," the Ambassador said, "if I may speak candidly."

"The Prime Minister is hoping for something . . ."

"With more immediate political payoff," the Ambassador said, making explicit what Patel could not bring himself to say. Patel grimaced at the coarseness of the statement but did not disagree. The Ambassador continued with just a hint of mock outrage, "A lot of people are going to die in the United States."

"And we would like to prevent that," Patel assured him. "That is why I am here. The Prime Minister is just hoping we can create a win for everyone."

"The polls I've seen suggest that public opinion in your country is strongly in favor of offering Dormigen to the United States," the Ambassador pointed out.

"Yes!" Patel agreed. "That's exactly what we would like to leverage. Can we make everyone a winner here?"

"What does the Prime Minister have in mind?" the Ambassador asked skeptically. He felt a warm glow of inner satisfaction. He had done it. He had taken the conversation in the direction it needed to go. He had arrived at the California Pizza Kitchen to ask for a donation of a lifesaving drug. And now, with the pizzas barely having arrived, Patel was beginning to look like the supplicant.

"We're being entirely candid here?" Patel asked earnestly.

"Of course," the Ambassador assured him.

"Something that puts him on equal footing with the President," Patel said. "Something that makes India look like an equal partner."

"We can make that happen," the Ambassador replied, though there was a coolness in his tone that suggested the opposite. "Obviously the President has some political sensitivities of his own."

"He does not want a poor country coming to the rescue," Patel offered.

"No, no," the Ambassador assured Patel in a tone that suggested, "Yes, yes." The Ambassador explained, "The President is very sensitive to charges that he left the country vulnerable—that he's responsible for this situation. He's trying to steer a delicate political path here."

"I can understand that," Patel said.

"Yes, well, if there is a very public display in which India delivers the Dormigen that the U.S. somehow could not produce . . ."

Patel finished the thought, his voice laced with indignation: "The President must be horribly incompetent if *India* is coming to the rescue."

The Ambassador said, "I'm just the messenger here. I think it's pathetic that thousands of people could die because of his political vanity."

"I understand," Patel said, his tone warming noticeably. "Of course, the President's not the only one with political vanity!" They exchanged a knowing laugh at the expense of their political over-lords. The waiter approached the table once again. Neither man had eaten more than a few bites.

"The food is okay?" the waiter asked with concern.

"Fine, fine," the Ambassador said. "Can I take mine in a box?"

"I would like a box as well," Patel said.

"I would like something sweet, however," the Ambassador said. "Do you have ice cream?" he asked the waiter.

"Of course, sir. Chocolate, vanilla, and mango."

"I'll have mango!" the Ambassador exclaimed. "I love mango ice cream. Are the mangos in season?"

"I believe so," Patel answered. "I'll have the same."

As the waiter walked away, the Ambassador continued, "Why don't you consult with the Prime Minister. Ask him what he feels he needs: a phone call with the President, maybe a public ceremony in which the Indian Ambassador comes to the White House for for-mal recognition . . . I'm just thinking out loud here. I will advocate strenuously for whatever the Prime Minister proposes because there is absolutely no reason politics should get in the way of saving lives. But, please, make the PM aware that the White House is going to push back against anything the President feels makes him or the country look like a supplicant."

"Well put. I understand completely," Patel replied.

The waiter returned with the ice cream. "Will there be anything else?" he asked.

"Just the check," the Ambassador answered.

As the waiter searched for the check in his small notepad, Patel produced a credit card. "Please, allow me," he said.

"Thank you," the Ambassador said. He leaned closer to Patel: "I think we can make this happen."

"I hope so," Patel replied. "I hope so."

76.

THE PRESSURE HAD BEEN BRIEFLY REDIRECTED FROM OUR team at the NIH to the biochemists, as we awaited their findings on the chemical structures of the virulent and indolent forms of the *Capellaviridae* virus. I awoke early and shared an awkward breakfast with Ellen. We watched television and said little to one another. I switched from channel to channel, eager to see how the Dormigen story was being covered. The Saudi Arabia hostage situation was the top story across channels. I imagined a crisis team like ours working in different rooms at the White House with the President yelling at them to make sure that no hostages were killed. The media seemed to have the bandwidth for one crisis at a time, so the Dormigen story had been bumped off the front page, literally in some cases, figuratively elsewhere. Most of the cable news programs were still using their "Dormigen Countdown" graphics. The White House had gained some traction in shaping the story. Our local morning program in D.C. did a story on a nearby hospital that was preparing measures to provide alternative care for patients who would be ineligible to receive Dormigen. That story, and most others, used our phrase "similar to a serious case of the flu" multiple times. But then they would cut almost immediately to Seattle, where Cecelia Dodds remained in an induced coma.

On the political side, there was a lot of waiting going on. The President had arrived back in Washington during the night. The Chief of Staff briefed him and others on what they were now referring to as "the California Pizza Kitchen Summit." The next move would have to come from the Indian Prime Minister's office. On the science side, we were also waiting. The NIH Director canceled our morning briefing, as there was little to discuss until we received more information from the biochemists. Meanwhile, Giscard had invited Jenna for breakfast, which she had accepted, much to my horror. So I was waiting for breakfast to be over, too.

The Speaker organized "No Rationing" protests in a number of cities. Several were scheduled for that afternoon. However, the agenda had been coopted by other progressive groups; the demonstrations now included protests against income inequality, domestic violence, sexual assault, and racial profiling. (The Democrats' progressive wing prided itself on a lack of hierarchy, which took a toll on focus and strategy.) A Palestinian rights group offered up several speakers to address Israeli land annexation in the West Bank. In the end, the disparate causes rallied under the banner of "A Protest Against Unfairness and Oppression." Predictably, no one without a nose ring showed up.

I was in no mood to see humor in any of this, but I now find it amusing that the Tea Party was blasting our Dormigen rationing plan at the same time. "This is exactly what happens when you put the government in charge of anything: *rationing*," populist radio host Chuckford Pickens told his loyal listeners. These anti-rationing diatribes bounced around the right-wing echo chamber for a while, though the sentiment wilted quickly when exposed to anything approximating logic. As the President pointed out in a moment of exasperation, the whole point of the free market is to ration goods, albeit using price rather than some other mechanism. (I vaguely recall my microeconomics professor saying the same thing.) Eleven thousand economists signed a petition affirming the importance of government patent protection to promote innovation, and government funding to promote the kind of basic research that often lays the groundwork for major pharmacological breakthroughs (like Dormigen). Chuckford Pickens disparaged the petition on his program, describing it as "more sad evidence that our universities have been totally hijacked by the left." Several callers shared stories of lefty academic exploits; one concerned an Oberlin professor teaching a course called Gender and Sexual Identity in *The Wire*.

"*The Wire*—like the TV show?" Pickens asked the caller incredulously.

"Yep," the caller affirmed.

"My God, it's not bad enough that you can watch television for college credit, now it also has to be about gender and sexual identity. You can't even get credit for watching straight people on TV anymore! Can you believe that?" Pickens exclaimed, clearly pleased with his own analysis of the situation. "You know what we should do, we should get a copy of the Oberlin course catalog. Can we do that?" he asked his listeners, though the question was presumably directed to a producer in the studio. The answer must have been yes, because Pickens continued, "We're going to do that." The supposed logic of this meandering conversation, as best as I could infer, was that a handful of silly courses at Oberlin College somehow obviated the collective wisdom of eleven thousand economists, including twenty-one from the University of Chicago (a bastion of free-market thinking).

For all that, the President's response to the Outbreak enjoyed reasonable support. He had never been personally popular. (Even before the Outbreak, fewer than half of those asked said he would be a fun person to have a beer with.) The "adults" in Congress had done a good job of explaining and defending the White House response to the crisis. The most idiotic ideas floated by other members of Congress, usually in front of a television camera, tended to sink on their own (e.g., using military force to procure Dormigen from countries unwilling to share). Policy types offered up numerous sensible reforms to ensure there would not be another Dormigen-type shortage in the future. Most of these recommendations had been filling binders and glossy reports for years. (The Brookings Institution had hosted three conferences over the previous decade on issues related to the development, affordability, and distribution of "uniquely valuable" prescription drugs; only eighty-three people attended the largest of them, including Brookings staff.) Of course, now that the milk was spilled, the nation was giving more time to those who had warned that the glass had been perched precariously on the counter. Still, the milk was spilled. Most reasonable people agreed with the President's effort to clean it up. One could argue the President's approach was sensible *because* it protected so much of the population. He was taking heaps of abuse for his proposed rationing, but, more quietly, he was also getting credit for the implicit triage. Most Americans were protected. The President had been elected by a coalition of voters exhausted by political nonsense; for the most part, they were sticking with him.

Around ten-thirty in the morning, I received a text from the NIH Director summoning me to a noon meeting. Tie Guy called me separately. "They found a difference," he said when I answered.

"Who?" I asked.

"The biochemists. The virulent form of *Capellaviridae* is missing a protein," Tie Guy explained. He was speaking faster than I had ever heard him speak, and my cell phone reception was choppy, so I could not absorb all the details that he was spewing. "This is what we've been looking for," he continued.

"A missing protein," I repeated.

"Yes," Tie Guy said excitedly.

"Which means the harmless form of the virus has an extra protein," I said, thinking as I spoke. "As if it had been neutralized by an antibody." That is how antibodies work: they attach proteins to viruses, rendering them impotent, like the key in a lock.

"That's what it looks like, more or less," Tie Guy said, growing calmer.

"It's consistent with our theory," I said.

"Yes, good work," he offered.

Our noon meeting was delayed, as the NIH Director finished a call with the Chief of Staff to apprise the White House of our latest findings on the virus. She and the Chief of Staff agreed that we were not ready to make a public announcement of the breakthrough. There were too many outstanding questions: What caused the difference in the two viruses? What role did the dust mite play, if any? And most important, how could this discovery help those who became sick with the virulent form of the virus? The President overruled their decision, ordering the Communications Director to put out a release immediately. "You don't think it will raise false hope?" the Chief of Staff asked.

"That's the point," the President answered, turning his attention to the Communications Director. "Say that scientists have—no, make it 'NIH scientists'—we might as well get some credit for government work. Say that NIH scientists have made a major discovery . . . something about why the virus turns deadly."

"The NIH scientists have identified the protein responsible for the difference between the indolent and virulent forms of *Capellaviridae*," the Communications Director offered.

"Fine, but don't say 'indolent' or 'virulent.' Use words that people watching *The Bevin Crowley Show* can understand."

"Okay."

"Then say that scientists are optimistic this will lead to a non-

Dormigen treatment for the virulent form of *Capellaviridae*—but don't say virulent."

"Dangerous," the Communications Director suggested.

The Chief of Staff warned, "That's a very strong statement. The NIH Director just told me they have no idea what accounts for the difference in the two viruses and they don't think they can develop a vaccine in three days."

"Do we want to create false hope?" the Communications Director asked.

"Yes, I just told you that," the President answered impatiently. Once again, he was playing political chess while others in the room were playing checkers. The press release went out shortly after noon in Washington. In New Delhi, where it was nearly ten at night, an aide to the Indian Prime Minister delivered the news to him: the Americans had cracked the code on the *Capellaviridae* virus. The Prime Minister was planning to phone the U.S. Secretary of State in the morning to offer a Dormigen shipment sufficient to solve the shortage (subject to certain conditions, of course).

"What if they solve this thing before we can offer them the Dormigen?" he asked his assembled aides. He really said that out loud.

77.

OUR EARLY DISCUSSIONS ABOUT DORMIGEN RATIONING HAD been theoretical, almost like an exercise in a college ethics class. It was no longer feeling theoretical. Those of us working closely with the President could see him carrying the pressure. He physically looked different, weighed down somehow. Even the sardonic humor was gone. The President reminded staff members that thousands of lives were at stake. Cecelia Dodds reminded us that each one of those cases would be a tragedy somewhere, regardless of how sick or old that person happened to be. People are going to die who do not have to die, he would intone to anyone whom he felt had become too insouciant with the situation. The staffer would apologize, surprised by the emotion in the voice of the President, a guy who normally guarded his emotions closely, especially around junior staff.

There were several White House interns whose job it was to sort through the mail (after the security screening). The President had a standing request to see a sample of the physical mail and e-mail flowing into the White House. The interns would select a handful of positive notes, a handful of critical ones, and then several selected at random. Under normal circumstances, the interns would also bring him a few from the "crazies"; the President found temporary amusement in letters from people who blamed him for the poor performance of the U.S. men's soccer team or warned him of an imminent Canadian invasion. One famous letter from San Diego—three pages, typed—complained that a neighbor's dog was "shitting all over a six block radius" and asked accusingly what the President planned to do about it. There were five pages of accompanying maps and several photos that appeared to have been taken by a drone. If the President was in a particularly good mood, he might dictate an ironic response. For example, he wrote a letter to the San Diego complainant informing him that the "defecating dog" was really a matter for Congress to handle. "Make sure you copy the Speaker," he told the staffer to whom he had dictated his reply.

Even during the Outbreak, the President was diligent in spending some time every day with his mail. While he was on Air Force One, he had letters scanned and e-mailed to him, as he wanted to maintain a feel for what ordinary people were thinking and feeling. Polls could give him a snapshot of national sentiment, but they were "shallow," as he liked to describe them. People around the country—those who bothered to answer the phone—were disturbed as they cooked dinner or watched television or surfed the Web. They answered the requisite questions, eager to get off the phone as quickly as possible. But the folks who took the time to write to the White House were different—whether it was an old-fashioned handwritten letter with an envelope and stamp (the President's favorite, even when they were critical) or by e-mail. They tended to express a thoughtfulness and depth of emotion that the polls could not capture.

Shortly after the President arrived back from Australia, one of the interns in the mailroom phoned the Chief of Staff. "I think you should see this," she said.

"Have you alerted security?" the Chief of Staff asked distractedly.

"It's not that. I just think you should see this, maybe the President, too."

"Can you just bring it up?"

"It's pretty heavy."

"What do you mean?"

"I mean it's too heavy for me to carry."

"Okay," the Chief of Staff agreed. In the midst of everything else that was going on, she could not have been happy to trudge down to the basement office where the screened mail was sorted, but that is what she did.

When the Chief of Staff arrived in the cramped office, a glorified closet with exposed pipes running across the ceiling, the intern pointed at a brown box about the size of a laser printer. It appeared to be full of paper clips of all colors and sizes. "Paper clips?" the Chief of Staff asked.

"Uh-huh."

The Chief of Staff ran her hand through the paper clips, letting them slip through her fingers. "Are you sure security cleared this?"

"It's from an elementary school outside of Chicago."

"I think we're fine on office supplies."

"It's based on a documentary," the intern explained. "I looked it up online. There's this film about a group of elementary school kids who collected six million paper clips, one for each Jew killed in the Holocaust."

"And this?" the Chief of Staff said, pointing at the box.

"I'd bet it's about forty thousand, one for each person who will not get Dormigen—"

"Of course." They both stared at the box for a while. "That's a lot of paper clips," the Chief of Staff said softly.

"Do you think the President will want to see it?" the intern asked.

"I do," she said. And then, "He should, in any event."

Later, when the President returned to the Oval Office from a meeting in the situation room, the Chief of Staff was waiting for him, along with the open box of paper clips that had been wheeled on a cart up from the basement. The President noticed the box immediately. "What's that?" he asked.

"It came from an elementary school near Chicago," the Chief of

Staff answered. There was a brief silence as the President waited for the balance of the explanation and the Chief of Staff decided how to couch it. "There's one paper clip in the box for each person who would be denied Dormigen—"

"Like the documentary," the President said.

"Yes, exactly," the Chief of Staff replied. He still surprised her on occasion, despite their many years working together. The typical day in the White House was a blur of fifteen-minute meetings; the President survived by exercising good judgment and knowing just enough about a lot of things. It was the opposite of her experience in academe, where her colleagues could spend hours drilling down on the most obscure of topics. She would sometimes forget that the President was a reader and a film enthusiast; it was his escape. After his divorce, he spent a long stretch alone in Washington. There had been a lot of media buzz in those years about his antics as one of the nation's most attractive bachelors, but the reality was that he retired most nights to his tiny apartment with a book or a film. Even in the White House, with the First Lady traveling frequently, he would do the same, after the Chief of Staff had gone home to her husband and teenagers. On occasion, the President would invite authors or directors to dinner—not the famous ones, as he had no particular affinity for celebrities, but a historian or an accomplished filmmaker. The Chief of Staff should not have been surprised that he had seen an obscure documentary about schoolchildren who collected six million paper clips, even though she was.

"Leave them here," the President instructed.

"In the middle of the office?" she asked.

"Somewhere everyone can see them," he said. The paper clips were different sizes and colors: big, little, metallic, green, blue, bright pink. There was one paper clip resting on top with a sticky note attached to it. The President was not wearing his glasses when he picked it up, so he could not read the tiny elementary-school handwriting. But he knew what it said: Cecelia Dodds. In subsequent days, when staff members would ask about the box, or make jokes about buying paper clips in bulk, he would explain their significance.

Not long ago, when the President was in the final months of his term, he visited the students who had done the Dormigen paper-clip project at their elementary school in a Chicago suburb. The President spent nearly an hour and a half talking to the student body and answering questions, an unheard-of amount of time for a presidential visit. "Your project was a crucial reminder for me during the Outbreak of how our decisions would affect real people," the President told the assembled students, most of whom were too young to appreciate the significance of what they were hearing. "That didn't make it easier—harder, probably. But we needed that. We needed a constant reminder that the decisions we were making would affect real people and families—thousands and thousands of them," the President explained.

The event garnered a great deal of national and international attention. To that point, the President had said relatively little about his decisions during the Outbreak. There was speculation that his elementary school visit would prompt some newsworthy reflection. By then, however, the President was thoroughly fed up with the media. He ordered the student assembly closed to the press, except for two reporters from the school newspaper, the *Springhill Chronicle*.* The balance of the media—over a hundred photographers, videographers, pundits, writers, and bloggers—were relegated to the school parking lot while the President spoke inside. Then, in a moment of delicious irony orchestrated by the President, one of the student writers for the *Springhill Chronicle* was deputized to give a pool report for the global media assembled outside.

"It's going to be a pool event," the Communications Director told the traveling White House press corps, smirking visibly. (When events were space-constrained, or when a large group of reporters might disturb an event, such as a visit to the bedside of a wounded soldier, the Communications Office would choose a single reporter and cameraperson to cover the event and share information and photos with the rest of the "press pool." However, the reporter designated for such responsibility was not usually an eleven-year-old writer for the *Springhill Chronicle*.) After the event, the President stood on a

---

* Some of the questions for the President, as reported by the *Springhill Chronicle*, included: "Why don't you have a cat?" and "What do you normally eat for breakfast?"

patch of grass outside the school, smiling and silent, as eleven-year-old Dan "Bucky" Riegsecker reported dutifully on what had been said inside. Correspondents from the *New York Times*, the *Washington Post–USA Today*, Home Depot Media, and all the major cable news stations—notebooks out, cameras rolling—lapped up the tidbits Bucky tossed their way.

78.

THE PHONE RANG AT THE U.S. AMBASSADOR'S RESIDENCE IN New Delhi around midnight. It was Sumer Patel requesting a meeting as soon as possible between the Indian Prime Minister and the U.S. Secretary of State. "The Secretary of State is in Bahrain," the Ambassador told Patel.

"It's just three hours away," Patel pointed out.

"Yes, that is fortunate," the Ambassador agreed. "I can't say for certain, but given the urgency of the situation, the Secretary of State might be able to get here in the morning."

"Yes, that would be perfect, if you can arrange it," Patel said.

"This is her top priority," the Ambassador assured him. The details for the meeting were fixed. The Ambassador immediately phoned the Secretary of State, who was attending a banquet hosted by the Royal Family. The paperwork for the flight to Delhi had already been prepared for this contingency; a pilot and flight crew were standing ready. The Secretary excused herself from the banquet, which had gone from tedious to excruciating over the course of the evening. And so, less than two hours after the Communications Director had issued the press release announcing a "scientific breakthrough" with regard to *Capellaviridae*, the Secretary of State and the Strategist were on an Air Force jet bound for India.

Upon landing in India, the Secretary of State found herself with a curious problem: she had no entourage. The American Secretary of State does not travel alone; no one on the Indian side would believe that she had been in Bahrain for meetings without a large complement of aides. The fact that she was traveling with the President's top strategist and pollster would raise even more questions. The Indian

Prime Minister was vain and self-interested, but he was no fool; if word leaked that the Secretary of State had been loitering in Bahrain without all the usual hangers-on, he would suspect a scheme. (Political schemers are, of course, most adept at detecting scheming by others.) The Ambassador solved this problem by "loaning" the Secretary of State eight embassy staff members, all with the requisite security clearance. "Follow her around, look obsequious, and don't say anything to anyone," he instructed them. Those eight "staffers" can now claim to be a footnote to one of the most famous negotiations in modern diplomatic history—as fake lackeys.

The Secretary of State was scheduled to meet with the Prime Minister at ten in the morning Delhi time. The Strategist would not attend the meeting; even his presence in India was secret for the reasons I alluded to above. Over breakfast, he coached the Secretary on strategy for dealing with the Prime Minister. "I've dealt with him on many occasions," the Secretary said, peeved by the suggestion that the Strategist's dark arts somehow trumped her deep knowledge of foreign affairs and diplomacy.

"You need to downplay this breakthrough on the virus," he continued, ignoring—or, more likely, oblivious to—the Secretary's vague hostility to his briefing.

"That's the only leverage we have," she said.

"No, no, no," the Strategist insisted. "No." He paused, like a professor who realized his student had not done the reading. "Look, the PM is a guy who's always worried he's getting played, because that's what he's always doing to other people. He's always got an angle, so he assumes everyone else does, too."

"I'm aware of that."

"If you walk into the room and declare that American scientists have figured out *Capellaviridae*, he's not going to believe you. If you tell him that we probably won't need extra Dormigen, he's going to ask why the hell you are sitting in New Delhi asking for it, right?"

The Strategist had captured the Secretary's attention, if only by the convoluted nature of what he was arguing. And he had been right so far. The California Pizza Kitchen Summit was brilliantly choreographed, she had to admit. (Upon hearing the recap, the Strategist had yelled, "Mango fucking ice cream! I love it!") The Secretary asked, "Our only leverage here is that we may develop some kind of vaccine in the eleventh hour—and I'm supposed to downplay that possibility?"

"Play possum," the Strategist instructed her. "Tell him you really don't think there's time to develop a vaccine. Scientists are working on it around the clock, but they're pessimistic . . . blah, blah, blah. That kind of thing."

"Okay," the Secretary said, still not sure where the strategy was headed.

"This is a guy who's always wondering if he's paranoid enough. If you tell him we're on the brink of developing a vaccine, he'll know you're bluffing. But if you downplay that possibility, then he's going to worry about the opposite: 'Oh, shit, what if they pull off the vaccine right as I'm about to ride my white horse down Fifth Avenue?'"

"You really think he's that callow?" the Secretary asked.

"What's so callow about that? We all want to be the hero. We've set him up to think there's a huge political payoff—which, by the way, there may well be. Just because we made up the poll numbers—"

"Stop," the Secretary said sharply. "I don't want to hear anything about that."

"Anyway, I think he's like anyone else. He doesn't want a lot of people to die unnecessarily in the U.S., but if someone is going to prevent that, he wants it to be him."

"You think this is going to work?" the Secretary of State asked.

"I have no idea, but I do know that if you're holding a pair of twos, you don't try and persuade people around the table that you've got four aces. You try to make them think that you're trying to make them think that you have a pair of twos."

"I don't play poker."

"Yes, that's apparent."

They were holding their discussion in a small, secure conference room at the U.S. Embassy (a curious building with offices arrayed around a large indoor fountain and pool that had allegedly inspired Jackie Kennedy to hire the same architect to design the Kennedy Center in Washington). The U.S. Ambassador knocked and then entered. "Your meeting has been pushed back to eleven," he told the

Secretary. "There was some shooting across the border in Kashmir and the PM is dealing with that."

"Anything serious?" the Secretary asked.

"No, just the usual," the Ambassador assured her.

The Secretary of State used the time to check in with the Chief of Staff, who pointed out a logistical reality that had not been top-of-mind. The U.S. was now, by our most recent estimate, three days from the point at which the existing Dormigen supply would have to be rationed. "Maybe a little sooner," the Chief of Staff warned. "Doctors haven't been as strict with Dormigen prescriptions as we had hoped." She walked through the realities of the globe: Delhi was an eighteen-hour flight from New York. It would take additional time to distribute Dormigen across the U.S., particularly to rural areas. The Chief of Staff connected the dots for them: "If the Indian Prime Minister is going to save the day, that Dormigen is going to have to be on a plane sooner rather than later."

79.

IN WASHINGTON, THE NIH SCIENTISTS WERE HOPING TO REP-licate the success of the Manhattan Project in a fraction of the time, albeit with the benefit of the Internet. The technical details of the most recent *Capellaviridae* breakthrough—the difference in the protein structure between the virulent and indolent viruses—were posted publicly with an invitation for teams of scientists anywhere in the world to explore the crucial questions: What caused the difference in the two forms of the virus? And how might the virulent form of the virus be rendered indolent? The hope was that "parallel science" might replicate the success of parallel computing, in which millions of personal computers linked together by the Internet had proved more powerful than even the largest supercomputer. The Scopes Foundation, a previously obscure philanthropy, offered a $1 million prize for a definitive answer to either *Capellaviridae* question, though the prize was quickly canceled at the behest of the Acting HHS Secretary, who feared that it would promote secrecy at a time when "massive openness" offered the only hope of a breakthrough in the little time available.

One bottleneck to this massive scientific effort was bizarrely low-tech: access to dust mites. The North American dust mite was not endemic to most of Europe, Asia, or South America (as the name would suggest). Even in the U.S., there was no ready supplier of dust mites for laboratory work as there was for mice or rats. A cottage industry grew up almost immediately, with the people who had been previously afflicted by the small, itchy bites suddenly able to cash in on the nuisance. (Despite the very clear description of the North American dust mite on the NIH website, eager entrepreneurs showed up at regional laboratories bearing everything from red ants to cockroaches.) The Midwest turned out to be the place where dust mites could be gathered most easily for research purposes. As a result, we leaned heavily on teams at Northwestern, the University of Chicago, and several of the other Midwest universities.

We set up a "war room" in the NIH headquarters to be the central repository for the myriad decentralized research efforts. Almost immediately we realized that we were lacking even the most basic tools for sharing the information that was being generated. The normal scientific process involves peer review, publication in journals, and presentations at scientific conferences—all things that take months or years. Now we had hours. "We need a place where everyone working on pieces of this challenge can post their progress," I explained to the Director. The NIH had internal sites where we posted this kind of information, but there was no way to grant security clearance to outsiders in a short amount of time (nor did we necessarily want teams of foreign scientists to have access to these sites).

"How much security do we need?" she asked.

"Not much," I figured. "We don't want anyone without access posting a lot of nonsense. Other than that, we just need a place to gather a lot of information." Even as I spoke, I was thinking of an easy solution, but it seemed too silly to mention.

"I'm sure somebody from the NSA can set something up for us," the Director suggested. "Or maybe we should call one of the big software companies."

"It will take three hours just to get the right person on the phone," I said. "Look, I think all we need here is a big Google Doc. We can invite people to join."

The Director was scrolling through messages on her phone, trying to manage other problems as she dealt with mine. My suggestion caused her to stop and look at me. "A Google Doc?" she asked incredulously. "That's what my daughter uses for eighth-grade projects."

At that moment, like so many other moments during the Outbreak, I was tempted to blurt out the obvious: "If you've got a better idea . . ." In fact, there may still be a commercial market for some product in this spirit—maybe an iPhone app with an elegant-sounding British voice that says, "If you've got a better idea . . ." at the push of a button—because if I learned anything during this ordeal, it is that the world is full of people who are very good at criticizing any proposed course of action and far less skilled at offering practical alternatives. To her credit, the NIH Director was not normally a naysayer, and she came around quickly to my suggestion once she focused exclusively on our conversation. "Really?" she asked. "Do you think that would work?"

"Why not?" I said. The Director gave a small shrug of approval. With that, the world's most intensive scientific effort since the Manhattan Project was launched on the same platform that the NIH Director's daughter was using to collaborate with three classmates on their U.S. Constitution project. We posted our plan on the NIH website and invited researchers to request access to the document. The timing was not good, as it was now nearly midnight on the East Coast. I worried that we would lose precious time since few scientists would pick up the news until morning. Still, we granted access to the document to thirty-one researchers in the first half hour; by one-thirty a.m., there were one hundred and twelve: biologists, physicians, biochemists, epidemiologists, virologists, evolutionary biologists. Giscard became the self-appointed master of the document, like a disc jockey managing the flow of information. I must admit that he was really, really good at it. The flow of data, questions, and theories was overwhelming. Giscard stood in the middle of this surging river of information, constantly directing the effort back to the questions that mattered: Why did the indolent form of the virus have a different protein structure than the virulent form? How did it get that way? And, of course, the holy grail of this whole endeavor: How could we render the virulent form of the virus harmless in the absence of Dormigen?

Almost immediately, we had our first breakthrough. A team from Rockefeller University in New York explained how the benign form of the virus could lose a protein, rendering it virulent. The long, scientific explanation for that process (which they would subsequently publish) involves changes that take place in a cell as it replicates (divides); namely, that parts of the cell break down after repeated replication. (This is the reason living creatures grow old and die; their cells degrade as they divide over time.) The shorter, more accessible answer to how the benign form of the virus could lose a protein is comically simple: it eventually falls off, "like a button on some pants that go through the washing machine over and over," as Giscard would explain to his social media followers.

There was euphoria in our war room as we celebrated this discovery—and the speed with which it happened. We were painfully aware of how little time we had left. The Army had provided us with a small logistical team that was offering guidance on everything from how long it would take to mass-produce a new vaccine (long) to what would be the best way to distribute such a vaccine around the country (UPS and FedEx). At every turn, the Army logistics experts told us things would take longer than we expected. Still, it was the middle of the night and we had just unlocked one of the key mysteries of *Capellaviridae*, which would in turn fuel insights by the other teams.

"Beautiful work, everyone," Giscard exclaimed to the room. I admired his confidence and extroversion. *We are going to figure this thing out*, I thought.

It was right about then that the French film crew arrived. I heard the NIH Director's voice before I knew what was happening. "You have got to be fucking kidding me," she yelled from somewhere outside the war room. The film crew was waiting down in the lobby: two camera operators, a producer, and a technician, all from a famous French news program.

Giscard, alerted to their arrival, stood up in the war room and said loudly, "We are in history!" A film crew was the last thing we needed in our cramped, hot, frenetic war room. Giscard had invited them, of course, with no approval from anyone. As obnoxious as that was, it was becoming increasingly apparent that we were participating in something historic. The next major discovery came around three in the morning, just after the start of business in Europe. A team from the Munich Institute for Tropical Diseases confirmed that *Capellaviridae* had indeed evolved from the influenza virus. Using DNA analysis, they discerned that *Capellaviridae* was a near-exact match for a flu virus that had infected Native Americans roughly nine thousand years ago. The German team found one other interesting thing: the benign form of *Capellaviridae* resembled a flu virus that had been neutralized by human antibodies. Less than an hour later, a team of evolutionary biologists offered an elegant explanation: The North American dust mite transmitted the flu virus to its ancient human hosts along with antibodies to neutralize it. "The North American dust mite evolved into the earliest known flu shot, thus bestowing an evolutionary advantage on the human populations where it was endemic," the lead Stanford scientist wrote on our Google Doc.

We were getting very close to the answer for one of Professor Huke's final exams, and we could feel the time slipping away. As we were celebrating our wiki science project, the Chief of Staff requested a moment alone with the President. "The doctors are going to bring Cecelia Dodds out of a coma," she informed him.

"That's great—"

"No," she said gently. "They don't think she will make it, and this will give her some time with her family."

"Thank you for letting me know."

80.

THE MEETING BETWEEN THE SECRETARY OF STATE AND THE Indian Prime Minister kept getting pushed back, first to eleven-fifteen a.m. Delhi time and then eleven-thirty. Just as the Secretary of State and her entourage were preparing to leave the American

Embassy for the Parliament building, the Secretary of State was summoned to a secure conference room to take a call. It was the Secretary of Defense, who had been consumed with the Saudi hostage situation, but was now insistent on speaking to the Secretary of State before her meeting with the Indian Prime Minister. The two cabinet members had a prickly relationship in the best of circumstances. The Secretary of State was still angry at having been left out of the China Dormigen discussions, something for which she blamed the Secretary of Defense (unfairly, I would argue). In any event, she did not welcome his reappearance in what was clearly a diplomatic process. "We think the Indians are going to ask for the F-80," the Secretary of Defense said without any prefatory small talk.

"And why do we think that?" the Secretary of State asked coldly.

"That's what sources are telling us," he replied vaguely. The F-80 was America's most strategically advanced fighter jet. The U.S. government had not offered to sell the jet to any other countries save for the Israelis, and even then some of the most important technology had been removed. "It can't happen," the Secretary of Defense said emphatically.

"The Indians are an important ally," the Secretary of State answered. "Maybe we offer to share some of the technology down the road."

"No," the Secretary of Defense said. "It will destabilize the entire region. The Pakistanis will go nuts." His voice was rising. "There can be no mention of the F-80—none."

The Secretary of State knew he was right but resented the lecture anyway. "How good is your intelligence?" she asked.

"The intelligence is good," the Secretary of Defense answered. "We know the Indian generals want the F-80. What we don't know is how the PM feels about it. We don't know if he cares enough to make it a negotiating point."

"He's ex–Air Force," the Secretary of State offered.

"I think that works in our favor," the Secretary of Defense said. The Indian Prime Minister had been a decorated fighter pilot and later a general in the Air Force. Conventional wisdom, at both State and Defense, was that politicians with a military background were less enamored of fancy, expensive hardware than politicians with no military experience. They also had more credibility when facing down the generals who were clamoring for such toys.

"I suspect he'll probe a bit," the Secretary of State said.

"You have to be very clear that it's not even a possibility," the Secretary of Defense declared.

"Obviously."

"You'll have to be prepared to walk away—"

"Yes, I understand that. I know how negotiations work. Is there anything else?"

"No, that's it. Sorry to have to drop this on you," the Secretary of Defense said earnestly.

"This is going to be China all over again, isn't it?" the Secretary of State said. "The price will be too high."

"I don't think so," the Secretary of Defense said. "The PM may be a self-interested bastard, but he still gets up every morning and reads the newspapers to see how he's doing. If rushing Dormigen to America plays well in the villages, that's what he'll want to do."

"That's what would happen in a Hindi film," the Secretary of State mused.

"With all the singing and dancing? I don't watch Hindi films," the Secretary of Defense replied. "But I am idealistic enough, or maybe just naïve enough, to think that democracy might work to our advantage here."

"That would be nice, wouldn't it?" the Secretary of State said.

"Good luck."

81.

THE SECRETARY OF STATE, THE U.S. AMBASSADOR, AND assorted aides were finally ushered in to see the Indian Prime Minister at around noon Delhi time. They met in the Prime Minister's capacious personal office, decorated with tapestries depicting various historical scenes, from the Moghul era to Independence. The Prime Minister showed the American entourage to a small sitting area with two stuffed chairs, one for him and one for the Secretary of State.

Their aides, including Sumer Patel on the Indian side, arrayed themselves awkwardly behind the two principals. There were not enough seats at first; an Indian functionary rushed to bring more. "Mr. Prime Minister, we have brought you a small gift," the Secretary of State offered, at which point an aide behind her produced an elegant wooden box about the size of a brick. The Prime Minister carefully opened a latch on the side of the box, revealing a small bottle of rare bourbon. "Ah," the Prime Minister exclaimed with genuine enthusiasm, "the British have their scotch, but the Americans do bourbon! Shall we try it?"

"How about if we celebrate with a drink after we consummate a deal?" the Secretary of State suggested.

"Yes," the Prime Minister agreed. "We are prepared to offer you the assistance you need. At first, we did not appreciate the seriousness of your situation. This is why . . ." He gave a wave of his hand to dismiss the Indian government's charades when they were first approached about offering up Dormigen. On this point, he was almost certainly telling the truth. U.S. intelligence reports—and plain common sense—suggested that many governments, including the Indian government, did not believe the American Dormigen shortfall was as serious as it had been made out to be.

"I appreciate your willingness to help," the Secretary of State said. "I think it could be an important step toward cementing our bilateral relationship. The President feels the same."

"As do I," the Prime Minister said.

"I have to be honest here," the Secretary of State said. "We have few other options and we are running out of time." In terms of playing possum, the Secretary of State was now lying on her back, legs in the air.

The Prime Minister looked skeptical. He proceeded to sniff: "There is an impressive scientific effort happening," he said, making it sound more like a question than a statement. "A new Manhattan Project."

"What we've learned about the virus is very impressive," the Secretary of State replied. "But it's hard for me to conceive of a situation in which the scientists can produce actionable results in the time that we have. Even if they were to come up with a treatment right now—this very minute—it would take days, if not weeks, to produce and distribute a new drug." Rarely had she felt so manipulative while speaking the absolute truth.

"Dormigen is a more elegant solution," the Prime Minister said.

"Of course. Absolutely," the Secretary of State agreed.

"This could bring our two nations closer together," the Prime Minister said.

The Secretary of State finished the thought: "This can be an opportunity to revitalize some of the bilateral initiatives that have been languishing for too long: our civil nuclear cooperation, the intelligence-sharing, the H-1B visas."

"Exactly," the Prime Minister said, looking over at Patel, presumably to acknowledge his work at the California Pizza Kitchen Summit. There were subtle nods of agreement among the aides in both delegations. Yet the Secretary of State was developing a bad feeling. The conversation had gone on too long—too many dates without a kiss, as one of her mentors at State would describe this kind of situation. The Prime Minister should have closed the deal by now; they had seemingly reached agreement. "We could do reciprocal state visits," the Prime Minister offered. The longer the conversation went on, the worse the Secretary of State began to feel, regardless of what the PM was saying.

"Sooner rather than later," the Secretary of State suggested. "The President and First Lady have a special affinity for India." *What is the holdup here?* she wondered.

The door to the office opened. An aide scurried to the Prime Minister's side and handed him a small folded note. "Excuse me," the Prime Minister said as he read. "My goodness," he exclaimed. "Your scientists are making great progress." The press was eagerly reporting our wiki science breakthroughs in real time. The NIH Director reckoned there was little hope in keeping the developments secret, and no compelling reason to do so anyway. It was not a surprise that the Indian Prime Minister was keeping abreast of these scientific developments; it was surprising that an aide had interrupted him with specific news. The Ambassador and the Secretary of State exchanged a puzzled glance. "This is very exciting," the Prime Minister said.

"We are still a very long way from having any actionable findings," the Secretary of State said, as if she were reassuring him that his magnanimity would not be supplanted at the last minute by some scientific miracle. Both the Ambassador and the Secretary of State later described this moment in the conversation at length in their respective memoirs, but somehow it got lost in the wider public discussion of the Outbreak. Our remarkable research efforts at the NIH and this bizarre diplomatic chapter in India were inextricably linked. Yes, they were two different paths we pursued for managing the Dormigen shortage, but they converged in the Prime Minister's office in those few delicate moments. The science—the possibility that our unprecedented network of scientists would render Dormigen unnecessary—offered the Secretary of State the only leverage she had.

"I think it would be to India's great advantage if we were able to assist during this crisis," the Prime Minister said, which was just a restatement of what he had been saying since the meeting began. The members of both delegations nodded in agreement. *More dating, still no kissing*, the Secretary of State thought. The Prime Minister continued, "Perhaps we could have a private session?"

"Of course," the Secretary of State agreed. Anything to encourage him to get to the point. The various aides began to file out of the room. *And if he's going to ask about the F-80*, the Secretary thought, *the fewer people in the room, the better.*

"Would it be okay for Mr. Patel and the Ambassador to stay?" the Prime Minister asked.

"Yes, of course," the Secretary of State said. Patel and the U.S. Ambassador moved their chairs closer to the principals. Neither one of them said much during the balance of the meeting, but we are fortunate that the Ambassador was there to substantiate the Secretary's account of the extraordinary conversation that followed.

The Prime Minister leaned forward, placing his fingertips together, almost like a little prayer. "This is very exciting, yes?" he asked. The Secretary did not know quite what to make of the question. She had spent every wakeful hour in recent days pleading with world leaders, fending off Chinese aggression, dealing with petty members of Congress, and squabbling with her fellow cabinet members. The most recent NIH projection was that between thirty-seven thousand and a hundred and eleven thousand people would die prematurely in the United States due to *Capellaviridae*. She could think of a lot of adjectives—"frustrating," "infuriating," "tragic," "exhausting"—but "exciting" was not on the list. The Prime Minister must have read her expression, because he added, "Not the Outbreak, of course, but that it can be a catalyst for better relations between the world's two most important democracies."

"I hope so," the Secretary of State said cautiously.

"I have two personal requests," the Prime Minister offered.

"Please," the Secretary answered, inviting him to continue. She had known something was coming, but a "personal request"? Her mind was racing. The F-80 would hardly be a "personal request." Did the PM have teenage children? How many times had she been asked by foreign leaders to get their children into Harvard, Princeton, or Yale?

"It would be very beneficial for India to assist the United States with your Dormigen situation," the Prime Minister said.

"Yes, I think we've established that," the Secretary responded. Patience is like a muscle; it grows stronger when exercised. But even the Secretary's prodigious patience, exercised constantly by rambling Russian diatribes and verbose NATO bureaucrats and lying Iranian negotiators, was growing fatigued.

"It would be good for me, too, politically," the Prime Minister said. The Secretary and the Ambassador nodded in understanding. He continued, "I would never put my political interests ahead of what is good for my country—*never.*"

"There's no reason they can't be aligned," the Secretary said, urging him along.

"Yes! Exactly." He seemed relieved that his visitors grasped this point. "In that spirit, I have two requests to help keep these interests 'aligned,' as you say."

"You are in a position to save a lot of lives, Mr. Prime Minister. I will do whatever I can," the Secretary said honestly.

"Hmm, yes." The Prime Minister was a remarkably articulate man, but he was clearly stumbling for words. "Well, first," he began,

"I would like to make sure that India gets the appropriate credit for this generous donation."

"Obviously," the Secretary said emphatically. She was still entirely puzzled as to where this was going.

"The scientific discoveries around this virus are moving very quickly," the Prime Minister explained. "That's a good thing, obviously. Please don't get me wrong."

Finally, the Secretary thought. So that was it: The Prime Minister was worried about being upstaged by some last-minute discovery. Not merely upstaged, but embarrassed. Nothing would be worse for his political standing at home than making a high-profile announcement offering assistance to the United States, loading up Indian cargo planes with Dormigen, and then having the whole effort rendered unnecessary—foolish, even—by this wiki Manhattan Project. India, the perpetual junior partner in the relationship, would have its planes loaded up with nowhere to go.

The Secretary of State felt a wave of relief. This she could manage. "I understand completely," she assured the Prime Minister. Because she did. Her job was to prevent any potential embarrassment for the PM or his nation. "I'm thinking out loud here, but tell me what you think of this," she said, pausing to gather her thoughts. "The President obviously cannot suspend the research efforts—it would be imprudent, and he couldn't stop the progress even if he wanted to."

"I understand."

"But he can certainly make a statement—an entirely truthful statement—telling the American people that those efforts have not yielded a Dormigen substitute and will not in the time we have left. They've failed. I don't think he would use the word 'failed,' because it's been a remarkably impressive scientific effort all things considered, but the time has passed for the science to bail us out."

"Yes," the Prime Minister said.

"And then he could couple that statement—"

"A live statement, not just a press release," the Prime Minister clarified.

"Absolutely," the Secretary of State agreed. "Perhaps a short address to the nation. In any event, I could imagine him coupling that dire news with the announcement that India will be providing the Dormigen necessary to ward off the crisis. That makes perfect sense to me."

The U.S. Ambassador interjected, "I can't speak for the President, but I'm sure he would be comfortable running the text of those remarks by you in advance."

"It would be the least we could do," the Secretary added.

"Excellent," the Prime Minister said, visibly excited. "Then I think we have a deal!"

"You had a second request?" the Secretary of State said, while thinking, *Please, God, do not make it the F-80, because then this whole thing will unravel, but what else could it possibly be?*

"Oh, yes, it's a tiny favor, I can't imagine the President would object."

Help me, the Secretary thought, because when anyone asks for a "tiny favor" it's usually a complete disaster, like when the bullying Turkish President tried to persuade her that arresting some of his critics in the U.S. would be "such a small thing"—

"I'd like to fly the Dormigen there myself."

"Pardon?" the Secretary asked. Her thoughts were racing so quickly that she had missed the essence of what the Prime Minister was asking.

"I'd like to deliver it myself—the Dormigen. I'd like to 'fly west!' as the President would say."

The Secretary of State was still struggling to catch up. The Ambassador, seeing her confusion, said, "You're saying that you would like to be on the plane that takes the Dormigen to the United States?"

"Exactly."

The Secretary of State felt a wave of euphoria sweep over her. *This was going to happen.* "The President would be delighted to have you deliver the Dormigen," she said confidently. "I'm not sure we can plan a state visit with two days' notice, but we will do everything short of that. We will plan an event befitting what you and your country are doing for the United States."

And you can wear a fucking superhero outfit, if you want, she thought. The Secretary of State is not a profane woman, but according to her memoirs, that was exactly what was running through her mind as she shook hands with the Prime Minister, consummating the deal.

82.

THE SECRETARY OF STATE IMMEDIATELY PHONED THE CHIEF of Staff, who was traveling with the President. "We did it," the Secretary of State reported breathlessly. The excitement in her voice was laced with fatigue.

"You're certain?" the Chief of Staff asked.

"Yes. We have a firm commitment: five hundred thousand doses. Technically it's a loan. The embassy is preparing the documentation. There are some other things: the civil nuclear cooperation—"

"He's not going to go back on his word?" the Chief of Staff asked.

"The Prime Minister? No. For all his foibles, he's rock-solid when he makes a deal. That's the military in him."

"Thank you," the Chief of Staff said softly. And then, after a pause: "I'm going to tell the President now."

The President was standing alone on the tarmac at Dover Air Force Base. He and the Chief of Staff had traveled there to greet the remains of the two U.S. diplomats who had been killed in the Saudi school kidnapping. The plane carrying their bodies was expected to land shortly. The families would be coming, too, along with a Marine honor guard. The President had been here many times before, greeting the fallen soldiers on their return at all hours of the night. He felt it was his duty; the families were always grateful, despite the horrific circumstances. He also enjoyed the solitude and used it as a time for reflection. On this morning he had made a point of arriving early. The Chief of Staff walked over to where the President was standing. The air was pleasantly cool and the sun was just coming up over a runway on the horizon. The Chief of Staff's heels clicked loudly on the asphalt. The President turned slightly as she approached, seemingly annoyed by the interruption.

"We got the Dormigen," she said without undue drama. "The Prime Minister is offering up everything we need."

The President nodded, betraying little emotion. "I need to call Cecelia—"

"Done. It was my first call."

"And?"

The Chief of Staff shrugged. "She's very sick. They gave her Dormigen immediately, but her daughter says it could go either way."

The President nodded in acknowledgment. "What does he want?"

"Who?" the Chief of Staff asked.

"The Prime Minister."

"No problems," the Chief of Staff assured him. "Just the stuff we talked about: civil nuclear, intelligence-sharing, visas—he didn't even ask about the F-80."

The President exhaled audibly. Someone watching from a distance would have no idea that he had just received great news, but the Chief of Staff knew him well enough that she could see some of the tension go out of his body. "We're not out of the woods yet," the President said. "We still have to make sure the Dormigen gets on a plane. There's not a lot of time, and it is India, after all. There's a big difference between offering five hundred thousand doses and actually getting it loaded on a plane and off the ground."

"The Ambassador is on it," the Chief of Staff assured him. She wished the President would take more time to savor what they had accomplished. "There's one other thing," she said.

"There's always one other thing. You know how I feel—"

"I think you'll find this amusing," the Chief of Staff said. "The Prime Minister wants to fly the Dormigen here himself. Apparently you've started quite a thing—this whole 'flying west.'"

The President smiled in genuine amusement. "Whatever makes him happy," he said. They stood in silence for some time, appreciating the peace. "There is going to be a lull, while we wait for the Indian Dormigen," the President told his Chief of Staff. "You should get some time with the family."

The Chief of Staff gave a short, sardonic laugh. "My daughter is failing trig. I think she's doing it just to get back at me."

"Does anyone really need to know trigonometry?" the President asked.

"Don't tell her that," the Chief of Staff replied, with a more mirthful laugh. "Dan's been a saint."

"Don't take that for granted."

"No."

Moments later a minivan arrived on the tarmac carrying the parents of the slain consular officer. They had traveled to Dover from a suburb of Detroit. Their son had been in the diplomatic corps for thirteen years, having done tours in Belgium, Ghana, Jordan, and then Saudi Arabia. The President walked purposefully toward the van. The Chief of Staff watched as he helped the couple out of the vehicle, hugging the mother and shaking hands with the father. She could see the President pointing toward the runway, presumably explaining that the plane carrying their son's body would arrive shortly. A few minutes later another minivan arrived carrying the second family.

83.

OUR "WAR ROOM" WAS BUZZING WITH ACTIVITY WHEN THE NIH Director walked in shortly after daybreak. The large conference room had no windows; the fluorescent lights bathed the room in bright light, disguising any sense of what time it was. Most of the scientists and staff had been there all night. The pace of discovery was intoxicating; even those who had planned to leave found it hard to do so. I was on the phone with a science blogger, walking her through all that we had learned in the past twelve hours. "This place smells like a locker room," the NIH Director said. The French camera crew, having tired of footage of slovenly people hunched over keyboards, eagerly turned their cameras on her.

"Give her a little breathing room, please," I told them. Giscard repeated my admonition in French (though I am certain they understood my instructions in English perfectly well).

"It's fine," the NIH Director said. And then, more directly to the film crew, "You'll want to get this." Everyone who heard that curious remark stopped working and turned to the Director. She continued, "Could I have everyone's attention, please?"

The clicking of keyboards slowed and then stopped. The two camera operators sidled even closer. "I just received a call from the President's Chief of Staff," the Director said, projecting her voice across the room. "She informed me that the Indian Prime Minister has offered the United States five hundred thousand doses of Dormigen.

That medicine will be on a plane bound for Washington shortly." A loud cheer erupted in the room, but there were also a few sighs of disappointment. We were all relieved, obviously, but we were disappointed, too. *We could have figured this thing out*, I was thinking, as were many others. Perhaps sensing this emotion, the Director continued, "The Chief of Staff asked me to tell the people in this room one other thing." She paused to put on her reading glasses and unfold an ordinary piece of copy paper on which she had scrawled several sentences. "This is an exact quote: 'Our leverage in the negotiations came from the blistering pace of progress we were making on the virus. Without that, there would be no Dormigen on its way to the United States right now.' The Chief of Staff asked me, on behalf of the President, to thank each and every one of you." There were hearty cheers. The French film crew turned their cameras on the room to capture the reaction.

After the Director left, our room was oddly still for several minutes. A few people, exhausted from the all-nighter, left to get real food or to go home for some sleep. But most of us did not want to leave. There was a unique bond in the room, holding us there together. The crisis may have passed, but the urge to figure out *Capellaviridae* had not. Less than fifteen minutes after the Director addressed the room, a group of biologists, a joint Northwestern–University of Chicago team, posted the most extraordinary finding yet: when the North American dust mite transmits *Capellaviridae* to humans, it also passes along an enzyme that destroys the older *Capellaviridae* viruses already in the body. "New *Capellaviridae* viruses get swapped out for the old ones, effectively," they wrote in the *What does this mean in plain English?* section of our Google Doc. We recognized immediately that this could easily be the piece of the puzzle we had been waiting for.

"Do they know?" Giscard asked no one in particular, his distinctive voice rising above the clatter in the room.

"What?" I asked.

"Do they know we have the Dormigen?"

"I'm not sure it matters," I replied. That reading of the situation turned out to be broadly correct. Our site had more meaningful posts over the next twenty-four hours than we had in the first twenty-four.

84.

THE INDIAN DORMIGEN PLEDGE SET IN MOTION A FLURRY OF logistical activity. The NIH was worried about Dormigen shortages in rural areas, even with the arrival of the Indian doses. It would be roughly thirty-six hours before the new Dormigen arrived on the East Coast, and then at least another twenty-four hours before it could be distributed to all parts of the country. Deep in the bowels of Homeland Security, some nameless bureaucrat opened up the electronic equivalent of a binder: Pandemic Drug Distribution. There were other such "binders": bioterror evacuation, and nuclear accidents, and dirty bombs. The people who prepared these binders went home at night hoping that nothing they ever did would be relevant.

But on this day, the "binder" came off the shelf. Once the Indian Prime Minister's plane touched down in D.C., the U.S. Air Force would take the lead in moving the Dormigen to the major metropolitan areas. From there, National Guard units would ferry it to more remote areas with the assistance of private couriers, as necessary. There had been simulations of this exercise before; now the contingency plan was set in motion for real. The Air Force began flying a massive fleet of cargo planes to airports in and around Washington, D.C. National Guard units in all fifty states were called up for duty. National Guard trucks and planes, with their respective drivers and pilots, were assembling near airports in the major cities. The maps and routes had already been drawn up. It was all in the binder.

The planning on the India side was more ad hoc. The Prime Minister requisitioned an Air India 747 cargo plane to make his historic flight and requested that the aging plane be repainted for the occasion. When he was told that a 747 could not be painted in twenty-four hours, he settled for having enormous Indian and American flags painted on the tail and fuselage. The hulking 747, a beautiful plane under normal circumstances, looked appropriately majestic for the PM's mission. The U.S. Embassy was testing samples of the Dormigen as it was loaded on the plane. This request had come from the CDC in Washington, where there was some fear that a high proportion of the Indian Dormigen might be counterfeit or expired.

Nearly all attention in India was now focused on the Prime Minister's "toilets and televisions" initiative. "I assume you're joking," the Secretary of State had said when an aide hustled into her temporary office at the embassy and described the program.

"Nope. Fifteen thousand villages in forty-eight hours," the aide said. "That's the plan."

Less than an hour earlier, the Indian Prime Minister had announced a plan to furnish fifteen thousand villages with a sanitary latrine, a television with a satellite dish, and a solar panel that would generate sufficient electricity to power the television. The Prime Minister proclaimed, "In the middle of the twenty-first century, no Indian village should be without a clean, sanitary toilet. And no village should be cut off from the rest of the country." He bypassed the legendary Indian bureaucracy and enlisted the Army to carry out his edict. A public school teacher in each of the designated villages was recalled to the nearest population center, where he or she was paired with a small contingent of soldiers who would return to the village—often hiking for hours to remote places with no road access—to dig the latrine and install the solar panel and television.

The Prime Minister called the program "Technology for India" or something like that; within a few hours, even he was referring to it as "toilets and televisions." His political opponents went ballistic, declaring the obvious: the PM wanted to ensure that even the smallest village (where voter turnout tended to be quite high) would be able to witness his heroic journey to the U.S. At first the Prime Minister's lackeys tried to argue that the program's timing was coincidental. Eventually that charade became impossible to maintain, since every village participating in the program was given a single sheet of paper with a description of three things in the simplest possible language: (1) instructions for the television; (2) an explanation of how and why using the latrine could prevent the spread of disease; and (3) a description of the PM's flight to America, including a photo of him posing in front of the 747 and its enormous Indian and American flags.

The new toilets turned out to be perfect insulation against charges of political opportunism; public health officials reckoned they would save thousands of lives in the long run. The solar panels, too, would be beneficial, as they could be used for other village functions, such as charging mobile phones and powering lights so students could study at night. In the end, the PM's opponents argued that if the program was so beneficial, he should have done it earlier—hardly a searing indictment. The most creative claim was that Pakistan would invade India while the Army was busy digging toilets in remote parts of the country. The Prime Minister, never one to shy away from adding more frosting to his own cake, phoned the Pakistani Prime Minister and asked him to do his best to deter any border provocations that might jeopardize the assistance plan for their mutual ally, the United States. We have no record of the Pakistani PM's response; we do know that Pakistan did not invade India while its Army was digging toilets.

It took about nineteen hours to gather the Dormigen in Delhi and load the 747 (plenty of time for the paint to dry on the large Indian and American flags on the fuselage and tail). The plane was scheduled to depart around six p.m. Delhi time. A small diplomatic contingent was invited for a departure ceremony. Takeoff was pushed back to eight p.m. and then nine; the Prime Minister's spokesperson did not offer a reason. The President phoned the Secretary of State to ask about the delay. "It's never too late for them to ask for the F-80," he said. "They've got us over a barrel now."

"I don't think the Prime Minister would do that," the Secretary of State assured him.

"We don't have a big buffer here. Tell them we need that plane in the air," the President insisted.

"I've made that abundantly clear," the Secretary of State replied. "If I were to guess, the PM is stalling for time so more televisions can get to the villages."

"You can't make this shit up," the President muttered.

The departure was postponed once again, this time until seven the following morning, putatively because of a mechanical issue with the plane. The U.S. Ambassador called Sumer Patel to implore the Indians to get the flight in the air. "Don't worry," Patel said. "The seven o'clock departure is firm."

"You think the mechanical issue will be resolved by then, do you?" the Ambassador asked sarcastically.

Patel laughed. "The Prime Minister wants ten thousand televisions installed before he takes off, and another five thousand in operation before he refuels in Germany," he explained.

The U.S. Ambassador did not know how to respond. Finally, he said, "*We have absolutely no cushion.* You realize what's at stake here?"

"Of course I do," Patel bristled. "And so does the Prime Minister. You'll get your Dormigen. Just let him have what he wants."

85.

THE DELAYS IN NEW DELHI NOW PUT THE DORMIGEN DISTRI-bution plans in the U.S. in jeopardy. An Air Force logistics officer arrived at the White House to brief the President on the disruption. She was a stocky woman with close-cropped hair who stood at rigid attention after the Chief of Staff ushered her into the Oval Office. The President was finishing a call with the Mexican President, who had called to express his displeasure with an immigration bill making its way through Congress. The President motioned the Air Force officer to a seat, but she remained standing. "I can't promise you I'm going to veto it—that would be unwise—but I can tell you that I think it's a lousy bill and I don't think it has enough votes in the Senate," the American President told his Mexican counterpart. He then listened for what appeared to be an excessively long time.

"Lots of translation," the Chief of Staff explained to the Air Force officer.

"I appreciate your thoughts on this," the President said in a tone meant to wrap up the call. He waited for assorted pleasantries to be translated, said goodbye, and then hung up. He looked at the Chief of Staff plaintively and said, "This isn't on the schedule."

"We've run into a snafu with the logistics for the Dormigen distribution," the Chief of Staff said.

"Why can't we get that goddamn plane in the air?" the President snapped. The Chief of Staff nodded to the Air Force officer, inviting her to speak.

"Sir," she began nervously, "even if that plane takes off right now, we are bumping up against the time we need to deliver the Dormigen to all the specified hospitals and clinics."

"How long do you need?" the President asked.

"Our plan requires thirty-six hours from the moment the Prime Minister's plane touches down in Washington."

"I was told twenty-four hours," he said angrily.

"That's to reach ninety-five percent of the population, sir," the officer explained. "That's typically how the logistical people—"

"Thirty-six hours?" the President exclaimed. "Are you kidding me? Are you delivering this stuff on bicycles?"

"No, sir."

"When is the Prime Minister's plane supposed to take off?" the President asked the Chief of Staff.

"Now they're saying seven a.m. Delhi time," she answered.

"And that's for real?"

"The Ambassador says it's firm," the Chief of Staff replied.

The President turned to the Air Force officer. "So what are our options?"

"I've prepared three plans," she answered, holding a briefing book out to the President.

"I don't have time for the bad ideas," he said sharply. "Just tell me what you think we should do. What's the best option?"

"Yes, sir. If we act reasonably soon, we won't have a problem, but we have to change the sequencing of the plan."

"What does that mean?" the President asked.

"I think she was about to explain that," the Chief of Staff said, trying to calm the President.

The Air Force officer continued, "We can take the Dormigen we have now and begin moving it immediately to more distant areas. Then when the relief shipment comes from Delhi it can be distributed relatively quickly to the major population centers. We would just turn the plan on its head, so that the shipments to our far-flung areas can happen before—"

"I understand," the President said.

"That's clever," the Chief of Staff added.

"It buys us a lot of time," the Air Force officer suggested.

The President nodded in acknowledgment. He was calmer now that there was a feasible option on the table. He began thinking out loud. "That's asking a lot: hospitals have to give up a dwindling supply of Dormigen for the promise of a replacement that's still sitting on a runway in Delhi."

"Do we even have that authority?" the Chief of Staff asked.

"Yes, ma'am," the Air Force officer said confidently. "I've consulted with the legal counsel at Homeland Security. The President has the necessary authority to set the plan in motion."

The President was still talking mostly to himself. "What if they don't give it up? I don't want to be in a situation where federal marshals are wrestling Dormigen away from doctors and nurses."

"Mr. President, if we go with this option, we'll have a cushion again," the Air Force officer said, gaining confidence. "We can afford to wait until the plane is aloft."

"Assuming it takes off at seven," the President said.

"Yes, sir, that's right."

The Chief of Staff offered, "Everyone would be much more willing to pass along their Dormigen if they were confident the replacement was in the air and on its way to the U.S."

"I agree," the President said. "Let's do that. And, for God's sake—"

"I will call the Prime Minister's office and tell them to get the plane in the air," the Chief of Staff assured the President, finishing his thought.

86.

THE SEVEN A.M. DEPARTURE WAS IN FACT FIRM. A SMALL group of diplomats assembled on the tarmac. The Prime Minister, dressed in his former military flight uniform, shook hands with each of the assembled officials. As a military band played the Indian national anthem, he climbed the stairs to the hulking 747 with his wife and two children. The Prime Minister's family disappeared into the plane. The Prime Minister paused at the top of the stairs, and as the band finished, he turned and briskly saluted the assembled guests (and, of course, the hundreds of millions of Indians watching on television). The door to the jet was closed and moments later the plane was aloft. Flying west.

It was nine-thirty p.m. on the East Coast of the United States; the major news channels all cut away from their normal programming to cover the takeoff. The President watched the dramatic departure in his study in the family quarters of the White House with the Majority Leader, the Strategist, and the Chief of Staff. They broke into spontaneous applause as the 747 left the ground. The news channels cut to the Seattle hospital where doctors reported that Cecelia Dodds was "responding to Dormigen" and had been upgraded from critical to serious condition.

"She's the toughest person I know," the President offered.

"She'll pull through," the Majority Leader said. "This calls for a drink."

"I'll go find some of the good stuff," the President agreed.

"This is great news," the Chief of Staff said. "I'm going to head home." She handed the President his schedule for the next day. In the morning, he would be making a brutal trip to California, where wildfires were ravaging eleven counties. He would tour the area briefly and then fly back across the country in time for the Prime Minister's arrival.

"The guy knows how to make a departure, doesn't he?" the President said. His mood was noticeably improved, almost buoyant.

"At least he's in the air," the Chief of Staff said. "That's precious cargo."

"Get some sleep," the President advised her. "Give my best to Dan and the girls." The Chief of Staff walked wearily out of the study. The President went in search of a bottle of rare Irish whiskey the Prime Minister of Ireland had given him on his last visit.

Twenty minutes later the President, the Majority Leader, and the Strategist were sipping Irish whiskey and watching cable news coverage of the Air India flight when the Chief of Staff walked briskly back into the study. "I thought you went home," the President said quizzically.

"We have a problem," she announced.

The President set his tumbler on the coffee table, leaned back in the sofa, and exhaled audibly. "Do you know what I dream?" he said with resignation. "I dream that one day you're going to come bursting in here and exclaim, 'Great news: Something went much better than we expected!'"

"Not today," the Chief of Staff said, unamused.

"What?" the President asked.

The Chief of Staff explained, "Three governors are saying they won't allow Dormigen to be moved out of their states. They're refusing to allow their National Guard units to participate—"

"Hold on," the President said. "Why does any Dormigen need to cross state lines?"

"The Homeland Security plan has Dormigen moving from metro areas to rural areas," the Chief of Staff answered.

"Okay," the President acknowledged.

"Well, look at a map," the Chief of Staff said impatiently. "The fastest way to get Dormigen to northern Wisconsin is from Minneapolis. If you want to get it to northern Mississippi, it comes from Memphis."

"Of course," the Strategist said.

"And three governors won't play ball," the President said, absorbing the situation.

"Correct," the Chief of Staff said. "The federal government can't tell them what to do, they have an obligation to protect lifesaving medicine from federal bureaucrats, and so on, all the usual claptrap."

"Let me guess," the President conjectured, "Hazlett, Goolsbee, and Spencer."

"Congratulations. A couple of others are making similar noises," the Chief of Staff said.

"Alabama, Mississippi, and Louisiana," the Strategist added. "I sometimes find myself wondering if we should have just let the Confederacy go."

"You're welcome to wonder that," the President said sharply. "I would appreciate it if you would not say it out loud."

"I've asked the General Counsel's office for our options," the Chief of Staff said wearily.

"I can nationalize the National Guard units," the President said. "Do we have time?"

"I've called some staff back in. They're working on it," the Chief of Staff answered.

The President sipped his whiskey and stared at the television. There was a graphic on the screen of the Prime Minister's projected flight path from New Delhi to Washington. "They're just trying to make a point, more partisan grandstanding," he said bitterly.

"This is more serious than they realize," the Chief of Staff replied. "If they mess up the plan, then the logistics go off the rails. *And if that happens, we run out of time.* Every hour means unnecessary deaths—"

"I understand that," the President said, his former buoyancy long gone.

"These fuckwits think they can have their Dormigen and flip off the federal government, too," the Strategist offered.

"They can't," the Chief of Staff said plaintively. "These are complex algorithms. It's not like we can just redraw the maps so that no Dormigen crosses state lines. Even if we could, if we make some concession to these guys, then every other governor will want the same thing. Then the plan unravels and people start dying because the Dormigen isn't going to make it to some places in time." She paused to breathe. She was worn out, and this political play—so gratuitous—felt like one more kick. "They're playing with a loaded gun," she added.

"But they don't think it's loaded," the President said. "That's what makes it so dangerous."

"That happens, you know," the Strategist interjected. "If you take the clip out of a semiautomatic pistol, there's still one bullet left in the chamber. Most people don't know that."

The President stared at him, too fatigued to tell him to stop talking. "If I have to nationalize the National Guard, so be it," the President said.

"If they resist, or even delay—we don't have hours to play with," the Chief of Staff lamented. "Every minute they dick around in front of the television cameras is going to put some areas of the country at risk." The room went silent as the four of them absorbed the potential cost of this political ploy. "*And it's totally unnecessary,*" the Chief of Staff added angrily.

"With respect, Mr. President," the Majority Leader said quietly, "I'm wondering if there isn't a better option here."

"I'm all ears."

"Can you get me an office with a phone?" the Majority Leader asked. "I might be able to persuade these esteemed elected officials—"

"Fuckwits," the Strategist declared.

"Yes, well, I might be able to get these fuckwits to think about the situation differently," the Majority Leader continued.

"You know who you're dealing with," the President said. His exhaustion was evident. For the first time during the crisis, there was also a hint of sadness, as if the ongoing parade of self-interest and narrow-mindedness and partisan grandstanding had finally begun to erode his belief in basic human decency.

"I do know who I'm dealing with," the Majority Leader said confidently.

"I'll get you an office downstairs," the Chief of Staff offered. The Majority Leader stood and retrieved his suit jacket from a nearby chair. He put on the jacket, buttoning it over his paunch. He picked up his empty whiskey tumbler and shook the ice cubes against the expensive crystal.

"Might I get a refill?" the Majority Leader suggested. The President fetched the bottle and poured two fingers for the Majority Leader. "Now, can someone get Governor Hazlett on the phone for me?" he asked.

"You're going to try to talk sense to Hazlett?" the President asked skeptically.

"He's the least decent of the bunch," the Chief of Staff said.

"That's exactly why I'm going to start with him. I'm going to talk his language," the Majority Leader said.

"In that case, here," the President said as he poured more Irish whiskey into the Majority Leader's glass.

The Majority Leader rattled the ice cubes gingerly in the expensive glass, creating a pleasant clinking. "Thank you. I'll be back."

As coincidence would have it, I was working on a press release on our new discoveries regarding *Capellaviridae* in one of the small communications offices below the living quarters in the White House.

The print media may have been dying a long, slow death, but Americans still liked to wake up to their news, even if it was no longer in a newspaper lying on the front porch. Tens of millions of Americans would start their mornings by checking their phones and tablets and computers. We were hoping to control that narrative, pushing out all of our good news through every possible channel.

The Chief of Staff appeared at the office door with the Majority Leader standing just behind her. "Are you using the phone?" she asked. I shook my head no and moved to a small chair in the corner of the office, so the Majority Leader would be able to sit at the desk. She turned to the Majority Leader. "Do you need privacy?"

"Oh, no," he assured her. "This will be a very public exercise. Do we have Governor Hazlett on the line?"

"He's not taking our calls," the Chief of Staff answered.

"Try again," the Majority Leader said confidently. "Only this time, tell him I'd like to discuss the Sea Snake Sonar appropriation." The Majority Leader took off his suit jacket and placed it delicately on the back of his chair. He loosened his tie and sat down at the desk, fully expecting the phone to ring. Sure enough, within minutes the Majority Leader was on the phone with Alabama Governor Sterling Hazlett. I continued to type at my laptop, but mostly I was watching the Majority Leader do what he does.

"Governor Hazlett," the Majority Leader intoned, "I don't have a lot of time for pleasantries. This is a courtesy call. I thought I would let you know that I'm withdrawing my support for the Sea Snake Sonar in the Defense Appropriations Bill." He listened briefly and then continued, "It's over budget and it doesn't work. You know that, I know that, the Navy knows that. I spoke to the Chair of Armed Services, and he agrees. We shouldn't be spending a billion dollars on a sonar system that can't tell the difference between a Russian submarine and a school of tuna."

"That's six thousand jobs," Governor Hazlett answered on the other end of the line, loud enough for me to hear clearly.

"I understand that, which is why I wanted you to be the first to know," the Majority Leader said with faux-sincerity. "You're going to want to do some damage control."

"Is this about the Dormigen thing?" Governor Hazlett asked.

"What do you think?" the Majority Leader asked coldly.

"I can certainly reconsider," Governor Hazlett offered.

"That ship has sailed, Governor," the Majority Leader said, "if you'll forgive the nautical metaphor."

Governor Hazlett began to protest, but the Majority Leader cut him off. "We have a lot going on here with this Dormigen situation. Thank you for your time." He hung up.

I stared at the Majority Leader quizzically. "He's not willing to participate in our plan to move Dormigen where it needs to go," the Majority Leader explained. Now, the good thing about crappy weapons systems is that they come in handy when you need to get rid of them. And it really will save a billion dollars."

After a few seconds, I worked up my courage to ask, "But you just hung up . . . Don't we need him to agree to the Dormigen plan?"

"Oh, no. This is about sending a message to the other governors," the Majority Leader said. "Sometimes you have to shoot someone like Hazlett in the head to get the others to pay attention. How do I get someone around here to issue a statement?"

I hustled down the corridor and returned with the Communications Director, who had been working to push out his own good news. The Majority Leader, leaning back in his borrowed chair, issued instructions: "Put out a statement over my name saying I'm withdrawing my support for the Sea Snake Sonar. It's over budget, it doesn't work, budgets are tight, blah, blah. Put a quote in there from the Armed Services Chair saying this will allow us to devote more resources to our troops. Then call the Armed Services Chair at home to tell him what he said."

"Do you want to look at it before I send it out?" the Communications Director asked.

"No, it's not that complicated," the Majority Leader answered jauntily. After the Communications Director disappeared, the Majority Leader sipped his whiskey with evident satisfaction. "Now we're going to use a little sugar," he said to me. "Can you have someone connect me with Charlotte Johnson in Texas?" He looked at his watch. "In about half an hour."

"It's late," I said, almost instinctively.

"Texas is an hour behind us," the Majority Leader answered. "I need Governor Johnson to learn about what happened to Hazlett before we get her on the phone."

I felt like I was a student in some kind of backroom political science tutorial. The Majority Leader sat patiently at the desk, sipping from his drink. He seemed perfectly comfortable with the silence, the waiting. After five minutes or so, I asked, "Is Governor Johnson refusing to ship Dormigen out of state?"

"Oh, no," the Majority Leader replied, eager to share his strategy. "Charlotte's a good egg. But she could waffle, and she'll feel pressure to follow these other assholes. Texas is big and important. *That's where we need to hold the line.* It's like Lincoln in the Civil War: he knew he couldn't afford to lose the border states."

We went back to our silence. After a few more minutes, a young aide stuck his head in the door. "Governor Hazlett is on the line for you. He said you and he were just talking and there was some confusion about the Sea Snake Sonar—"

"Tell him to hold," the Majority Leader said, exchanging a knowing glance with me.

"Of course," the aide said compliantly.

The Majority Leader and I both looked at the phone on the desk, where a small red light began blinking hypnotically. "That's Hazlett?" I said, pointing at the light.

"I would assume so," the Majority Leader said. He sipped his drink.

The minutes passed. I finished my press release. The small red light continued to blink. I have never watched anyone sit still so contentedly. The Majority Leader did not check his phone. He did not make notes to himself. He did not feel compelled to make small talk. He sat stiffly in the chair, sipping his drink periodically, but mostly just still, like a hunter in a blind. Eventually the aide reappeared. "We're going to place the call to Governor Johnson in Texas. Shall we send it in here?" he asked.

"Yes, please," the Majority Leader said pleasantly. The small red light on the phone panel was still blinking. After a minute or so, both because I was uncomfortable with the silence and because I was curious, I asked, "How long are you going to keep Governor Hazlett on hold?" But before the Majority Leader could answer, the phone rang and he picked it up.

"Charlotte," the Majority Leader said warmly. "It's so good to hear from you." He listened to pleasantries on the other end and then continued. "The President is up to his eyeballs in this Dormigen thing. He needs all the help he can get." The Texas governor, not nearly as loud or as agitated as her fellow Alabama governor, said something about the Texas National Guard. "You are absolutely correct," the Majority Leader assured her. "But as a personal favor to me, can we have that conversation another time?" he asked. The Majority Leader laughed loudly and warmly at whatever Charlotte Johnson said in reply. "Yes, that's right," he continued. "News travels fast. That Sea Snake system never did work." He looked in my direction and gave a little smile. "Why not save the taxpayers some money?" the Majority Leader told the Texas governor, laughing some more. "Look, if you could spread the word among your buddies that the President could use a favor on this one, I would appreciate it. I owe you one, and the President owes you one." He listened, nodded, and then chuckled. "My God, you really are something, Charlotte. Yes, that's two favors: one from me, and one from him."

After the Majority Leader hung up, the aide stepped back into the doorway and said, "Senator, I just want to remind you that Governor Hazlett is still on hold."

"I'm aware of that."

"Line one."

"Okay, thank you."

The Majority Leader stood and carefully lifted his jacket off the back of the chair. He was clearly invigorated by the phone calls. He put on his jacket, buttoning it deliberately. He was not a thin man, as I have noted, but he must have had a good tailor, because the jacket fit neatly over his sizable girth. The aide continued to linger in the doorway, looking at the phone on the desk, where line one was still blinking red. As the Majority Leader buttoned his last button, he looked at me and said, "There are sandwiches upstairs in the kitchen. Are you hungry?"

87.

THE PRIME MINISTER'S FLIGHT—DESIGNATED AIR INDIA One—landed in Germany and refueled without incident. The camera crew on board broadcast footage of the Prime Minister and his family resting comfortably in a small compartment built especially for them at the front of the cargo plane. There were beds, a bathroom, and a makeshift shower. The Prime Minister walked the camera crew through the cargo hold, showing off the pallets of Dormigen. "Five hundred thousand doses," he explained to the viewers. "Each with the potential to save an American life." As Air India One left Germany, the President was landing in Orange County for his tour of the areas that had been wiped out by the wildfires. "The Dormigen flight is on schedule. No more delays," the Chief of Staff informed him.

"Then let's make sure we stay on schedule," the President replied. He wanted to be back in D.C. with a comfortable cushion for the Prime Minister's arrival. The California visit went as planned—some pro forma visits to damaged areas, a breakfast with firefighters, meetings with local elected officials, and most important, a declaration of the affected counties as a federal disaster area. On the flight back to Washington the Chief of Staff briefed the President on the process for distributing the Dormigen upon the Prime Minister's arrival. "Governors Goolsbee and Spencer are back on board with the plan," she said.

"They had a change of heart, did they?" the President replied. "What about Hazlett?"

"He's been very cooperative."

The President laughed. "He's not getting the Sea Snake Sonar back," he said. The Chief of Staff shrugged. That was a problem for next week. "I'd like to send the Majority Leader a bottle of that Irish whiskey," the President continued.

"That's a nice idea," the Chief of Staff agreed. "I'll do that."

With that, for the first time since the beginning of the Outbreak, the President found himself with nothing urgent to do. He watched a romantic comedy for a while and then drifted off to sleep.

The Indian Prime Minister, however, had not played his last card.

88.

OVER THE NORTH ATLANTIC, ROUGHLY TWO HUNDRED NAU-tical miles off the coast of Newfoundland, the Prime Minister took the controls of Air India One. The President was working in his office in the family quarters of the White House, having showered and dressed after the whirlwind California trip, when the Chief of Staff burst in. "Turn on the TV."

CNN was showing live footage of the Prime Minister at the controls of the 747, ostensibly flying the plane. He checked several gauges, conversed with his copilot, and generally went through the motions of flying a plane. A banner along the bottom of the screen explained: "Indian PM takes the pilot seat on historic lifesaving flight."

"He's a pilot," the President offered.

"Does he know how to fly a 747?" the Chief of Staff asked.

"God, I hope so."

"It's probably on autopilot, don't you think?" the Chief of Staff said optimistically.

The two of them watched the live broadcast, transfixed like so many other viewers around the world. Some four hundred million people were watching in India as the Prime Minister piloted Air India One toward Washington. Even in bustling Mumbai, where business types typically dismissed political shenanigans, groups of people gathered informally in front of televisions in restaurants and cafés to watch their Prime Minister at the controls of the 747. The film crew on board broadcast the cockpit audio, so that viewers could hear communications between the flight crew and air traffic control, beginning when Air India One made radio contact with the air traffic station in Gander, Newfoundland.

"Greetings, Air India One," a voice crackled over the radio, with a hint of a Canadian accent. "Maintain your current altitude and bearing."

"Roger that," the Prime Minister answered confidently.

Soon thereafter, the plane was handed off to the FAA Washington Center in Leesburg, Virginia. "Washington Center, this is Air India One," the Prime Minister said loudly.

"Go ahead, Air India One," a female voice responded.

"We are requesting permission to enter American airspace."

"Roger that, permission granted," the woman replied. And then, with over a billion people listening, she continued, "On a personal note, Captain Joshi, may I be the first to officially welcome you and your crew to the United States of America."

"It's an honor, ma'am," the Prime Minister replied.

In the White House, the President said, "The guy is a fucking genius—a political genius."

The Chief of Staff replied, "I just hope he doesn't crash the plane. That would be a sad end to all this. Seriously, do we know if he can fly a 747?"

"I do think it's on autopilot."

"What about landing? You know he's going to want to land it himself," the Chief of Staff worried aloud.

The phone in the President's study rang, interrupting their conversation. The President answered, listened for a moment, and then said caustically, "Of course he has." He turned to the Chief of Staff and said, "The Prime Minister has requested a flyover of the Capitol."

"At what altitude?" she asked.

"I don't know. Would you know the difference?"

"No, but I have a bad feeling about this."

The President went back to the phone call. "Look, I don't care about the noise restrictions. We can apologize for that later. But could you please inquire discreetly whether this guy really should be flying a 747?" The President listened for a while and then hung up, turning back to the Chief of Staff. "They say he's really good. He flew jets."

As the President and Chief of Staff nervously watched the news coverage, the phone in the President's study rang again. A White House operator informed him that Cecelia Dodds would like to speak with him. "I was worried we were going to lose you," the President said when she was patched through.

"I'm not that easy to get rid of," Cecelia Dodds replied warmly.

"How are you feeling"? the President asked.

"Like someone backed over me with a truck. They told me I'm not supposed to be on the phone, but I felt I owed you a call."

"Are you watching this flight?" the President asked.

"The Prime Minister really knows how to make a point, doesn't he?" she said.

The President laughed loudly. "Coming from you that's high praise."

"My intent was never to make things harder for you," she said. "I hope you understand that."

"Of course," the President said honestly. "You didn't make things easier, necessarily, but you know that. Sometimes I appreciate the moral clarity. Not always . . . Moral clarity is not usually the currency of choice in Washington." It was not clear from the President's tone if he was answering her question, musing aloud, or both. Cecelia Dodds listened, in any event.

Air India One did a low (1,750 feet), slow flyover of the Capitol Mall, dipping its wings as it passed over the White House. Tourists gawked at the enormous 747 flying bizarrely low over the city. Government workers hustled outside to witness the arrival of the historic flight. The Prime Minister was at the controls the whole way. Moments later the plane landed without incident at Joint Base Andrews. The landing and subsequent arrival ceremony was the most watched television event in Indian history—half a billion viewers—with many viewers in remote villages watching on their new televisions. The jumbo jet and its precious cargo taxied to a halt in an area where the President and First Lady were waiting. Seats had been set up on the tarmac for other VIPs. The entire NIH crisis group was there, as well as the White House staff who had worked on the Outbreak and the senior diplomats from the Indian Embassy. I was sitting in the second row with Jenna. The NIH Director, part of the official delegation welcoming the Prime Minister, stood slightly behind the President. Rows of Army trucks were parked near the terminal building, ready for the Dormigen to be unloaded and then reloaded onto the Air Force cargo planes that would fly it to the major population centers. One could feel the logistics folks ready to spring into action; the President had ordered them to stand down until the Prime Minister had his moment in the spotlight. (Of course, no one in the White House had anticipated how good the Prime Minister would be at shining the spotlight on himself—all down the Eastern Seaboard and over the Capitol at 1,750 feet.)

I found it all thrilling. The disappointment that we could not ward off the crisis with a scientific miracle had given way to the realization—valid, I still believe—that we had been part of a successful team effort. We were watching history, like being at Cape Canaveral when the moon shot was launched. The 747 taxied into position, the huge Indian and American flags on the fuselage gleaming brightly in the afternoon sun. Was that choreographed, or was it just luck? In any event, the perfectly illuminated flags provided an idyllic backdrop for the subsequent photos. A Marine band struck up a tune, something I could not identify but that felt vaguely familiar. The staircase was wheeled into position as the jet door popped open. The Prime Minister appeared and waved jauntily to the crowd.

The President walked to the bottom of the stairs, leaving the First Lady (wearing her wedding ring once again) and the others in the welcome party behind. The Prime Minister descended slowly, pausing about halfway to give a crisp salute in the direction of the Marine color guard standing at attention on the tarmac. The President, almost instinctively, began to climb the stairs so that the two men met on the second step. The Prime Minister extended his hand, which the President grasped, pulling the Prime Minister into an embrace, almost like two children. This was the photograph broadcast around the world: the two leaders locked in a bear hug. The Prime Minister was looking over the President's shoulder, beaming at the adoring crowd. The President had closed his eyes in an expression that looked like profound relief.* Two politicians. Two statesmen, I suppose, though even now I would be hard-pressed to explain the difference. "I'm very glad to see you," the President whispered to the Prime Minister, who laughed heartily.

"It's good to be here," the Prime Minister replied. "Yes, it's good to be here," he repeated. "And how are you doing, Mr. President?"

In a moment of candor—one elected head of state to another—the President of the United States replied, "I'm very tired."

---

*   This photo would win the Pulitzer Prize that year for Best Spot News Photography.

EPILOGUE

THE FOLLOWING EVENING THE PRESIDENT HOSTED A DINNER at the White House for the Indian Prime Minister. It was not an official state dinner. The exact protocol of that was lost on me, other than it meant I could wear a suit rather than having to rent a tuxedo. The guest list included White House officials, the Washington diplomatic corps, a handful of CEOs, prominent members of the Indian-American community, and an array of celebrities, including some Indian film stars. I took Ellen as my guest—I figured I owed her that much—though I spent much of the evening talking to Jenna. We would start dating several weeks later. Giscard was there, of course; he spent most of his time hitting on an Indian film star. I could not say that I had come to like him, but I had grown to appreciate his force of personality. He was wearing a burgundy suit with a matching scarf—always the scarf. Who else could pull that off?

The Chief of Staff was there with her entire family: her husband and two daughters. The daughters looked like they would rather be anywhere else. At one point I watched the Chief of Staff tell the older one to put her phone away, which apparently prompted some snippy response, because the two of them argued briefly before the daughter went storming off, high heels wobbling slightly, as only a teenager (in the wrong) can manage. I found the whole scene oddly reassuring, even sweet. It made me feel like life was back to normal.

There were elaborate toasts before dinner. By then the Indian

Dormigen had been distributed across the country with relatively few hiccups. The American supply would be back online in hours. The crisis was unequivocally over. "This is the beginning of a new chapter in American-Indian relations," the President declared in his toast. I had been around him enough to know when he was being sincere and when he was going through the motions. This felt genuine to me, not least because the world is a dangerous place and I had been persuaded that the world's most powerful democracy and the world's most populous democracy ought to be close allies.

The Strategist was there, basking in the success of the fake polling that had set the India strategy in motion. "I got it wrong," he said with false modesty (to the small group who knew about this activity). In fact, the Prime Minister's heroic flight to the U.S. had been even more popular than the Strategist's fictional polling had suggested: 91 percent of Indians supported the Dormigen donation to the U.S.; 83 percent felt relations between the two countries should be closer. I said hello to the Strategist and exchanged pleasantries. "What do you think of my date?" he asked, nodding toward a large-breasted woman in a very short dress who had to be at least twenty years younger than he was. "She's a professional," he said with a wink. I had no idea what to say. I think he was telling the truth.

The menu was vegetarian out of respect for the Indian vegetarians among the guests. The centerpieces were made of lotuses, the national flower of India. (I did not notice this detail; someone pointed it out to me.) I was amazed by what had been pulled together in thirty-six hours. The President had nothing to do with the planning, obviously. There was an entire White House office for this kind of thing: flowers, food, seating arrangements, protocol. The President did make one specific request for the evening: the Speaker of the House and the Chinese Ambassador were seated next to one another. I could not help but look at them as they sat there glumly all night.

We would eventually unravel the mysteries of *Capellaviridae*—and of lurking viruses more generally. It would take more than a year for the pieces to fall into place, with many significant discoveries along the way. To the surprise of no one, Giscard was the lead author on the article that wove the intellectual strands into a coherent theory, though I think he deserved the credit for this one.

In the end, we confirmed most of what we had hypothesized in the early days. Over the course of many millennia, the North American dust mite had turned *Capellaviridae* into an instrument for its own survival. The dust mite bite transmits the indolent form of *Capellaviridae*, which is essentially a flu virus with antibodies pre-attached. Eventually, as the indolent virus replicates, the proteins that render the virus harmless begin to detach, creating the more virulent form of the pathogen. *Unless . . . more dust mite bites.* Each bite transmitted more *Capellaviridae*—benign—as well as an enzyme that destroyed any of the viruses that had turned virulent. In other words, the best cure for a North American dust mite bite was more bites. That is how the dust mite made itself invaluable to humans.

"Fantastic!" Professor Huke exclaimed as I walked him through what we had learned. He had invited me to campus for a lunch with students. From an evolutionary standpoint, what we had discovered was fantastic. And it was consistent with the theory I first formulated while sitting at my dining room table: The North American dust mite effectively holds its human hosts hostages; *as long as I'm fine, you're fine.* When humans tried to eradicate the dust mite, or when they moved away to an area without them (which from a biological perspective was the same thing), *Capellaviridae* turned dangerous.

Our discoveries paved the way for other important work. The enzyme the dust mite uses to eliminate the virulent form of *Capellaviridae* has enormous medical value. It is essentially a targeted assassin, which may transform some kinds of cancer treatment. Meanwhile, our "wiki science" has become a template for how cutting-edge research ought to be shared. We are now using more sophisticated platforms than Google Docs, and there is recognition that peer review is still an essential tool for validating work, but our *Capellaviridae* "war room" demonstrated the power of openness and collaboration. Last year the National Academy of Sciences promulgated a set of standards for sharing scientific work in parallel with the peer review process.

Some months after the dramatic Air India One flight, those of us who worked on the scientific effort during the Outbreak were invited to a small White House reception with the President. The event was postponed twice—once during the intervention in El Salvador and again when the First Lady had her cancer surgery. Eventually we gathered at the White House. The NIH team was there, along with the other principals who had been involved in the response: the Acting HHS Secretary (now retired), the Secretary of State, and so on. The President and First Lady welcomed each member of the team as we entered the East Room; the NIH Director stood at the President's side, introducing each of us as we reached the front of the receiving line. "You remember our expert on lurking viruses," the NIH Director said to the President as I stood in front of him, offering my hand.

"Of course I do," the President said, looking down subtly at my name tag. "Thank you for your service."

I moved along to the First Lady. "So nice to meet you," she said. "The nation owes you a profound debt." Jenna was right behind me. I waited for her as the First Lady said, "Thank you for your important work."

Jenna was chuckling when she joined me. "Hah," she said, "the President forgot your name."

"No," I replied with a smile. "He never knew it in the first place."

ACKNOWLEDGMENTS

———

I TYPICALLY WRITE NONFICTION—BOOKS ABOUT ECONOMICS and statistics and monetary policy. Bringing a novel to fruition was an entirely different undertaking. I am deeply appreciative of those people who guided me through this new process. As always, it has been a pleasure to work with W. W. Norton, a partnership that is approaching two decades. John Glusman steered me expertly through the new territory associated with fiction. His faith in the story and its characters made the book possible. Helen Thomaides is the one who made the production process run far more efficiently than the rest of my life. I owe a special debt to copyeditor Dave Cole and his remarkably careful eye. This is a complicated story that takes place in the future over a handful of days in multiple time zones. Dave was the one who made sure that the details were consistent and always supported the larger narrative.

I wrote this book while traveling around the world on a "family gap year" with my wife, Leah, and our three children. Leah is a remarkable partner in all that I do. She had the imagination and energy to make that family trip happen. She was the first person to read an early draft of this book—before there was even an ending. Her encouragement inspired me to keep going. Our children—Katrina, Sophia, and CJ—were fun and adventurous travel companions. If I am being honest, however, their primary contributions to this book were fits of teenage behavior that drove me to cafés and other isolated places where I was able to get a lot of writing done.

I showed up in New York at the end of our family gap year and informed my agent, Tina Bennett, that I had written a novel. (At least I did not present her with poetry or watercolor paintings.) She was remarkably supportive; as a result, we now have a book. Tina and I have brought a diverse array of projects to fruition. It has been a privilege to have her at my side along the way. And thankfully, Svetlana Katz has been at Tina's side to round out a great team.

My day job is teaching public policy at the Rockefeller Center at Dartmouth College. (Anyone who did not see a lot of public policy themes in this book did not look hard enough.) Andrew Samwick is the one who brought me to the Rockefeller Center. He has encouraged my eclectic projects at every turn. He also made possible our year of traveling, which in turn made possible *The Rationing*. It is a joy and a privilege to be a part of the Rockefeller Center and to teach Dartmouth undergraduates.

I want to thank Joyce Gerstein, a family friend since I was in high school. For as long as I can remember, Joyce has worked at the Book Bin, an independent bookstore in Northbrook, Illinois, where I grew up. When my mother gave Joyce the manuscript, Joyce read it promptly and pronounced that it was a book she could sell. That was high praise coming from someone who loves books as much as she does; it also motivated me to move the project forward.

Thanks also to my mother, who gave the manuscript to Joyce without my permission. That's exactly the kind of thing mothers are supposed to do.

'Sorry?'

'*Agora* …' She grabs another cereal bowl. 'It's the Greek for marketplace. Agora-phobia: a fear of the marketplace.'

'I see.' Gene is nonplussed.

'There was a woman I visited while I was in training up in Sheffield. Her name was …' She thinks hard for a second as she looks down at the cereal bowl then notices a small food remnant still gracing its rim. 'Nina. Late thirties, early forties, unhappily married. Her husband was incredibly overbearing. Didn't take the condition seriously – just thought it was yet more evidence of a basic lack of moral fibre …' She places the bowl back into the sink, and then stares, glumly, through the window. 'I think it was him who got the church involved, although it wasn't an especially successful manoeuvre. She just really seemed to resent it.'

Sheila raises a hand to her face but Gene cannot tell – from the rear – if she's moving aside a strand of hair or wiping away a tear with it. 'Not my greatest piece of Community Outreach work, as I recollect.'

Her voice starts to shake a little.

'This woman I met today – this agoraphobic …' Gene is about to confide in her about the meeting with Valentine (the broken meter, the strange bruise), but then – in the light of the whole Stan farrago – he suddenly thinks better of it and falls silent.

'This woman you met today …' Sheila prompts him.

'Uh … Yeah. She'd done something really strange to herself,' Gene improvises.

'Really?'

Sheila glances over her shoulder at him, her powerful, dark eyes dulled with a profound indifference.

'She'd tattooed a brick on to her leg,' Gene expands. 'Several bricks. Incredibly lifelike …'

'Bricks?' Sheila echoes, blankly.

213

'She's an artist. It was some kind of an art statement, I suppose. She showed me this photograph. It was really beautifully taken …'

'Ah …'

Her eyes suddenly glimmer with a momentary show of engagement. '*Women Who Marry Houses*,' she muses.

'Women who …?'

Sheila returns the tea towel to its hook.

'It's the title of a book I salvaged from the church jumble a couple of years back. Looked intriguing. There was a quote on the title page by Anne Sexton – one of the women poets I wrote my dissertation on at Oxford …' She picks up the four, dry plates and places them into a cupboard. 'It went something along the lines of …' She frowns as she struggles to recall it: '*Women marry houses. It's another kind of skin.*'

She shrugs. 'An odd concept, really, but it's always stuck with me for some reason.'

Gene gazes at her as she speaks – slowly drinking in her ragged fringe, her deep frown lines, an area of inflammation in the centre of her right cheek, a suggestion of staining on one of her front teeth – and suddenly feels an incredibly powerful rush of emotion towards her.

'You're amazing,' he says, his voice low and unexpectedly guttural. 'So bloody wise.'

She turns to look at him, shocked.

'Don't be ridiculous!' she snaps, then pats him on the shoulder, straight after, almost as an afterthought, before heading off, morosely, to Evening Service.

'I'm sorry …' Valentine stares at her brother, her cheeks flushing, her expression one of complete bewilderment. 'What kind of therapist did you say he was, exactly?'

214